The Local

Keith Wild

Pen Press

First published in Great Britain by Pen Press

All paper used in the printing of this book has been made from wood grown in
managed, sustainable forests.

ISBN: 978-1-78003-528-4

Printed and bound in the UK
Pen Press is an imprint of
Indepenpress Publishing Limited
25 Eastern Place
Brighton
BN2 1GJ

A catalogue record of this book is available from
the British Library

Cover design by Jacqueline Abromeit

Author's Notes

The Local is the third book in my drama trilogy based in current times and set in different locations in Surrey, UK.

This story describes how a violent death can change a life overnight. Alan Fisher, a local man who left the army early to take up a civilian career, had help from old friends and acquaintances in finding out the truth about what happened concerning a mysterious family death, and one friend has an unlikely job for him.

Almost everyone has a local public house, even if they don't use it regularly. Some are in the same street and others within walking distance, and many are a short drive away. As surveillance by the police on the lookout for motorists driving while over the limit became much more vigilant, and cheap alcohol increasingly easy to obtain from supermarkets, drinking and meeting habits changed dramatically from the end of the nineties, and the future of the local was in great danger.

By 2009 as many as three pubs a week were closing countrywide, and many others were on the brink of bankrupcy.

The Brown Cow Inn, a small and quaint establishment owned by Larry Nixon and situated just two minutes off the main road between Leatherhead and Dorking, was not exempt from the downturn and its prospects for the future were looking bleak. Larry was determined to avoid the closure of his pub, as he knew it would be followed by a messy and shameful bankruptcy. He had no plans on the table, but he would seek help and advice from his accountant friend in order to find a buyer or partner to possibly turn the pub more into a restaurant, or fast food outlet. At the same time, he knew that he needed other help too, as an old illness had become more urgent with the stress of his failing business. The cards were on the table for Larry, and as a matter of urgency he had to play the right hand to save his business, his home and his marriage.

Chapter 1
Speeding
Surrey, November 2009

'What do you think, Cheryl?'

'I don't have time at the moment to think; slow down, please. I hope this car has good brakes: the Leatherhead bypass is not a racetrack, Alan, and the police live on it.'

The Mini Cooper was not the latest model but its power and the 'hunger for speed' speech by the salesman had worked well on Alan, convincing him to buy a car that he could only just afford. The garage had given him a good price, and it needed to be, as the insurance was a month's wages and he would have to pay for both the car and the insurance in instalments. His job in the local planning department was not a high payer, but he was a determined young man and one day he wanted to be a chief planning officer. Alan Fisher was academically well qualified and army combat trained. After leaving the services he used his background and the confidence it had given him to retrain. Now after only two years in the planning department, he was dealing with many of the smaller planning applications.

Alan was 33 years old, the second son of Fay and Gordon Fisher. Gordon had recently retired from his role as a Judge Advocate, and was now concentrating on upgrading their 1920s house on the Tyrells Wood estate in Leatherhead. He had served in the RAF, and then as a barrister both overseas and in the UK. The reality was that he had been working in front-line disciplinary situations based first in Bosnia, then the Middle East (and specifically Iraq after the Gulf War), and then during the fall of Hussein. His friends and relations knew he was a military Judge Advocate, but they were unlikely to ever find anything out about his work; he lived a very private life and his premature retirement had been accelerated after he was diagnosed with heart problems, which meant a complete change of lifestyle for him. Gordon had a special job, and his family and friends sometimes found it difficult to understand how a military court worked in dealing with disciplinary issues relating to servicemen.

Alan, his youngest son, joined the army at 18 and after ten years' service he declined further promotion. An invitation to join the security services followed, but he could not be persuaded, although the door was left open should he change his mind. He had no encouragement from his parents to stay in the army for another term: they gave their view and it was clearly 'Get out and stay alive.' His father had seen death and misery at first hand, and Alan knew that his own survival had only been good luck, when bombs had ripped apart buildings and roads in areas where terrorists thrived.

Although Alan knew his father worked in the judiciary service he never discussed it with anyone, even close friends, although a Google search gave a brief summary of Gordon's early career to professional nosey parkers. In Alan's case a careless slip of the tongue could have resulted in problems for Gordon; his upbringing had taught him to preserve a strict wall of silence about his father.

After a good education and joining the army hungry for action, he had quickly learnt his role in live operations. His quick mind, combined with good fitness, made him a prime candidate for quick promotion, and if the devastating events had not occurred he would have been a senior officer by now. But fate changed everything, and he could not carry on for another term. He looked at several opportunities, but quickly selected what he saw as an easy career; more like a stopgap whilst he got his head back in order. He would discover that it was more complicated than he expected, and he would soon grow to like it.

As his basic qualifications were good, he soon passed the entry examinations to become a planning officer one day. He was a versatile and logical thinker, but now he had to learn the rules on something new, although then again this was a normal challenge as it was something he had done for years. His superiors in the planning office were impressed by him; they saw how quickly he adapted to a desk job dealing with colleagues and members of the public, some more difficult than others, were a credit to his army training, and a development request could land on his desk for a group of lockup garages, or the destruction of several trees to make way for a new path, or the conversion of a property from one use to another.

It was one of these planning requests that saw him at Mandy's Beauty Salon in Tolworth Broadway, a stretch of road with many different types of businesses from cafes to video shops, all of which lay in the shadow of the famous Tolworth Tower, a landmark for travellers along the A3 road south. Mandy Rix was the owner of the salon and the flat above it, and she was a 55-year-old divorcee with many a story to tell. Her shop was her share of the divorce settlement from her ex-husband, and together with her daughter she offered a range of beauty treatments from simple nail painting, to waxing and all types of massage. She wanted desperately to get away from Tolworth, and had sublet the flat over the property to a variety of people, but none of them seemed to stay very long. The Thai couple currently in situ were slow to pay and there seemed to be more occupants every week; she was convinced they were up to no good but she needed the money. Parking was becoming almost impossible on the Broadway and she found attracting new business very difficult. Over the years many of her regular clients had moved away from the area, and much of her business now was passing trade and youngsters who worked in the tower.

Her plan was to buy the old antique shop next door to her house in Oxshott, a small town in Surrey with many wealthy locals. At the same time she would apply for planning permission to alter the layout and extend it ready for a change of use to a beauty salon; she would then offer the 'complete service' as she was doing in Tolworth, but this time on her doorstep.

The day Alan turned up to discuss the plans for her house, Cheryl Rix was in charge as her mother had been delayed. It was love at first sight. He asked his standard questions about the plans that had been submitted, but didn't take any notes; he worked it so that he had to come back the next day when Mandy Rix would be available for more detailed questions on the change of use in the Oxshott shop. He wasted no time and was back at the shop early the following morning; Mandy was still not around so he plucked up courage and asked Cheryl for a date the following day, which was also the day he would be collecting his new car. Cheryl was his first passenger as he collected her from Tolworth.

'Still a bit quick, Alan – you are bloody well over 40!'

'Sorry Cheryl, I totally forgot my speed and yes, you're right, but this car does have good brakes; they're discs all around. Watch how it stops.'

'Christ Alan, that's good, but don't look now; there's a copper on the inside of the corner.'

'Bugger it – he's coming after me.'

The officer pointed to the lay-by and Alan followed him as he parked his motorcycle and entered the car details on his computer, then walked to the car.

'Sorry officer, I was just testing the brakes. I only got the car today.'

'Yes, I guessed that. I didn't need a computer check to work out you were a new owner – how long do you expect to stay in one piece, driving like that?'

'A long time hopefully, officer?'

'To do that, sir, you need to drive more safely, not fast and then screeching to a halt like a teenager would do.'

Alan avoided the subject of his speed; he knew he was not much over the speed limit, if at all, but he could still be done for driving without due care and attention. His father had told him how to deal with speeding offences, but not on braking too quickly.

'Look, I see your name is Alan Fisher; it is your car and I know it's taxed and insured. That's all in your favour, but stopping quickly like that is just stupid; the guy in the van behind you nearly landed on his bonnet.'

'I...'

The conversation stopped as the motorcycle policeman saw a squad car go racing past. He turned to face Alan, and after a brief conversation on the phone started his bike.

'Please take care, sir. Life is too short. If I see you again doing tricks like that, or speeding around this area, I promise I will book you.'

The officer rode off, and Cheryl leaned over to Alan who looked stunned; the date was only an hour old, but she grabbed his head and planted a kiss squarely on his lips.

'Sorry, Alan – that's all my fault for asking about your brakes.'

'Don't worry Cheryl, I was being stupid. Let's go for a drink at the Brown Cow; it's just down the road. By the way, I don't drink and drive so it's just orange juice for me.'

'Then I will make up for that and have a large gin and tonic. Come on, let's go.'

'Just one thing: we may see some of my old army mates in the other bar; they can walk to the pub as it's only a short distance from the training camp.'

'It's a bit early for that, Alan. Can we avoid them?'

'Yes, sure – we can go to the next place I know. It's just past Box Hill and should be pretty quiet on a Monday; we can leave the Brown Cow until another night.'

The Mini hugged the Box Hill road as if it was on a wire until they passed the summit, then the road levelled out as the road humps killed any speed. They passed the mobile home park slowly, and pulled into the car park of the Hand in Hand. Alan parked the car at the front so he could see his new pride and joy through the window. He really wanted a strong drink as the events on the bypass had shaken him up, but he kept to his promise and abstained.

The evening passed quickly, but in the time the couple were in the pub they could hear several sirens in the distance from police cars, ambulances and even a different noise, probably a fire engine. Something was happening very close to the Brown Cow. Alan became concerned and wanted to leave. Cheryl had spent the past two hours just staring and continually chattering excitedly to her new boyfriend, and she could not believe her luck. Alan was Mr Perfect, but he hadn't met her mother yet and when he did it would be on business. She was worried that her mother would be aggressive, especially if the planning permission was turned down or they had to spend more on the Oxshott move.

She had left many boyfriends behind her, and at 29 years she was seriously looking to get hitched. She had a nice feeling about Alan, but she didn't want to rush things in case he had a history. She knew he was older; had he been married before, or had he been in jail? All she knew about him was that he had been abroad for a long time, and not much else. At least she could talk to her mother first and warn her that if she was rude to Alan Cheryl would be finding another job; but then she wondered what she would do for an income. She hoped Alan was not sensitive as she stared out of the side window as the car slowly went back down the steep Box Hill and towards the main road.

'What are you thinking, Cheryl? I can hear the wheels turning in your head.'

'Nothing – just hoping you will get on all right with my mum.'

'If she's like you I will, but I guess from your concern she isn't?'

'Wait and see; you are coming back on Wednesday, aren't you?'

Alan just nodded as his attention was drawn to the roadblock on the bypass. The motorcycle policeman from earlier that evening saw them and walked down to the car.

'Hello again, Mr Fisher. There has been a terrible incident not far from the pub; you'll have to go back into Leatherhead and through the back roads to get home.'

'You know where I live, then?'

'Yes, of course – I saw your address when I checked you out and it's an address we know. Off you go, please – you haven't been drinking, have you?'

'No, definitely not, officer.'

'I didn't think so. Please take the young lady home; then I suggest you return immediately to your own home.'

Alan didn't hesitate. He passed over the M25 at Leatherhead and took the side road to Oxshott, concerned that the policeman had known his address off by heart, and by the tone of his voice when he told him to go home.

They stopped outside a small house in Oxshott High Street, and Cheryl leaned over and wrapped her arms around him and gave him a long kiss. It had an instant effect on him – normally on a first date he wasn't sure, but she already ticked a lot of the boxes for a relationship. As she broke away from him his trouser zip was bursting at the seams, but he knew it was not the time or place. She guessed what was happening and decided to go inside her house before she also lost control; her third gin and tonic had hit the spot.

'Call me tomorrow, you promise, Alan?'

'Yes, sure – your number's on the front of the file.'

'No, no – here, this is my mobile number. Put it in your phone.'

Alan had switched his phone off. When he opened it again he had three voicemails, all of them from his uncle's number.

'Sorry Cheryl, I'm needed – maybe my uncle wants a lift. Speak to you tomorrow.'

She climbed out of the car and waved as Alan pulled the door closed and drove around the corner. Whatever the message, it was not for Cheryl's ears tonight.

'Uncle Ted it's me, Alan – you wanted me urgently?'

'Yes, come home now, Alan – I am outside your parents' house, and there's been an incident. Come quick.'

The line went dead as he went through the country lanes. He decided not to ring back as the phone was not hands-free – the journey took less time than it should have and he was already ignoring the policeman's warning. As he pulled into the road leading to the family house, the scene was like a war zone. The view of the house was one of total devastation to his parents' garage and the side of the house attached to it. Paramedics were carefully removing the remains of two bodies from a smouldering Mercedes which the fire brigade had covered in foam; the house and garage were sealed off with yellow tape. Alan's Mini screeched to a halt; he stared at the sight but he couldn't take it in. His uncle Ted was stood next to the gate using it as a support, and he grabbed his nephew and hugged him.

'It's awful, Alan – some bastards have blown up your mum and dad. I just can't believe it; look at the mess. Why the hell has somebody done this?'

Alan was speechless. He left his parked car and jumped into his uncle's 20-year-old Jaguar.

'Take me to your house; I feel like I'm going to collapse. If the police want to see me, give them your address. Let's get out of here.'

The pungent smell of burnt flesh and debris from the garage filled the air as they drove away; the police took Ted Fisher's address as they passed the front gate. It would be the last time Alan visited the house for many months.

Chapter 2
For Sale

'You're early today, Bill – it's only 11.25am.'

'I know that, but when I show you the accounts you will need a drink as well, Larry.'

'Come in; sit down – pint of Courage Best, I assume?'

'Yes Larry, but listen to me now, and at the same time look at this summary.'

Larry Nixon knew what Bill Knowles wanted: he had done six months' accounts for Larry and the Brown Cow pub was seriously in the red. Beer sales had plummeted; food sales were satisfactory, but he had no room to expand the dining area so alternative sources of revenue were needed, and quickly. Bill had turned up to spell out the bad news.

Larry studied the spread sheet as if looking for a major mistake, but the figures were clear and spoke for themselves.

'It's a mess, Larry: I can't see any hope and there's only one thing you can do.'

'What's that, Bill?'

'I see nothing else really other than shutting this place down; you own the freehold on the buildings and also that bit of land at the back. It has a value to somebody; you can't continue to trade insolvent, Larry, and worst of all you'll need a lot of money for tax in two months. It's a pile of shit and I have no ideas that currently spring to mind.'

The pint disappeared quickly down the accountant's throat, and he went to his pocket for money.

'Don't be silly, Bill. I owe you well over £1,000 already and I can't let you pay – the beer is free. I will come and see you on Friday, and if I can't come up with a plan we'll have to shut it down.'

'Look, I'll ask around, Larry – you need about £200,000 to clear all your debts, pay the taxman and have enough to get a new start somewhere, probably renting until you find a job. This place is probably worth about the same. I'll see if I can find a buyer for a quick sale, but I'll have to move quickly.'

'Yes, but that'll be a difficult one to take – I can't live off my pension and Jill doesn't get much for her paintings when she sells one. If that's all I'll get for the pub I need to talk to her and choose my time. I'll need a job and I don't want to sell.'

'OK, but Friday is probably too soon for us both – talk it over with Jill and I'll come back and see you on Monday. I've asked around about valuations on pubs and it's grim. Sorry that I can't be more optimistic, but this situation is a nationwide one and I hear of pubs closing down every week. See you on Monday.'

Once back in his car and out of earshot, Bill dialled a number on the car phone.

'His face is showing panic; I think we'll get it for around £200,000. Come to my office and we can work out how to put it to your client. I may need your help; after all it was your idea for me to hit him with it head-on.'

Bill Knowles, a local 44-year-old widower, had a good living as a chartered accountant and an eye for a deal. His endeavours had started to make him serious money, buying out bankrupt companies and selling them on to eager asset buyers. He only dealt in business property, and the Brown Cow at a giveaway price was right up his street. He was assisted sometimes by Alice Smith, a self-employed girl about town with quite a few different sources of income. She was well educated, her work was varied and she could turn her hand to many things if it paid well; this included private investigating, debt collection and sourcing land for development. Her diverse talents for finding an unsuspecting sucker fascinated Bill Knowles; he had tried to get closer to her in more ways than one without any success.

Knowles regarded it as unusual for a woman to work in the cut-and-thrust world of land acquisitions, building regulations and finance, as they were a complicated mixture and required many interpersonal skills to close a deal and make money. She seemed perfect for doing the legwork before he got involved, and between them, in the past three years they had made several very profitable quick deals, operating just as middle men without the need for much capital. Her dynamic, outgoing personality was obvious, and she was the life and soul of any party or pub gathering. Nobody ever seemed to get to know her as she kept her private life to herself and she never discussed her family, her business or her friends. If she had a history, it remained firmly inside her sizeable breasts.

Larry Nixon thought Bill worked for him and technically he did, but Bill had seen the possibility of a deal to buy the pub and sell it on immediately: no risk with a simultaneous sale and purchase. Alice Smith was the key to making it all happen, with her and Bill earning a fat profit at the end, and all parties happy.

The Saturday lunchtime diners had left the pub, and Marie the barmaid was on her own as Larry and Jill had taken a break before the evening rush.

'Thank God for Saturdays and Sundays, Jill. It's just a pity that it's dead in here for the other five days.'

'There must be something we can do to save this place, Larry.'

'If there was, dear, I'd do it – don't pressure me, my mind is totally blank. Bill says our cash position is not improving, so unless we do something we'll go broke in less than six months.'

'Remember we do own this place – but then of course, we borrowed against it to buy Spain. Perhaps we should just sell up and move out there?'

'Yes, that's worth considering but will we have enough to live on? How much more do we need to survive?'

'Not sure; I haven't told Bill Knowles about Spain as there's something about him that always makes me a bit nervous.'

Jill Nixon liked Bill Knowles from the first time she met him in the pub; she had flirted with him at parties and it had gone further. She knew she was too old for him, but it didn't seem to bother either of them and her visits to his house had become a very regular event.

'There's one thing for sure, Larry: I'm not keeping up this seven-day working, especially as we aren't making a penny after all our costs. I want to retire and paint. By the way, while I remember: can you stop touching Marie's backside? I know she's a sexy Polish girl but she may get the wrong idea; don't think I haven't noticed.'

'Don't be silly it's just a bit a fun.'

Jill just wagged her finger, then laid down on the bed. 'Join me, you randy old man, and I will give you something to stop that eye wandering.'

Larry's mind was elsewhere. Some of his thoughts were about the meeting with Bill: he wasn't sure about him, and he was thinking about getting a second opinion on the pub value without his accountant knowing. After his wife's words, his main thoughts had drifted to Marie, his new employee. At 25 years old she was just like Jill had been 25 years before, and just as sexy.

17

'What are you thinking, Larry? Come on now, please – get on with it or I'll be asleep.'

'Yes, sorry darling; I was thinking about the pub.'

Jill just smiled; she knew her husband well and she also knew she would have to keep an eye on the young lady behind the bar.

Larry was first back into the bar as Jill slept on; it would be a late weekend night so she would have an extra hour's sleep before showering and changing into her kitchen clothes. Food sales were a priority: most of them were cash and some of the proceeds went into a small nest egg, which even the accountant did not know about. Only credit cards and a few meals went through the books. Marie knew this as she saw Bill put the money into the safe every day. She knew where he kept the key and she had decided that it was her insurance policy if the Nixons ever fired her. She saw only the cash, not understanding what the couple were doing; if Larry let her down she would steal the money and leave for Devon where many of her friends worked.

'Hi Marie. Take a few hours break, we seem to have a few bookings for tonight already.'

She smiled, and as he passed behind her at the till he squeezed her backside, then pushed himself against her.

'Again and soon, please, Larry?'

'Yes, very soon, Marie. Go now and have a rest and I'll take over.'

Over the years the regulars had kept the pub going, but habits had changed and now there were not enough of them left. The period an hour or so before dinner was the busy time, with customers who were dining arriving and ordering pre-dinner drinks mixing with regulars. Harold Penny was one of the few faithful who came into the pub every evening. He had two pints of Guinness, which he made last an hour and a half as he talked endlessly to Bill as he served the one or two other regular customers.

'You know, Harold, I don't know what I'd do if I didn't see you every day – that is of course excluding holidays and your occasional unexplained absence to the Hand in Hand.'

'Things aren't good, are they Larry? I can tell you look much older every day I see you.'

'Well that's obvious, Harold; we are getting older and you're bloody ancient. How old are you?'

'I don't normally discuss my age with anyone, but I'll make an exception with you, Bill. I am actually 74 years old; some days I feel it but as I've played tennis and walked regularly for the past 50 years I must be fit, but not young. I can still manage a couple of pints, of course.'

Larry leaned over the bar and whispered in his elderly customer's ear. 'Yes, but can you still manage *it* – and by the way, can you loan me £200,000?'

'Yes, don't be silly – of course I can! Sometimes it's a long wait, but my old friend still works, at least I think so, last time I tried. More importantly why do you need the money?'

'At least you're still in action, Harold – must be the 14 or so pints of Guinness you drink every week. Well done; perhaps I should try that medicine. It may improve my brain power and then I can find a solution for this pub.'

'You don't need Guinness surely, Larry, with that young lady behind the bar rubbing her tits against you every day.'

'Chance would be a fine thing, Harold.'

'So Larry, I ask again: what are we talking about; a loan or women?'

Harold Penny was a retired lawyer and his speciality had been divorce, but he dealt mainly with probate cases in his latter years. He had seen many scenarios in his working life and many of them repeated themselves; he could see the way the young girl looked at the pub owner. He concluded that Larry would not be normal if he didn't fancy the foreign girl, and he guessed the tall, middle-aged publican was in her range as well. The dark side of Larry was his terrible temper, and many customers had not returned after seeing at first hand arguments and scenes involving him for little or no reason. Changing the subject quickly, Harold sat on a bar stool and put both hands on the counter.

'Now, young man, please tell me why you need as much as £200 grand?'

'To keep me young Harold; this place carries a huge debt and I need to do something about it, and quick. I could try and raise money by selling it, but then I'm back to square one. We would be left with a tiny two-bedroom apartment on the Costa Brava and my small pension to go with it – by the way, that's confidential.'

'Yes of course, everything you say is for my ears only. I guessed business was not good; what options have you got?'

'Very few, Harold – my accountant Bill Knowles would like me to sell it and he said he will probably be able to get me around £200,000 for a quick sale. It all depends on timing; if I wait too long it may be taken out of my hands.'

'Let me think about it for a couple of days, Larry – no, better than that, I'll come back tomorrow at the same time. If the idea I have is interesting to you I'll introduce you to some people; buy me a beer then and we can talk more in private.'

'You have an idea already, Harold?'

'Yes, possibly, but I need to think it through, so don't do anything rash. I'm off now – see you tomorrow and keep your hands off that girl or I'll soon be asking you what it feels like.'

'Thanks Harold – can't wait; I promise to be good!'

As Harold left the pub, Larry decided that he would keep their discussion a secret from his wife, and when the lawyer came back he would make sure Jill was occupied before having a discussion with him. He knew very little about Harold Penny, but what he did know was that he was a very wealthy man. His children were married and lived abroad, he had four grandchildren whose education he paid for and his house in Leatherhead was worth several million pounds.

The first dining customers came in as Harold left, so Larry's attention was diverted to pub activities and he left thoughts on the discussions with the retired lawyer and his accountant until later.

'Good evening, is it a table for two?'

'Yes, the name is Parker.'

The couple were most unusual. They did not look like Parkers: they had slightly brown Mediterranean looks, and were dressed very smartly and far too well for the Brown Cow, where jeans and tee shirts were normal dress. As far as Larry was concerned they were just paying customers, but he would remember them – a talent any good landlord should have. But as Larry was a troubled man, his pub was not the main issue in his confused head. He had nightmares at least once a week that were linked to memories and situations in the past; the same mutilated faces peering at him, and he wasn't sure if the people were dead or alive. Each time he prayed to wake up, and when he did he was soaked in sweat. The dreams were not new, but they were getting more frequent, and linked to the same memories that had haunted his career.

'Two gin and tonics please, with ice and lemon. Can we order here at the bar?' The customers' accent was unfamiliar to Larry; he had heard many but this was a new one.

'Yes, sure, that's fine.'

'Is everything OK, Larry?' Jill called.

'Yes, darling; I'll come and collect the menus – can you put the specials on the back?'

'Sure – five minutes.'

The couple took their drinks and tried to avoid Larry's line of sight. He went behind the bar and put his head in his hands; did they really want to eat or was it connected to his past? His paranoia had got to him again. He poured himself a large Scotch and drank it in two gulps, then pushed his nails into his palms and talked to himself.

'This is stupid, everything is OK; it was just another death in action; I must not keep thinking about it. I didn't kill those people; I am not even involved, not me. Why did the bastards do it? Didn't they realise they killed and maimed innocent civilians?'

'Larry, for goodness' sake forget it and take the menus to the table, please. It's simple of course, it's what we do every day, but with new fancy names, just differently typed.'

Jill saw the sweat on her husband's forehead. She knew the signs of one of his panic attacks, and the best thing was to keep him busy. They were getting more frequent now, and when they happened they were usually very bad. She became very frightened sometimes as she felt she could see death in his eyes, and she just wanted to get away from him as soon as possible. She knew he needed help but he rejected all her suggestions, so she didn't mention the attacks to anyone as she didn't know how he would react.

'Yes, thanks darling – I'm OK now, just a minor wobble. I'll get the food menus on the tables.'

Jill Nixon was a local girl who had been to catering college and worked in a top restaurant before she met Larry. He knew little of her past, but the marriage had worked. She knew when she married him that he would be away a lot of the time due to his army career, but she continued with her job and brought up two children who had studied and got good degrees before moving abroad. They had bought The Brown Cow before Larry retired from the army, and she had had many anxious days and nights when she did not hear from him. He was away so long she never really knew where he was or what he did, other than that it was dangerous. She always half-expected a knock on the door or a phone call, but thankfully one never came.

When he retired suddenly she was pleased at first. As the children were grown up, owning the pub and an apartment in

Spain should have given them a good life, even though they had some borrowings, which she thought were not excessive. In the beginning, His army pension and pub takings made them well off, but as business became difficult tensions between them started to increase, especially with Larry's panic attacks becoming more frequent.

'Take the order from the Parkers and the two girls sat in the window seat please, Larry – come on darling, we need to get the show on the road. Marie can handle the bar herself; she only has a couple of customers.'

Larry grabbed another large Scotch, which he downed in two mouthfuls. Obeying his wife's instructions, he took the orders from the early customers.

'Well, it's fish for the couple and steaks for the girls; the guy has chosen that expensive Merlot and with fish, but I'm not complaining. I suggested the Chablis, but he was very insistent. The girls want Caesar salad starters, and to follow, sirloin steaks cooked medium. They're holding hands under the table, Jill – we've got the lot in here tonight. A couple of Arabs called Parker plus Pinky and Perky holding bloody hands out of sight.'

'Don't be silly Larry; they're paying aren't they? It's not a personality competition, they're probably just good friends. I really doubt if they are gay.'

'No, you're right; it's just no way are the other couple called Parker. Someone's taking the piss.'

'They might be, Larry; don't be so dismissive of people with darker skins – you're becoming a racist. Wait until they pay; it's sure to be by card, and then we'll find out their real names.'

'You should have been a detective, darling, not a bloody chef.'

'Larry, get out of my kitchen – you have another couple in the bar and remember we have that party of six lads in half an hour.'

The Scotch had taken effect, and Larry felt good. He was not an alcoholic, or at least he didn't think he was; he drank every day but rarely too much. His inability to ever fully relax was due to his history, and when he was alone in the bar or cellar the memories of the past flooded back. He served the drinks and decided that the Arab-looking Parkers were definitely from the Middle East. Could Parker be their real name? He hoped this would be confirmed later, one way or another, on the credit card receipt. He thought they acted British, but he wasn't sure; there was something about them that irritated him more than usual. From the brief conversation Larry had had with them, the man had told him they were both professional people, but they were not specific which area they worked in. When he asked where they came from, they were very direct with him and just said that their parents had lived in Cyprus, but they were now dead and they had decided to come to live in England. No details or explanation were given, and Larry decided not to ask.

He felt foolish. Every day he expected a visitor, and he doubted his fear would ever leave him. He would have another Scotch, then concentrate on the arriving group of six, the local lads just starting the evening with pints of lager and shots of vodka and Red Bull. Larry would have loved to join them, but then he realised Jill was frowning at him through the kitchen serving hatch. He waved his pad at her and gave her a V sign without a smile. The lads all laughed; they knew Larry and they would spend lots of money. All he needed was more customers like them every day and he would get solvent.

The girls finished their meal and sat in their car just like Thelma and Louise planning their next move.

'Well, what do you make of the pub then, Alice?'

'I like it, and I see it becoming a Michelin star restaurant. As a pub alone it's finished, but considering the geographical position, with the right sort of décor and management it could be very successful. Downside is that it would need a great deal of money spent on it, as the dining area is not large enough and I suspect the same will apply to the kitchens.'

'Have you met Larry Nixon before?'

'No, Sheila – that's why I held your hand. I wanted him to be distracted; he started to look at me before but as soon as we moved together he scuttled away.'

'You don't, though, do you?'

'Don't what, Alice?'

'Fancy me, Sheila – don't you remember we did a few things together with a couple of your customers once?'

'No, don't be silly. I'm dead straight, Alice, but sometimes I'm a bit over-tactile with my girl friends and it gets me into trouble. I assure you I'm absolutely straight and have eyes only for men.'

'That's a big relief.'

The girls laughed and Alice started the engine.

'Pity we don't do this more often, Sheila, but then restaurants aren't something I deal in most of the time. But I found out a lot tonight; I'll meet up with Bill Knowles again tomorrow and we can see if the figures work out. What do you think?'

'Not much to say really, other than thanks. It was OK Alice; I like being taken out for dinner. Take me home and I'll make you some coffee.'

'You're on. We can phone Aaron Parker from your place to see what he made of it.'

'Are he and his wife really from Cyprus?'

'Yes, I think they lived there for a few years, but not originally – their family were definitely from the Middle East but then they finished up in Cyprus. For some reason they got married in Nicosia and came to England about ten years ago.'

'But then the name Parker can't be true unless his father was British.'

'Yes they must have changed their name at some stage. No idea why; Aaron has never told me, but he has a British passport and so has his wife Leah. I would guess they are Iranian or Lebanese. What I do know is that their parents stayed in Cyprus and when they died Aaron moved here with his wife, but he told me he and his family were always protected by the British before and after they came here.'

'Bloody hell, why?'

'Look, I don't know everything but he told me he had a very special job; I guessed security or something similar. I'm very careful what I say to him; we just talk day-to-day stuff. He really is a man of mystery, but a pleasant one, and he always comes over as the complete gentleman, and he pays me very well.'

'That's why I rang you about him after his call last week, as he specifically asked me to look into Larry Nixon's pub. I told him that I had heard it may be for sale and I knew you would be the one to set this evening up, and he's paying.'

'I'm jealous, Sheila; he kept looking at you.'

'Yes, he shouldn't do that, Alice; it makes me blush.'

'I noticed, but why? Surely you have nothing to worry about – you're so cool I didn't even realise at first that he was the customer you frequently mention. You are so smart, and of course you must be giving him a special deal.'

'We see each other regularly and as I said he is very generous, so it's a good business relationship for both of us.'

29

Alice smiled and looked forward carefully as she accelerated from the sliproad on to the M25 motorway. She was also wondering about Aaron Parker, and how she should play her next meeting with him. She was a little concerned about her friend Sheila, and she decided that she would only tell her a very limited amount concerning her business deals. Alice wanted to know more about Aaron Parker as she was attracted to him, but then she knew any approach to him could mess up her friendship, so she decided to stick to business for the moment, and if a deal could be done with him and Nixon for little work, she would be more than happy.

Chapter 3
Randalls Park Crematorium
Leatherhead, December 2009

'I thought this ceremony for Gordon and Fay Fisher was meant to be a private one for family only, sir, but I see detectives, uniformed coppers and lots of blokes who look like the security services. This place has got to be far too small for Gordon and his wife. The family have known about the funeral for several weeks, so I wonder why it is still being held here?'

'It's safe, Norman; if you look at the front row, Alan Fisher and his Uncle Ted are the only family attending. It's our job to protect the two of them today, and the only way we could do that was to keep everyone away, which unfortunately includes some other family members and old colleagues. They'll have another ceremony: not here; maybe not even in the UK – probably in Jersey, and we are not invited to that under any circumstances, but his old friends from the military and SIB will be there, as, no doubt, will the Security Services (MI6) and his old legal colleagues. He was very well known and respected.

'The local people here just know that Gordon and Fay Fisher were attacked by supposed terrorists and murdered by a bomb blast in their own home just months after Gordon had retired from the service. The PM will speak again to the House of Commons tomorrow and make another statement. The words in the speech will be carefully put and sympathetic, but actually will mean nothing. At this stage many organisations are under investigation worldwide and there is a lot of speculation, so that will be his main point.'

'I understand, sir, and I just hope we can find the killers before any other bombs go off.'

Chief Superintendent Dick White turned to his colleague Detective Inspector Norman Hubbard and clenched his tightly-closed fist in front of his face; a spontaneous gesture of anger from the big man, but one his DI thought was a bit unnecessary.

'The security light is on red, Norman – we have no decent intelligence yet. The investigation has several threads, but nothing concrete. Gordon worked all over the Middle East and made few friends; he helped to convict the few bad guys in our ranks and saw they got the punishment to suit their crimes. Your team will report directly to me on this case; is that clear – we are just waiting now for SIS?'

'Yes sir. No DCI?'

'No – I prefer a small team, then there are no cock-ups, like what happened with Sutcliffe when nobody in the force talked to each other.'

White had his plan, and changing the subject, he turned the discussion straight back to the Fishers.

'The bottom line is that Gordon's job was vital in allowing the soldiers to do their work and make the world safer. If we ask the question who and where are his enemies, probably many are unknown to us, and with his job they are almost too numerous to list; but someone has to find out who, and that might be us but I'm not yet sure. Maybe we will never find who did it.'

'That's a strange view, sir. Do you know something?'

'Look, Norman – we should continue to send copies of all our findings to SIS for the time being.'

The inspector detected that his boss knew something that he wasn't telling him, and if SIS handled the search for the killers he would probably never find out what his boss knew about the deaths.

'I am told by SIS that nothing will happen soon, and we shouldn't be surprised if it turns out that this is not an investigation for them to be totally involved in. What the hell that is supposed to mean, other than that they are saying that the investigation could all end up in our lap, I'm not sure. If that happens it means almost certainly, Norman, that the deaths were not at the hands of terrorists.'

'It sounds like they're keeping us in the dark, sir, and then they'll wash their hands of it. Could it be that they just can't be bothered with the murders? Surely not, sir?'

'No, no, Norman – it's just the way they work; they are straightforward, and decisions are based on what they know. Unless a terrorist link surfaces I'm sure it could be totally our problem; sooner or later we'll know what they're doing, but I suspect it will all come back to us. We will be ready – or you will be, Detective Inspector; keep all that work you have done as this could be a murder case to make your name on, and I'm sure you're up for it.'

'Yes I am, sir. I hope everyone cooperates.'

'Not sure what you mean Norman, but remember: you tell me everything. Do you understand me?'

Hubbard just nodded, then looked away. The tone of Dick White's voice worried him; he wasn't sure if his boss even liked Gordon Fisher, but he certainly seemed anxious to know exactly who killed him and his wife before anyone else did.

Dick White was at the end of his career and it seemed to a few people that he had almost become over-involved in the case. It was obvious that he would have liked SIS to blame one of the known Middle Eastern terrorist groups, but there was no evidence, and the call he received from the Home Secretary had not been a friendly one. The Home Secretary had spoken to White's boss, the chief constable, and he would hear directly from him very soon that with the full cooperation of the SIS, the Surrey police, headed by White, should be ready to take full responsibility for the investigation, and he wanted a result quickly. An unusual call from a politician, but the Home Secretary knew Dick White, and his message was without doubt to make him understand that he did not want any cross-department fighting. On behalf of the Prime Minister, who was abroad, he would make a clear statement to Parliament in two days' time that the killers were probably not terrorists.

The four weeks' delay with the post mortems and funeral permission for Gordon and Fay Fisher appeared painful and unnecessary to Alan and his family. Nobody gave Alan straight answers; then suddenly he received a call from the police that he could finally move forward and set the date for the funeral in Leatherhead. Alan would never be told directly, but suicide had to be considered and he was intelligent enough to guess it would be a line of enquiry for the inquest. Nobody close to the Fishers would believe that outcome, but the post mortems hopefully would reveal all.

In the weeks since the bomb blast, Alan had tried hard to work even though his employer had told him to take a few weeks' compassionate leave; he would take the leave soon but he was desperate to have some solid clues on his parents' death first. The situation was very sad and frustrating for him, and he wanted to rip someone apart. In order to keep sane he increased his gym routine to nearly every day. He knew he had to carry on and complete his grieving. His brain was working overtime on why on earth his parents had been so brutally killed; in his mind with no apparent reason. His army career had in many ways prepared him for death, but not the deaths of his own parents. He had a note in his hand suggesting a meeting, and as he stood in the exit to the crematorium, he waited to speak to Dick White.

'Dick, don't say a word – you knew Mum and Dad as well as me; today belongs to them and tomorrow I will see you in the SIS office at Vauxhall Cross. I feel nothing now but anger and the need for retribution. I know in time it will become just a horrible, nightmarish memory, similar to the one I left the army for three years ago, but this time it's much worse.'

'Yes, Alan; we all feel the same as you, and I have an idea. SIS could pass the case back to us tomorrow, but let's wait and see. I will see you at 10am in London.'

The police chief did not want to linger; he had things to do before the next day and that included reading in detail once more the information about Gordon Fisher's career from his comprehensive file in advance of his next meeting. For his own reasons the file on Gordon would be one he would be pleased to see closed.

The remains of the front right hand side of the Fisher house was a ruin. The bomb had been planted in the garage, and the police forensic staff confirmed it had been triggered by the electric door closer signal, which was radio operated; the couple were killed instantly the button was pressed to open the door. In the darkness of the garage Gordon Fisher would not have noticed the marks on the wall where the device had been tampered with. The killer would also have known – or been told – that the couple were going out together that night, and that they would get into the vehicle by going through the house door, and then open and close the roller shutter after the car had left the garage. The homework had been done well, but for a professional it would only have taken a couple of days' surveillance.

The police had mentioned to Alan that a secondary explosion, again triggered by the door closer, occurred simultaneously and wrecked his father's office. It had obviously been intended to destroy the contents of the office, but Gordon Fisher kept little or no current papers in his house, a rule he had followed all his working life. Very little of the office remained, but what was left had been taken for analysis. The forensic team had instructions from SIS not to make public any details of the couple's death. The coroner would have to be satisfied on the completeness of information from the post mortems and the forensic report of the garage scene before an inquest hearing could commence. A few days after the deaths, the coroner would open the inquest, but in this case he would immediately adjourn it until the pathologist's work was complete and the cause of death was as clear as possible from the mutilated bodies.

The only known fact was that the garage and car had been destroyed by a bomb of the type known as an Improvised Explosive Device. Could the couple have died before the bomb exploded? A revolver had been found in the car with four bullets in the magazine and two empty slots. What had happened to the other two, and why was Gordon Fisher keeping the gun in the seat pocket? IEDs were well known to the armed forces; they could not be bought ready-made and thorough knowledge was needed to assemble one. Amateurs varied the explosive mix and detonation devices, often with disastrous consequences. This resulted in the bomb disposal teams having their work cut out until the device's maker could be identified, or the style recognised by the men who seemingly had no fear, and bravely disarmed bombs by hand or through controlled explosions in war zones.

The jury at the inquest could have several possible verdicts to consider, the most likely one being unlawful death by explosion caused by person or persons unknown. Another could be suicide, but good reason would be needed for this almost unthinkable outcome.

Chapter 4
Office of the Home Secretary
Whitehall, London

'So, gentlemen, what can you tell me before I'm hit by a barrage of questions in the House of Commons tomorrow? The PM has told me he wants an official statement about the death of the Fishers, and I'm to deliver it. What he has had from me already was very little. Hopefully you have something concrete I can give him?'

The chief constable nervously coughed, shuffled his papers and looked up at the Home Secretary.

'The police view is that the bomb could have been made by terrorists, but not necessarily planted by terrorists. The materials used must have been supplied by someone who knew exactly what they were doing – it wasn't something made in a garage by a novice with weed killer; it was grade A plastic explosive and a sophisticated trigger device, but from the blast area it looks like the packing fell apart seconds before the explosion. This tells us that whoever set it off was not experienced. From the forensic photographs we have also discovered some evidence on the position of the explosives: they were hidden under the front car seats. This leads us to believe that the killers were definitely targeting both Gordon and his wife. For some reason Gordon had a revolver in the car. We are checking that out; maybe he expected visitors. The garage and a large part of his office were badly damaged and the force of the bomb was so strong the house will most likely have to be demolished soon as it is unsafe. Then it's up to the son, Alan Fisher, if he rebuilds it or not.

'I personally have not seen a bomb do so much damage since the IRA bombing in Brighton. I am told the amount of explosive used was massive; the bodies were mutilated. Army links are a possibility, but not one we can talk about. If anyone asks you, sir, it's safest to reply that we are following many lines of investigation, which in itself is not untrue. The eldest Fisher boy, Ben, was killed in Kabul by friendly fire; the younger son, Alan, left the army and we know one of the reasons was his brother's death. He is, as expected, cooperating with us fully. He now works in the council planning department and is local if we need his help.'

The Home Secretary put his hand up to interrupt. 'I went to the funeral as well yesterday. I saw you guys there, but thankfully as I sat behind you with my detective, nobody approached me. It was a sad day, and not one for questions and answers by the press. I knew Gordon Fisher well before he was a Judge Advocate, and of course we bumped into each other several times after he took the job. In case you are asked why we met up

40

recently, it was to discuss a private matter and it has nothing to do with this investigation I assure you, he seemed quite normal; he was retiring and looking forward to the future.'

'We knew you were at the crematorium, sir, and don't think we left you totally alone with just your detective. We had men behind you.'

'I know, I saw them, and thanks.'

'Sir, if you know anything about Gordon you think may help us, please let us know. We need details of things he said to you recently about his job.'

'No, it wasn't about his job: it was about a dinner party. Fay Fisher was a cousin of mine, and I was around when Gordon met her. We used to meet a couple of times a year.'

The Home Secretary, for his own reasons, would not say any more, and his visitors dared not push him on the subject. He knew that one day he might have to give more information, but not at a meeting of many people.

'What is the SIS view today?'

The director lifted his head. He did not like the current Home Secretary due to the hard time he had given him over his own boss, the chief of SIS, who was supposed to write a statement for the House of Commons. The meeting prior to the statement being prepared was unusual in that the top man in SIS had suddenly become unavailable, and sent his London-based director. The

41

chief had given no explanation for his late withdrawal from the meeting; just a brief apology.

'John Wickham sends his apologies for not being here, but something has come up that needs his personal operational involvement, sir, and he said he will call you later.'

'Bloody hell, this is an issue of national security; Fisher was a judge! I'll call him later; now get on with it.' The Home Secretary was agitated, and his face was turning purple as the SIS man spoke.

'Our position is clear: today we started passing any information we have on the death of Gordon Fisher and his wife to Surrey Police. We have said internally to anyone that has asked that in our opinion a terrorist group was not responsible for the deaths. Since the day of the bombing I have had two case officers working on the evidence, and we are certain that no splinter groups, activists or anybody who is a known threat to the UK now or possibly in the future is involved.'

'That is a very broad statement. Have SIS some evidence that tells us you are 100% certain that is the case, and that I can tell the PM so we can all relax in our beds tonight?'

Nobody smiled, and the director started to get annoyed.

'Sir, this is a grotesque double murder and no other words can describe it. Given Gordon Fisher's background, he would have been vulnerable to an attack from someone he had passed sentence on in a court martial. That is the line of enquiry we have recommended the police to follow. To make certain, though, we are in daily contact with our foreign base staff – mostly targeting officers – to see if anybody is commenting about the atrocity, and the Americans are doing the same.'

The Home Secretary had heard enough and his irritation at the comments was clear. He interrupted the speech.

'Why the fucking Americans? They should have enough to keep themselves occupied.'

The director replied calmly, almost before he had finished the question.

'We share information with them, and if something is mentioned in their domain it will bring up a red warning on their screens, in case there is a copycat or a previous death investigation that mentioned the Fisher name, or in fact anything that could lead to a similar crime in the USA. I've prepared a statement for you and the chief constable has agreed its content; it is a joint communiqué, as you would expect. If required we will put as many resources behind the capture and conviction of the killers as needed, but the main enquiry will be done by the police, and I stress, with our total cooperation if specifically requested. Later today I'll meet with Alan Fisher as he has asked to see me – his father and I were friends. I'll give him an outline on the case but no detail; I understand that the murder team in Guildford have their best men on it and they'll need to interview Alan soon. Hopefully something will break soon on the actual reasons for the bombing, but in the meantime I'll send a report of my meeting with Alan to the police tomorrow. Finally, the red national security alert we had in place has been dropped back to yellow, and the extra security people patrolling Heathrow and the Channel Tunnel have been stood down.'

'Thank you, but aren't I usually consulted on that first?'

'You were, sir. I gave you the basic information; you just nodded as you were on your way to question time.'

'Yes, sorry – I do remember now. I won't tell the House anything unless they ask, as the opposition get awkward with red or yellow, or any other bloody colour. Now, Mr Chief Constable: do you share the views of the SIS, that this is another situation where you guys closely cooperate with each other and that applies to MI5 as well? To hell with the politics, I'll handle that; you just have to quickly find the bastards who did it, and why.'

The chief constable wriggled on his chair, as the speech from SIS had made it clear that the investigation would now continue firmly with the police.

'We have a very experienced team set up to investigate the murders, led by Chief Superintendent White. At this stage I agree with SIS that any statement for the House of Commons should be kept simple and without any speculation; if you have not done it, sir, please do it as soon as possible. We are aware of the government's concern but the need to keep anything we learn quiet is of utmost importance, without it seeming that we are keeping them in the dark.'

'Don't tell me what to do, please, but I do get your point. It's on the agenda now for tomorrow; I'll tell the PM in a routine call tonight.' The Home Secretary was already reading papers for his next meeting. Then he stood up and shook hands with his visitors. As he got to the door he spun on his heels and pointed to the group, but at no one in particular.

'Do you think it could possibly happen again? Separate answers, please; you first, chief?'

'Unfortunately yes. The killer may have other targets but somehow they will have a link to Gordon Fisher. We're checking out everyone he knew well and dealt with, and that's a lot of people.'

'Thank you, and the SIS view, please?'

'Again, yes – Fisher may be one of several targets, and the police are correct that his friends and connections probably hold the key to the bomber.'

'Keep me posted. Let's keep a yellow status for the time being, please, and don't argue between yourselves.'

The two men left and had a brief discussion on the steps of Whitehall.

'It's almost if he knows something we don't.'

'I hope not, if he does know something we may have to get some help.'

'Look, my boss and the PM meet occasionally at No 10; if we feel that SIS is not being told something by the Home Secretary, he will get involved and find out what it is. That doesn't mean we will get it; if it's relevant the PM will decide.'

'Thanks. I have Chief Superintendent White, one of our top men, on the case and I think you have met him already. If you feel he needs a push, let me know.'

'Hopefully Parliament are sensible and just let us get on with it.'

The two men left Whitehall separately, but as soon as their drivers had left central London they both made phone calls. The call from the SIS director was to Jason Harris, a senior case officer.

'Jason, come and see me in my office first thing in the morning. There's something about this Fisher bombing that's bothering me, and someone is rattling the Home Secretary's cage.'

'OK, sir; I'll see you about 9am. What's the agenda?'

'This is the story: I had a call from our Turkish station on that piece of news we had from the US, and it's all making sense now. Look up everything you have on the man; find out who we have that can speak Turkish, and also someone who knows that specific area of Turkey and Iran.'

'I have just the team for you. Shall I call them in?'

'Yes Jason, but not if they're all our men; some might have to be anonymous.'

'Not sure on that one, sir – the files will be on your desk in an hour.'

'Get Brian Wilson involved in the morning as well; brief him first before I get into the office. I will explain the anonymous requirement when I arrive.'

'I assume the second man is the one we discussed? He is very close to you.'

'Never assume, Jason, in your job, but yes, call him and make sure he is coming.'

Chapter 5
SIS (MI6) HQ
Vauxhall Cross, London

The three men sat round the oval table without a smile between them as the director broke the silence.

'Alan, this is our third meeting now and from all the information we have gathered we have reached the following current opinion on your parents' deaths. It is most unlikely that their deaths were the result of an action by a known terrorist group; I say known as sometimes we have a renegade or splinter group that do something unexpected, and when we finally track them down they have usually already been killed by their own people or are awaiting trial for some other capital crime. We cannot be 100% certain that your parents' deaths were down to someone else other than a terrorist. We will therefore continue to seek information on all links to your father's previous activities, but mainly supporting the police, as it's ultimately their investigation. We have a specialist here in SIS who does nothing all day and every day but turn over stones and search via computers, phone taps, newspapers and CCTV – information most people never see, so hopefully Molly will find something.

The analysis of the explosive device is that it was an IED wired to the detonator set off by a radio signal in the garage door opener. This was most unusual; we think someone designed it with specialist knowledge in explosives and bomb making, and we know only a few people who could have done it. Research is now being carried out, but more on that in a minute.

'Bombs are daily occurrences in war zones and the IEDs are crude in their construction, but deadly for the bomb disposal guys. The bomb in the garage was very well made, and of a construction we hadn't seen since the Northern Ireland Troubles. The secondary device was more incendiary and it started the fire – we have come across this before when the objective was to destroy the contents of a room, and in this case an office. It had been set up to detonate a few seconds after the first blast; we are not sure why, other than it could be that whoever did this got hold of ready-made IEDs and altered them to do the job.

'Now back to the door closer trigger: we found the device almost complete, and although it was the normal opener it had been modified to the frequency of the detonator, very much like some we have seen in Iraq. In the poor light your father would not have noticed the scratch marks where the closer had been opened and modified. The explosion in your father's office was not positioned very well, as the safe almost protected the filing cabinet due to the positioning of the incendiary device. Our view is that although it was very much a professional device, the person who placed the bombs was not experienced. A professional would have hidden it in case your father had returned to the house, but not behind the safe. So, Alan, we are saying that it would need to be someone with very good electronics knowledge – in my opinion, with army or special forces experience – to set those devices up, but not necessarily plant them.

'Finally, our opinion is that the killer watched the explosion: we couldn't find any tyre or footprints in the garden but that means nothing; this person would have been making sure the bomb went off before he made his exit. It's speculative I know, but to go to the lengths he or she did with the door closer and the fire bomb, they would want to make certain it all happened first time around, as perhaps material was not available to repeat the process. I must now ask you a question, then I'll hand over to Chief Super White, but Alan, please don't be angry.'

Alan guessed the question, but waited for the words.

'Do you think your parents could have taken their own lives?'

'No. I'm not angry; it's a logical question and the coroner will probably make that point at the inquest, but to me it's just cold-blooded murder. I don't care if it is SIS or the police find the killers, but someone has to tell me the reasons why. It's eating me up.'

Alan paused and drank his coffee down in one gulp. He walked to the window and spoke as he moved towards the sunlight.

'I have no doubt that at some stage the coroner will ask me if they were unhappy or showed any signs of distress, and my answer will be a very big *NO*. They were very happy; I saw them the day before it happened and they told me that they were just about to book some holidays. My father had just retired and they had lots of plans; I'm very sure that they were settled and looking forward to the future. The only problem they had was the memory of my brother's death hanging over them, but recently they even seemed to have come to terms with that.'

Chief Superintendent Dick White took his turn to speak.

'I agree with you, Alan – suicide is very unlikely, but as no motive is on the table for the deaths we have to ask the question. What happened to your brother was a terrible thing, as is any death in action.'

Alan nodded. 'My brother Ben and I both joined the army after our education. He was a high-flyer and was promoted several times before he was 30; we were not in the same regiment, but unknown to our parents we did meet sometimes in the Middle East. The last time I saw him was in Turkey at a US airbase where I worked for a period before I finished up in Baghdad. My battalion were on a clean-up trip to Iraq, but Ben had a girlfriend in Istanbul and he was on special leave before he left for

Afghanistan. My brother had somehow found out where I was, and we met and had a meal and a few beers at the base before he went back to his platoon. He couldn't tell me what he was doing, so we talked mostly about football, home, girls – you know, the sort of stuff men discuss. During our meeting he was on edge; he mentioned some sort of threat he had received but he said it was not for me and he was dealing with it. As he left the café he said a strange thing: "Look out for Mum and Dad if anything ever happens to me." That wasn't like Ben – he was usually very happy-go-lucky and outwardly he seemed to have no fears, but this time he must have been pretty afraid of his next mission in Afghanistan. I said the same; we shook hands and he left. I never saw him again.

'He was killed the next week in Kabul by a stray bullet. The report said he was just walking to his tent after attempting a recovery of four stranded local Afghan soldiers; two made it, but two didn't. One of the Afghan sergeants he had rescued shot him by mistake as he cleaned his gun; a round had been left in the breech. It was a terrible accident and definitely one that should never have happened. But that was of no consolation to Ben or the rest of us. He got a medal and a free ride to Brize Norton; naturally we were all devastated at his death. My mum and dad took it very badly, but they never asked me to give up. I had an opportunity to leave before I signed up for a longer stretch and although I didn't fancy a 9–5 job I wanted to stay alive, so it had to be a career outside the army.'

The director stood up and served the coffee.

'Did you really think that, Alan? You were known to me as Alan Fisher, a man of action, and one I was possibly grooming for SIS.'

'You mean, sir, that my father was bending your ear; it sounds like he was trying to push my career along. He knew I was good on intelligence, computers and hi-tech equipment, so he had this vision of me in SIS.'

'Alan, please be straight with us. Why did you leave the army?'

Nobody spoke. Alan stared at the ceiling; he had faced interrogation techniques in his training and his tactic was to say nothing, as they would only have to look in his file for the answer.

'OK Alan, we know we can find out, but our guess is you were threatened after Ben's death that unless you did something your parents would be attacked. Probably not related to your brother's death, we guess.'

Alan Fisher's face showed no emotion; not a muscle moved in his body. He had been trained by an elite army unit, and to leave it and become a planning officer or a surveyor was like moving from one end of the earth to the other and into a dead-end job. His face told the story; he was with some of the most important men in UK security and the police, but he could not give them the answers they wanted. He now had his own agenda: to deal with the killers of his

53

parents without any mercy and as quickly as possible. He would take the compassionate leave from his planning job, and with the help of an old friend or two, follow the few clues he had.

'I'll say one thing: that's not why I left; please read my file.'

'We have, Alan, and it's not specific; it just states that they were personal reasons. If you are going to do what we think you are, please be very, very careful; leave it all to the police. We are stepping back from the case, but we know the police will be keeping an eye on you for your own safety. I want you here in SIS one day, not frontline. Your technical brain is our requirement as a case officer, and I promise you it's better paid and with opportunities to go as far as you want. I also promise you it will be much more interesting than town planning.'

Alan found a smile. The prospect of a job at SIS was far from his mind, but he would not write the idea off.

Chief Superintendent Dick White broke up the meeting. He had not liked the suggestions made to Alan by the director of SIS, and he would phone him later and tell him so. Fisher was a civilian now, and in White's view, he should remain one.

'I will drop you back to Leatherhead, Alan. Where are you going to live?'

'I always had my flat in Epsom but never lived in it; I just let it out. When I left the army I terminated the letting agreement and now I live in it. Please drop me in Epsom town centre; I'm going to the gym now and then I'm seeing a friend.'

Dick White gave Alan an old-fashioned look; he knew that he did not want the policeman to know where he lived.

'I can find out where you live, Alan, when I need to. I have your mobile; keep it on at all times, and I mean all times.'

'Thanks, my dad was always talking about you. He said you fancied his job.'

Alan had touched on something, as Dick White changed his tone and pointed at him.

'Look, Alan, from now please call me Dick when we are on our own. Have you thought about joining the police instead of the security people?'

'No, Dick, and not even SIS, but you are aware of my priorities and I am sure at some stage I may need you. Don't worry, I'm not keeping any firearms.'

'Alan, you don't need firearms, and please don't try anything.'

The warning was lost on Alan: he would do what was needed when the time came, and he was sure that it would. He left the policeman's car and entered the gym; grabbed his clothes from his locker, changed and met Cheryl, who was dating a rowing machine.

'Speed it up or you'll stall.'

'Hi lover boy, how is it with you?'

'Fine. Much as I expected, I'm signed off from work for a month and I've a few things to do. The inquest will be soon, and afterwards I'm going to demolish the house and maybe sell the land or rebuild it. I've already had an offer on the land yesterday.'

'Bloody hell, I'm going to stick hold of you, mate.'

'You bet you will, and tell your mother not to start any work in the shop until the plans have gone through and been approved. I finished the approval document before I saw my boss and everything should happen soon, but she must wait.'

'That's brilliant Alan, thanks. Did the funeral service go OK yesterday?'

'It was as sad as it can get, Cheryl, when people die before their time. My parents deserved a long retirement and I still can't believe it happened.'

'Come here and give me a hug. I left you alone as I know your Uncle Ted was looking after you. He reminds me of my dad, but much older.'

'Yes. Now get the machine going; we're not going for dinner until you have done 2,000 metres. I need you to keep that body in trim.'

'Why, you cheeky sod – just so your mates can lust over me?'

'No, Cheryl – so I can.'

Cheryl stopped her gym programme and grabbed a towel, the clock said 2,000 metres.

'I think I'm in love with you, Alan Fisher.'

Alan just smiled. She was a great girl, but he did not want her involved in his plans to find the killers. He knew he would probably need to restrict his time with her in the coming weeks; the killers were an unknown quantity and he could not put her at any risk.

'I don't have any transport as the car is at home. Why don't we get a bus and go to The Brown Cow and have dinner, then come back to my place?'

'Yes, great idea; I'm actually going to see your new place which you have been putting off showing me off for weeks. My mum thinks you live at the YMCA.'

Alan just smiled. He had deliberately delayed showing the girl his place; so far she had passed his tests, but he knew people changed after the initial excitement of a new relationship had worn off.

'Alan, do you think you will ever get over the death of your parents and brother? I can't believe so much has happened to you. How do you really feel?'

'I learnt a lot in the army, Cheryl, and I saw death all the time. When my brother Ben was killed that was enough for me; I'm not a coward, but fighting for hopeless causes really got to me and I didn't want a new long-term stint in the war zones. Army life is great, but you live in barracks or camps and you forget what it's like to have home comforts; many of my friends are locked in to five or ten more years of standing in a shooting gallery and hoping nobody finds them and pulls a trigger. My parents understood, and this civilian job has taken me two years to get the necessary training completed. During that time I lived with my parents, so at least I had some quality time with them before it all happened.'

'The way you talk it's as if you expected something to happen. Did you?'

'Don't be a detective, Cheryl; I'll tell you one day. All I'll say is that I'm a fatalist and yes, my Dad made some enemies when he was working as he was in the front line of military justice. I think, though, that the killer or killers are here in the UK, and with help from the Met, Surrey Police will hopefully track them down. It may take a year, but I'm certain it'll happen one day.'

'Sounds like you may be helping them.'

Alan avoided a direct answer.

'Just going to check a few things in my parents' possessions, but then I have a job to get back to as soon as the compassionate leave is over. I'm not used to doing nothing; it makes me think too much, so don't worry – I'll be going back to work for certain.'

Cheryl was already getting to know her boyfriend much better, and his determination to succeed in life was written all over his face. She had not slept with him yet and he was not pushing her; it did not matter to her at this time, but she resolved to encourage him as soon as the inquest was over. Maybe then he would relax a little bit more.

The Brown Cow was very quiet as Alan and Cheryl grabbed a couple of bar stools. The only other person at the bar was the retired lawyer Harold Penny.

'Evening Harold; in pole position for a pint, I see.'

'Yes, but service is non-existent; Larry is ill and Jill has taken him to the quack. He should lay off the whisky, he's probably drinking what little profit the pub is making, if it's making any at all.'

'Is he very ill?'

'Not sure. He has problems but what they are is a mystery; he keeps everything to himself. It's probably linked to this place; I promised to see him tonight about an idea I had, but he must have forgotten.'

As Harold spoke, the barmaid (and now assistant chef) Marie burst into the bar.

'I'm sorry, gentlemen, I'm on my own and I've had to make some sandwiches for the couple over there. What can I get you?'

'Pint of bitter for me please, Marie, and a gin and tonic for Cheryl.'

Cheryl had already taken a dislike to the Polish girl as she saw how she looked at her handsome boyfriend, but then Marie noticed and turned to her.

'Hello, I'm Marie. We haven't met before.'

'Yes, that's right; I'm Cheryl. Are you totally on your own tonight?'

'At the moment nobody else is here, so I can only do cold food if you want to eat.'

Alan smelt danger and interrupted.

'I'll tell you what, Marie: we'll have a couple of ham salads, but don't worry, I'll keep an eye on the bar. It's not exactly crowded.'

Harold laughed as Marie went to the kitchen, leaving Alan to do the drinks.

'Give me a pint of Guinness then Alan, as well as your own drinks, and keep a glass to put the money in for Larry.'

A few more people came into the pub and Alan suddenly found himself busy. He had no idea of the prices, so he just rounded up to the nearest pound what he thought it should be and made a note of everything so Marie could sort it out when she had served the food.

The entrance of Larry Nixon was like something from a cowboy film; he burst in through the side door as he had seen Alan behind the bar and wondered what was going on.

'What the fuck are you doing, Fisher?'

'What does it look like I'm doing, Larry – helping you out! Have you got a problem with that?'

Larry's face was creased with anger as he looked around the pub at his customers, all of whom were looking at him. He lifted the counter flap and just pointed to Alan and then the door, gesturing him to get out of the pub. Alan was convinced that Larry was going to explode, and if he attacked him he would have to defend himself. If that happened the landlord was in serious trouble; he was obviously not a well man. Larry had been in the services, but he was in poor condition. Alan was a trained fighting soldier, and he knew he would have to get out of the pub quickly. He grabbed Cheryl's arm and they left the pub.

Jill Nixon and the barmaid Marie caught the end of the confrontation, and both of them glared at Larry as he put the cash Alan had taken into the till and slammed it shut. The customers in the bar all drank up quickly, and apart from Harold Penny, left within a couple of minutes. The atmosphere could have been cut with a knife, and the two women were afraid of what Larry would do next, but he surprised them by suddenly laughing and turning the incident into a joke.

'Running my pub, Harold – what will the Fisher boy do next?'

'You'll soon be running out of friends and customers, Larry, if you continue to behave like that. The boy was just helping you, couldn't you see that?'

'No, he was just taking the piss because I wasn't here.'

Jill decided to be brave and she put her hand around her husband's shoulder. He was shaking like a leaf.

'Come on, let's have a cup of tea and Marie can handle the bar.'

He pulled away from his wife and poked Harold in the back.

'Don't you want to talk to me, Harold, like you said yesterday?'

'Definitely not, Larry. I'll come back sometime and if you're in a better mood we can discuss something.'

'No way – fuck off, Harold!'

Harold didn't need any more encouragement; he was leaving anyway, and he almost ran out of the door to get away from the mad landlord.

'You've done it now, Larry – you've cleared the pub completely. We had eight customers ten minutes ago.'

Larry ignored his wife and grabbed a bottle of Johnny Walker whisky and a glass. He poured a large measure, then went upstairs leaving a frightened barmaid and a crying wife to clear up the empty pub.

Alan and Cheryl had no car, so they decided to walk into Leatherhead and go in the first pub they came to. They were both in shock and Alan was very quiet, but since his brother's death he coped with anger much better than he had as a boy. Alan had been a hot-headed youth until he had a reality check when he joined the army. He soon discovered how precious life was, and in his mind sad dickheads like Larry Nixon had no place in his life.

The couple found The Eagle, a modern gastropub in the town, and were soon tucking into a bar meal and a drink in a place that actually welcomed their business – unlike The Brown Cow, a pub that Alan was convinced was doomed to closure.

'Thank goodness we got away in one piece, Alan – that guy is mad.'

'I don't know Larry Nixon very well, but my dad went to the pub quite a lot. Not sure why he stopped but it must have been due to that bloke. . .but I can't ask him now, Cheryl, so let's forget it.'

'Yes, sure. So tell me about your meetings - was it the police?'

'Later, Cheryl darling, not now.'

Alan did not want his girlfriend to know anything at all about the investigation into his parents' death; if she didn't know anything, she wouldn't worry. His problem would be explaining some of his movements to her over the coming weeks, as they were likely to get very complicated. The couple finished their meal and got a bus to Cheryl's home. Alan kissed her goodnight and continued on to his apartment in Epsom. He needed to get things down on paper: who did his father know, who were his real friends, did he have obvious enemies? There were many questions, and he would start in the charred remains taken from the house by the police and spread out in a police warehouse in Guildford. Alan completed three pages of his notes, then fell asleep with his mind working overtime. The nightmare of the bomb returned to him; he could have died as well if he had been in the house. He jumped up in a sweat, and a thought came to him: whoever planted the device wanted to destroy his father's office papers as well, or at least make it difficult for anyone sorting through the remains. He would see what was left, there must be a clue or two in the Guildford warehouse.

The noise of his mobile phone woke him up, and when he looked at his alarm clock it was 8am. The number was blocked and that pissed him off; if it was someone selling double-glazing or life insurance from India he would tell them where to get off. But the smooth voice of the SIS director was instantly recognisable.

'Alan, I have a busy agenda but I just noticed something after reading the report again that may be relevant. We know the first explosion killed your parents, and we also know that there were two explosions; the second one, probably an incendiary, didn't explode properly. In the debris the forensic guys found an unused detonator – the bomber must have been disturbed and he panicked as he was setting it up and damaged the detonator. He then replaced it with a second one, leaving the first on the office floor. As we mentioned to you before, the killer must have put the device behind the safe so anyone looking into the room wouldn't see it. We have checked out the detonator and its origin and without any doubt it's one of ours. A few of our lads brought back trophies – stupid really, but this could be one of them. The plastic explosive we are convinced came from Ireland, but that of course usually means it originally came from Libya.'

'Thanks, but why are you telling me all this?'

'Two reasons, Alan: one, we didn't want you digging around on things we know; we have our work cut with terrorist scares, and we didn't want you asking the wrong people about explosives. Secondly, we had a meeting after you left our office; we do want you to join us here in SIS, firstly as a case officer, but then in the field. It will take six months to get total clearance for you, and I'll meet you next week at a neutral location and not here in London. You don't have to make a decision now.'

'OK, thanks. I'm not committing myself as I already said at the meeting, but we can talk.'

'I'll be in touch. Bye.'

The abrupt end was typical of the director, and Alan knew that for security reasons anything in detail he learned from him would be in person and in total privacy. Alan had been in Iraq before he left the army and knew what detonators looked like, but so had hundreds – perhaps thousands – of servicemen, so anyone could have brought the trophies home. From his father's address book he made a list of ex army contacts; it would be a long job sorting the book and an even longer one finding the people in it. As he prepared for the day and took a long shower he missed another call, and this time when he got to his phone he recognised the number. It was Harold Penny, and he returned the call.

'Harold, I saw you called me.'

'Yes, Alan; I'm really sorry for that nonsense last night. Larry Nixon has always had the tendency to go off into a rage about something and nothing, and nowadays it's happening more and more. The man is going broke and he needs to find a buyer for the pub to clear his debts; I had a couple of contacts to give him, but after last night I walked away from the pub. I'll give it a week or so before I go back. His wife is a darling and Larry can be charming, but I think he's screwed up about something in his life other than the pub, and it's affecting him and he's drinking too much; maybe because of that Polish girl, who I'm sure he's seeing on the quiet. Jill is no fool, so next time I go to the pub it'll be on a Tuesday when he plays snooker in town. No doubt if I talk to her for a bit, she can tell me more about the pub and if it's worth giving Larry my contacts' names.

'Anyway, I didn't phone you up to whinge about Larry – I've done as you asked and started to put together your parents' estate. This is a special one, Alan; you know I'm retired but when you asked me I had to do it – still, this really is my last job. It's the saddest one I've ever had, and not a probate that I ever expected to be doing, but nevertheless I promise you I'll be thorough. I'll warn you, though – it'll probably take me a long time. Can you come and see me tomorrow? We can discuss the will itself and the estate; there's a lot of tax to pay soon unfortunately, but we'll see how we can handle that and the property. A valuation on a bombsite will be tricky.'

'Thanks, Harold. I'd almost forgotten about The Brown Cow; I was only trying to help but in future I'll steer well clear of Mr Larry Nixon, so I'll need to find a new local. Do you think he'll find a buyer for the place?'

'Yes, but not sure if it'll clear his debts – that's one for Bill Knowles, his accountant. I'm never sure about him either; the word is he's already working with some property people, but I don't know any details.'

Chapter 6
Office of Bill Knowles

'Come in, Alice Smith; really nice to see you again.'

'What's got into you, Bill; why are you being nice to me? You're usually such a rude bugger.'

'I smell a deal with Aaron Parker; my nose tells me he wants Larry Nixon's pub. I worked hard on convincing him to have a look and he's keen. He'll be here in a few minutes to see you. Remember, though – it's Leah who holds the purse strings on releasing investment cash; he told me that.'

'Sounds interesting. Is he stashed?'

'Yes. I don't know where from – he looks like an Arab and we know his family was from the Middle East, but it stops there. He moved to England with his family years ago; I don't know exactly when. His name is on a couple of restaurant investments in Surrey, with a share of the places but not total ownership. I think he's testing the market. It's the usual deal between you and I, Alice: you do the legwork and deal with his questions; arrange site visits and the usual searches to make sure Larry and Jill Nixon do own the joint and the land behind. I have put some numbers together as Parker will be here soon; we can ask him how he intends to finance the deal. Then I'll do my bit and hopefully make it all work.'

'What's Larry Nixon's situation, Bill?'

'Not good. He owes around £180,000 so by the time he's paid me and all the legal costs, he will be wiped out. Now comes the sting: I'll let things get really bad over the next month and Larry will get a couple of writs. He'll panic – he's a nervous guy anyway and he'll be desperate – and then I'll make him an offer he can't refuse; probably around £200,000 but it's worth loads more. In the meantime, you warm up Aaron Parker; it's essential that you sell him the location; the land to build, etc. We can tell him later that we've got him a good price as Larry Nixon is on the rocks. In other words, I buy the place and do a back-to-back transaction with Parker.'

'Can you do that, Bill? Won't Larry know what you're doing?'

'No – there is a way, and the for sort of price I'll buy it for, it's worth the risk.'

'So what's my cut then, Bill? I do have quite a lot of work to do.'

'Depends on what I get the place for, but between £8,000 and £9,000; and that includes a bit for your mate Sheila, providing she continues to keep close to Aaron. You know what I mean, Alice: she keeps *very* close. How you divide it up is down to you.'

'If you do the sting and get £250,000 from Parker, I want another £1,000 as you'll be making around £50,000. Tell me more about how you can control Larry Nixon to get what you really want.'

'I have a way and she has a dress. I know everything he wants.'

'No, I don't believe it, Bill – not Jill Nixon?'

'Next subject Alice, please; leave it now.'

Alice laughed at Bill. He had it all worked out, but that did not mean it would happen. She would get a letter from him about the commission; she didn't trust him, and they agreed she would collect the document the following day.

Sheila Hamilton was waiting for her in her car outside the accountant's office.

'That didn't take long Alice, what's in it for me?'

'It'll be worth having, I promise, but you have to keep sleeping with Aaron now and then and keep very close to what he's doing. Ask him questions when you are together; anything we can get could help Bill to close the deal.'

'No problem, that's what I do anyway; I see him regularly but tell Bill I want £500 for my expenses now. That bloke has expensive tastes, and I need to get cabs most of the time. I'm skint.'

'Is your hostess job with him not paying, then?'

'No, it's OK – that's how I met Aaron, and he's sort of told me it's him only and I don't take any other punters, which is rubbish. He does look after me but I need more money, as that arrangement restricts me a bit.'

'How much does he give you, Sheila?'

'£1,000 a time plus dinner; I usually see him a couple of times a month, sometimes three – all cash; not enough for me to live on in my place as it's bloody expensive, but it's a good start each month and I've a couple of other customers to keep me in champagne.'

Parker was something of a mystery man and it was difficult for Bill Knowles to find out exactly where he lived. He owned an apartment somewhere in Reigate, which Bill guessed might be in his wife's name. Information on them was difficult to get, and he asked a couple of local friends about them in person to see if anyone knew the couple, but nobody could be found, or maybe they just were not saying.

An AMG Mercedes pulled up under the front window of Bill's office. The accountant was green with envy as the shiny silver door swung open and the tall figure of Parker climbed out of the vehicle. Bill opened the office door and smiled at Parker.

'Nice set of wheels, Mr Parker.'

'Call me Aaron, and yes, just got it and I'm frightened to leave it anywhere.'

'Come into the office. Do you want tea or coffee?'

'No thanks, let's get straight down to business. I briefly spoke with Alice at the pub and also in the car park after the meal: yes, the place has possibilities. What do you think? You know the area better than me.'

'Yes, it has potential, but it's on the catering side rather than just as a pub; this has been done on a couple of places locally and they're very successful. The problem will be that if Larry Nixon, the owner, knows you are the man interested then the price will rocket. My suggestion is that I front the deal so Larry sells to me – I'm his accountant and I think he trusts me. The place as it stands is probably worth around £350,000 but it's small and needs at least £60,000 spent on it.'

Parker showed no emotion on Bill's price summary. 'What are your ideas for it?'

'You may know that I own a share in a couple of places a few miles away and my plan is for a Mediterranean restaurant, tapas and wine bar. Old English pubs selling just beer and a few heated-up bar meals don't make money. It will be a top quality restaurant and I'll eventually be looking for a Michelin star. I'll build a dozen or so rooms on the back so we can do overnight accommodation as well; all the small hotels are full in this area and I think we will be expanding it within two to three years. We'll need planning permission but that's my risk; I'll get an architect to look it over once you have given the go-ahead from the owner.'

72

'How are you going to fund the deal? That's the key to getting the best price.'

'No problem: it'll be a cash deal if the values are correct. What's your fee?'

'Ten per cent of the sale price to you; I don't do legal, Aaron, so you'll need a solicitor for the conveyance. My part is the introduction and helping to smooth the process.'

'Too much, Bill – 5% is my figure. Your suggestion is wrong; it's just an intro fee we're talking about and that is much lower. It's straightforward and you have little to do, now give me a better rate.'

'You need more from me on this deal; that's why I want 10%. I have people to pay as well for background work and they will need expenses.'

'No, it's 8% so if it's around £250,000 you get around £20,000. We shake hands now.'

Bill grabbed his hand before he changed his mind. He knew his big money would come from the sting, but he'd tried to make the man understand he wasn't a pushover and failed. Parker was firmly in control.

'How can I reach you, Aaron?'

Parker handed him a piece of paper with some scribbled writing. He was not a man for business cards.

'Use this address, it's my PO box; or just send me a note by email and I'll contact you immediately.'

The apartment address was obviously linked to the PO box, but Bill already had the actual address. Parker was not giving out phone numbers to anyone.

'Alice Smith has a way to contact me in an emergency. Call her and she'll contact me immediately through a friend; I'll then call you.'

Bill was frustrated that this man was not opening up to him, and if the deal he had planned was to work he had to be sure that Parker would come up with the money at the right time. His manner gave the impression that money was not an issue, and his car fitted his image.

'Have you always lived in the UK, Aaron?'

'What is this, *Police 5*, or are you a detective agency as well as an accountant?'

'No, just trying to get to know you a bit. I know nothing about you and we're soon to have a deal between us.'

'I'm just a very private person, Bill. My background is complex and my family moved my wife and I here many years ago; we are both British citizens now. We had a few enemies in the Middle East as my father was, let me say, *a trader*, but he made sure we were safe by sending us here for your government to watch over us.'

'Bloody hell, you must be important to them.'

'Not really, now – my father always helped your country and I followed him in business in the Middle East and learnt a lot from him. I helped save the lives of many of your countrymen. I still have some enemies as well out there but I'm pretty sure most of them are dead. But as not all of them have gone, I keep my life very private just to be on the safe side.'

'I understand, Aaron, and thanks for telling me. All that makes me more comfortable.'

Aaron Parker almost smiled as he left the office.

'Just one thing, Bill. People don't double-cross me – never. You understand, don't you?'

'Yes, yes, Aaron; don't worry, I understand. I'll be in touch soon.'

Bill all but pushed the arrogant visitor out of his office, and turned to his secretary as she entered the room.

'Phew, Betty – that bloke is some scary client. Maybe I shouldn't have got involved; he worried me when he started talking about the Middle East. I started to think about Gaddafi and his cronies.'

'No, I didn't like him; he's scary, but don't you think you are way out of your depth, Bill? After all, you are just an accountant.'

'Don't say it like that – my inferiority complex will take over. I may be just a simple bookkeeper but I know a deal when I see one. Larry Nixon is desperate; he owes me money so I feel I need to help him, and by doing this deal we're all winners.'

'What will Larry do once he's paid everyone off?'

'Don't know, but hopefully he'll go to Spain immediately and live in his beach hut. His moods are getting worse; I'm convinced the man is mentally ill. Jill has her work cut out with him.'

'You fancy her, don't you? Does she feel the same about you?'

'Since my wife died, Betty, I've tried to immerse myself in work and it's helped me get on my feet again. You know that, and Jill has helped me as well on more than one occasion.'

'I get your meaning, Bill, but remember: she's still married and if Larry is as ill as you say he is, I'd watch your back.'

'More warnings – this is becoming a day of them. Make me some coffee whilst I think about the logistics of this deal.'

'Yes sir, will do.'

Betty saluted her boss and went to the office kitchen. She had been with Bill for 20 years, and she helped keep him on the straight and narrow when things went wrong. She saw trouble ahead, but she was not sure if this time he would listen to her and that made her frightened for him. Not that she liked him, but as a single mother she needed her job.

Chapter 7
Police Storage Warehouse
Guildford, Surrey

Alan parked his Mini in front of a row of old army huts protected by a high fence, barbed wire and two seriously large gates. Chief Super White followed him into the car park, then walked to the gate with a bunch of keys and opened the first gate manually and the second from a digital keypad. He did not want Alan to see the code. Normal procedure had gone out of the window as he was allowing him to visit the site without official documents, but then the circumstances were special and Dick White would vouch for the visitor.

'You didn't waste much time, Alan; I was just about to check out our new computer centre. Thanks for your call – it gave me an excuse not to go.'

'I appreciate your help. Can we have a look inside? I won't keep you long, provided I can come back again.'

'You can only return when I can make it. This is a tight investigation, and the fewer people involved, the better.'

Alan nodded. He doubted the police were hiding anything, but he thought it would be nice to have a rummage through his parents' effects on his own. Keys would be a problem, but a

77

small one – he had memorised the code on the keypad from the position of the numbers.

The large warehouse was almost empty. Signs bearing names and dates hung from just three areas, and he found his parents' area right at the front.

'What is this place? What are all those shrink-wrapped parcels?'

'It's a MOD store, and believe it or not, this was stuffed with kits in case of nuclear war. Not sure what help metal pans would have been – a cooking set and a blanket would have been issued to everyone if someone had dropped a bomb; amazing, really. Take your time, I can give you an hour. I'll sit over here and make a few calls on my mobile, but sorry, I can't leave you alone.'

Alan nodded as a rat shot across the floor and into a drain. He looked at the damp walls and muttered to himself: what a place to store crime scene material! Surely it would be put somewhere better, later on? He pretty quickly found what he wanted; the most important paperwork had been checked thoroughly by the police forensic team, and all the floppy discs from the metal storage box had gone. His solicitor Harold Penny had the majority of the legal documents, but many tax and copy share certificates had been badly charred by the explosion, making Harold's job more difficult.

'Dick, my father had a Perspex box with loads of pictures in it; he was in the process of scanning them all onto the computer so they could be categorised and run as slide shows. Do you know where it is?'

'Yes and no, Alan – the explosive device must have been put almost underneath the box as it was behind the safe. We thought the killer probably put it there so it would take the full blast and the contents would be wrecked, and 95% were melted and way beyond recognition.'

'You said 95%. What about the other 5%?'

'Just a book with a list of the files and a code against each one. Frankly, we couldn't make it out, other than that it did have a sequence which we think was related to the photographs. Actually there were 3,000 of them, but apart from very small pieces they were destroyed in the explosion. Your father must have only just started the job of computerising them, as we found nothing on the computers or even on hard discs in case he had hidden them.'

'Can I see the computers? There should be three and a laptop.'

'Yes, all here on that shelf; we've taken all we wanted off them which was virtually nothing. The emails are still being checked out.'

Alan needed a diversion; he wanted to inspect the computers without the beady eyes of the policeman watching over him. He was just thinking about asking for a drink or some similar distraction when Dick White's mobile phone rang. He turned away to speak in private, and Alan had his opportunity to go to the computers without any interference. He went straight to the Apple Mac and smiled when he saw what he wanted. The floppy disk slot was a special one – the machine was a prototype that had been given to his father in the USA, and the disk slot had the facility to take two discs instead of just one. The key to open the disk slot and give the user access was a manual operation: a button under the keyboard had to be moved to the left. His father had shown him this device, just the week before his death. Alan had come prepared, and he pushed the small blade of his pocketknife into the button, lifting the keyboard as his father had shown him. A blue disk popped out. Written on it with a black marker pen in bold capitals were the words *BACKUP. SEE HAROLD IF NEEDED*. Alan had just enough time to put the disk in his pocket when Dick White turned around.

'Found anything we missed?'

'No, Dick; if you have the hard discs, that's everything. I want to read these house papers – my solicitor has copies, I'm sure, but in any case I want to know that these will be kept and eventually given to me. Give me a few minutes, please.'

'All right Alan, you have 15 more minutes. The stuff will be boxed and archived; I'm not sure how long they will keep it but if we can solve the crime it all becomes very important, especially at a trial. You can have it all back eventually, or as much as you want.'

80

He did not find anything else he wanted: paid bills, magazines and legal books formed the bulk of the office, and he did not really want it back, but as it was all personal stuff he needed to make sure it was destroyed properly. Alan Fisher was not a religious man, but he repeated what he'd said after his brother's death, then took a few minutes with his eyes closed to reflect on his wonderful parents. Thinking about his need for closure; possibly a new life with Cheryl, and maybe a new job – he had lots of thoughts, and said a simple prayer as he left the building.

The two men shook hands as the policeman locked the gates. Alan wasted no time leaving the drab warehouse, and his rapid exit caused some concern with Dick White. Due to the speed with which he left, the policeman was suspicious, and he wondered if Alan had learned something he was not telling him. He'd seen him studying the computers, but why? He would check if he had moved any of the machines, and if Alan was keeping something from him he would be right back to him.

'Yes, Alan, OK. You can come now.'

After leaving the warehouse, Alan immediately contacted Harold Penny and told him he was on his way to see him with some important information. Harold was intrigued, and put the kettle on as he awaited the young man's visit. He lived on his own in a large detached house in the Tyrells Wood estate in

Leatherhead, not far from Alan's parents' house. His wife had died five years before and the house was far too big, but he had lived in it for 40 years and he was not leaving until he had to. His office was as big as most living rooms, with shelf upon shelf of legal books and many others.

'Come in. Tea or coffee?'

'Tea please, Harold; no sugar and a drop of milk.'

'I like a man who knows what he wants. So what is this revelation you have driven ten miles to tell me about? Couldn't it have waited until tomorrow?'

'You have a box of disks which my father gave you, Harold, and I have a disk which I'm sure should contain the password to open each of them and give us access to photographs and descriptions of many people. If you wind your old Dell up and put in the disk, we can take a look.'

'Right, Alan, here goes – what are you looking for, then?'

'That's a leading question. My father wouldn't have given these photos such an elaborate filing system if they weren't important. We don't need to go through more than one disk today to get an idea of what he was doing, and that may give us a clue to any secrets he was hiding.'

'OK, I'm ready. Here we go.'

The computer whistled and clonked into action, and when Alan inserted the disk it asked for a protection code, which he entered from the other list taken from the warehouse disk.

'Bloody hell, it's one of Dad's operations. This one is in Ireland, and according to the menu it has 50 photos and a report – presumably this is the same format for the rest of the codes. This is really interesting stuff. I think each file is a person or persons – look, Harold, I want you to keep everything in your safe, and don't download any more to the computer; make a copy of the warehouse disk and hide it somewhere away from this office. I'll keep the original.'

'Was your father a keen photographer, Alan? Why keep reports in this way?'

'No, he probably had a special photographer to do the majority of them; they're very good pictures, and with my father's reports the incidents or cases could be correctly filed, especially when many of his court martials were in war zones. If you look at them you'll see both captured enemy soldiers and our people, mostly uniformed – that disk we looked at gives each picture and has a summary of who's in it. The only chance I have is if I recognise someone. It looks like I have a few months' work here, but I'm hopeful that I can find the killer.'

'Are the court martials still done abroad?'

'No, Harold – my father was working here since they changed the procedures a few years ago; the three courts were Buford, Catterick and Colchester, with one joint venture in Germany. I don't think we'll find anything about the UK cases on the disks. My father was one of seven Judge Advocates, but I think the

Judge Advocate General gave him the complicated trials, which he thrived on. I never heard him complain – quite the opposite; he enjoyed his job but not always the result. Remember, though, that the judges also worked the circuit, so availability had to be taken into consideration.'

'If procedures changed, would that have been a problem for your father, Alan?'

'No, on the contrary: he was in favour of the changes, as from a safety point of view he knew the UK would be better than Tehran or Kabul.'

'So are you are ruling out terrorists?'

'No, not at all, but if it had been a terrorist they would have been boasting about it, that's a certainty. The killer, I believe, is just someone with a grudge. To destroy what they believed to be Dad's records tells me that they know that if someone – like me, or one of Dad's work friends – saw the pictures, it could give them a trail. That is my line of thought; I have no idea who it can be, but the case starts now for me. Both Ben and I were threatened, Harold, and the messages came thick and fast; there were two to Ben just before he died, and one to me just before I left the army. It was one of the things that made me quit. After Ben's death, the threats kept coming to my father's home from a withheld number. We got the calls checked, but the caller was clever and kept changing the phone line. They were always the same: the caller sounded Irish, and he just said, "You are all dead."'

'What did your father say about the threats?'

'In Ben's case, he didn't know until after his death, when I told him about the two calls. He went white and told me to be very careful, but he knew something; it all makes more sense now.'

'I see, Alan; that all sounds very frightening. I'll help you as much as I can, but if bullets start flying or bombs go off I'll be on a plane to my place in Bermuda, quick as a flash, until the dust settles.'

'Yes. Sorry, Harold, I'm getting carried away – after all, you are my solicitor and that should be all, but apart from Cheryl, my girlfriend, who will know bits and pieces, you are the only person I'm confiding in. To keep you safe, nobody else will know what I'm doing, and what I tell her and you will be a mixture of need-to-know and how to contact me in case of an emergency.'

'All right son; I'm happy with that, but come back tomorrow and we can talk about the summary of where I'm up to with probate and your parents' estate. By the way, this just came through the post so you won't know about it, but the inquest is a week on Friday. I suggest we go together as it's at the Surrey Coroner's Court in Woking. Will you pick me up that day?'

'Yes, sure, Harold. I wonder if anyone we know will turn up? Apart from my uncle and a few of Dad's friends, and no doubt the police with their notebooks.'

'Alan, don't upset them – they want to solve this crime as much as you do. I heard over the grapevine from some old police friends that Chief Superintendent White has already suggested that the killers may never be found. A strange statement, and one that doesn't inspire confidence. Maybe he'll be replaced.'

'Don't get me wrong, Harold; I'll involve the police when I can, but I've got my own agenda as well. I want to make sure the killer is convicted, but what I'm very much aware of is that I could be the next target, so I've got to be on my guard.'

'That never occurred to me, but you're right; watch your step Alan.'

'I will. I was trained well in the army and you never forget it.'

'Were you trained to kill?'

'Of course, as a last resort or for a specific reason, and I killed several times but always in self-defence. That's why I left the army; I had enough of it when Ben died. No more questions, please, and I'll see you tomorrow.'

'There is one more question, Alan: several people have asked about a remembrance service for your father. It's in his will, actually, and he said that after a period of four months from his death, you as executor should hold a service on the island of Jersey. Full details are in a sealed envelope at your parents' bank.'

'I wonder what my father was thinking when he did that letter. Collect it for me, Harold – I'll call the bank and tell them you'll be there next week.'

Alan went home and sat in his armchair. His mind was racing, and again the thought occurred to him – did his father know his own life was in danger? But why, and what did it all mean?

Meanwhile, Harold grabbed a Scotch, which soon turned into two and then three. He sat in his office thinking only about Alan: the boy needed a friend – and he was still a boy even though he had served in the army and seen a lot of life – and now he had no shoulder to cry on. Harold knew that it was partly Alan's anger that was keeping him going, and somehow Harold had to help him bring matters to a conclusion. If Alan got it wrong, there could be more deaths. Alan did not know the full amount he would inherit from his parents' estate, although he knew it was a considerable amount. In rough calculations, the solicitor had noted £10 million in property and investments, and £2 million in liquid cash. Even after death duties Alan's wealth would be considerable, and he would have no financial need to work again. Harold was determined to help him plan his investments and savings, and in their meeting the next day he would spell it all out to him. There had been a case or two where sons had killed their parents for money, but the police would have made their own early conclusions on that line of thinking and Harold was convinced that they would have dismissed the likelihood of the scenario as zero.

The solicitor had no immediate family, and had similar wealth to his client, so apart from his charities he had nobody to benefit from his estate. He had thought that maybe he should buy a pub to keep him occupied and give him company, and the crazy idea to buy The Brown Cow had lasted only 24 hours, though why he had thought of it in the first place he could not imagine. The surprise of the day had been a call from one of the customers of the pub, a nice young lady called Alice Smith, who asked if he could recommend a solicitor for a potential buyer of the pub; a wealthy man from the Middle East. She told him that this man's wife was a solicitor but she needed help with the conveyance paperwork. Harold's answer had been no; he didn't recommend anyone as he was retired, but he was interested in what the man would do with the pub. Perhaps he would turn it into a harem – was that legal? No, surely not in Leatherhead, and anyway, it would not be for Harold; he was far too old to turn up and ask for a pint of Guinness with extras.

The whisky had got to him, and he decided he was lonely and fed up; yet he looked forward to the next day when he would be helping Alan. As he climbed the stairs he missed the dark saloon car parked badly across the road, with an occupant dressed in a baseball hat and hooded jacket. It was not until he turned on the bathroom light that he saw it again, and at the same time the occupant saw him looking; the face was slightly familiar, but the whisky blurred the image. He switched the light off as he entered his bedroom, and the car left. It was unlikely that Harold would remember it in the morning, but he would when he saw it for the second time later that week. That was how his memory worked.

Chapter 8
Cheryl and an Old Friend

'So where have you been hiding then, Alan – with another girl?'

'No; really sorry, Cheryl, I've just got back from Harold Penny's house, and I've had an interesting day. How about you?'

'Yes, Mum was like a machine today – we had loads of clients and everyone wanted their nails done; goodness knows how many we did. We desperately need to move and get that extra space; will she hear from the council soon?'

'She should do, but I can't make any promises. I'm confident they will give her the permission, but they may ask her to amend some small parts of the application – that can usually be done quickly by the architect, though. Are you coming over? We can walk into Ewell and get some food, or better still, shall I make a chilli and we can stay in?'

'Yes, come and get me; I don't fancy a red bus tonight.'

The drive to Oxshott took 15 minutes, and Cheryl was waiting on the shop step. She kissed her boyfriend like it was the first time she had met him. The more she thought about him, the more she loved him; *What could go wrong?* she thought, when she couldn't sleep. Only the business with his family, which was still big news everywhere, and the word had soon got around that she was dating Alan. Most of the time it was people in the shop just expressing sympathy, but then she got the occasional doom-and-gloom person telling her that she would be in danger if she ever got close to him. It all went over her head, and as the shop was so busy the negative discussions were soon forgotten as the nail paint dried and the client gave her a nice tip.

'Alan, do you remember a girl called Sheila Hamilton?'

He hesitated with his reply, which Cheryl noticed.

'Not sure, who is she?'

'She's just a client.'

'I guessed that, Cheryl. Why do you ask; is she a problem?'

'No reason really, but she came in for nails and a facial; Mum did her facial and I did a manicure and painted her nails. She's a really pretty girl with great skin and hands. She didn't stop talking all the time she was with me; she asked about you and if you ever go to the pub. I told her about our brief visit, and she said that she heard Larry Nixon was getting worse, and that her friend Alice is pushing hard to find a buyer for the place. It seems she helped introduce a *friend,* a bloke called Aaron Parker, and he's interested.'

'No, I don't know him. Who is he?'

'He's a businessman from the Middle East and he's looking for property to buy. I think Sheila may be a hooker, and a high-class one at that; I'd say some uptown escort agency with clients that have more money than sense, and Aaron Parker is probably one of them.'

Alan knew a Sheila Hamilton; he remembered her from a few years back, and he tried hard not to look interested.

They approached the car park behind his apartment and stopped next to a black series 5 BMW. The driver turned away as he saw Alan, and left the car park at high speed.

'He was in a hurry; almost as if he saw us and went. I don't like it, Cheryl; I didn't see his face or the car registration number. All I know is that it was a series 5 Beemer; probably black, but at least a dark colour.'

'Not much of a description, Mr Detective.'

Alan scoffed; he was annoyed with his own suspicious nature. Was the driver watching his flat, or was he just being paranoid?

The car was soon forgotten as the smell of the chilli hit them from the kitchen. Alan just rescued it before it totally dried out, and quickly heated some pitta bread and boiled some rice.

'Not bad, Alan; slightly overcooked but it adds to the flavour. What else do you do well?'

She was teasing him, and she wondered to herself if the time was right to stay over with him; but then she would need to tell her mother and the safety lecture would follow even though she was 29. She had been out with many boyfriends but only one that was serious; they had slept together after just four weeks of dating. With Alan she would take her time until she felt they were in tune with each other. A kiss and cuddle was on the agenda as the chilli breathed fire at each of them, and Alan's body made Cheryl sweat in anticipation as they did everything other than the complete act. She was satisfied and so was he for today, and as he drove her back home she almost fell asleep in the noisy Mini. Alan delivered her in his arms to the front door and rang the bell.

'Delivery of one sleepy young lady for you, Mrs Rix.'

'My goodness Alan, you do tire your girls out. What's your secret?'

'Not me; must be you getting her to paint 15 sets of nails today. She must be sniffing the fluid.'

'Get home, Alan Fisher, and come to lunch on Sunday. I'll see if I can cook something without poisoning you.'

'Yes, great, see you then – oh, and thanks, Mrs Rix.'

'Alan, my name is Mandy; only be polite to me if you have done something wrong otherwise I'll be suspicious. Good night.'

Alan took the back roads to his flat as he wanted to check out a house that an army friend lived in. He had not seen him for two years, and he drove past slowly to see if he was still around. It used to be easy, as Charlie's love was a 1972 Ford Mustang that never seemed to move off the front drive. As the road narrowed, Alan caught a glimpse of the car, and even better, his old friend was climbing out of it. He stopped and shouted from his car.

'You haven't still got that pile of Yank shit, have you?'

'Alan, bloody hell, great to see you! How's life now? I was really sorry to hear about your parents.'

'I'm OK Charlie, or at least I think my sleep is improving. The council have given me some leave of absence and once the inquest is over I have a few things to catch up on.'

'Have you got time to come in for a coffee?'

'Yes, would love to, mate.'

Alan parked behind the Mustang, his Mini looked like an invalid carriage against the frame of the muscle car.

'Go in the lounge and I'll stick the kettle on.'

'I see the car is still in good nick.'

'Yes, I do my own maintenance and other than the left hand chair it's a perfect posing car, but very thirsty so I go to work by motorbike.'

'Are you all right, Charlie? You're shaking.'

'Yes, just got a bit of a cold. Where have you come from?'

'I've a new girlfriend; her mother runs the nail place in Tolworth Tower and I just came from her house in Oxshott.'

'Where did you meet her?'

'I've a job in the planning office at the council and I was checking out her mother's application to turn the place next to her house into a shop, and that's how I met Cheryl.'

Charlie opened the front door and pointed to the lounge. The semi-detached house was typical of that part of Chessington; the area was developed between the two World Wars, with rows and rows of properties now just about affordable for young couples and their families. Charlie Baxter had served in the army with Alan Fisher; they left at the same time, but he was a few years older than Alan. He didn't need to retrain when he left; he was a specialist in electronics and walked straight into a job, and the army had kept his knowledge up-to-date with constant training courses, almost as if he was still with them.

'How's your job then, Charlie?'

Charlie paused, which Alan noticed, then sat down and looked directly at his friend.

'It's OK. I was on the hushed-up stuff at first, keeping our jet fighters flying with updated software to operate those clever weapon systems. That only lasted a year due to cuts in RAF requirements, so I now have a new job.'

'Still into the dangerous stuff, Charlie. Have you signed the Official Secrets Act?'

'No more questions, Alan; I could be saying too much to you already. Are you working with SIS?'

'No I'm not, but in passing I did speak with them about my parents' death. They said they were sure it wasn't terrorists who killed them, or anyone else under their remit, so the case has been passed back to the old bill.'

'It sounds like you could be doing your own investigation, and knowing you it'll be way ahead of the police.'

'I doubt I'm ahead of them, Charlie, but yes, I'm unofficially helping them without them knowing. I'm trying to ID some people who could have been mixed up with my dad; it's a big job but over the next few weeks I'll be looking at old pictures and documents, so maybe I'll find a clue or two.'

Charlie Baxter went pale. Something Alan had said had hit him between the eyes, and he was clearly shaken up.

'Charlie, how much do you know about explosives? If I show you a picture of one we found damaged and unused in my parents' study, could you give me anything on a possible supply route?'

He almost didn't answer, and went to change the subject.

'Sorry Alan, I'm out of that now. So is your job permanent?'

'It's a good job, and I like it apart from local politics sometimes interfering with my planning applications. Mostly anything I recommend gets through, but then occasionally they throw a few back; I think it could be just to make sure I don't get it all my own way. Anyway, for now my career is on hold until I get some satisfaction from the investigation; since my parents died I've lived very much week-to-week.'

Charlie looked grim. 'All right, I'll explain a bit more about my job: I work on missile guidance and armaments, including drones; that's it, Alan, so you understand the need to keep quiet on the subject. To protect me I've limited access to anything other than the device operating systems; it's routine electronics for me but not something I talk about. Anyway, if anyone grabbed me I'd be of little use, unless they had stolen the gear first. The army give me plenty to do, so I don't think much about security.'

'I hear what you say, mate, but don't underestimate your skills. You'd be useful to any enemy. Can I ask a favour and bring a photo of a detonator found at my parents' house, plus a few photos of other small bits of the device to see what you make of them?'

Again Charlie hesitated, and Alan noticed.

'Are you all right mate; have I upset you turning up like this?'

'No, detonators are not my area anymore.'

Alan decided to leave; he had touched something his old friend did not want to or could not discuss, and he was not going to push him.

'Thanks, Charlie; great to see you again, and regards to Ann.'

Charlie had said that his wife was away with the children, but the house showed no signs of either children or his wife: there were no photographs or toys, just spotless rooms like an army barracks.

'See you mate, you know where I live now; hope to see you again.'

Alan left his friend's house. He was very worried about Charlie. What was the matter with him; had he been thrown out of the army, or had his wife left him? Alan tried to get him out of his mind, and to do so he started to think about his visit to Harold Penny.

Alan was desperate to start work on the photos the next day. For almost the first time since his parents died he felt he was not alone, as Harold would help with his mammoth task. He drove the two miles slowly as he thought about the good times he had with Charlie in the army, and the nights out they had together. Alan liked male company, although it helped that Cheryl was filling a partial void in his life. He needed mates as well, though, and he was determined to see his old army pal again soon, even if it was only to find out what was bugging him.

The lights were out as he swung past the Beech Letting Agency building in Epsom; the top letting company in town, and the one he had used to let his place when he was away. The road narrowed past the railway station, and at the first turning he parked in a bay below his flat. As he got out a car accelerated quickly away from the block with its lights out; Alan noted just the *56A* on the number plate in the dim light. He did a double-take: was it a couple having sex and he had disturbed them, or was it someone watching out for him?

Chapter 9
Photos and Diaries

'You're early, Alan – it's only nine o'clock and I'm still in pyjamas! Make some tea and I'll start up the computer; as you know it takes some time.'

'I think you should buy a new machine, Harold, with up-to-date programs. You may find a widow or two to chat with if you search the find a friend websites.'

'Alan, it's early – buzz off and let me get dressed! I don't want any widows of any description; my time with women is probably over.'

'Never, Harold; you're always looking at the ladies in The Brown Cow! So what are you going to do now if you've given up thinking about buying the pub?'

'Find another pub to drink in, at least until Nixon leaves. He has to find a buyer otherwise it will just close down and he will get 10p in the pound. Something has to be done, and quickly, but that's not my business. By the way, I have something to tell you; just give me ten minutes.'

Alan had not studied Harold Penny's old house before, but as he waited for him he realised how many things needed replacing. The structure of the place was sound and could be made fabulous if refurbished; a project that he thought could be of interest to him one day. Harold said he was happy with the house, but then he knew he had to be practical and downsize before he got too old.

'That was a long ten minutes, Harold.'

'They always are when you're old, Alan. I had to get all my papers. Now before you start on the pictures, two matters of interest for you: firstly, it could take two years to get probate fully sorted. We will have to pay inheritance tax before then, so we should discuss that with your bank – they will probably take a legal charge against the land of your parents' house; it seems it's worth about £2–3 million. They will then lend you the money for the tax at some exorbitant rate secured against the land, but I've a better idea.'

'What's that, Harold? Surely I can't sell the land until probate is granted, and the tax people will no doubt want loads of my money.'

'You're right. The tax due – even after the deduction of all allowances, and taking into account some planning that your parents did – will be around £3 or 4 million.'

'Blimey Harold, so I'll be worth about £8 or 9 million after tax?'

'Possibly, Alan, but your uncle was left £1 million of it in the will; I hope he can pay the tax. As you can see it's all very complex and I need your permission now to administer it, and your uncle's part as well. As I've known you since birth, I'm prepared to help you. I'll loan you the money to pay the tax and charge you 5% interest per year, which I'll total up and you can give it me at the year's end. If I die in the meantime, you'll have to find another lender or a bank. Fortunately your parents' will is very specific, so I'll get the wheels moving straight away and I'll send you a fee letter this week. I'll charge mates' rates, Alan, but we need to get on with it so call me as soon as you've read my letter.'

'I understand, Harold. I have this time off now so can I come round again tomorrow; I've a meeting now and can't stay.'

'Yes of course, but not too early.'

'All right; ten o'clock, then. I don't want to take the disks away to view because you have the safe, and I know I'm sounding paranoid, but we must keep them really secure until we've had a good look. Also, you know many people my dad knew, so you may be a help.'

'I doubt it, Alan; I can't remember what day it is sometimes.'

Alan's phone burst into life. He had received a text message to meet a Detective Inspector Hubbard for a chat in Wetherspoons in Epsom Upper High Street. He didn't know the man; only that

100

Superintendent Dick White had already delegated the investigation to a young high-flyer. Alan had heard about Hubbard, but he had never met him. He parked the Mini in the multi-storey car park and walked down to the pub. He'd never seen the policeman before, but it took him five seconds to find him sat in the corner with a coffee.

'Alan, pleased to meet you. I think I spotted you first?'

The policeman was already trying to score points, and he was about to make it clear to Alan that he would be in charge of the investigation from now on.

'I must stand out then, mate. Were you in the army?'

'No way, I'm a police career boy and I don't intend to be an inspector very long.'

Alan ordered and paid for his own coffee, and sat facing the door. He had already spotted another policeman who kept trying to look away.

'Why don't you tell the copper with the spotty face to go and sit in your car? You're quite safe with me.'

'OK, if he's bothering you.'

Alan nodded; he hated anybody watching him from behind.

'Jack, go and sit in the car; I'll be about ten minutes. Now, sorry Alan, but can we go straight to the death of your parents?'

Before Alan could speak, the policeman carried on.

'Firstly, I express my deepest sympathy; secondly, I need you to tell me why you think they were killed. The team dealing with the murders have almost exhausted their enquiries, or at least the obvious ones: terrorists, gas leak, and even possible suicide.'

The message was delivered as if he was reading it off a prompt card.

'I heard that from your boss, Dick White, but you must have some ideas, Inspector?'

'Our job is to stick at it until we've got something; like the pathologist we need to give a full report at the inquest. If we haven't got it right for the coroner, he could just adjourn the hearing again until we have.'

'OK, I understand. If I think of anything I'll call you.'

'I'm not sure about that, Alan; from what I hear you usually sort out your own problems. In this case we may have a bloody fruitcake planting bombs, and it's one for us alone to deal with. I'll find the bastards, and if you can cooperate a bit I'd appreciate it very much.'

'Of course, I'll work with you and I'll go through my father's papers – or what's left of them – and see if anything hits me in the face.'

'I assume you have photos that we haven't seen?'

'What do you mean, Inspector?'

'Don't play games. I have asked around, and your father had many photographs of his career and we've found only family pictures; the ones you know we have.'

'I repeat what I said: I'll go through anything I find, and if something turns up I'll let you know.'

'Why am I not convinced? But enough for today – take my card; I'm based in Guildford, so let's meet again soon. I'll call you.'

No goodbyes from the arrogant policeman. Alan sniggered to himself; he was determined not to tell him anything until he had some good clues, and he knew it would be one-way traffic until Hubbard loosened up, or had a suspect.

Alan went back to his flat and looked carefully through his father's last diary. He had done it many times before, but as the police had now taken a copy he could study the original in detail and in private. He had only read a few pages when his phone rang.

'Alan, it's your Uncle Ted here.'

'Hello Ted; good to hear from you. Anything to tell me?'

'Yes. Straight to the point, Alan: your father made several trips last year to the Middle East, when he was supposed to be retired. It seems someone called him back to finalise a job he had been doing; he was bloody pissed off about it, but said he had to do it. I suddenly remembered this last night; does it mean anything?'

'No Ted, but I'll check it out. Harold Penny may know; he could have been just visiting someone – an old friend, maybe. It must have been official business, so better still I'll ask his old boss the Judge Advocate General; he's likely to come to the inquest and if he does I'll try and corner him afterwards.'

'So what news have you got, Alan?'

'Off the record, Ted, we've found all Dad's photos on a computer; also there were two bombs at the house and the second one was, I think, aimed at destroying as much of my dad's paperwork and photographs as possible, but they didn't get everything. If that's the case, someone didn't want to be recognised in a photo. I knew a bit about Dad's job; not from him, but from the newspapers, as it was public knowledge. So I have to look for someone that firstly I recognise, and then find out what he did for my father to explain why Dad had a photo of him. I'm going through everything and I need some luck; Harold Penny is helping me, so we'll call you when we've finished and could you then have a look as well, please?'

'Yes, of course. By the way, I hear from Harold that I am a beneficiary in the will?'

'Sorry, Ted, I should have told you and not Harold, but he likes to do everything by the book. Did he write to you?'

'Yes, he sent me a letter, but with your Aunty Clare in the care home the money will all go to looking after her. I've everything I need, but she needs 24-7 attendance now.'

'Will she ever recover?'

'No, that will be her last home. I've come to terms with it all and I really do want to help you, Alan; I need something to occupy my mind.'

'I'll have something for you later, Ted, when I rebuild or buy another property. In the meantime, can you help me sort through everything that is left from the house? The police have quarantined a lot of material, but as they release it can you list it and then we can decide what to do with it? You never know, we may find something that wouldn't mean anything to the police, but it might to us.'

'Thanks, Alan, but listen to me for a minute: I know you have enough money now and you don't need to work again, but you're a bright lad and I think you need to keep working; don't stop you'll get bored. The other thing is, do you think your parents' deaths will be the end of it, or could the killer come after us as well?'

'Both things have occurred to me, Ted. Yes, I'll still work, but it's at the back of my mind; I've got to get the next few weeks over and then make some plans. I don't know if we're targets, but watch your back. It feels like someone is following me, but then it could be the police or just my paranoia.'

'Yes, that's understandable, and I'll keep my eyes open.'

After he hung up the phone, Alan sat and pondered his uncle's words. Ted was the only member of the family who hadn't worked or served in the army or police: he was an engineer, having been born with a deformed arm which prevented him from following his brother into the army and beyond.

Before he knew it, Alan's day was about to get worse: the cocky Inspector Hubbard had reported back to Superintendent Dick White, who then called Alan. At the same time, Cheryl had fallen out with her mother, as a new planning officer had turned up and asked lots of new questions in Alan's absence. Alan decided to have a hot shower and then continue to go through his dad's diaries; much would be day-to-day information, but he had something to look for now that his uncle had mentioned the recent visit to the Middle East, and the rough dates when it occurred. He phoned Cheryl to come and help him, and she told him she was already on her way to his flat.

The bathroom overlooked the car park, and Alan had just opened the window slightly to let the steam out when he saw a silver car parked in the corner, and a man inside it, looking at his flat. Alan ran down the stairs just as the car screamed past him. He had noted the number, and he rang Inspector Hubbard.

'It's Alan Fisher here, Inspector.'

'That's quick, have you got something?'

'I forgot to mention it this morning but I had a feeling somebody was following me. I was just about to have a shower and I looked through the bathroom window and caught this bloke in a silver Audi looking up at me. I ran out to tackle him, but he was too quick. The car number is G-something-0-something

106

5HY, and it's a dark silver Audi A4. Can you see who it belongs to, unless of course it's one of your lads?'

'No, Alan; not one I know of, but we'll check it out. I'm beginning to worry a bit about you, mate.'

'What do you mean?'

'When I sent my colleague back to the car this morning, he said a guy sort of ran away when he saw me leaving the pub. It's rare for coppers to be followed, so we can only assume it was someone watching you, Alan. They don't want you to see them, or at least not yet; they want information on you and who you're seeing, and it's got to be linked to your father. Leave it with me; we'll keep you posted after the car has been checked out. Stay in tonight so we can talk later.'

'OK, I'll be here.'

Alan hung up and went to his Mini in the car park, where he put a trace seal on the door handle, just to see if anyone tried to break into it. The transparent seal would break if the door was tampered with; he had nothing to steal, but hidden bombs worried him a lot.

Cheryl met him on the stairs.

'Bloody mother just phoned to apologise – the bloke from the council just phoned her to say everything was OK now with the plans and she would hear from them soon. You'd already told her that, so why couldn't she accept it?'

'Sit down, Cheryl. I'm sorry I didn't think about what you said earlier; now what did this bloke look like?'

'He was about 6ft tall, in his 40s I would think; grey hair and glasses. I thought he was a bit scruffy for a council man, and his hair looked like a wig.'

'Unless he's new, I don't know anyone at the council who looks like that. Hang on a minute, I'll phone the office now.'

The brief call and the look on Alan's face indicated that the visitor was not from the council's planning department.

'Did he speak to you, Cheryl?'

'Yes, all the time; he sort of ignored my mother which made her even more angry.'

'I want you to sit down and give me the best description you can and I'll draw him on this sketch pad.'

Cheryl was very specific on the details; she had a good memory for people, especially ones that stared at her. Alan was good at drawings and he quickly put together a picture. They altered it several times before Cheryl was happy that it matched the man.

'That's it, or very near it. Do you know who he is?'

'No, unfortunately not, but the police have good equipment to match photographs to identikit drawings if it's someone they know or have had dealings with. I'll talk with your mother in a minute, but make me some tea and I'll get my new police friend working on it.'

Mandy Rix was even angrier than before when Alan phoned to tell her the story.

'I'll break his arms if I ever see him again – what a fucking cheek! What did he want, Alan?'

'Wish I knew, Mandy, but I promise you I'm on the case. In future ask for ID; if they haven't got it or they seem dodgy, don't let them in or just phone the police. I'll give Cheryl the special number for you.'

'Thanks, Alan; as I said before, come over for dinner on Sunday and I may have calmed down by then.'

'Yes, thanks – that'll be great. I'm sorry about this; it may be something to do with me and my parents' death, but we'll sort it out, trust me.'

'Don't worry son, I'm a big girl and I can handle myself, but I hate shit like this. See you on Sunday.'

Alan hung up the phone. 'Your mum will be fine, Cheryl. I'll take my drawing to Guildford now; get some food from the Co-op on the corner and I'll be back in two hours.'

'Alan, I really love you; I want to stay here tonight. I told my mum and she's cool about it, in fact she was even pleased. She's a tough old bird and nobody frightens her, and she probably feels that I'm safer with you tonight.'

'Sounds good; come here.'

Alan planted a long kiss on the pretty girl's lips, then grabbed the drawing and phoned Inspector Hubbard to tell him that he was on his way.

The photo check lasted longer than anticipated, so Alan called Cheryl to make sure she was OK and said he would be back by 8.30. Hubbard was waiting for him when he hung up the phone.

'Alan, I was worried about you this morning, but I can see now that you are trying to cooperate with us. Still, although this is a good drawing it doesn't match anything we have; your girlfriend might have it slightly wrong, but my guess is that the specs, hair and clothes were a disguise. He obviously wanted to meet your girl, but what he was thinking of doing next beats me. So this is what we do, Alan: a watch will be put on Cheryl and her mother's shop for a week; anything out of the ordinary will be noted, and we'll meet again in seven days' time, unless something comes up.'

Much as he wanted to find the killers on his own, Alan realised that it was almost an impossible task. For now he still had to check the photos, and that would be the next task at Harold's house.

Chapter 10
An Interesting Meeting

The bar of The Brown Cow was its usual sleepy self as Larry Nixon polished a dozen pint glasses for the second time since he removed them from the dishwasher. He stacked them carefully behind the bar, hoping they would all be used that evening. He had lost more customers through his strange moods and violent temper, but some customers prevailed and the flow of them to the dining area allowed him to pay his expenses, although there was nothing more for him and his wife after bank interest had been paid.

The slightly dark-skinned man walked into the empty bar.

'Yes, sir, what can I get you? Don't I know you?'

'I have been here before and eaten in your restaurant.'

'That's right, with your wife I believe; sorry, I assume it was your wife?'

'Yes, it most definitely was. I'll have a pint of your best bitter, please.'

'Are you eating with us, Mr. . .?'

'It's Aaron Parker, and no, I'm not eating here. I want a chat with you, Mr Nixon; it's about this place.'

'OK, good; I'll just get a barmaid and then we can talk.'

Larry Nixon's heart started to race. Someone really interested in his pub: up yours Bill Knowles, and maybe some big money. His brain was bursting as Marie went to attend the empty bar, and he ushered his guest into his small office behind the bar.

'So, Mr Parker, what's your idea?'

'My ideas are just for me. As far as you're concerned, I may make an offer for this place after I've had a good look around, which I'll do now. We'll start outside first; show me your land.'

Larry was shocked at the man's direct approach, but at least he had someone interested in his pub and land other than his accountant. The tour of land and buildings lasted only 20 minutes; Aaron Parker didn't take any notes and his main interest seemed to be at the rear of the building. No doubt he was thinking how he could extend the place.

'So, what do you think? Come and have another drink.'

'No, I've seen enough. I'll send you an offer shortly; the deal will be cash, with no mortgages or surveys, just a visit from my architect. Have ready all the paperwork relating to the place and I can get things moving quickly; if you don't accept my offer you won't get another and you won't see me again.'

Larry was beginning to get annoyed with the arrogant man, and he dug his nails into his palms to keep in control. He would have liked very much to kick him out of his pub and wipe the slimy grin off his face, but he knew he had to keep calm. As long as his money was good it didn't matter to him who bought the place.

Parker turned to leave, and didn't offer Larry a handshake.

'Just one thing, Mr Nixon: your accountant tried to double-cross me yesterday – he gave me a high price for this place, but he was going to buy it and then sell it on to me. He must have thought I was born yesterday; watch that man, he seems like a crook.'

Larry didn't even acknowledge the remark; he just turned and went back in the pub as Parker's Mercedes pulled out of the car park.

'I'm going out, Marie, and I'll be back in an hour. Mrs Nixon is shopping and I've an errand to run.'

'What's an errand, Larry?'

'It's when you have to do something that can't wait. See you later.'

He wouldn't warn Bill Knowles he was on the way. Maybe Aaron Parker had got it wrong, but then he wanted Larry to know about it, and the foreigner sounded genuine enough.

The front drive of Bill Knowles' office was empty. Larry parked his ten-year-old Ford under the window and marched in without ringing the bell.

'Mr Nixon, what do you want? Mr Knowles isn't here.'

'When will he be back in the office, Betty?'

The secretary paused to think. She know what her boss was doing, and it was not something she could tell Larry Nixon about.

'I don't know, but shall I give him a message?'

'I'll call him later. His mobile is switched off; is he playing golf?'

'No, as I said, he didn't tell me anything.'

'Betty, that's a lie and you know it. You have covered for him for years when he left to see a lady friend or play a quick round between clients; probably charging them for the time he spent away from the office as well. I can never get hold of him since his wife died – what's he up to?'

'He's very busy, Mr Nixon.'

'OK Betty, I'll talk to you then.'

The tone of Larry voice quickly changed; his headache was getting worse, and he needed a drink or his tablets, or maybe both. He pulled up a chair and sat next to Betty, taking her hand and squeezing it.

'Don't do that.'

'What do you know about a Mr Aaron Parker then, Betty? Tell me, please.'

Betty was not sure what her boss had told Larry about the back-to-back deal, but she suspected he had said very little, and that Larry was likely to lose out just because he owed money to Bill.

'Come on, what do you know?' Larry was almost shouting and his headache was getting worse.

'He came here the other day and they had a meeting. Bill was pleased, and said they shook hands on a deal to try and buy your place. I didn't like the man and I got the impression he might have just been using Bill to get information. The introduction was from that flashy girl Alice Smith, who in my suspicious mind always spells trouble.'

'Thanks, Betty. Don't tell him I've been here.'

Larry left without any message for his accountant, and decided to drive past the golf club and Knowles' house in case he should see his car. He had to have this business sorted out as he was beginning to think his friend might be stitching him up. The drive to the golf club was only a few minutes, but there was no sign of Bill's car, but when Larry turned into the side road beside Bill's house he saw a car he recognised. He did a double-take: was it his wife's car? Once he saw the number plate up close there could be no mistake; he knew she must be in the accountant's house. In some ways Larry was relieved as it explained a lot about how Jill had been behaving, but for today he decided to go back to the pub. He would not tell his wife about Aaron Parker, and just see what would happen when Betty told Bill about Larry's visit. She had her faults but he was her boss and she knew she had to be loyal to him.

The pub car park was empty when Larry arrived back.

'That didn't take long, Larry. I've only had one customer and he's gone; can we close for an hour? Nothing is happening.'

'Good idea, Marie. What time did Mrs Nixon say she'd be back?'

'Around 4 o'clock.'

'Good. Come with me.'

He grabbed the Polish girl's arm and all but dragged her upstairs. Larry was a strong man, but she wasn't resisting. Without speaking he pushed her on the spare room bed and without any ceremony he rapidly removed her clothes. The sight of her naked body almost made Larry spoil the event, and he lasted only a couple of minutes before satisfying himself, then immediately got out of the bed. Marie would have preferred a lot more, even a kiss from the middle-aged Larry, but he was already in the shower and plotting what he should do next. His life was upside-down, but maybe this was the opportunity he had been waiting for. One by one his problems were coming to the surface, and the confidence to deal with them was coming back to him. He was back on duty; he looked into the steamed-up mirror, stood to attention and saluted. The headache had gone; the sweat he had left in the shower; Marie lying on the bed with her hands behind her head would on most days have meant another act from him, but today he was too busy. He had to make phone calls, and then he would have his first large Scotch of the day. It would be a better day than he'd thought, since his meeting with Aaron Parker.

Chapter 11
A Bit of a Cock-up

'Who's going to tell Alan, you or me?'

'On this one I'll do it, but then carry on pressing him on the photographs. He must find someone that he recognises.'

'It could be, sir, that Gordon Fisher upset someone big time, maybe locals in Iraq or Kuwait, and they've followed him back here to get even.'

'No, I don't think so; SIS say the chance of that is unlikely. Not impossible, but unlikely.'

'That tells me, sir, that SIS aren't 100% sure.'

'Politics maybe, but we continue our enquiries and keep tabs on Alan, but now more openly, like a chat with him every few days. Try to speak to him on his territory and not over the phone, unless it's urgent.'

Chief Superintendent Dick White had the short straw. The surveillance on Alan Fisher had been compromised; the police had used different cars and officers, but Alan was sharp and he had guessed that it was probably them.

'Alan, it's Dick White, sorry to phone you in the evening but we have something to tell you. It's slightly embarrassing.'

'Hi, Dick. I know you're following me, and you've worked out that I've rumbled you.'

'There you go, I told Inspector Hubbard you would know, but it was more for your own protection than anything else; we've been keeping an eye on you since just after your parents' death. Anyway, that's it, we'll stop now. Keep in contact with Norman Hubbard and if we get any new clues we'll tell you. We have to crack this together.'

'Yes, it would have been nice to know that it was you. So who was the bloke in Cheryl's mum's shop? Your people in Guildford couldn't match the face; Norman knows about it.'

'Hang on, Alan.'

Dick White covered the phone up. 'Norman, did you get any further with that sketch picture Alan did of the bloke in his girlfriend's mother's shop?'

'No, and it's definitely not one of us. We aren't watching her, that's certain.'

'Alan, that wasn't anybody we set up. I don't like the sound of it at all, so keep me informed. We'll ask around locally in Tolworth as well. Have we still got the picture?'

'Yes, you have a copy. Bloody hell, who is that bloke and why was he in Mandy Rix's shop?'

'Don't know, but we're on the case now.'

Alan put the phone down after promising Dick White that he would keep him informed if the man turned up again. If it was a disguise it was either a criminal or a weirdo, and Alan did not like the thought of either near the two ladies.

Chapter 12
A Mission

'We had a meeting this morning with all parties, and the general view is we go ahead with the plan; the message comes right from the top, and with Westminster approval. The problem could be that although they are both trained soldiers and have special skills, they are now civilians, or at least one nearly is; but that might work in their favour, especially if someone was to grab them.'

'Why do we have to use so-called civilians on such a mission? Isn't it all a bit far-fetched for us to ask them to do such an important job?'

'Jason, nobody in SIS knows that area of Turkey like Alan Fisher: he lived with the locals and was our ear there for nearly three years and would probably still be there if his brother hadn't been killed in action. The other man, Charlie Baxter, is one of the best in his field; army trained and technically brilliant, so he'll be able to check the guy out so we know what we are getting. He'll do the initial interrogation, and if the guy's a fraud or someone the Iranians are using to infiltrate us, we'll leave him in Turkey. The interrogation will be as soon after the rendezvous as is practical in order to ascertain if information useful to us or the USA has found its way into this Turkish man's hands.'

'You know Baxter well, sir?'

'Yes, I've come across him several times, but not recently. An SIS case officer working for me in Southampton met up with him on a computer course and he sent his regards to me, so I pulled him in for a chat. He left the army sort of secretly; I can't get the full story but they are saying he's a good man. He probably left or went on extended leave after pressure from his wife, who had been on his back to pack it in. The promise of a safe, well-paid local job had some attractions, but I doubt a man like Baxter will be happy for long – remember he did that Dubai job for us three years ago? He also speaks fluent Turkish.'

'I hadn't forgotten that, sir. I know he's a clever bloke, but I just wonder if he's up to this type of operation. You know he got pulled in by the Kingston police for threatening his neighbour in a dispute about noise, and his old commanding officer said he was good but he had a habit of losing his rag with people. Why did he leave the army, sir? We need to check that out properly before we offer him the job. Did he really leave?'

The chief frowned and put his palms flat on the glass table. The two men jumped.

'Listen, don't waste time checking Baxter – he's expendable and that's the point. You can read about what happened to him; I think it's on this file. He knows Alan Fisher and that's good enough, plus we know he needs the money. I can't spare any men for this operation, and Jason, you will not travel unless it all goes wrong – just Brian; he'll be the link man. We know Charlie Baxter will do the job and get a nice fat cheque for two weeks' holiday, then if he comes back we'll leave him to his missile systems until the army or a company give him a job. Alan Fisher also needs to get away from the UK for a bit as he is giving the police grief with his one-man crusade to find his parents' killers. Gentlemen, it sounds very hard and cold, but due to our limited resources we're doing this assignment at arm's length; if it goes wrong we're one step away from it and the Americans will be the same.

'Now let's go through the plans. Brian, on the logistics front, what's the cover story for Alan Fisher? It's not essential they travel to Turkey together.'

'Simple, really, sir: he's just a tourist on holiday, travelling BA economy class, then a Turkish Airlines internal flight from Istanbul to the East; booking, of course, a return ticket. He meets up with his old buddy Charlie, who will fly to the small US airbase on a Hercules from Brize Norton on the weekly supplies plane. We've only got one seat from the RAF and it's too far to travel lying on the floor, but I'm sure Alan would have done it. Baxter can't go on a scheduled flight: he had a run-in with the police there a few years ago; they're still looking for him and him turning up at Istanbul Airport would mean he would have a welcoming committee. Via Brize Norton, nobody will see him. They'll probably both return with the third person on that plane four or five days later when the job's done, but that will depend if their visit becomes public or not.'

'I see. Brian, discuss the schedules with the RAF lads and see if they can be flexible with three seats on a day coming back if we need it. Jason, go and see Alan immediately. He may not want to help us as he's still grieving over his parents' deaths, but a week's work for us will not change things. I'll tell Chief Superintendent White he's doing a small job for us, but give no details; he doesn't need to know any more.'

Jason Harris smiled. 'He'll be thrilled about that as Fisher is turning over lots of his parents' stuff, but working on his own. Did we drop out of the investigation entirely, sir?'

'We did, don't you remember? But something new has come up and I'm passing it on to the inspector on the case; purely by accidentm we stumbled on something when Gordon Fisher was leading a court martial in Baghdad. It may be a waste of time but we'll leave that to the police.'

'Not a local terrorist then, sir?'

'Most definitely not a local terrorist, but someone who knew about terror in Northern Ireland, Jason. I'll tell you about that later, but now let's get moving on this. Both men will go to Sandhurst for a couple of days, then fly out. I want the whole thing wrapped up by month end, which is in 16 days' time. Any questions, gentlemen?'

Both the SIS men looked concerned. They knew what the government wanted, but they were uneasy and apprehensive about the way it was going to be done. Jason Harris was one of the best case officers in the SIS; multi-lingual, with a sharp brain and an expertise in planning operations for the Target teams. The subject of this operation was an engineer with a Turkish passport who was working in an electronics plant in Iran. The engineer wanted to come to the UK to live; he had contacted the CIA initially for a deal, and the small amount of information he provided indicated that he had knowledge of components and equipment being supplied to a nuclear plant. The CIA passed the task over to the British government, who agreed to arrange his unofficial extradition to London. He claimed that he could provide full details of plans that could be used to make a nuclear bomb, and the stage the Iranians were at. The deal was that if he gave useful information he would be accepted into the UK, and the exchange would result in his protection through a change of identity, a payment and accommodation. A USA agent had already checked the validity of his claims, and the information on his workplace was of interest to both the UK and USA security forces.

Jason collected his papers up, went to a private office and closed the door to make the call. 'Is that Alan Fisher?'

'Yes, who's that?'

'I'm Jason Harris and I work for the government. I need to meet you today; can you be at Leatherhead Leisure Centre at 7pm?'

'Possibly, but what's it all about? Who actually are you?'

'You'll find out tonight, Alan. Ring this number; you'll recognise the voice. You know the person, and he'll verify that I'm not a journalist or a nutcase.'

'OK, but I'll check with this bloke first. If I'm happy I'll see you there; if not I'll ask him to call you. Does he have your number?'

'Yes. See you later.'

Alan was puzzled. After the nonsense with police surveillance, now he had another odd contact; must be to do with the police again, but he could meet the guy and then carry on to Oxshott and see Cheryl afterwards, so it would fit in with his evening. He had a brief phone conversation using the number given to him, and a call back from a security services officer who told Alan that he had nothing to fear, as for once his services were urgently needed. He was intrigued, but would arrive early to observe the man and weigh him up before they met. Alan decided to tell Cheryl his movements as a precaution in case he was late.

'Hi Cheryl, I'll be around about eight. I have a meeting with a police bloke at Leatherhead Leisure Centre at seven, but my phone is playing up so I may not be able to contact you if I'm late.'

'Yes, OK darling. I'm still tingling from last night; can't wait to see you.'

Alan put the phone down, then switched it off – the signal was poor, the battery kept running down and the line crackled. He was lucky he got the call after all the interference. With careful use of tweezers, he moved the components around to see if he could spot a problem; he knew the exercise was probably pointless, especially as he hardly knew anything about phones. The small orange piece of metal soldered to the inside was definitely not part of the phone. What the hell was it, and how did it get there?

Alan tried to think back when the phone had been out of his sight: he always had it with him in his breast pocket or by his bed. Then he remembered Cheryl had picked it up by mistake and she had it for a few hours in the shop before she noticed; when she drove over to give it to him he hadn't even noticed it had gone. He could see small marks on the case, which looked like they had been made by a screwdriver – someone had planted the orange strip, but why, and what did it do? Alan decided to move the SIM card out of the phone and into a spare handset, then take it to a friend who worked in a phone shop the next day, to see what he could find out about the mystery piece of metal.

He had decided that he would spend all day at Harold Penny's house, and as Leatherhead was on the way he would grab a sandwich on the way.

'Hello Alan, come in. What have you got in the packed lunch or dinner?'

'I suppose it's lunch, Harold. I've been so busy with looking through my dad's papers that I forgot about food until my phone rang.'

Alan told Harold about the orange metal in his phone.

'Very strange, Alan, it's like your sandwich in that thick cardboard pack: you can't see what's in your phone until it's all been opened up.'

'Yes, good point Harold, but what is it? Was I meant to open the phone up and find the metal bit? Is someone telling me something?'

'I doubt that it does anything other than interfere with your phone; whoever planted it is saying, "Look, I can get near you." Think again: other than Cheryl, who could have had access to it?'

'It's the killer, Harold; the police are right, someone here is out for us Fishers. But why?'

'Did your brother die in combat, Alan?'

'He died from friendly fire. I'm going to dig out the report they read out at the inquest on his death and read it again. There's only my Uncle Ted and I left in the family now, and of course you – not family, I know, but still a dear friend, you old fart. You're all precious, and I need to sort this business so that we all stay alive.'

'You didn't come here just to eat your sandwich, Alan. What's up?'

'Lots of things, Harold. I'm meeting another copper at seven who wants to see me urgently, or at least I think he's a policeman; the security services know him and he sounded OK, so I'm waiting to see what he wants. The other thing is going back to what you said about my brother: I know my dad was in charge of a few court martials during the war in Iraq. One was held there but the remainder were held here, and he might have made some enemies. I want to start going through the photos of that period; can we get that old computer buzzing, please?'

'Yes, here's the safe key get the disks out, and that master one is in a Jiffy Bag under the settee seat cover.'

'Bloody hell, Harold, that's a terrible hiding place.'

'I know, but if I got burgled they would be looking for the safe keys and if they found them they would get anything in it; it's too obvious they wouldn't look there.'

'Look, the computer has the files; all the disk does is open them for us, and I'm going to make it safer by copying all the files from the computer and then deleting them. They're no use without the master anyway – they'd be impossible to open. Then I'll put them on my machine at home, and put the master disk in a secure place for when I'm working on it. I haven't time yet, Harold, but I'll start it at the weekend.'

'Oh dear, does that mean you aren't going to come here anymore, Alan?'

'No, Harold – we are going to see a lot of each other; I have an idea for the future, but let's wait a few weeks until I've done my best to find my parents' killers.'

'What's that noise, Alan?'

Alan reached into his pocket. 'It's my spare phone; it has a different tone to the old one.'

'Alan, it's me – Uncle Ted.'

'Hi Ted, how are you?'

'I was all right until I found out somebody has killed my cat.'

'How do you know the cat was killed, Ted?'

'Because it's dead and stiff; not run over, which is the usual thing on the estate – how do you think I know, son?'

'No, Ted, you got it wrong; it could have been natural causes.'

'Alan, it's got a bloody rope round its neck.'

'It must have been kids, Ted. Don't get paranoid.'

'No, course I won't, but Alan, what a dirty trick to play on an old man. When are you coming to see me? I want to talk to you.'

'Soon, Ted. Are you going to get a new cat?'

'No. Maybe a very big dog instead. Don't worry, though – I just had to tell someone.'

'OK Ted, I'll see you soon.'

Alan laughed. His uncle was just like his father for turning sadness into fun, but the cat's death was just another thing that concerned him. Was it another message?

'Come on, Harold, let's think what the following have in common: my parents' death by explosion; plastic detonated by door closer in the car and and secondary explosion on same circuit but in the office. A mystery man turns up at Cheryl's mother's shop, in disguise we think. My phone tampered with and a blind device fitted, or at least we think it's blind, but I'll be getting it checked. Ted's cat is strangled, although I doubt that's connected to the others.'

'Alan, the thing that bothers me is that man you say was in disguise. Have you swept the shop for devices? He could have planted something.'

'No – shit, you're dead right. I'll go to the shop now. See you Saturday.'

Alan wasted no time; he broke the speed limit again on the A3 to Tolworth and parked down the road from Mandy's shop on a yellow line.

'Hi darling, no need to panic. Is your mum here?'

'Yes, I'll get her.'

'Alan, nice to see you, lad. What's up? You seem anxious.'

'That bloke who came here – did you leave him alone anywhere? I want to check to see if he left something, like a parcel or a box.'

'Blimey, it's like *Spooks*. Now, let's think: he was in here most of the time looking at Cheryl's tits, but he did use the toilet and wash his hands in the kitchen.'

'Just lock the door for a couple of minutes while I do a search.'

Alan used his car torch and checked likely places for a device to be fitted, and had almost finished when he noticed a radio on a shelf.

'Does that work, Mandy?'

'Where's that come from? Do you know, Cheryl?'

'No idea, Mum, I thought you brought it in.'

'It's the first time I've seen it. Is it dangerous, Alan?'

'Go outside into the street, well away from the shop windows.'

The two ladies ran out of the shop as instructed as Alan checked the small radio. It had no external wires, and apart from some spots of paint it looked like a normal transistor radio. He carefully climbed up on a chair to look at the back. Something worried him: he remembered he had seen a device like this before, but what was it, and how was it triggered? The one thing he decided was that it was not for him; this was bomb squad stuff. He carefully closed the kitchen door and joined the others outside.

'Here are your handbags; we can't go in there until that radio is checked. I believe it could be a bomb, but have no idea how it's detonated. If it's real it could be detonated by a radio signal.'

Alan's phone rang. 'Alan, it's the guy who's meeting you tonight here. I'm stuck in traffic in Kingston, so I'll be another 30 minutes. Wait for me, though – we are coming.'

'Look, I've a situation here: I'm outside my girlfriend's mother's shop in Tolworth Broadway, just off the A3, and I think someone has planted a device in the kitchen.'

'OK, you're talking to the right people. Explanations later; I'll get the police down there to seal off the area double-quick. Get at least a hundred yards away, and we'll be with you in ten minutes.'

The police arrived at the scene in three minutes and evacuated the whole area within 150 yards, including all the people in the Tolworth Tower. Then they sealed off the roundabout, and all paths and roads around the area. Once the area had been secured, one of the policemen ran across the road to Alan.

'Sit in the patrol car, Mr Fisher, and take the ladies with you.'

'Yes, fine, but I've two guys coming in a few minutes who are bomb experts.'

'We know that – we've had a message; they'll be here on that side road in three or four minutes. They're from SIS, I'm told; not their business, but the bomb squad are also on the way.'

Alan smiled. He should have guessed who the mystery caller was. 'I need to talk to them when they're all here. I have a clue about the radio; I've seen a bomb set up like this before.'

'Are you an expert as well then, Mr Fisher?'

'No, I just used to be in the army and I think I've seen that type of bomb before. The secret is that it doesn't look like one: it's disguised as a radio, but inside it will have no components other than a dial and a speaker grill. The base of it will have plastic explosive, detonated by an external device.'

The area was ablaze with blue and yellow lights when two men jumped out of a car and ran towards Alan and the ladies.

'Charlie, what the hell are you doing here?'

'I'm with Jason Harris to talk with you, but more on that later. We've got to sort out this bomb of yours.'

'OK then, here goes: it's a transistor radio without wires on the top right shelf in the kitchen of the salon. I believe a bloke in disguise planted it a few days ago. The radio looks to me like a type I saw in the Middle East during a drill. From memory I think it's detonated from a remote signal hidden in a watch or a phone. I had trouble with my phone today and when I opened it up I found this small, round piece of loose metal inside, painted orange. It could be that somebody was going to do the same as they did to my parents and blow me up here in the Broadway. All it would have needed was for me to be picking Cheryl up – which I do most days at the moment – and the device would have gone off, triggered by a signal from my phone.'

'Look, the bomb squad are here; let's brief them and see if we can find the answer before we go near the device.'

The three men ran to the bomb squad jeep and told them everything they knew, and the sergeant in charge took over.

'I'm Major Fred Leech, gentlemen, and from what you've told me I think Alan may be right about the bomb, but we need to be sure. Let's have a look at the inside of the phone under the strobe light.'

In case Alan was right they handled the phone extremely carefully. Alan shuddered, as he had kept the dud phone in his pocket all afternoon and it had rattled around with money and keys.

Major Leech looked up and sighed. 'Somebody is playing nasty tricks. This is a crude trigger device, but it's not been soldered, and it's probably just metal; not a chip. The person planting this would know what he was doing, and no way would it work without solder in two points and an actual transistor. Also, I guess if it had been set up it would only have a range of about 30 yards. It's a joke, and a very bad one.'

'How do we handle it then, Fred?'

'My opinion now is that a detonating device was never made. I doubt it's a bomb, and I'm confident it was just made for Alan to think it was one. We'll still take no chances: let's suit up with the full kit and go and get it. We have to be sure, and if necessary we'll move it outside the shop and do a controlled explosion. We'll get to work in about 25 minutes, but first we need to check those service plans to make certain we operate well away from

135

the gas main. Then we'll go inside the shop and down the path to that field over there to do the controlled explosion if we're doubtful. Get the police to move everyone back another hundred yards, totally close the A3 and make sure everyone around here has their mobile phones off.'

Alan, Jason and Charlie went back to the squad car as the police started to move back the spectators and a couple of stranded vehicles. Two other police cars had blocked the northbound carriageway of the A3 and the slip road, and all traffic was being diverted through Hook and Surbiton.

The bomb disposal chief shouted to them. 'I suggest you move the Mini back at least another 50 yards, Alan.'

'Oh yes; sorry, I forgot about it. I'll do it now.'

Alan jumped in the car and saw what he thought was a parking ticket under the front windscreen. He found a place in the bank car park round the next corner, and locked the car. Stuffing the paper in his pocket, he ran back to the squad car. The bomb squad officers raised their hands and the police officers gave thumbs-up sign back: nobody was using mobiles and all radios had been switched off. The SIS man saw Alan pick up the piece of paper.

'What was on the paper? Did you get a parking ticket?'

Alan pulled the paper out of his pocket and read it.

'Quick – tell the bomb disposal guy to stop.'

Jason Harris waved at the leading officer who was walking very slowly across the main road; he stopped the other two officers behind him and walked over to the three men. The suit restricted the movement of the second bomb disposal officer, and through the special Perspex screen, he could read the message on the piece of paper.

'What does it say?'

Alan didn't reply, and just passed the note to Jason Harris. The note was handwritten; it wasn't a parking ticket. The message was short and very clear:

No bomb; stop snooping everywhere or next time it will be real.

'We can't trust that message,' said Major Leech. 'We carry on expecting it to be a bomb.'

The three officers went to the building. One went inside with a tool resembling an apple picker, and he carefully locked the jaws of the tool onto the radio, then extended it to its limit of five yards. He passed it to one of the other men, who took it to the path and carefully placed it on the open ground in the field.

'No need to blow it up, lads; the scanner shows it's totally empty. Let's open it up.'

The men were still cautious; one checked out the remainder of the shop and gave it the all-clear.

'Nothing in the radio, boss; it's totally empty. Do you think it was being prepared for a bomb or not?'

'Probably not just for this show; it's a style of device used in the Middle East. They were left in buildings – they were lethal until we worked out the disguise, and at first nobody bothered with them in a building search as they looked just like normal transistor radios. A couple went off and we lost men, and then we knew what we were up against. The metal piece in Alan's phone would have been the trigger unit; probably activated by pressing "answer" on the keyboard if the setup had been completed. Did you leave your phone here unattended?'

'Yes, I forgot it, but how did the bloke know it was mine?'

'At first sight, a guess, maybe. It could have belonged to anybody; even a kid could have checked the memory in seconds and it would have shown incoming calls and you contacts list. If it was you he was after, he did everything other than set it up to kill. I know who you are, Alan, and I'm very sorry about your parents' deaths. Please ask Inspector Hubbard to call me in the morning and I'll brief him on my report which will follow in a few days.'

'What will it say?'

'The bottom line is that it was a dummy, and in my opinion a warning to you personally not to get involved in trying to find your parents' killer. The person who planted this dud could be involved with the bombing at your parents' house, but that's speculation and I'm sure Norman Hubbard will check out that possibility. I'm sorry we can't allow any of you back in the shop today; the police will tape it off and forensic will go through it with a fine-toothed comb; they'll tell Mrs Rix when she can return – usually 24 hours if they don't find anything.'

'OK, I'll tell them; they're in the pub down the road. Thanks for your help tonight. I'm very worried about all this but it won't distract me; I want my parents' killers found.'

'Alan, leave it to the police – it's safer.'

The bomb disposal team packed up and left, and the area started to return to normal, although they left behind a fully-equipped Jeep and an officer to stay overnight with the police squad car. They didn't expect any further issues that night, but the shop had to remain sealed. As Alan and Jason walked to the pub, there was no sign of Charlie.

'Did I see Charlie Baxter with you?'

'Yes, it was Charlie, but he seems to have gone to the pub already, he lives near here and we were taking him home from a job he did for us.'

Alan was suspicious and would follow up on the presence of his old colleague when he had the time.

'OK, I'll just quickly speak to Cheryl and her mum; they've another car here so they can drive home, and we can have our discussion as soon as they've left.'

Cheryl and Mandy Rix left the pub and Alan promised to call in to see them after his meeting. Charlie appeared from the toilet, apparently not interested in what had happened.

The SIS man sat next to Alan. 'So, Alan, after all of the excitement of tonight, our plan for you could be a light relief.'

'Plan for me – what do you mean? Haven't we had enough drama for one day?'

'Firstly, I think proper introductions are needed. I'm Jason Harris, a case officer Middle East; one of many. I believe you know Charlie Baxter very well?'

'Yes, but you've made me very suspicious already – spill it out, Jason; get to the point please and tell me what you want.'

'Really simple, Alan: we – that is SIS – need the services of you and Charlie for one week. You haven't signed the Official Secrets Act recently, I know, but I'm going to take a risk in telling you this as it's a very unusual task. We need to help an engineer with a Turkish father and American mother to leave Iran and deliver him back here; his name is Deniz Korham. He has been working at a plant, making components for nuclear energy equipment, and from information he's given us it's possible the components could be used to make a nuclear weapon, so we need to go through his drawings, photographs and verbal information to be certain of him one way or another. If the Iranians are making a bomb at or near the site he works at, both the USA and our own government want to know about it before they hide the production underground and make it impossible to trace with aerial photography. We are told Korham wants to come here to live, and it appears he has

140

family in the Newcastle area. In any case he may finish up in the USA where he was actually born.

'The operation needs two specialists: one who knows the area between Van in Turkey and Northern Iran well and has combat experience in poor conditions; plus someone who can verify what this man has got and is prepared to hand over. Even if it's just a vague chance the components could be designed for a weapon, we want him. The factory where he works is in a town called Lasop in the north of Iran, and he's free to leave the plant but his apartment is situated on the site. It's a high-security place so he has to file details of any trip he makes outside the site to get approval, which he says is usually given. This type of security check would be normal practice for anyone working in a nuclear energy plant or its supply chain in a country like Iran, and possibly here as well. So that's why we need you two: Charlie has done several jobs for us since you saw him last and they've gone well. You'll be paid well of course, but my director has said if you cooperate he will get more involved again in your parents' murders – unofficially of course as it's now a full police enquiry. That would involve the photos you have. We have ways to check them for matches against people we know; a job that will take you years if you try it. He needs just a range of specific dates, then he will put it to one of our case officers who is a specialist in identification.'

Alan was silent, and Charlie Baxter frowned.

'Never enough money from you lot, Jason. This one is going to cost you double.'

'I've a budget, but we can talk about it. Alan, what do you think? Are you with us?'

'I don't like the SIS tactics sometimes, Jason, although I realise you're not trying to win a popularity contest. You guys drop out of my parents' case and leave it to the police; then when this assignment pops up you suddenly want to help me.'

'Frankly, Alan, you're right, but it's a question of resources and I know it sounds a bit crass to say that if you help us we'll help you, but that's the situation, like it or not. We're fundamentally looking at overseas projects; this one does overlap a bit.'

Charlie Baxter listened intently to the SIS man. Other than money, he had no reason to take the assignment. He had told his wife he'd left the army, but SIS guessed that he was still on their payroll, and nobody was asking why, other than they knew Charlie had special skills. He was beginning to think that one day he should go back full-time, if it was entirely his decision. In reality the help he'd been giving SIS was very dangerous and he hated working in hot climates, but on a good day he viewed it as cash for little work, provided that he stayed alive. His wife Ann was not told anything about what he was doing unless it went wrong; those were the terms Charlie agreed to when he was signed up. He had not divulged to any of his friends that he had a major problem and that he needed money urgently. SIS knew his situation and they were willing to pay him well for special assignments without any risk to their own men.

Alan had listened carefully to Jason Harris' summary without much comment. He knew what was required, and much as he didn't like the situation, the bait they were offering meant he had to accept.

'Charlie, can I talk to you alone for a couple of minutes, as I assume Jason wants a yes or no tonight?'

'Correct, Alan; I need to know your decision now. I'll go to the car for ten minutes.'

Jason drank up his soft drink and left the pub.

'Things are moving quickly my old mate, what do you reckon?'

'Tell me more Charlie – what do they want us to do?'

'I shouldn't tell you because it's all top secret, but broadly, you fly out as a tourist to Istanbul, then get an internal flight to a place called Van; then they will send a car to collect you from the airport to an unspecified destination. I'll fly into the base on a Hercules from Brize Norton and join you on the same day. The next day we'll study our route to Lasop, which is over the border in Iran; an area which you know pretty well, I think?'

'Yes, I did the trip a few times, both during the day and at night.'

'Why; what was so interesting to us that you risked certain jail or death if the locals saw you and informed the authorities?'

'I can't tell you, other than it was simple surveillance; you probably wouldn't come with me if I told you now.'

'That sounds very dodgy, Alan, but you're going to look out for me, aren't you?'

Alan saw fear in his friend's face. What was his problem? He had to find out.

'Yes, mate, and don't worry – provided this Turkish bloke goes to the place I tell him we'll be OK. The area is mainly mountains, and the tricky bits will be avoiding a couple of towns.'

'How long will it take to get there and back? I'll need a few hours to check his drawings; fuck knows what we'll do if he's of no use to us.'

'Jason says we have to bring him back or kill him.'

'What? No way – when we get back someone else can deal with him after we've arrived in Brize Norton. Shit, I hope they're paying you well for this job?'

'Yes, they know my fee; they'll give you the same but I'm not doing this for money, Charlie – I don't need it, my parents left me enough. I just want the bastard who killed them and it's better to have SIS working on it; that's the only way I would accept this job.'

Jason returned to the pub. 'Time's up, guys: what's your decision?'

Both men nodded, and all three shook hands.

'Thanks, Alan – these are the dates we're looking for on the photos; if you can find as many as you can before you leave we can get working on it. We have a nice young blonde graduate with long legs who joined us a few weeks ago, and she knows what we're looking for.'

They all laughed at the sexist remark, and Alan guessed that Jason was already doing homework with her.

The three men left the pub together. Charlie and Alan were expected at Sandhurst at 9am on the following Monday; the 25th January. They were not given any further information, which suited them; both had the weekend to make their plans, and Alan his careful apologies. Alan dropped Charlie off at his home in Chessington; little was said in the car, as if both men had suddenly woken up to the reality of what they had agreed to do.

'See you next week then, Alan.' He sounded strange.

'What's the matter, Charlie?'

'Why did you just turn up at my place, Alan? What did you want?'

'What the fuck is the matter with you? I came to see you as I was just passing and saw the car – you're really jumpy, mate.'

As if nothing had happened, Charlie turned to Alan and pointed at him.

'Call me on Sunday and we can check out that list of things we need. My memory of Sandhurst is sweat and more sweat rather than just a refresher; some of the two-day programmes could be a bit energetic. I don't think we'll be spending much time in the gym; no doubt the idea is to give us a weapons update and then we'll probably spend time on the latest satellite navigation gear we could be using. I've got my own gear and will take it with us.

'Alan, you need to know that as I'm technically still in the army I've got most of my stuff; they call me a consultant, or in other words I know things that they don't and they may need me sometime. The agreement was that I would never be active again in the front line; it suits me and I even get paid a good retainer. I don't regard this mission as front-line and I hope I'm right. They way I see it is that the tricky part could be working out if the drawings and notes this bloke Korham is supposed to have are any good or not. They'll be in the local language so I was going to get a translation done on key words next week, but it may not be needed after what Jason said. I wonder how good this bloke's English really is? I suppose if he spent time in the USA he'll be reasonably fluent. I speak Turkish, but not Persian or local Kurdish dialects. Do you speak any Turkish, Alan? You were there a few years; you must know some words?'

The comment concerned Alan. If Charlie spoke to the man in Turkish, he would have no idea what he was saying. Alan was nervous, and he didn't want Charlie to talk to the man in Turkish or any local language unless it was totally necessary; if it happened he would have to find a way of recording what was said, as he was not sure he could trust his old friend.

146

It was almost as if nothing had happened as the two men said their goodbyes and Alan went directly to Cheryl's mum's house. He had a strange feeling about Charlie but he couldn't work out what it was, so he dismissed it as just fear. He could help him, but he needed his trust and he hoped he would tell him when he got the opportunity. Mandy Rix opened the door at the sound of the Mini pulling into the drive. In her almost see-through dressing gown, heavy makeup and stockings, she needed only a red light over the door to confirm her status.

'Hi Alan, we thought you'd been arrested.'

'No, just talking to the police Mandy; no need to dress up for me, but it's a nice outfit.'

'Maybe one day before you marry my daughter I'll dress up for you; just once Alan, and I'll show you a thing or two.'

Alan laughed and stepped back; he was uncertain if Mandy was just joking or if she really meant what she said.

'Don't let Cheryl hear you say that. I'm not saying anything about marriage as I've to sort out a few things in my life before I marry anybody.'

They both burst out laughing as Cheryl appeared from the bathroom.

'What's the joke then, can I share it? Was it about bombs in our shop?'

Mandy Rix had always had men, but not many stayed very long. Cheryl's father had left and nobody knew if he was dead or alive; Alan wondered if Mandy had worn him out, and one day he might ask her.

'No, it's no joke or a bomb, Cheryl – the police reckon someone was giving me a warning; it has to be as no explosive was found in the radio, but they have no ideas who did it. They treat all bomb threats very seriously, and especially after what happened to my mum and dad, it was good that the disposal guys reacted so quickly. I'm sure the people who did it will show their faces again; we have to be vigilant and let me know immediately if you seeing anything at all suspicious.'

Mandy swung her dressing gown around her and started to climb the stairs.

'I'm off to bed, looks like we can't use the shop tomorrow so I'll ring up all the people we have booked in from the appointments in my diary. This bloody thing is going to cost me money; if you find the joker let me know, Alan.'

'No, I don't want you taking the law into your own hands, Mandy. Leave it to the police, and if by any chance that guy turns up again, lock him in the toilet and ring them.'

Cheryl almost pushed her mother out of the room, then grabbed her boyfriend.

'What a terrible day. Have you any idea who that man in disguise could have been – that's if it was a disguise? Do you know, Alan, I've seen someone walk like he did and I can't think where it was. I think that his hair was real. Maybe I saw him when he was collecting his wife from our shop, or saw someone using your gym when I've picked you up.'

'Think hard, Cheryl, please; try to remember where you saw him. If he planted the dummy bomb and then sent me a threatening note he'll do something else soon. I would think it's someone who's watching the shop.'

'No, you're wrong – I think it was the gym. There was a guy hanging about; I saw him on two consecutive nights when your car was in for service. He didn't go inside the building, and the minute you turned up he walked away quickly. That was the funny walk, I'm sure.'

'If you ever see him again, don't go near him; promise me, Cheryl.'

'I promise I'll just phone up the police number on that card you gave me for DI Hubbard, and you of course.'

'Correct; in that order. I've something to tell you, Cheryl: I'll be abroad for a week from Monday. I may not be in phone contact but if I can get a signal I'll try to call you.'

Alan would not have his UK phone with him on the operation; he would be using a satellite phone so definitely not a unit to call his girlfriend on unless in an emergency.

'An old army friend needs some help abroad with a building project and wants my advice, it's in the middle of nowhere so I decided to take a break and help him.'

'Yes, fine, but it's very short notice – is he after planning permission?'

'Well, yes, in a way: he needs to make sure his foundations are correct in the sand before he starts the next part of his plans.'

Alan was a bad liar but his girlfriend bought his story. She had no choice.

'The council have given me time off, so I'll take the opportunity to chill out as well and have a break.'

Cheryl put her head on his lap.

'There's one condition, Alan, to get my approval.'

Cheryl folded her arms and smiled.

'Yes, and what might that be?'

'I stay with you tomorrow night.'

'OK, that's great; I had the same idea. We can go to that Japanese restaurant near the theatre first – I must get back now as I've to start thinking what to take on this trip, and I need to get the washing machine going.'

'OK then, you perfect domesticated male, see you at the station about 7pm.'

Alan laughed as he went to use the upstairs toilet and Cheryl switched on the television. As he flushed the toilet the door swung wide open and he had a clear view into Mandy's adjoining bedroom. The image of her middle-aged body lying on her bed with her massive breasts hanging down and her knees drawn up to her chin would keep him thinking for at least two weeks. *Hell,* he thought, *I'm going to marry Cheryl*; but should he take the bait one day, she did say once only.

'Like what you see, Alan?'

Alan looked at her and just gave a thumbs-up sign as she rolled over onto her stomach and lay on her hands. He nearly fell down the stairs as Cheryl opened the front door. Cheryl kissed him and smiled.

'See you tomorrow, darling.'

Alan was confused. What on earth was he thinking about? Maybe he needed a few Sandhurst cold showers to get the older woman out of his mind.

By the time he got back to his flat he was thinking about who had planted the fake bomb and the one that killed his parents. It had to be the same person, and Alan was all but convinced it was someone who was not working alone. He felt he was making progress; the protection his father had given to the photo files and the interest from SIS must mean that the pictures contained some enemies. Then he remembered someone else who might be able to help. His priorities were clear, and as soon as he got inside his flat he rang Harold Penny.

'Harold, I'll be over first thing tomorrow – I'm going away but the police have given some dates to check the photographs. I'll use my copy, but in your computer, then when I find them I can show them to you. How are you, anyway? Is your peg leg OK?'

'It's fine, Ala,n provided I don't walk too much. Maybe I'm just imagining it but I still think somebody is watching my house. See you in the morning; if I'm not here I'll just have popped out for a paper and I'll get you some breakfast when I'm back. Have you still got that key?'

'Yes, Harold, thanks. See you tomorrow.'

'Just one thing, son – sorry, I forgot. The coroner's office phoned and confirmed that the inquest has definitely been adjourned again. The coroner isn't happy about something; he must still be waiting for more information on your parents' deaths.'

'I almost forgot about it as well. Was it supposed to be next week?'

'Yes, they say too much detail is still missing; we may know more when you're back from your trip. I think they should just get on with it – odd, really; it's as if someone has asked them to delay. But I'm sure the coroner wouldn't stand for any interference, Alan, that man or lady has a lot of power.'

'What, even if the country's interests were affected?'

'See you tomorrow, Alan.'

If Harold knew something, he didn't want to be drawn on the subject by Alan or anyone else.

Alan put the phone down and bowed his head. With all the events of the past two days, he'd totally forgotten about the inquest and all the dreadful details of his parents' deaths as they would be presented to the jury. His knew his nightmare would continue until the killer was found and convicted. He picked up the phone and dialled Ted Fisher's number.

'Uncle Ted, it's Alan.'

'That's a coincidence – I was just thinking about coming to see you. I've had an idea or two.'

'I'm going away for a week's break. What did you want to tell me? Will it wait?'

'Yes, of course, but briefly: your dad was a bit rattled about something just before the bombing. He rarely told me anything about his working life, and it was unusual for him to mention anything about the past. One day, about a week before his death, he was here reading newspapers and drinking coffee with me, and we were talking about retirement life when he suddenly pointed to a man in a photograph. He tapped the paper and stood up quickly, then turned to me and said, "Ted, that's a death a lot of British people would approve of if they knew what he had done."'

'Go on, Ted, who was the man?'

'Sorry, Alan, I can't remember. All I know was that he was Irish but I got the impression it was someone your father knew well and was pleased he was dead.'

'While I'm away could you check the date of that meeting with my dad and then see if you can get a copy of the paper? It may mean something to SIS if he died violently.'

'Yes, he died violently; just like my cat.'

'Surely not by strangulation? That would be unusual.'

'Yes, with a wire or cord I believe. At the time I didn't think too much about it until my cat died and then I kept thinking about what a horrible way to die it was.'

'There you go, Ted, this is important; did you discuss with anyone what my dad had read in the paper and his reaction?'

'Probably, but you know me: when I've had a few beers, I tell the same story many times but this time I really can't remember. I promise you I'll think about it carefully. Call me when you're back.'

'OK, but this could be an important clue; please don't talk about this to anyone. I'm pretty sure it wasn't the same person who killed your cat.'

'No, you're right: several were killed in this area by some nutcase who dislikes animals; the police and RSPCA got him last week, so pretty certain he wasn't the guy in Northern Ireland.'

'There you go again, Ted – you just told me a bit more! Come on; where in Northern Ireland? My dad may have commented on it.'

'He did, I remember – it was Belfast.'

'This makes it much easier, Ted – go and see your mate across the road with that new computer; ask him if you can use it to check your bank or something in private, I'm sure he'll understand. When you're on you own, enter into the Google search engine "Irish man strangled Belfast"; you're certain then to get something back. Send me a text message next week and we can discuss anything you've found out when I'm back, but don't involve the police.'

'Understood, Alan; it's nice to be doing something to try and find your parents' killers. I've felt so helpless since it happened.'

'Me too, Ted. See you soon.'

Chapter 13
An Eventful Weekend

'Bill, we've got to stop this: I creep out of the pub at times when Larry can't leave it; we have sex twice, lasting almost exactly 30 minutes including a cup of tea; then I go shopping and go home. I'm not sure if I love him anymore, but because of all this shit connected to the pub I can't leave him now. I'm eight years older than you – why do you want me?'

'I want you, Jill, as much as a friend as a lover; since Harriet died I've been lost. You've helped me recover, but at 48 it's not dial-a-date but dial-a-crisis, and all the contacts I've had apart from you have issues with something or other.'

'I understand, but don't give that excuse to Larry if he finds out about us.'

'If all goes well the pub will be sold in a month or two, then we can make some plans. My worry is that Larry will not accept that you're leaving him, and you know how violent he has become.'

'Yes, but he's never hurt me. I'm sure he's having an affair with Marie the Polish barmaid, though – she can't look me in the eye. She is twenty-odd years younger, pretty and wants security;

frankly I don't understand what she likes about him. Some days he just behaves like a mentally ill pig.'

'Harsh words, Jill, but one thing at a time; let's get this sale moving then we can make a plan. I'm going into the office now even though it's Saturday to catch up on the paperwork, and I'll be over later to discuss the pub with Larry. Off you go before my cleaner arrives – she's convinced you live here.'

Jill Nixon drove away to Sainsbury's; she would hit the lunchtime rush but she needed Bill Knowles' company. She had few friends, and at least he listened to her.

She went to the cash machine to check her bank balance and took out the last £150 – both she and her husband often dipped into the spare cash from the safe, but as business was poor she needed cash for the shopping. She turned to hide her PIN number, and as she pressed buttons on the small screen a man bumped into her.

'Hello, it's Jill, isn't it?'

'Yes; you're Alan Fisher.'

'I am, and I used to come to your pub.'

Alan told Jill the story of how her husband had all but thrown him out for helping behind the bar when he was out. She didn't need a reminder: she well remembered that day as one when Larry lost his rag.

'I'm sorry, Alan, I really don't know why that happened. Please come back – Larry plays snooker in town on Wednesdays so come in with your girl after seven o'clock and we can have a chat.'

'OK, you're on, but I'm away for a week so it'll be towards the end of the month.'

'Any Wednesday. Must go now, Alan.'

The supermarket car park was full when Larry Nixon drove past; he wanted to catch his wife before she went into the shop as they had run out of potatoes and he needed some urgently for the lunchtime meals. Jill had switched her phone off again – why did she do that? She wasn't on a golf course, and the excuses she gave were ridiculous; he was convinced she did it just to annoy him. He saw her turn away from the cash machine and speak with Alan Fisher. His mind was working overtime as he saw the pair smiling at each other. He spun the car around, and as he drove away he knew what his next step would be. Larry laughed to himself. He would put a stop to his wife's games once and for all. His temper was taking over his senses, and he drank a large gulp of whisky from a small bottle he kept in his car.

He drove to Bill Knowles' house and parked at the opposite end of the street; found an old envelope addressed to the pub and he scribbled a message on it.

Your friend Jill has a new toyboy: Alan Fisher.

He put the envelope through the letterbox and drove back to the pub. He was happy he'd done something, and he knew it would set the ball rolling on making his wife regret her affair.

Bill Knowles had a draft contract ready for the sale of The Brown Cow public house and the adjoining ground, left by his secretary for editing. He picked up the document, and in his haste at first he missed the note left by Betty. As he read through the contract he made a few alterations in red pen, then left it on Betty's desk for correction. Then he saw the note and sat down to read it.

Bill, you had a visit from a very grumpy Larry Nixon. He nearly made me cry, but that's not important – what happened was that Aaron Parker has been to see him direct about buying the pub. He said that Parker had told him you were going to double-cross him and make a big profit with the back-to-back deal. He said he was going to your house to look for you; that was about 2.30.

See you Monday.

Betty

Bill came out in a sweat. He was with Jill at 2.30, and Larry must have driven to his house, seen the car and left. He knew he had to see Larry, but he had to think what to do first, especially about Aaron Parker – he had to find out more about the man, and if he could rubbish him but then maybe it could save his business skin. He then had the more complicated situation with Jill, but

159

maybe now was the time to come clean and get her to ask Larry for a divorce. On his journey home he had the basis of a plan, until he read the piece of paper stuck in the letterbox. Bill looked to the sky and started to shake and sweat again for the second time within an hour: he was running out of ideas, but he needed to talk to someone soon. He found the number for Alice Smith.

'Alice, it's me, Bill; I know it's short notice but I need to talk with you urgently about Aaron Parker. I'll pay you more if you can help me with some information.'

'Bill, I'm not sure I know enough about him to tell you anything you don't know already, but wait a minute – why don't you speak with Sheila Hamilton? She knows him very well.'

'Could you set up a meeting around five today, say, the King's Head in Epsom? It's about halfway for her – please, Alice, I'm pretty desperate.'

'Yes, unless you hear from me meet us at five; bring £150 and that should cover an initial meeting. If you like the information she will probably give you more but you can ask her yourself; it'll cost you, though.'

'Thanks Alice, see you both later.'

Bill felt a slight relief, but it only lasted a few minutes. He had been in many scrapes but this was the worst one ever. He worked out that Larry had to know he was seeing his wife, but then he'd said as well that Jill was also seeing Alan Fisher, and if that was the case Jill really was putting it about. The way Bill saw it, he had no future if Alan was serious, and he could get a kicking from Larry just for the hell of it. Other than Jill, Bill was one of the few people who knew the landlord had a violent and uncontrollable temper. Bill did a double-take: surely he had got it wrong on Alan Fisher? No way would he get involved with Jill, except maybe for a quick one, but then even that seemed far-fetched. And on top of all his women problems, Bill's new client Aaron Parker could turn nasty now, and he was surprised that he hadn't heard from him already. He put the phone back on the receiver, with sweat dripping down the unit and onto the hall floor.

He tried hard to think what he had on Larry that he could trade with: he knew all his tax fiddles, but then he was a party in them, so it was a bad idea to even mention they existed. Maybe Jill could tell him something – what Larry did before he was a landlord? Larry and Aaron Parker could certainly make a good deal without Bill; the introductions had been made and all Larry would need was a good local conveyance solicitor.

Chapter 14
Preparing to Leave

Alan Fisher arrived at Harold Penny's house and found the front door open. From his army training he immediately thought danger until proved otherwise. He grabbed a thick walking stick from the hallstand and went through it to the lounge area. The stick was not for self-defence, just to push doors open; Alan had been well trained in self-defence and unarmed combat, and anybody attacking him would almost certainly come off worse unless they had a firearm.

The whole of the ground floor was empty, but the kettle was warm. As Alan tiptoed up the stairs, he heard a noise in the bedroom Harold used as an office; he pushed the door open with the stick and saw that the noise was the wind blowing the curtains outwards from a fully-open sash window. As he turned into the room, he saw a sight he didn't want to see. Harold Penny was on the floor with blood dripping from a wound to his forehead.

'Harold, wake up.'

Alan could feel a good pulse, and he was breathing. He found a whisky glass and filled it with water from the bathroom tap, and when he got back in the room Harold was sitting up.

'What happened to you? Are you hurt?'

'No, Alan; I came in here because I heard a noise, and this bloke pushed me and I fell backwards. I'm just a bit dazed. He climbed out of the window with my computer; it was so heavy he threw it on the lawn.'

'Bloody hell, Harold, I'm really sorry. This is all my fault.'

'No it isn't, I wanted to be involved. It was my choice to work with you and together we're going to get this bastard. He must have guessed that I'd have stuff on your dad; we moved it just in time.'

'Yes, he won't be able to open those files even if he finds them – I copied them, then deleted them from your machine, and then I cleared the delete file but the computer system still holds them somewhere on the hard disk. Only an expert could get them back, but nobody could open them without the code on the floppy disk we have. Now, my friend, I'm going to call the police and then we need to check you out at the A&E unit down the road.'

'No, you're not going to tell the police – we know what's going on. We just need to go through the photos and try and find someone, or maybe a group, that your father really sorted out, or tried to. Have you any ideas who they are, Alan?'

'Only one lead from my Uncle Ted, but whoever these people are they won't rest until they've finished the job. That fake bomb business was just a warning about what they can do. Come on, we're going to the A&E, Harold; I'll close the window. Look at this on the windowsill: as your visitor climbed out he must have caught his belt and the buckle's snapped off. What do you make of that?'

'No idea – can't tell you, son; my glasses are in my bedroom. What is it?'

'It's an army belt buckle; I've not seen one like it before but we could have a clue here, and a big one. We'll sort you out, then I'll call at Office World and buy you a new computer – that guy did you a favour, pinching that pile of old rubbish.'

Harold didn't protest. He had delayed shock, and Alan left him at the hospital with a story of falling out of bed. The wound was just a scratch but he had mild concussion, and the doctor made him stay the night. Alan had guessed that they would keep him in and drove back to his house and grabbed pyjamas and a change of clothes from his bedroom wardrobe. When he got back to the hospital Harold was in a private room.

'I'll pick you up in the morning – your house is all locked up but I'm pretty certain your visitor won't be coming back.'

Harold just nodded; the hospital had given him a sedative and he waved to Alan without protest, then fell asleep.

Alan checked the garden to see if the intruder had left any further clues, but apart from boot footprints he found nothing. He went to his car and collected his new Nikon digital camera, and took several photographs of the footprints to study later. On his journey back to his flat he changed his mind about a new computer: he was going away for a week and Harold would be resting; he had all the disks that he had copied secure and he had taken the one with the code from the safe when he went back to get Harold's clothes. The furniture, home safe and personal effects salvaged from his parents' house had been moved by the police, on Harold's instructions, to the depository on the Ewell bypass. Alan had a key to his father's charred but empty safe, and he placed all the disks inside: they would remain there until he returned.

His day cut short, he parked behind Epsom High Street and went to Millets outdoor shop and bought some new shirts and walking trousers. He decided to use his old boots rather than break in new ones on the foothills and rough mountains of Turkey and Iran. On his way back to the car he was distracted by a woman's backside in front of him, and he smiled to himself, wondering what she looked like from the front. He was soon to find out as she bent down and unlocked the white Audi TT with a personal plate.

'Sheila? I haven't seen you for years, do you remember me?'

The girl looked hard at Alan before she answered.

'Yes, blimey I do – you're Alan Fisher; could I ever forgot you? I saw you in Sainsbury's in North Cheam a few weeks ago, but you'd gone before I could talk to you – come here!'

Before he knew it Alan was in a clinch with the beautiful Sheila Hamilton, and he didn't want it to end as she pushed her body tight against his.

'So what's your story? I heard you left the army; you were away a long time.'

'Yes, that's history. I work for the council planning department now, how about you?'

'Just modelling and a bit of PR work; it pays well.'

'Yes, nice car – you must be doing OK. Any men about?'

'Yes and no: they come and go; nothing permanent, but I've got a mortgage and a dog to feed so I need to work until Mr Right comes along. How about you, then?'

'I've a steady girlfriend of about six months – not sure how it'll work out, but we'll see.'

'That's OK, I would expect you to have someone. Anyway, would you like to meet me for a drink one night?'

Alan paused, and the girl noticed.

'Yes, love to, Sheila, but I'm away on business for a week. Give me your number and I'll call you when I'm back home.'

'You didn't sound sure at first, Alan. Don't worry, I'm not going to seduce you in the pub.'

'That's a shame. I was looking forward to seeing your body again.'

'You obviously remember that night.'

'Do I, but I was on leave and I went back to my unit like the cat who had just drunk all the cream.'

Sheila laughed and hugged him again. 'That good, was it, big boy?'

'Sure was, and from memory even though I'd had a few beers, there were definitely three of us. I believe your friend Alice Smith joined in as well.'

'Yes, what a good memory you have; we did work together once or twice but she always had her own job. She'll surely remember you, but I may keep you to myself this time. Here, take this card with my number: I have to get out of here as my ticket is well over the time. Bye, Alan; great to see you.'

'Same here. I'll call you, but why are you here? I thought you lived nearer London.'

'My mother lives here so I do her weekly shopping. Must go, she'll be waiting on the front step.'

The minute he left Sheila Hamilton, uncertainty crept into Alan's mind. Yes, she was fit, but then did he want a glamour girl? He decided to call into the Rainbow Centre and go into the gym – he needed a change of thought and he knew an hour pumping iron would sort him out.

167

As he left the gym, his phone vibrated in his pocket as he had switched it to silent. It was Jason Harris from SIS.

'Hi Alan, sorry to ring you but I need a quick answer or two from you on something now.'

'OK, what is it Jason?'

'Firstly you have to sign the Official Secrets Act on Monday; no choice, but then I'm sure that's OK for you?'

'Done it before, Jason. You said two things; what else do you want?'

'I want you to ask a few of your mates – very discreetly, of course – if any of them knows a guy called Aaron Parker or his wife Leah. They were last seen in your area but nobody can trace them. He is slightly dark-skinned, about six feet tall with short black hair; very well dressed all the time and he drives a large Mercedes, or he did six months ago. His wife is the same skin type and colour; five foot four inches tall and has long straight black hair; very pretty, I'm told. The sort of place they hang out in will be upmarket clubs or restaurants; not many in your area so hopefully someone has seen them. The address we have for them is let to someone else and the Parkers have moved on. If I put someone on it we could track them down eventually, but it's a lot of time and effort to put a simple question to them.'

'Why do you want to see them?'

'As I said, just a quick question; let's just say that the police are supposed to be looking after them but they haven't bothered, and now when we want to ask them something they say the couple have moved and gone missing. We know they're still in the UK but have moved flats without telling us – it's all very embarrassing, really. The only thing we know from snooping around a bit is that the Parkers were recently checking on the title of a property; they made the application but then a girl called Alice Miller made an application on the same day, and she gave an address near you in Epsom. The girl also asked for the details in Parker's name, so one of our admin girls passed it to me as a connection to Parker – just shows, our systems work most of the time. The address she gave was 16 West Hill, which on our equipment shows up as just across the road from you.'

Alan was for once lost for words. What a coincidence! Two hours before, he would have had to think hard about a girl called Alice, but since the chance meeting with Sheila Hamilton he was sort of up to date. Could her mate Alice Smith be Alice Miller?

'Is she really called Miller? I know a girl called Alice who lives near me in Epsom, but her name is Smith. I'll check her out for you but don't expect anything from me until I'm back from the assignment.'

His reply was non-committal; by the time he was back home hopefully Jason would have found the Parkers.

'Yes, Alan, I think the name Miller is right, but then she could have changed it. Anyway, thanks – I won't be at Sandhurst on Monday; Brian Wilson, one of my colleagues, will be doing the briefing. He is a targeting officer in Turkey and will go with you for some of your journey. I'll see you in a couple of weeks with Mr Deniz Korham.'

'He sounds like a footballer.'

'Definitely not, Alan; wait until you see him, then you'll see why. Take care, and watch your back.'

'I will, and this is just a one-off, remember.'

Jason said nothing and rang off.

Alan drove into the flat car park and followed his habit of checking for people sat in cars, or anybody who could be watching him. Everything was fine. He washed and changed, then started to gather a pile of clothes to fit in his rucksack for his departure on Monday. Alan still had to tell Cheryl a little more about the trip, and his story would need to be a good one. He put everything in the spare room and closed the door tight.

Cheryl's unmistakable hair was visible on the station stairs before he saw her. She knew he was going away and her outfit was set to kill: high-heeled black leather boots, tight jeans, open-necked blouse and fitted leather jacket. She was certainly dressed to impress her boyfriend.

'Wow, Cheryl, you look nice. I feel really scruffy.'

'That's very polite, darling; I wanted to look special for a change in case I've any competition.'

Alan felt guilty already, and so far he had done nothing wrong.

'Come on, let's go for a drink in The Old Bank before we eat. I have to tell you what I can about the trip.'

'Oh dear, aren't I going to like it?'

Alan ordered two glasses of wine and they found a corner away from the local lads watching the football.

'Some of this you aren't going to like, but I'm doing it for one reason and one alone: if I agree to it, the government will help me find my parents' killers, or at least try a lot harder to find them if I help them. It's bizarre, I know, but SIS had passed everything on to the police and now they're getting involved again; it's not their brief really but someone thinks it could be a security issue and they're checking up on everyone they know had connections to my father. I had them on the phone a few hours ago checking on a guy that could live locally who must be involved with terrorism as they were protecting him, and now he's gone missing. They're anxious to keep close to me and I reckon they're finding excuses to call me.

'I leave on Monday for a week, but first I've to stop on the way to see some people in the south, and then I go to a destination a few hours away by plane. I'll have an English colleague with me; we were in the army together. The reason we've been asked to help them is that we've specialist knowledge of the work we have to do.'

'That sounds very much like a James Bond film.'

'More like a backpacking trip, Cheryl: no girls, no booze and lots of walking. That's all I can tell you; as I said yesterday I probably won't be able to communicate with you, but a man called Jason Harris has your number as well as my Uncle Ted. In the case of an emergency he will ring you.'

'I'm frightened, Alan.'

'Don't be. I'll see you two weeks from tomorrow.'

The doubts in Cheryl's mind were not helped by Alan just having two small glasses of wine and insisting on an early night. As arranged, she stayed overnight, but neither of them could sleep: Alan's mind was in Turkey and Cheryl was worrying about everything.

Early on the Sunday morning Alan packed his bag and took Cheryl home. He wanted to avoid her mother, and dropped Cheryl outside the house: she might ask more questions, and the less she knew about his mission the better. He collected a revitalised Harold Penny, and they discussed the burglary and the latest analysis of his parents' estate, until Harold remembered he needed to do some shopping and left Alan alone in his flat. He was beginning to feel apprehensive about the whole mission, and regretting that he had agreed to go. He was pleased that Charlie would be with him: he used to be cool-headed, and was once a man whom Alan could trust in any physical situation. Now he was not sure, and while they were at Sandhurst he would try to find out what was bugging Charlie. He was certainly different from the man Alan used to know.

When he arrived back at his flat he tried to sleep, but the adrenalin was already pumping through his veins. He remembered the call from Jason Harris and the chance meeting with Sheila Hamilton, and decided to fire up his small notebook computer and see if either Sheila or Alice appeared on any of the social networking sites like Facebook or Twitter. Nothing at all on Alice Smith or Miller that matched the Alice he knew in Surrey, but then he found Sheila Hamilton; she had a short profile and an email address that he could pass on to Jason when he got back, and it could be a way for the SIS guys to track down the elusive Alice.

As he returned to his bed he found something hard on his pillow in his handkerchief – he had almost forgotten about the belt buckle, and put it in his rucksack so that he could ask the Sandhurst people to try and identify it for him. His mind suddenly switched to the note left under his windscreen on the night of the fake bomb: what would the mystery person do next? If he thought that Alan had stopped looking for his parents' killer, he might just forget about him.

Alan couldn't decide anything until this mission was over. He took a pill and was asleep in minutes.

Chapter 15
The Parkers

'Aaron, the drawings on the pub have come from the architect.'

Leah Parker continued to open the large brown parcel as Aaron read the rest of the mail.

'OK, spread them out on the table so we can see his ideas. That looks fabulous; it's a very clever design, Leah – all he's done is take the old building and rework it, and look, he's avoided demolition other than that one internal wall; he's basically just made three conservatories. Clever, especially as he didn't take any measurements; just had a couple of beers and walked around outside the place.'

'Yes, it looks good; his design is simple. Will it keep building costs down?' asked Leah.

'We'll need some new foundations in places; lots of glass, heating and many blinds. The bar stays as it is but we'll refurbish that kitchen and create some serving space; the kitchen wall comes out and the cooking will be visible to the customers.'

'What's the new capacity, Aaron?'

'About 80 covers; currently they have a job to do 25, and some have to eat their food at the bar with the miserable man Nixon staring at them.'

'Can you do a deal with him?'

'Yes, I'm sure I can, but I've to get rid of his accountant first, or maybe Nixon will do that for me. Either way my price is no more than £240,000 and around £80–90,000 to do it up including expanding the car park; if times were not as hard it would fetch over £350,000. The council may insist we expand the parking area, but we've to do that anyway and we can use some of that land at the back.'

'What are you going to do next, Aaron?'

'Confront Knowles; I'll go and see him today. I'll stay away from the pub for the time being until I know it's clear to deal direct with Nixon. I'm not going to sign anything with Knowles, as I'll drop him when we're ready. Can you check that Nixon hasn't got a mortgage? I've a feeling he may have borrowed some money secured against the place. We don't need a paid solicitor, you can do all this.'

'No thanks, I'm a lawyer, Aaron, not some tart doing lousy conveyance.'

'You're still very negative, darling, do you miss the Middle East? I thought you would be OK over here after living in Beirut and Cyprus.'

'I like staying alive, that's all, and you know we could never go back without changing our identity or even splitting up for a time; not even to Cyprus, for it's a certainty that someone would recognise us.'

'You're probably right, but remember I was working for peace; many of our enemies are now dead and most of the others in jail.'

'You know yourself Aaron that some are still out there – you were their weapons and explosives supplier! If we went back they would rise up again as they know you can get hold of what they want; they would start a fresh load of new trouble in the Middle East.'

'That's why the time isn't right, we have to continue to invest in business in the UK. Later we'll review what we can do back home; it's in my blood, Leah, you know that.'

'I know, and that frightens me; I worry about how safe we are here. The good thing is the immigration people are tough here, and it was a good job we had all that paperwork when we first arrived to get our pretty red British passports. Since we had those meetings they seem to have forgotten that they agreed to keep contact with us; someone was supposed to be providing us with the protection we were promised, don't you remember?'

'Yes, I remember very well, but we don't know if they are watching us or not. We've been very discreet and it's important we keep a low profile. The responsibility will have been passed to the police or even a detective agency, but if nobody has arranged it my guess is nothing will happen. I had one call six months ago from a chief superintendent, a man called White who I know vaguely from the past; he said people would keep an eye us but I'm not convinced they're doing it.'

'That's before we changed our address and phone numbers. Why didn't you tell the security services?'

'That policeman White knows my phone number and I've got his; that will be enough if we have a problem.'

'They need us here, Aaron, we're an insurance policy if things go badly wrong and they have to find a source of explosives in the Middle East. Without us being involved in the supply line, any uprising would get out of hand pretty quickly.'

'Yes, you're right. I'm still in contact with everyone, Leah, and as you know I've some emergency supplies available if needed.'

'Have you sold any, Aaron?'

'Not a question I'd like to answer. I could have sold some recently to get some cash, and the least you know about it the better.'

'I knew being married to an arms dealer would not be simple. You are your father's son, but remember he got blown up and I don't what that to happen to us.'

'Stop worrying, everything is under control. I'm off to see Bill Knowles and it should be interesting.'

'Don't say everything is under control; you keep so many things to yourself I wonder some days what my role in your life is. Do you still love me, Aaron?'

Parker hardly lifted his head to answer. 'Of course, Leah; I'm just protecting you from bad people.'

'Do you think we've any real enemies here in the UK?'

'Possibly, but we can never be sure. I think everything has been dealt with, or at least everything I know about has; just relax and do some emails to your friends or go on the internet and find us a nice restaurant away from Surrey for Saturday night. I've people to see; now don't worry.'

Aaron Parker left the flat quickly. He never told his wife the full story on his business or his extra-marital activities, because if he did she would worry herself crazy about money and maybe leave him if she knew where he disappeared to a few times a month. They both had good health and sizeable bank balances, and the investment in the pub was just a game for Aaron Parker, but something they could be proud of in the company of foreign visitors.

Parker drove quickly to Bill Knowles' office, and it was not surprising that he had six penalty points on his licence for speeding offences. Everything he did was at high speed and without any real fear of the consequences. As he pulled into the parking space outside the accountant's office, he gathered his thoughts. Knowles would surely know by now from Larry Nixon that he knew he was double-crossing him; maybe he had paid a visit already. He rang the doorbell. He knew Knowles was in even though it was a Saturday, but he could see no sign of the accountant through the window so he rang again. After a long wait, the door opened and a horrible sight greeted him.

'Mr Knowles, what happened to you?'

Bill Knowles' face probably did not illustrate his worst injuries. He couldn't sit down, and he held his testicles like he had been kicked by a horse or been through a vasectomy operation that had gone wrong. Both his eyes were black and his top lip red and blue; he had tried to clean himself up but his clothes were covered in blood.

'Let's just say, I didn't fall down the stairs; the deal with you was only part of the problem and I had other issues with my ex-client. Why did you go and see him?'

'You know why, Mr Knowles; you were taking me for a fool. I saw through what you were doing in five minutes so I went to see him and am sure I can do business with him. I'll pay you an introduction fee if it all goes through, and more than you would expect. Look, I don't have much time, but to get those injuries you must have had a visit from Larry Nixon. Don't bother to tell me, I can guess – were you screwing his wife?

'My wife is a solicitor and she'll do some of the legal work if I buy the pub, but I need you to tell me Larry Nixon's exact financial position and also any other information about him that could give me problems with the pub later; I think he's a man who might have a few skeletons left in his cupboards. I will pay you £10,000, so there we are, Mr Knowles; things aren't that bad are they?'

'Thanks, that's great. I need the business and I can bring his books up-to-date in a day or two, check on his tax position and dig around a bit to get his career information. I know one person who will help me, especially when she sees the shit state I'm in.'

'I'll contact you on Monday, Mr Knowles, and my advice is don't ring the police – too many questions. If you need your balls checking out I've a friend who's a doctor, but from my personal experience if you aren't peeing blood then don't worry about it. Take some aspirin and get some sleep; you should be fine once those eyes start to recover, but get some dark glasses or you'll frighten your secretary.'

After he'd left, Aaron decided to call Larry Nixon from the car.

'Yes, Mr Nixon, it's Aaron Parker. I've prepared an offer for your building and my wife will deliver it on Monday. If you agree with the offer, which in my opinion is a very generous one, I'll need the name of your solicitor; a verbal acceptance will be fine with me. As I said before, it's a cash deal and I can move quickly.'

'I'll study your offer, Mr Parker, and get advice on it so don't expect to hear from me until the end of next week.'

'That's what I expected; you have seven days, until a week on Monday, and if I don't hear from you by then I'll look elsewhere for a similar purchase; I'm told there are many pubs on the market.'

'Yes, but not like mine, with land and a good restaurant.'

'Both those things aren't relevant: it's market price and condition that count, so think carefully before calling me.'

Parker's arrogance put Larry Nixon into one of his turns. He started to sweat and shake as Parker spoke, and all he could think about was smashing his pretty face like he'd done to Bill Knowles.

'Just one other thing, Mr Nixon – I really feel as if we've met before the meeting this week; I'm good on faces. Do you remember if we've met and when and where it was?'

'No mate, I'd never seen you before this week.'

'I must be mistaken; that's unusual. Anyway, read the proposal and contact me, and I'll see you soon, I hope.'

Aaron put the phone down, not giving Nixon time to reply. He had said all he wanted to.

As he drove back to his home, he tried desperately to place where he had seen Nixon. Not many people ever called him "mate", and the man's manner stuck in his mind; he knew he would remember one day, he always did. It had to be the Middle East or Northern Ireland; he would check if he had been in the army. He phoned his wife from the car.

181

'I'm going to London and I won't be back before dinner, Leah. I've spoken to Nixon and told him you'll deliver the offer on Monday, make it £5,000 less than we've discussed as he's desperate, so subject to a survey, £235,000; we can knock some more off later when we have the survey details. Have you met him before, other than when we ate at the pub a few weeks ago?'

'No, I've only seen him the once.'

'The only time I possibly could have met him or heard about him was in Beirut or through Paddy Mulligan or one of our other Irish friends – call them and check; it would be nice to know if we have mutual acquaintances. See you later.'

As he drove through Putney and Chelsea his mind was working overtime on when he had met Larry Nixon before. If it was on a business assignment he knew he would have to be very careful in case Nixon knew his history, or could find out about him. The ringing of his car phone changed his line of thought.

'Aaron, it's Mohammed here. How's your assignment going? We hear you've been busy.'

'I'm in the car, Mohammed, so I'll call you later but yes, everything went to plan and I'm working on the next move now. I have to go, the phone signal is not good. Just one thing: please check out a guy called Larry Nixon; he owns a pub called The Brown Cow near Leatherhead in Surrey. I want to know if we've dealt with him at any time, not in Pakistan, but in Beirut.'

The Mercedes swung into the courtyard at Chelsea Harbour and Aaron took the first turning into the residents' underground car park. He waved the card at the reader and the barrier lifted. He pressed the button on the panel and a voice came on the intercom.

'Hi, come up, but mind the dog – he's sitting outside the lift door.'

The usual feeling of excitement hit his stomach; he had visited Sheila Hamilton many times and he stayed overnight occasionally, yet still on every occasion she made it feel like the first time. One day he would have to deal with her, but provided everything was kept confidential his visits to Chelsea would continue. She was expensive, but that didn't matter: she was cheaper than a night at the casino and he always felt good when he left.

15
Enough
The Brown Cow Pub
Leatherhead, Surrey

'You're hurting me; don't hold my arm so tight! Larry stop, please, stop.'

I should break it, Jill, and your nose! How long has Bill Knowles been giving you one?'

'Let me go, Larry.'

The bedroom door was locked and Larry Nixon had his unfaithful wife pinned down on the bed. She had no chance of getting away; he was foaming at the mouth and she feared for her life. Bill Knowles had already had a visit from a mad Larry and he had been lucky to escape with just minor injuries, but it was different for Jill; she lived with Larry and unless she did something to defend herself he would make her life a misery.

'I want a divorce, Larry. I know you're having sex with Marie behind my back – do you think I'm stupid?'

'This is about you, not me and I haven't decided what I'll do with you yet, Jill. What I do know is that when this place is sold in a few weeks you won't see a penny, I promise you, and that applies to Spain as well; you'd better see if your lover will take you in. No, thinking about it, that's too good for both of you – get him to fix you up with a flat; you could be a kept whore.'

Larry stood up and towered over his wife. His anger was boiling over; he was losing control and needed a drink. He unlocked the door and called for Marie.

'Come here, Marie; you're in charge now. Mrs Nixon is taking a holiday to her sister's in Brighton; order a cab for her, take £150 out of the till and bring it up here for her, then take over in the kitchen.'

The Polish girl didn't speak. She had guessed what had happened: the secret of Bill Knowles was not a good one, and many people knew about the affair. The young girl was almost regretting that Larry was using her for everything he wanted. The bedroom door was slammed in Jill's face, and she went to the wardrobe to get her clothes. Her husband was on the verge of losing control and for her own safety she had to leave and quickly. To avoid the customers she left the building via the fire escape and met Marie and the cab at the front door of the pub.

'Listen to me, Marie, my marriage could be over; I have to go away to think what to do. Mr Nixon is a sick man and my advice is get away now as well or you may regret it.'

Marie seemed to understand. She took Jill's hand, then pulled away quickly.

'Thanks, Mrs Nixon. I've no plans but I think I'll make some soon.'

'I have to leave here or he may hurt me; he's crazy! I know you're having sex with him, but you can do better, Marie. I'm not sure when I'll see you again, if at all, but really I don't want to see you.'

The cab left the lane and joined the main road. Jill had her bankcard with her, so at the first cash point they came to she got the cab to stop. Larry would not have had time or even the thought to freeze the account, and anyway, as it was a joint one she was within her rights to withdraw the limit of £500, which was all they had in the account. Jill phoned her sister Wendy from the cab and told her she was on the way to Brighton and would be with her in just over an hour. Wendy was supportive; she had never been sure about Larry, but he was her husband Dermott's friend and she put up with him on the occasions he turned up and they went drinking together. Jill knew she was welcome to stay with her until she had decided on her next move.

'All of you get out, we're closed.'

Larry didn't need to shout; the three customers had seen Jill leave and heard the noise from upstairs. He locked the front door as the last customer left and switched the lights off.

'Marie, come here.'

'Don't hurt me, Larry, I've done nothing wrong.'

'Just shut up and get undressed. I want you and that's all I can think about at this moment.'

At first Marie started to cry; then she started to think how she could make the best use of the situation. Her brother Mark was working in the gym in town, and he would help her. She had to stay calm and give Larry what he wanted, and before they started she made him drink two very large whiskies, which she hoped would soon send him to sleep. The sex was rougher than usual and totally without any meaning; for Larry it was just a small release of tension. As he had drunk so much whisky she knew it would only be minutes before he would roll over and pass out.

Marie pulled away from Larry as his body had started to drip sweat all over her breasts and navel; he smelt bad and she had to slide out of the bottom of the bed so as not to disturb him. He started to snore the second she pulled the duvet over him. Larry was a big man and Marie could not move him more than a few inches; she was half-hoping he would fall out and hurt himself. She hated him, and she knew what she had to do. For Larry Nixon life had been one big injustice, and his wife leaving was the final straw. Marie picked up her mobile and dialled her brother.

'Come round to the pub now, Mark, I can give you some beers and spirits for the weekend. The pub's closed; Larry's ill and asleep. I know where the key to the safe is, but I don't think there's much money in it now.'

'I'm on the way, Marie. Take some money from the till but leave a little; if he's as bad as you say he may not remember anything tomorrow.'

Mark Waleki was Marie's 21-year-old brother. He was unemployed, but somehow through his many casual jobs he managed to find enough cash to pay the rent on a one-bedroom flat in Leatherhead and have enough left to enjoy himself. He knew The Brown Cow pub well, and when it was busy in the summer months he had started to help out in the bar and the kitchen. Larry Nixon liked Mark, and they often drank together after closing time and discussed schemes to make money. After the summer Larry could not give him any more work, but the boy still kept in contact and occasionally they went out together. Marie was suspicious that they were involved in some criminal activities, but she never asked either of them where they went and what they had been doing.

Mark arrived ten minutes after his sister's phone call.

'That was quick. You obviously didn't come on your bike?'

'No, I borrowed this van.'

'Who from? You haven't stolen it, have you?'

'No, just borrowed it. I had a job to do and needed transport.'

'Like hell you've borrowed it. Quickly, take all that booze and some crisps; take this £50, that's all I have. The safe is empty; be quick before someone comes.'

'Is Larry really ill or is he just drunk?'

'He's sick in the head, Mark; you must keep away from him, and yes, he's pissed and will sleep until tomorrow. His wife has left him and when he wakes up he'll be angry and dangerous.'

'He owes me money. I did a couple of jobs for him and he hasn't paid me.'

'Keep away, Mark, I'll let you know when it's OK to talk to him but that could take a few days. Go quickly now, in case someone turns up for the pub and you're seen here.'

'OK Marie, thanks; come into town on Sunday if you can.'

'I doubt it; Mrs Nixon has gone to stay with her sister so I'll be doing the cooking, that's providing the pub is open. I think Larry has a buyer so he'll need to keep it open, but maybe not. He could close it, I'm his only employee now.'

Chapter 16
Discharged

Harold Penny had been discharged from hospital, and apart from a plaster on his head he showed no signs of his fall during the burglary. The loss of the computer was not a problem, as he hardly used it. His neighbour, Janet Ash, a retired civil servant, looked after his correspondence; a part-time job that worked for both of them. The taxi dropped Harold outside his house, but he had to borrow £5 from Janet to pay the fare.

'What on earth happened to you then, Harold?'

'I had a burglary, Janet, and they stole my computer.'

'Was that all? Surely they took something else?'

'No, just the computer. I disturbed him, but I fell over and hit my head. I was just coming round when Alan Fisher turned up and he sorted me out. Did you see anybody lurking around, Janet?'

'No, I didn't. Come on, let's go in your house; I'll make you a cup of tea.'

Janet Ash opened his door with her spare key and immediately they knew something was wrong. The sight made them both stand back against the door. The floors and stairs were covered in papers and storage boxes; books had been stripped from the shelves and cupboards ransacked.

'Who did this, Janet? I'll kill them.'

'Don't be silly, you're an old man. Somebody wants something you've got, and obviously it wasn't on the computer. I'll phone the police; let's go into my house now.'

'No, phone Alan Fisher – he goes away tomorrow and I need to talk to him. This is the number.' Harold produced a piece of paper from his wallet, and Janet dialled the number.

Alan answered straight away. 'Yes, I understand, Mrs Ash; thanks for phoning me. I'll call the police and explain why we hadn't reported the burglary, and once they've been and taken a statement just pack a bag for Harold and send him over here to Epsom.'

'That's a good idea, will he stay with you?'

'Yes, in my flat while I'm away; in the meantime please can you sort his house out? I'll pay you.'

'No, that's not necessary; I do some work for Harold already, so I'll be pleased to put everything back in place. My sister will help me, she's staying with my husband and I for a few weeks. Are you going on holiday, Alan?'

'No, just a trip with a friend to look at a property abroad, but it's remote so you won't be able to contact me. Harold should stay here in Epsom until I'm back, but I know what he's like and maybe in a few days he'll want to work with you in his house during the daytime. I've a feeling that what the burglar wanted is not there, and he's had good look and couldn't find anything so he may give up now. I'll give you a phone number for a policeman; he's not normally involved with burglaries but he will be when I've spoken to him. His name is Inspector Hubbard; please call him if anything at all happens. I'm almost ready to leave, but a spare key for my flat is with my girlfriend Cheryl; she works in the beauty salon in Tolworth Broadway and I'll tell her you'll collect it. Please bring Harold here with some clothes and his wash gear. I'll have everything else he needs left out on the spare bed, and the library is just a few minutes away so he can walk there for the exercise.'

'OK Alan, off you go and have a good trip. I know the beauty salon; Cheryl's mother does my nails. Oh, Harold wants to talk to you.' She handed the phone to Harold.

'So, Harold, you're coming here to Epsom; don't argue, I could hear you in the background. Calm down and get ready for your holiday here.'

'I'm bloody angry, but Janet's helping me. Have a good trip; I'll water your plants.'

'Thanks Harold; take care, stay close to my flat for a few days and go home when you're ready. We still have a lot of things to work on together.'

'Did I tell you, Alan, that the man who stole my computer shouted when he caught his belt on the window catch and he had an Irish accent?'

'Thanks Harold, I've noted that. See you in a week's time.'

Alan hung up, and Harold turned to Janet. 'I just wish I was 20 years younger; I'd stay here and get that burglar should he try to get in my house again.'

'No you wouldn't, leave it to the police.'

'You don't understand, and I can't tell you, Janet.'

'I don't want to know your secrets, Harold; I'll leave that to Alan. If it involves the deaths of his parents, that of course is very important indeed, but it must be handled by the police.'

Harold nodded and started to pack his holdall. The more he thought about the burglar, the more he was convinced that he had got nothing of value from his house – Harold kept everything of value locked in the safe, and apart from the mess there was no structural damage to the safe itself.

'I didn't set my alarm, Janet, but I will now.'

'Why not? It's crazy to have one and not use it. Set it now and let's go.'

Chapter 17
Briefing

'What do we do then, Charlie – just turn up at the front gate?'

'No, look for a sign with this emblem on it; no words. It's an entrance for special guests and people who don't want to be seen by everybody.'

'That's a new one, mate; not like when we joined up. First thing I remember was that punch-up with that skinhead bloke.'

'Alan, we were all skinheads the following day. That bloke was OK, he worked with my brother for a time; he was just bloody rude to everyone but it was always in fun. You took him too seriously when he laughed at your clothes.'

'Yes, but we did make it up; I was nervous and he was cocky. Is he still around?'

'Not sure; I didn't come across him again once we left here. What was his name, can you remember?'

'Yes, Corporal Robert Button; Bob to his mates.'

'Memory is still good then, Alan.'

'Yes, and at the moment it's having its biggest test ever.'

Alan stopped at the small gate and the two men got out. An armed guard gave the Mini the once-over: inside, outside, underneath, and under the bonnet and even the spare wheel.

'Bloody hell, Corporal, are you expecting to find something?'

'I expect to find something every time I do this, sir – that's the job. Maybe one day I will, and then it will all be worthwhile, but it's more likely I'll be dead before I get my medal.'

'Yes, sorry; you were doing your job and well done, but why didn't you inspect our bags?'

'Because we've been briefed on your arrival and we're just checking for anything someone else might have planted in your car. I assume you two packed your own bags? All right, I cocked up – bloody hell, I should have checked the bags as well. Please don't report me, sir.'

'Of course we won't do that, Corporal; we understand why you didn't check our bags, but next time do it. As a matter of interest, my colleague has a detonator and some metal in his bag – we believe a bomb-maker dropped the detonator so we're bringing it here for identification.'

'Blimey, I'd have been in the shit if that had been found by another security post.'

Alan smiled. 'Look, just record it now and send a note of it by email to the security supervisor. You spotted it and you told him, so let's see if he asks us about it.'

'Thanks, sir. Take the second road on your right and go to building C100; leave the car on the other side of the road. Please report to the reception area; that building is your home for a couple of days so take your bags in as well.'

As they drove away, Charlie turned to Alan. 'You should become a training officer.'

'No, but maybe one day our words will keep him alive. There's no point being thorough with a security check if you don't check everything. That's why the majority of our bomb disposal guys are alive: because they check every single detail.'

'Right as usual, Alan. Let's see what they've got for us.'

A smart young man stood on the step of building C100, holding with a metal box and a large briefcase.

'Good morning, gentlemen.'

'Charlie, this is Brian Wilson of the SIS. Do you know each other?'

'No, and I've only met Alan briefly at our HQ. Welcome back to Sandhurst.'

'Thanks. I assume as this is just a short assignment and unlikely to be repeated that we should use our old army ranks, Brian?'

'Only here, but in the field you are exactly as your passports, just British citizens; that's why your cover is perfect. Come on, we're wasting time – let's go inside and go through the programme.'

Alan and Charlie looked at each other. On the outside they both appeared calm and professional, but inside they were very nervous men. They both knew that once the presentation of the plans was completed they would just want one thing, and that was to get the job done and to get back home.

They hardly had time to put their bags in the small rooms before Brian Wilson shouted.

'Come on, the film's starting.'

The subject of the amateur movie was Deniz Korham. Both men knew his name from the meeting with Jason Harris, but now it was of more interest as the film rolled.

'A brief background on your target, gentlemen. Deniz Korham was the son of a Turkish hotel owner, who met Anne Lambert, an American, after she came looking for work in Istanbul to fund her travel plans. Anne married him two years later, and old man Korham sold his hotel and gave the couple money to leave Turkey for what they both believed would be a better life in Detroit, Michigan. The marriage was a disaster for Anne: she loved the handsome Turk dearly, but he couldn't settle in the USA. He had the money from his father in Turkish currency safely hidden, but because it would be devalued if he converted it to US dollars he wouldn't even have enough to buy a car. At first he was patient and he tried many jobs, but he became restless for his home country.

'The couple had a boy called Deniz, and when he was six years old his father decided he had had enough of Detroit and the

USA. After a violent argument, the couple split up, and before Anne knew what was happening, Deniz was snatched from school by his father who had carefully planned their return to Turkey on a merchant ship. Anne managed to contact her husband after a few months, but apart from a couple of heated phone calls she lost touch and died soon afterwards. Her death was recorded as suicide, and her friends confirmed to the coroner that Anne had a broken heart and could not take in what had happened.

'When the boy was 18 years old he started to argue with his father. He knew what he had done to his mother from a relative, and he was grief-stricken. The boy had completed his secondary education and was ready for the army. According to the information we got from the Turks, he spent most of his time as a translator as his English was first-class. We then have a gap until he turned up in Iran about five years ago, and we aren't sure if the family were originally Kurds or Turks; that'll be one of the questions to ask him.'

Wilson started the film, pointing at a boy on the screen.

'That's him as a boy. These pictures were taken from a cine film, and as you can see he was in Turkish army uniform, but they are the only ones we have of him growing up. The film shows some video footage taken by friends in Tehran just a few months ago; listen and I'll put the sound on.'

Deniz Korham faced the camera and spoke in clear English, without much of an accent. 'My name is Deniz Korham. I'm 32 years old; my home was Istanbul and I'm a Turkish citizen. I had an American mother but she's now dead. My father and I don't speak as I was taken from the USA when I was young and never saw my mother again. I can never forgive him for that. I have been in Iran for more than four years. I was approached by an Iranian company on the recommendation of my commanding officer in the army. They had an office in Istanbul, and they wanted someone who spoke good English, and who also had my skills.'

Wilson paused the film. 'Notice that Korham referred to his skills. Who taught him sophisticated electronics and the process for manufacturing nuclear energy? These subjects are not normally offered to a young sergeant, especially in the Turkish army.'

'Carry on, Brian; we may get a clue soon.'

Wilson restarted the film.

'I was moved to Tehran and then later to Lasop I am a specialist and well paid, but I want to move to England or the USA. My mother's family live in New York and I have contacted them; I also have relatives in Newcastle. I'll help you with information on the Iranian nuclear project if you can get me out of this country; the file I sent you is my ticket. That's all. I fear for my life if anyone other than my two friends know my plans.'

The screen went blank, and Wilson returned his attention to Alan and Charlie.

'OK, that's his story. He sent us a five-page file in the Persian language, which we have managed to decipher and a copy is in the folder we will give you. Don't take it out of this camp: if you were caught with it in Iran it would be your death warrant. Read the translation and tomorrow we can discuss it in more detail. It gives us enough information to know that your trip is vital. Charlie will recognise most of the stuff, and we'll go through a small list of questions for you to take to Korham.'

'Why not ask him now?' Alan asked. 'It'll make our job easier, especially Charlie's. If we know some key thing that relates to a nuclear bomb, we'll feel a lot happier that he has the information you want.'

'You saw the film, Alan, this guy is shitting his pants at the prospect of getting caught, so we can't ask him any more questions. Charlie is good at his job and within a few minutes of meeting him he'll know if he's genuine or not.'

'I hope so, Brian – I don't want to have to put a bullet in his head.'

'No, that would be messy; we're pushing our luck already with the Iranians and if they got hold of you two it's likely you'd be in Iran for some time, and not in a five star hotel. So that's all for now, gentlemen; get some lunch from the canteen next to your block and you'll be collected by Lieutenant Grove who will be responsible for your luggage.'

'What luggage, Brian? Remember I'm on BA to Istanbul.'

200

'Yes, Alan, most of your stuff will be with Charlie; later at your rendezvous point we'll show you your route in detail, and then he'll pass over everything you need.'

'I don't get it – why do I have to go on a normal commercial flight when Charlie hitches a lift on a Hercules?'

'I thought you might have asked more about that already, Alan. You're too polite.'

'No, not polite, just bloody suspicious; that's how I stayed alive in the army.'

'OK, this is the reason. When we first asked you to do this job for us we were concerned that your parents' killers had not been identified; not found, but not even identified. That is still the case, and after discussions with the police we strongly believe that the killer or killers are still here in the UK. We have some intelligence and we think you are being watched; we followed you here from your home today and we're certain you didn't have a tail on your car. If you had someone following you, you would have been replaced; don't ask why as the answer is clear: we want you to remain a planning officer who takes a holiday to Turkey to see friends, not Captain Alan Fisher turning up and possibly being watched during arrival. This cat-and-mouse business is for your own safety, and especially Charlie Baxter's as he's still in the army – we know he may not have told you much about that, but again that was for your own safety. His work now is all in the UK and he works for army security, making sure that all the secret equipment in our rockets and missiles remains a secret.'

'Charlie, I thought you were joking – no, not really but I was suspicious, especially when I was told that the Hercules only had one spare seat. It makes sense now.'

Charlie clapped a hand on his friend's shoulder. 'Come on, let's get our lunch and then we can go and see Jack Grove to get our wiring, phones and some weapons sorted out for you to practise with.'

'I know I have to do this, Charlie, but I'm getting more nervous by the hour, especially now we're practising with loaded weapons.'

'Just a precaution, Alan.'

The door of the meeting room burst open, and a civilian girl handed a piece of paper to Brian Wilson. He took ten seconds to read the message, then turned to the girl.

'Thanks; I understand. Reply by secure phone, understood and will action. You will not be here after today, gentlemen: Deniz Korham is being moved to Tehran at the weekend and my office is convinced that something is happening on the nuclear project; maybe the big underground hole they were supposed to be digging is ready. You have to leave tomorrow; all the details are being arranged and this afternoon we'll go over the route from Turkey to Iran thoroughly. I know you're very familiar with it, Alan, but we have to be sure that you find this guy first time.

Leave your car keys and we'll deliver your Mini back to Epsom; we know the address.'

'Sounds like a bit of tidying up. It's as if I won't come back.'

'Not at all, Alan, but if we leave it here the tank guys will think it's for target practice as we take in lots of cars and yours is the right colour.'

The first humour of the day from the SIS man brought half a smile from Alan and Charlie. The fate of his car was the last thing Alan was concerned about.

Chapter 18
The Parkers' Apartment

'Aaron, I've got all the searches on the pub and a copy from the Land Registry and everything seems in order. The property has a mortgage and I'm just waiting for a rough figure, but that loan will have to be cleared on completion. From what I've found out from the paperwork, it seems that Larry Nixon is the sole owner.'

'That keeps it simple then, Leah. Have you delivered the offer?'

'Yes, I put it through his door personally; then he rang me and said it was too low.'

'That's fine, if he'd accepted it first time he would have been hiding something, like damp or a problem with the drains.'

'Yes, the survey was done today and the surveyor phoned to say that he would email the report: he had a few points but nothing to revalue it, and he remarked that your offer price was much too low at £230,000.'

'Did you tell him the figure, then?'

'Yes, but he said that if we get it for less than £300,000 we'll have a very good deal indeed. Nixon is desperate to sell; get the contracts prepared and leave the figure out and I think he'll be back to us in a couple of days or less. By the way, Aaron, I had a bit of a shock today.'

'Why?'

At first Aaron's guilt complex put him on his guard; surely Leah had not found out about Sheila Hamilton? He had always been very careful that she didn't know anything about his girlfriend.

'I phoned Paddy Mulligan about the explosives as you asked me to do and he had his answering machine on. I got a phone call back from a man who said his name was O'Brien, and the bad news is that Paddy had been found dead; he was strangled with a wire last night. I couldn't get O'Brien off the phone, and he started to ask questions about how I knew Paddy and what did I want from him. I finally got rid of him without giving him any answers.'

'Well, that's not unexpected – Paddy had it coming, Leah; he must have supplied someone with explosives and I guess they probably didn't work or they needed to silence him, or most likely he was killed to stop him revealing his buyer. It would definitely have been the last of that big consignment that came from Libya.'

'Thank goodness we haven't dealt with him recently.' Leah paused, eyeing her husband closely. 'What's the matter? Why are you shaking your head?'

'I did buy some plastic explosive from him recently – it was a batch I'd supplied to him a few years ago, but it went straight to the Sudan, or at least I think it did; their agent in London paid for it and I heard nothing else.'

'Do you ever get pangs of conscience about what we do, Aaron? For 20 years we've lived on deals from weapons and explosives, most of the time to fuel civil war groups and at other times supplying both sides in a war.'

'It's a business that has to be done, and at least I do it with the knowledge of the British government; remember, until recently they still bought arms delivered away from this island for special situations. My rocket launchers are the best in the world, and Argentina will not be invading the Falklands again while my equipment is pointing in their direction. As a precaution, if that man O'Brien checks back our number and calls us, just switch the phone to the answer machine with the usual message that we aren't in and nothing else; don't mention our name. We'll use the fax line for a few weeks until I find out what really happened to Paddy Mulligan.'

The phone burst into action as they were in the process of switching on the answerphone.

'Let it ring twice, Leah, then switch the machine on.'

The machine told the caller to leave a message. A strong Irish accent followed. 'I don't know who you are, but I'll find out. I want to talk to you about Paddy; you know he's dead and I want the killer. Ring Paddy's phone soon and wait; I'll be there.'

The caller hung up and the Parkers stared at each other.

'I'll phone him,' Aaron said, 'but not from here. I'll use the public phone in the library tomorrow.'

'What will you say to him? He sounds very nasty.'

'As little as possible; just that we were friends with Paddy, but nothing about business or our name. If our Paddy was killed because of what he did we may be in big danger as well. For today we'll do nothing more on the pub apart from you seeing the surveyor – don't wait for his report; call up Nixon with a few questions and I'll go and see him tomorrow.'

'Yes, fine, but I hope he's still around.'

'What do you mean?'

'Nothing, it's just that the surveyor said that Nixon was supposedly abroad. The Polish girl phoned him and he spoke to me on his mobile.'

'Did she give you his number?'

'No, she said it was private.'

'I hope he hasn't got another buyer. I don't trust that man, his eyes are full of hate.'

'Maybe that's because his wife just left him.'

'You didn't tell me that.'

'Sorry, I didn't think it mattered, especially as she has no share in the property. He must be having an affair with that Polish girl.'

'I think it could be the other way around. I was in Bill Knowles' office and you know that sometimes I'm a nosey

Parker. When he left his desk I saw a note which said *Ring Jill* in rough scribble. Knowles isn't married; his wife died and I suppose it could be anybody, but when he got back to his desk he saw me looking at it and he immediately screwed the paper up and threw it in the waste bin. Guilty people do strange things and I'm convinced he had an appointment with Jill Nixon.'

'What do we do about Nixon then, Aaron?'

'We do the opposite to what he will expect and pull out of the deal to buy his pub as we don't think he'll go through with it; that excuse must be made clear. He'll come back to us quickly, I'm sure, and we'll get him to agree the sale price. We can sign and exchange contracts and complete in a couple of weeks. Any problems with his wife are not relevant.'

'I'm afraid they are, Aaron: she's the registered licensee and it takes time to change into another name. I'll check the procedure today but if we're to complete quickly we may need her to work for us for a few weeks.'

'I know someone who can help us with all this; she's called Sheila Hamilton and she's a good problem-solver – you met her in the pub the night we ate there. She was sounding the place out for us; she's spent quite a bit of time working in pubs and restaurants, so she'll know how to get around the rules on a licensee.'

'Yes, I remember her and her friend. Are they lesbians, Aaron? They seemed to be very close.'

Aaron knew his reply would be scrutinised by his alert wife, and he wondered why he had made the mistake of suggesting Sheila to help them.

'Doubt it, but lesbian or straight, it's not our problem; we just want information from Sheila so we can find out how we do things without it costing lots of money. We need to know if Jill will help us or if we should just close the place down and then apply for a license when we're working on the refurbishment, but all that has to be checked out carefully. I'll be back in two or three hours; I need to check that we have the money ready to do the deal. You know what you have to do, Leah?'

'I hope I get paid?'

'You will, my darling, in everlasting love.'

'Sometimes I don't believe you, Aaron. Now off you go.'

Chapter 19
Gordon Fisher, Judge Advocate Military

Ted Fisher had a letter with a new date for the inquest into his brother and sister-in-law's murder. It was now going to take place at Surrey Coroner's Court in two weeks' time, and he decided to send Alan a text, which he hoped he would pick up on his travels. Ted knew that Alan was on a special trip, but the less he knew, the less he had to worry about his nephew. The whole business of the bombing was like a bad dream that came true, and even worse in reality. Since his wife's death Ted had spent more time with his younger brother Gordon: they had played golf twice a week at the local club, and along with Gordon's wife Fay they'd played cards every Saturday evening. Ted could walk to his brother's house and passed it every day; he couldn't imagine how anyone could have done such a thing as blasting his brother and his wife out of this world. His sadness was turning to anger; he had to help Alan find the killer. Many times he went over in his mind the discussions he had with his brother concerning the possible danger of his job. Gordon had made a few enemies following the advice he gave to a military jury on the adjudication they were about to give, and he was a fair man but in many cases he had no hesitation about pointing the jury towards a conviction. One large gap existed in Ted's thoughts: he would have to check the dates with Alan when he returned as there had been one period when Gordon was very distressed. It was an incident with a soldier and a civilian death, and a painful decision for Gordon to make.

Gordon Fisher's career started after university. He went directly into the legal profession, and had planned to follow in his father's footsteps as a barrister. His mother and father were very disappointed when after years of studying he suddenly changed direction. In his spare time he had already obtained a pilot's licence and was an accomplished flyer, and the offer of a life of adrenalin and excitement in the RAF suddenly changed his direction in life.

The RAF was not quite what he expected. Although he loved flying, the dangers of the job came home to him and he sought a desk job. The RAF recognised his potential, and after just nine years he became one of the youngest squadron leaders ever appointed. But Gordon continued to look over his shoulder for another challenge, and soon he thought that maybe it was time to change his career again. It was not long before a new role found him, and he was recommended by his commanding officer for judiciary work. Gordon accepted the new opportunity as a major challenge, and moved back to the courtroom.

After a lot of work behind the scenes and practical experience in court, he took a role in the military judicial system, handling cases from combat incidents to desertions. Within four years he became one of the most respected military judges in the service; he had a quick mind and soon acquired a reputation for ensuring a fair trial took place for any charged serviceman who had been brought before his court. Military law is clear in its definition, and since 2009 all three services came under the Armed Forces Act. Gordon Fisher was responsible for dealing with soldiers brought before him by the Special Investigation Branch. Once a charge has been made against a military person, the rules under the Act dictate that the offence be discussed firstly with his or her commanding officer. If the offence were serious, the CO's powers would be limited, and in nearly all cases the result would be a court martial. This was under the military judicial system headed by the Judge Advocate General, an appointment made by the Queen; the General would appoint Judge Advocates to the role that Gordon Fisher had performed and define which cases they would preside over.

The court martial would be headed by Gordon with a jury (known as a board) made up of five officers and warrant officers, and held in the new courts built in the UK. The court had the power to impose a sentence of life imprisonment in a UK civil prison on any person found guilty of a capital offence, and dismissal from the service. Less serious offences usually resulted in imprisonment in the UK at the Colchester Military Corrective Training Centre. Gordon's early life had prepared him well for the role, although he would discover it to be a very challenging job, and one where friends could be limited.

Chapter 20
Incident
Baghdad, 2008

Through the smoke and the searing heat, the smell of death lingered in the main street. A soldier held his head in his hands; the armoured car was a total wreck. Nobody could possibly have survived the blast of the massive IED bomb; his two buddies were the sole victims. He jumped to his feet, knowing he had to do something: he knew the pattern, and the killer could still be close and watching the carnage caused by his work. The car bomb was one of several to explode that day; the bomber had dropped some detonators near the scene. The soldier collected one in his desperate need for clues on the perpetrators.

The result of the explosion was carnage: his two colleagues had been on their way back to barracks when without warning they drove over and triggered the device. They were just kids; both 20 years old with limited experience, and it was their first tour in the war zone. The soldier was grief-stricken; he had been trained to kill, but not to deal with this situation, and he knew he had to control his anger and just get on with his job. He took two ground sheets from his jeep and covered his colleagues' bodies, or what was left of them. He then radioed a detailed message to his command centre; they told him to wait as a medical crew and backup were on their way to the scene. Medication was a waste of time. The soldier leaned against the wall, and as the smoke and dust cleared, peering at him from about 35–40 metres away was what he thought at first was a woman; he could only just see the face uncovered under the traditional dress. He saw her pull something from inside her garment: it looked like an automatic rifle. She turned towards him, and without hesitation the soldier put his own gun to his shoulder, aimed and fired at her, and she collapsed in a pool of her own blood.

Silence returned for only a few seconds, then a group of local men arrived at the scene and tried to attend to the woman's wounds. They were too late; she was dead. In the resulting chaos caused by the desperate mourners, the soldier suddenly found himself under attack from the angry crowd. He fired into the air to protect himself and the people ran away, throwing stones at him as they left. The army ambulance arrived and all three bodies were wrapped in black bags and driven from the street at high speed as more shots could be heard from the adjoining streets. The ambulance men just nodded to the soldier as he got into his own vehicle. They did not comment on the woman's body; they would just report what they had seen.

The same evening, the soldier was questioned at the camp by his commanding officer, Colonel Richard Walsh. He explained the incident in detail: the car bomb, the woman, the crowd and the horror of all of it.

'Did you see a gun, Sergeant?' said the officer.

'Yes, sir, I most definitely did; the woman went to lift it to her shoulder and I opened fire in self-defence.'

'Can you be sure? Did she or did she not actually move the gun to her shoulder? This is critical, Sergeant.'

'I'm sure she was going to, sir; my instincts told me she was going to shoot me.'

'We have inspected the area near the scene of the blast where the woman stood and no weapon could be found. We believe the woman was going to the shops, as we found a bag with a handle in the gutter.'

'I'm sorry she's dead, sir, but I'm even more sorry about my dead colleagues. She had a rifle, and one of the locals must have taken it away from her.'

'You're likely to face a charge of unlawful killing, and I've made a report for the SIB people; they'll arrive here very soon. They will study the facts, and in my opinion you're likely to be charged and sent for trial. Unlike in civil courts, before reaching a verdict they will know your history of violence; it's all in your file and they may think it relevant. The shooting of an unarmed woman is the third act of third-party violence you have been involved in, Sergeant. There was the young boy stealing your provisions and the prisoner who swore at you; I know you didn't kill either of them but beating them up was serious enough, and how you avoided Colchester I don't know.

'I appreciate that you have saved many lives, but that is part of your work. Killing and maiming civilians is not acceptable under any circumstances. That's all from me, Sergeant. You'll stay here under guard and leave Iraq immediately after a decision on your future is made, even if you are found not guilty. Have you anything to say?'

The soldier didn't reply immediately; he just bowed his head. It was clear that his commanding officer was not supporting him, and he had to hope that somehow the court martial would go in his favour. Either way it was obvious the army didn't want him; he might get a small pension due to his length of service, but nothing else. He was a bitter man, and his mind had been badly affected by losing so many close friends. Nobody could help him, and he had to pray for leniency.

'The only thing I have to say, sir, is that the woman had a rifle. She lifted it to her shoulder, so I fired in self-defence.'

'I'll put that statement in my written comments now, and if you've nothing else to say, go back to your mess room. Your captain has found you something to do for the next few weeks; the outcome will probably be that you'll soon return to the UK under guard.'

The colonel did not regard the soldier as a risk if he was not on duty, so he confined him to the temporary barracks and the officer reluctantly took a job as an assistant in the small army gymnasium until the investigation team arrived to decide his fate.

The jeep pulled up outside the colonel's quarters: a building constantly on the move in order to avoid rocket attacks. Once it was known that the building contained the top soldier in Baghdad, it became a prime target.

'Welcome, Gordon; good to see you again.'

Gordon Fisher was not new to Iraq: he had worked on several court martials as Judge Advocate and had gained a reputation for fairness in dealing with soldiers who had for one reason or another broken the rules. Now his job had for the most part been moved back to the UK, but this case was one that the Judge Advocate General had decided to hold in Baghdad, as several local witnesses were required to give evidence.

'Thanks, Richard; you are one of the few commanding officers who greet me. Most of them just delegate my arrival to the duty sergeant, who's normally awkward as he regards me as bad luck. Joking, of course.'

'This is a nasty one, Gordon, and SIB have taken full control. Come inside and I'll brief you. Have you got accommodation?'

'No – just a room to work in and a decent bed, please; I'll read the report and your comments this evening and then I'll meet

SIB. The JAG asked me to be involved as I have adjudicated here before in similar cases.'

'The facts are in this folder; some I know you'll have read in the newspapers. It's a sad case, Gordon, but aren't they all? The sergeant had a good record, but recently he's gone totally off the rails. Normally we don't see this stuff until the hearing, however in this case I think you'll agree these incidents may be relevant. His captain will give a character reference at the right time, but it's sure to be brief and non-committal: the man has got to leave the army and serve his time in jail; his crime appears to be nearer to a murder than unlawful killing.

'We shouldn't jump to conclusions, Richard; as you know it's my job to ensure the soldier gets a fair trial. SIB may come up with something, so let's wait and see, please.'

'I'm sorry, I was jumping to conclusions. It's bad enough losing our own men fighting, but having to deal with cases like this just proves how futile this whole war in Iran is.'

'Not just Iran. I'm learning fast, Richard, that with some careless attitudes to fighting that started maybe in Vietnam, more innocent people are getting killed. I hope my two sons leave the army when their terms are up. They're both doing a good job, but now Fay and I want them safely back in the UK.'

Chapter 21
Sandhurst Barracks, Surrey

'Charlie, we've got to talk, mate – you're shouting in your sleep; not just a few words but a bloody speech about the army. None of it made any sense, thank goodness. Did you know about it? Have you got a problem?'

'Alan, please can you mind your own business? We have to do this mission together and that's what we should concentrate on; not my sleep patterns. I'm sorry if I kept you awake but I can't do anything about it. From a personal point of view you know all I really care about is the money and getting back here in one piece. As you heard again yesterday, I'm still in the army but all the papers are going through for my discharge; I've had enough. SIS have promised to help me find a new permanent post if I play ball – it won't be operational, but in a top electronics outfit that supplies them with gear.'

'This is all very odd, Charlie. You didn't tell me when we met up that you're still in the army, then as soon as you discovered we would be working together again you've gone all funny on me, and now I find out that you are still in the army. What did I do?'

'Alan, it's me; I'll never be able to tell you the issue as it comes under the official secrets umbrella, but I'm fit for this last field job and then that's the end of my active service and we say goodbye.'

'What did you do, Charlie? Tell me.'

Their discussion was interrupted when Brian Wilson burst into the mess room.

'Right, you two, we've to go early. Typical security service change of plan; not one to confuse the enemy as we don't really have one with this job. The flight from Brize Norton has been brought forward; no reason given, but that's normal. Your four days here are at an end. Alan, you're going on the Hercules as well – give me your BA ticket as someone is sure to ask me what we did with it. I doubt we'll get the money back, though, but maybe we got it free anyway. It's your role that we've yet to go over, so I'll travel with you in the car to the airfield and we can do our best to cover the plan for your mountain trek.'

'Yes, fine; I'm fed up of hanging about here.'

Alan's body language indicated to the SIS man that all was not well between him and Charlie, but it was too late now for him to change one of them. The drive to Brize Norton was less than two hours, and Wilson had covered the routes, the questions and the return journey after they had found Mr Korham. He had not, however, expected a phone call.

'Yes, sir, I understand; we're just in time. They're both in the car with me so I'll advise them now of Plan B. I'll be back in a few hours.' Wilson hung up. 'Gentlemen, the shit has hit the fan and is now going in two directions. Firstly, the Iranians are continuing to refuse to cooperate with NATO and in particular with the Yanks. The information they had promised to provide on their nuclear plants has not been given in any detail, and a lot of threats have been made today by both sides. That's only part of the story, though: our target Deniz Korham has decided not to wait for us to get him out of Iran. He left this morning for Turkey and the last message was that he was in the mountains in some safe house awaiting your arrival.

'This presents us with the logistical change we just discussed. I didn't know the reason until now, but that's the reason Alan no longer needs to travel alone on a commercial flight. It all makes sense, and that's why the Hercules will leave earlier; we've no time to waste. We told the Turks a white lie this morning which for the moment makes them more comfortable: we've told them that the mission is off and that you aren't going to Turkey. A returning countryman from Iran is no problem for them, but it could be if they find out he's been working in a plant that could be making a nuclear weapon, and also that a bunch of Iranian soldiers could be hot on his trail. If they know that, they could become a bit unhelpful, and if they find out about you now it would be embarrassing all round, but from my understanding that

222

doesn't mean that if you're in real trouble they won't help you, although we'll only ask them as a last resort.

'The bottom line is that the Turks will not be expecting you, so you can slip in and out quietly and hopefully with Korham. In the long term they're sure to prefer him here rather than be a liability in Turkey. Is the message getting to you loud and clear, gentlemen?'

'Yes, Brian, it is to me; and you, Charlie?'

'Provided I get paid I don't care if we have to kill the guy.'

'I do hope that won't be necessary, Charlie – you just have to look at what he's got, then hopefully if it's good enough, dump him onto the Hercules back to here; if he's a fraud it's unlikely he'll want to see his family in Newcastle or the USA. We don't want any deaths on our hands on Turkish soil; sorry to repeat myself, but it's vital.'

Alan just smiled and made no comment. His worry was Charlie, not Deniz Korham, and he knew that somehow he'd need to tell Wilson about Charlie's behaviour in case anything did go wrong. He hadn't expected that their arrival at Brize Norton would result in him having to warn them about Charlie: they already knew his history and they probably regarded him as expendable.

The gates to the outer area of the airfield opened without them waiting; the car was expected, and at the security post inside they would be thoroughly checked.

'Just routine, gentlemen, but got to do it all, I'm afraid. You're expected here, but then strange things have happened on these checks; even one guy who turned out to be a woman but his pass was made out to a man. He really had been through a sex change; we were nearly caught with our trousers down.'

The security officer's joke was lost on the three men, and only a polite laugh was returned as the man opened the gate to the hangar where a Hercules was being towed out to the runway.

'Off you go; have a good trip. Oh sorry, guys, can my dog have a sniff? He's looking for explosives but he also likes cannabis and cocaine; strange animal but bloody good.'

The men stopped and the dog sniffed each one in turn, including an embarrassing crotch inspection for Charlie which made Brian Wilson burst out laughing, although he quickly stopped when the dog barked and looked at the guard.

'That is what he's trained for. Are you guys testing my dog and me?'

'What you mean, can he smell something?'

'He sure can and it's a lot, come into this room, sir, remove your trousers and sit on the bed.'

Charlie Baxter went bright red. He took off his blue corduroy slacks and a packet fell on to the floor.

'What's that, Charlie?'

'Look, don't piss about with me, Brian – you know I take a bit of coke now and again; it's my medicine.'

'It's an illegal drug, Charlie, and if the Turks did pull you in we'd have to disown you.'

The security guard interrupted the interrogation as the dog was still barking at the crumpled trousers.

'What's his problem now? This is getting beyond a joke.'

'He's smelt something else. Put the coke on the table; we'll have to confiscate that, of course. As you're on a mission the next step is down to Mr Wilson. More seriously now though, my dog's telling me that those trousers have recently been in contact with explosives.'

'Look, guys, I'm getting fed up with this. Yes, I did have a bit of coke but no more than you can get in most London clubs for £50. The trousers are a spare pair that were hung up in my bedroom cupboard at home; I haven't used them for a long time and when I wore them last I was handling a lot of explosives.'

Brian Wilson made a quick call away from the security post as the others stood around like footballers waiting to see if the culprit of a bad tackle would get a red "off the field" or a cautionary yellow card. He returned, waving a piece of paper in his hand.

'Right, we've sent the report on what the dog discovered to my office, and here are the details; you'd better read it Charlie. The powers that be here will also be told what's happened and it'll all be documented for later. We must go now or we'll miss the plane.'

'Fuck you, Wilson; I've had enough. I'm going home.'

'I don't recommend that, Charlie; if you stay the police will be called and you'll be nicked for having the drugs. You're doing the job as agreed, but your possession of cocaine will stay on the record and I promise you if you get caught again you'll be done. The explosive on your trousers is odd but we can talk about that later and hopefully the dog was wrong. Is that all clear?'

The security guard shook his head as he waved them through. *What a pile of shit*, he thought to himself. He did the job he was paid for and 99.9% of the time he had nothing to report, then he gets double trouble and he's told to let the man go.

Alan said very little. He had now become more worried than ever about his friend, and he knew that he had to continue to watch him very carefully. The coke he could live with, as he had seen many of his friends and colleagues in the army take it. In a bizarre way he regarded a sniff or two before a mission as more acceptable than facing a stale smell of booze on the breath of a soldier with an automatic rifle in his hand.

Wilson pulled Alan to one side as Charlie Baxter went to the jeep waiting on the tarmac.

'Go to the toilet, Alan; the plane is one of the oldest and the bog is like one from a campsite. Now listen carefully: you're the top man on this trip; I hope Charlie behaves and I think he will, but let me tell you a little story. The captain of an Australian warship was on an exercise a couple of years ago with another vessel near Tasmania. We believe he was drunk and had also taken drugs, but whatever he took clouded his judgement and he told his First Officer to turn in a direction aimed at the other ship. They collided, the ship sank, and many lives were lost including the captain. We know we can rely on you, but if Charlie gets pissed or high on drugs you have clearance to deal with him.'

'Not a situation I'd expect, Brian, but I get your point and I'll take any action that's needed. Is this something that's happened in SIS or is your Australian example a bit extreme?'

Wilson half-smiled and pointed to the tarmac.

'Come on, we've work to do.'

Two identical Hercules were parked on the tarmac, the first one preparing to leave, full of servicemen and equipment. The plane moved slowly to the runway and then paused for a moment; it seemed as if the pilot was deciding whether this great lump of metal would ever get off the ground. In reality he was doing final checks, and Alan and Charlie watched as the engines were opened to take off speed and the pilot released the brakes. It seemed as if the plane defied all forces, and took off in an amazingly short distance and climbed into the clouds.

'Have you done this before, Alan?'

'Yes, Charlie. These aircraft are incredible; I'm told by Brian Wilson that the one in the air is going to Kabul, full of new recruits who have no idea what they're in for. All we can do is pray they don't return in a coffin.'

'So is the Hercules a safe plane? I've never been in one until today.'

'Yes, very safe; they even practised landing on the sandy beach at Saunton in Devon. In the hotel there you can see the picture of when they landed and took off several times, practising for the desert.'

The three men walked to the second plane, which was being refuelled.

'This has just arrived from an unknown destination,' Brian Wilson explained. 'Nobody talks destinations here when a plane is on the ground; we know where we're going but some of the lads on board don't know too much. They are what we call IR troops.'

'What does that mean, Brian?'

'Thought you might guess that one, Alan: they're men who've been in the army long-term; you must've met some when you were in Turkey.'

'I did, but I still don't know what a thousand or so men were doing in a camp in Turkey with Yanks.'

'I'm not going to tell you; all I'll say is look at the geography with Iraq, Iran, Syria and then Israel, all within a couple of hours' flying time. Does that make sense?'

'Yes, it does. So IR means "if required"?'

'No, Alan: "instant response". If you get in trouble they'll be called in to help, but please try to complete the job yourselves. This is an SIS operation, not an army one.'

The Hercules was full of servicemen, and a couple of civilians who looked like reporters but were probably just bean-counters or nosey parkers from the MOD. Brian Wilson made sure the three men sat well away from them to avoid any questions, or even small talk. Wilson was still fuming about the debacle at the security post. Initially he would have travelled the next day on a commercial flight, but now he had been told to travel with the two men and stay local to the airfield in Turkey until the job was done. Alan and Charlie had changed into the supplied combat gear before they boarded the plane, their arrival clothes were all left behind at the airfield in a locker and the two men travelled light with just a pair of specially equipped rucksacks for the mission. No weapons had been issued in the UK, and Brian Wilson told them they would collect what they needed from a local contact in Turkey. The check done by the security guard was not ignored, and once the plane left the lockers at Sandhurst would be opened and both men's clothes thoroughly checked again for explosives. The equipment to make the checks was very sophisticated; it had to be so that suspect traces could be totally accurate, and if the traces of explosive were recent Alan Fisher would have to know.

As the plane crossed Europe, the three men slept. The noise from the four engines was quite loud, but in some ways soothing and sleep was inevitable. An hour before landing the crew gave weather and landing details to the passengers, and as the runway came into sight, dawn rose behind the mountains surrounding the town of Agri. Alan almost felt at home. His past base was only 50 kilometres from the airfield, and he knew the area well. His mind was jumping around in all directions: Charlie, his parents, Cheryl and the SIS; and then his training took over and he knew he must keep focused. He grabbed his own rucksack and threw his colleague's at him, and Charlie almost managed a smile. Was he with him or not? In Alan's mind he wasn't, but in order to survive the mission they would have to work as a team, and Alan knew that at the first opportunity he would have to get close to Charlie and find out his problem. If it was drugs it would be awkward, but then Wilson would have to find him a supply if he couldn't operate without a daily fix.

An army lorry with canvas sides was waiting outside the airfield with its engine running. The driver pointed to the back of the vehicle, and then climbed in and dropped down a small ladder. Charlie Baxter scowled and kicked one of the truck's rear tyres.

'This isn't for us, surely – it's for cattle! Couldn't we have had a taxi or something better?'

Brian Wilson shrugged his shoulders. The local arrangements were not part of his brief.

'No, gentlemen, this is your taxi. I'm not coming to stay with you, but I'll be at the house at 9am tomorrow to go through final plans. You'll be greeted by Almas Mehmet, and she'll look after you both. I think you know her, Alan, but please be professional.'

Charlie burst into life. 'An old flame, Alan; girl in every port?'

'Yes, mate. She's OK, looking forward to seeing her again.'

'She's left the army now but she still does the occasional job for us. She's married now, Alan, but I don't think she has any kids as she can be called in at short notice. As you no doubt remember, she's clued up on the geography of the area and she'll help you plan the route. She'll fix you up with some weapons. For lots of reasons we're keeping it simple: the tools she'll supply you with are identical AK47s and automatic Beretta handguns with silencers. You can practise this evening in the old basement range but remember your ear defenders otherwise you'll be permanently deaf; it was not designed as a firing range, just as a wine cellar. Off you go, I'll see you both tomorrow.'

Wilson left quickly, without goodbyes. He would see the men before they left for their mission and he wanted to avoid any more awkward questions or complaints about the transport arrangements. The driver looped the string and fastened the cloth door cover and then drove very slowly to the highway. No checks or security posts on the route out of the airfield: they had left by the back entrance and the staff on guard duty did not know they even existed.

After driving east for an hour through a valley surrounded by mountain ranges, they arrived at a small village just one kilometre from the main road to Patnos. The weather was mild and the town and the small food market in the centre were bustling with farmers setting up stalls with fruit, eggs and locally-grown fresh vegetables; the lorry containing the two men was like any of the others unloading, and a perfect disguise. In theory nobody other than the UK security services knew about their mission – the Americans would have been informed, but they would have put the details on file in case they were needed later.

The airfield and the adjoining base they had left a few hours before was one of several concessions courtesy of the Turkish government, and neither the UK or the USA wished to abuse it. With its strategic position it was valuable to both countries in the event of a crisis in the surrounding countries. Both countries now knew they were on dangerous ground, as the SIS target Deniz Korham was in Turkey and would inevitably be hunted by Iranian forces. If the mission failed, questions to the British Embassy in Ankara or SIS field contacts would be difficult to answer, as even with Turkey's general cooperation the plans to help Korham out of the country without local knowledge would have been prohibited. SIS had ignored protocol and rubber-stamped the mission and that was enough for the director. His use of Alan Fisher (a civilian) and Charlie Baxter (who would soon be a civilian) was a risk he was prepared to take.

The area they would be working was used to conflict. Turks and Kurds were uncomfortable neighbours, and acts of terror often occurred – usually aimed at Turkish interference – but very little was made of it in the world press. Deniz Korham had managed to send a brief text message that morning to a local contact stating that he was in the safe house; the contact had instructions to forward it, encoded, to the SIS. Worrying – but not unexpected – information from a CIA agent in Iran came to Brian Wilson via London that a platoon of border soldiers had been sent to find him. Nobody could be certain, but both the CIA and SIS were confident that Korham really was safely hidden at the meeting point and awaiting the imminent arrival of Alan Fisher and Charlie Baxter.

The lorry pulled into the drive of the large stone house just behind the main street. The gates closed behind it, and once inside the men jumped out of the back of the vehicle. Awaiting their arrival on the front step was Almas Mehmet. The woman was older than Charlie and Alan at 38 years, but she had looked after herself and her figure and complexion were those of a much younger lady. Her khaki army trousers, boots and shirt did her no favours, but it was obvious she had worked on her hair that morning and added some makeup in preparation for the Englishmen's visit.

'Alan, how nice to see you again! It's been a long time.' She politely turned her cheek so he could kiss her, then turned to Charlie. 'Who's your friend?'

'This is Charlie Baxter; we were in the army together a few years ago and we're working together on this job.'

She shook Charlie's hand and pointed to the inside of the house.

'I know you've had an overnight flight so I suggest you have a shower then I'll make you some lunch; afterwards I'll give you everything for your trip and you can have a practice downstairs in the cellar with the guns I'll give you. Once it's dark I'll take you to a small local restaurant, then I suggest an early night – Mr Wilson will be here early tomorrow, and then you leave for Patnos as soon as he gets his instructions.'

'Thanks; I see your English is better than ever, Almas. Who do you work for now?'

'Nobody full-time, Alan; my husband has a good job in Ankara, so I only see him at weekends when he comes here. I left the army when I met him and got married, but occasionally I still do some jobs for the government. Today, though, I'm just looking after this house and any visitors we have. That's why it helps to be in uniform: nobody argues with me in town and I get concessions on food and feel safe. It's a small place and everyone knows each other; they'll know about you already and be puzzled as to why you're here. Don't worry, I'll deal with that; you won't come to any harm in this place. Remember we are Kurds (the mountain Turks), and we always have to be alert to our enemies, so it suited me to retain this job here, especially as the place is used mostly by British and American people. Generally my husband and I feel as safe as we ever can, but he has to keep

234

quiet on his background or he could lose his job in Ankara or suddenly disappear.

'Sorry, I'm talking too much, so enough for now – please make yourselves at home. Your rooms are on the first floor; numbers ten and twelve; Alan you're in ten and Charlie in twelve. You'll find night clothes for your trip as it can be very cold, a towel and some booklets to read; Alan has a head start as he knows some of the information on this area, so before lunch we'll discuss what you may find a problem. The first one will be language, but I have been told Charlie speaks some of the local language.'

'Yes. Thanks, Almas. So tell me why you fear for your own safety; is it because you're on your own here during the week?'

'My husband and I try to avoid confrontation but it's near impossible; as I said we're safe as long as the Turkish government allows your country and the USA to be here. If that changed, we would have to emigrate. Once my husband was in the Workers Party, the PKK – no longer, though, for many reasons, but people have long memories and we're always watching our backs, as you say.'

Alan and Charlie climbed the stairs of the old building and found their rooms.

'You first, Alan; I need a sleep. I'll catch up with you later.'

'OK, but don't sleep all day: we've our meeting with Almas over lunch, then we've got to test the weapons.'

235

'Keep your hair on! I'll be ready.'

'Don't be awkward, Charlie. I don't know what the problem is with you but I'd sure like to know. See you later.'

Charlie closed his bedroom door and locked it, then took out his UK mobile phone, which he was under strict instructions not to use unless in an emergency. He sent a text:

We see the guy in next couple of days. Hope to get him on his own to get info; will let you know.

Alan started his shower and let the water pour over his body for a couple of minutes while he thought about Charlie. The mission to the mountains to meet, interrogate and bring Deniz Korham back to the house was a tricky job anyway, but with Charlie on board he was very concerned that it could all go very badly wrong. He decided all he could do was to get Brian Wilson on his own before they left and see if he had any knowledge about Charlie and his strange behaviour.

He wrapped the towel around himself and opened the window slightly. He could see the mountains and little else, and he was lost in thought when a smooth but firm arm slipped around his waist and inside his towel.

'I didn't think you were coming, Almas?'

'Don't speak; your friend may hear.'

The towel dropped to the floor and the naked lady took his hand and pulled him through the adjoining door to bedroom number nine. She pushed him onto the bed and he offered little resistance as she climbed on top of him and made love to him as if it was a daily routine.

'The unforgettable Almas.'

'The incredible Alan.'

Alan started to laugh, but Almas put her hand over his month and whispered in his ear.

'Get dressed; lunch is ready. Maybe again when we're back from dinner tonight, but you need to keep all your energy for the mountains.'

'Have you any children, Almas?'

'That's a good question. I want kids and my record in your system shows I've had two: this allows me certain freedom in my liaisons with your country and generally stops me being "chatted up"; your words, I think. Maybe one day it'll happen, but we've been trying for years, my husband and I. It's me, I'm told; we try a lot without success. I'm going now, so lean over – I want to give you a long kiss.'

The kiss was so good Alan nearly started again, but she grabbed his hand and expertly pushed him back into his room. He fell on the bed and smiled back at her without a word as she locked the interconnecting door.

Charlie finally arrived for the meal after sleeping for four hours. The three sat around a table in the dining room and consumed a traditional salad dish, accompanied by bottled water.

'I hope you enjoyed your lunch, gentlemen. Come into the next room, please, and collect your weapons.'

The AK47s were Russian issue, and the mark on the Beretta handguns' butts showed a flag which confirmed they were also of Russian origin. The weapons were old models but they looked unused; Almas explained that they came new and she had tested them with a hundred rounds each, and they were in perfect working order.

'Charlie, you first, please: answer these questions for me from the literature I left you, and Alan tell me where the places on the list are.'

The two men scribbled for ten minutes then handed the papers back to her.

'Alan, you got two places slightly wrong and one of them is the place you're going; please study the journey again and note the grid references. You'll be blind as everything looks the same in that area, so that's why you need to know every checkpoint. Charlie, for someone who's just read the literature for the first time you did very well. When did you learn Turkish?'

'I had a girlfriend from Istanbul and they say that the best way to learn a language is to have a lover.'

'I thought so. Now as I mentioned earlier, you must try not to speak unless in an emergency, or you'll be instantly recognised.'

'Understood Almas, but what about the satellite phone we were given by our security people?'

'Yes, that's all right, but make check-in calls only to your people or me; I'll programme the number, but with three digits missing in case it gets lost. Remember: be brief and move away quickly from the point you made the call in case the signal is picked up. That brings me on to the last thing: Charlie, don't use your mobile again; it can be tracked quickly. I've some equipment in my office and I know you called or texted someone from here today. Leave your phones with me, please, then go and test your weapons downstairs and then clean them and pack for your journey. Brian Wilson will have the latest information for you; the weather, the route and any new information on Mr Korham.'

'Has he said how long we interrogate him for and what the hell we do if he's a fraud?'

'No, Charlie, that's between you and Alan, but I think you know that we don't want any deaths on Turkish soil.'

'Yes, I know we must get the bloke back to the UK quickly. I'm sure he'll be useful.'

Charlie's eagerness to get Deniz Korham back to Brize Norton worried Alan; he would mention it to Brian Wilson before they left for the mountains.

The two men were like kids with new toys. Both had fired similar types of guns to the ones they had been issued, but nothing of comparable quality to the AK47.

'This gun is so good I feel like I've used it all my life. It feels light but it's not; hope we don't have to use it as I doubt I'll miss anything that stands still long enough for me to point at.'

'They're just for insurance, Charlie; anyone we have to shoot with these guns would have to totally disappear otherwise there would be an international incident, but we can't go on this trip unarmed otherwise we could be the ones to vanish from the earth.'

The guns were cleaned and locked away until the morning. The lorry was to arrive at 9am the next day with Brian Wilson as a passenger. He would give them a final briefing on the trip details he mentioned during the Hercules fight. They would be expected to arrive in Muradiye on Friday to meet Mr Korham. He would be waiting.

The dinner planned by Almas at a local restaurant was quick but substantial; no alcohol was on offer and the three were back in the house by 10pm for an early night. Almas felt guilty about making love to Alan again, and a brief discussion ended with a kiss and a 'Maybe when I see you at the end of the week.' Alan knew it was just casual sex but he found the Turkish lady particularly attractive, and he thought that if she hadn't been married perhaps he would be returning to Turkey on his own.

As he closed the bedroom door something bothered him. His mind was playing tricks on him again, and he saw images of his parents. In the excitement of the day he had thought only about the mission, and that had been good for his sanity. The Turkish house reminded him of his happy family home, but now he had no family apart from his uncle. He couldn't sleep, and the noise of the AK47 still rang in his eardrums as he put his head down onto the pillow. The lovemaking earlier in the day had relaxed him, but now he was ready to start the job they had been sent to do. He got out of bed and paced out the room, then sat in an armchair to read the maps and make sure he had enough information on the first night's checkpoint, which consisted of a shed a thousand metres above sea level at the start of the pass leading to Muradiye.

The next thing he knew, Charlie was banging on his door. He must have slept in the chair for seven hours; maybe longer, as his neck hurt like hell.

'It's 8am, Alan; I'll see you downstairs. Wilson's already here and chatting up our landlady.'

'OK, see you in 15 minutes.'

Alan would not be rushed; he needed to pack his gear carefully and make sure everything was ready for the trip. His doubts had vanished now, and he knew he had to be a soldier again; in his mind it was like running out onto the pitch to play rugby. He dressed and cleaned his teeth, no shave or shower. Beard stubble could help as a disguise and soap left a smell; the only smell he would carry for the next four days would be his own body odour. He checked his room out of habit, made up the bed and used the toilet; his home routine, and one he had done every day in his army years. He had a feeling he would see Almas again, but then asked himself if he really wanted to. She might not be around when they returned and the lorry would probably take them straight to the airport: no goodbyes, just a rapid exit. He made his mind up that he would try and work it that he would see her before they returned to the airfield, even if it was only briefly.

Downstairs, Almas stood next to the table in her overalls; Charlie and Brian Wilson had their noses into plates of meat and bread.

'Morning Alan – grab your breakfast; your provisions are in these two packs and your water's in the lorry.'

Brian Wilson nodded a greeting. 'Morning, gentlemen. First, a message from the UK: overnight a Mr Harold Penny phoned our office to say that the coroner at the Surrey County Coroner's Court has fixed the date for your parents' inquest in seven days' time; the 8th of February at 9.30. I told him to tell them you'll be free to attend.'

'Yes, I'll be there, but he's already told me that before I left. He's getting a bit forgetful.'

Charlie Baxter heard the message, but his head didn't change position from above his plate.

'So, gentlemen, these are the final details: Almas has left your weapons in the next room, so when I've finished, check them and the ammunition; usual procedure for you army boys. You've to be in the lorry ready to leave at nine, so no time for anything other than simple questions; I'm just passing on what I've been told. Look at the map in front of you, Charlie – it's unmarked apart from here and the destination. Alan has a marked copy, so in the lorry you can mark your map up together; he knows the area and will tell you about different features on the route, and the stopping points. Once we leave you the road will change into a narrow dirt track for ten kilometres before the main road comes into sight again, just before the village where Deniz Korham is waiting: this has to be approached in darkness tomorrow night.

'This mission is codenamed *Clee*; if you get in trouble use the satellite phone, dial the emergency number and say the word. This will put you on to a CIA agent in the area who will help you. Korham won't know this word when you meet him. Tell us when you're ready to return; if everything is OK with Korham ask him the code name – it's *Jell*; intentionally different from the actual mission codename. The lorry will leave here and be waiting for you when you reach the main road. If you're late he'll be hiding camouflaged off the road; he'll wait 30 minutes then leave if you don't turn up.

'Under normal circumstances locals and bona fide visitors can pass through the area you are working in quite freely, but

243

frequent checks are made to prevent Iranian criminals escaping over the border and travelling on to the major centres of Turkey. We're assuming Korham has no residence in Turkey, but he probably has a passport, although it could be in another name. The Yanks say he has a US passport, and if he has he'll have had to relinquish any others. That's one of the reasons why they're on our backs to help him. Whatever his status is, once you have him safely back here we'll be getting him out of this country as quick as possible. From the apparent safety of the mountain ranges between here and Iran, at some stage any traveller has to pass through two major checkpoints. Anyone without the correct documents is driven back to Iran, and every week some ten or so illegal visitors are returned to face certain imprisonment and sometimes death. You'll see those places clearly in daylight; sorry guys but you have to navigate around them otherwise we'll have too many questions; they could shoot you before we find out they've detained you.'

The briefing turned out be worse than Alan and Charlie had anticipated: the whole trip had to be done in three days and two nights, walking a distance of approximately 22 kilometres with some low-level climbing through difficult mountainous terrain.

'Finally, gentlemen, the Turkish army are going to start an exercise in the area in the next few days with two hundred armed soldiers covering the mountains playing war games. If I'd known about these manoeuvres before today I'd have asked London for advice, but it's too late now; you have to go, and be quick but careful. Any questions?'

Alan put his hand up, shaking slightly.

'I have my statutory questions; if Korham answers them all correctly do I give him some different ones to make sure he's going to be of use to you?'

'Yes, Alan, I leave that to you. What he doesn't know is that Charlie speaks Turkish and he will ask separate questions in his own language, then there won't be any translation surprises later. You then talk to him in English, which I'm told he can understand very well as he started life in the USA, but use Charlie as well and write down what he translates; the Turk isn't good at writing anything in English as it's been so long since he did.'

To have the meeting mostly in Turkish worried Alan; he was not sure that he could trust his colleague, and Charlie could ask Korham anything. Alan went to the toilet and called Almas, explaining what Wilson had said.

'Record all the conversation on your phone recorder without Charlie knowing, then call me and play it back on the sat phone. I'll be waiting, now go before they know you called me.'

Alan closed the toilet door behind him just as a worried-looking Charlie appeared.

'You OK, Alan, have you got the shits or something?'

'Did have, but now I'm good as gold. Let's go and grab the guns and get on our way.'

245

The three men shook hands and Brian Wilson went inside the house to make a phone call as the lorry started its engine and crashed and banged down the road to the mountains.

'They left sir, all OK; I hope they don't run into any Turkish soldiers in the next few days. Anything new back home?'

'Let's hope not, Brian. Nothing new here at the moment – are the two men fully briefed on the timescale?'

'Yes, Alan Fisher's good at logistics and he knows the area, hopefully well enough to avoid trouble. Just one thing: I don't think Baxter likes Fisher. I thought they were mates but I feel something wrong between them, or at least from Baxter's side.'

'They're probably just a bit jumpy about the trip. Give me a call when they're back or in any emergency situation; I want to know quickly before Whitehall has the Turkish Embassy on the phone.'

The director didn't want to pursue the information he was being given about his nephew Charlie Baxter and Alan Fisher. He just had to pray the two men would deliver.

Chapter 22
Information

The director left the secure phone room and sat down with his staff in the reporting room.

'Brian Wilson arrived safely in Turkey with Alan Fisher and Charlie Baxter. It seems the security dog at the airfield took a fancy to Charlie's trousers; the report I got said he had some coke and his trousers smelt of explosive.'

The man in charge leaned back on his chair and took a moment to speak.

'Are you OK, sir?'

'Yes, I'm fine. It's no secret that Charlie Baxter's my nephew; I thought he'd been clean of drugs for over three years, but his wife has a medical problem and he's taking it badly. When I spoke to him he seemed fine – did he say anything to you Jason when we hired him for this job?'

'No, sir, on the contrary: he seemed very upbeat about it, and he said he liked working with Alan in the past.'

'But he didn't work with Alan; they were in the same division but they only met through the bar.'

'He was keen to do this job with him. So do you reckon there's a problem, sir?'

'I bloody well hope not, but Brian Wilson smells a rat – speak to Charlie's employer, and also that Major Barrington he worked under just before he left the army.'

'You mean Bomber Barrington, sir?'

'What's the "Bomber" bit, Jason?'

'You must remember it, sir: we suspected him of sympathising with the IRA. We never approached him; just usual surveillance for a few months and we saw and heard nothing unusual. Barrington got his name from his bomb disposal work; Charlie did a stint with him in Belfast when he was still in the army.'

'Yes, I remember him now – a bit eccentric. He left the army, but my nephew stayed attached in a specialist role with another guy; what the three of them called "consultancy". I didn't believe them, and that's when the surveillance took place. I got Charlie on his own and he said they were just friends; not sure I believed him then but I let it go. Our contacts in the army said with what Charlie knew it was in their interests to retain him: his knowledge of hand-fired rockets and similar deadly weapons made him useful to have available. Not sure what they pay him; his knowledge is getting out of date so I doubt if he will be paid very much.'

'He was lying to you, sir. Barrington was the brains of the operation, and the other two did the work, whatever it was. From

248

what you've said I would guess bombs and advice on how to use them; the trousers Baxter had on at the airfield must have been those he used when working with Barrington. The smell can last a long time, especially if he hadn't worn them until the other day.'

'Who was the third guy in Barrington's little group? A leading question, and one I think we need the answer to quickly: if Baxter is in the front line with Alan Fisher it could all go very badly wrong in Turkey. Molly, please spend time on this as a priority; we want as much information as we can get on Barrington, Baxter and the third man. Just a hunch, Jason: maybe number three is financial, or God forbid even a politician; ask your friend Linda in MI5 just to see what she has in that direction. I'm not at all close to Charlie but he is my sister's boy; I don't want to talk to her yet but if anything goes wrong or we find out anything new about him I'll be making an urgent journey to Cardiff to see my relatives.'

'OK. Just one other thing, sir?'

'What's that, Jason? Be quick.'

'A long shot, I know, but Alan Fisher must have those pictures DI Hubbard keeps going on about. Get a picture of Barrington and when Alan gets back set up another meeting with him and tell him there could be a connection. It's a lot to tell him sir; we can't be sure yet that Barrington was involved with his parents' deaths.'

'Come on, Jason, let DI Hubbard do the dirty work. We'll be one step behind as now the third man could be in a photo; get Barrington and Baxter's army records and check if Gordon Fisher ever worked with them, or even if he was involved with them in an investigation. I smell a link. Yes, Molly – sorry, I'm not ignoring you. Please speak.'

'Changing the subject, sir, Deniz Korham sent another message last night: he's OK and waiting in Turkey in the safe house. He suspects his company in Iran have already sent people to find him and some may have already crossed the border.'

'That's what we expected and with the Turkish army on manoeuvres it could get pretty crowded over there. I hope my dear nephew keeps off the coke until he gets back; we have to keep our fingers crossed otherwise Alan will have to deal with him.'

'Finally, sir?'

'I hope not, Jason, but if there is a danger of national security being compromised he will need to have a temporary illness; just one to get him back here on the plane, remember he's family and my sister must never know he worked with us. I'll help the lad all I can but I can't live with a traitor.'

The big wheels moved very quickly in SIS. Molly Smart was good at her job, and with a name like that she had to be. Within hours she had details of Barrington and Baxter, Gordon Fisher and pictures of all three: none with them all together, but many shots of Baxter, Barrington and others. The others were being checked out from army records, but the key pictures had to have Gordon Fisher in them and someone wanted them desperately. The break-in at Harold Penny's was not SIS, but it gave them a clue or two as to who it could possibly have been.

'We have to do some more work on the Gordon Fisher case as I see an overlap of situations looming; Jason, get in touch with DI Hubbard, I know I said step back but with what we're hearing about my nephew we have to be involved. Get the photos; we have some already and Molly will collate them.'

'Are you going to inform Chief Super White that we're meeting Hubbard again?'

'No, on this one let's see if we can find the lead on Gordon Fisher and his wife's deaths. Then we can have a scrum-down with Dick White.'

Chapter 23
Another Chance?

The dimly-lit alley in the old part of Brighton was typical of the area known as The Lanes. The small terraced house owned by Jill Nixon's sister Penny Donnelly and her husband Dermott was a simple two-up-two-down Victorian cottage with a bathroom and toilet built on as an extension in the 1980s when the area had become the "in" place to live. In recent times prices in The Lanes had rocketed, and a house in good condition fetched a very high price. The older properties were still much sought after, and a similar house in the next street had recently been sold for over £400,000; enough to buy a sizeable semi-detached modern house in other parts of the town.

Penny was near retirement but still helped out part-time at the local hospital: she was a qualified midwife and her experience was invaluable to the over-stretched maternity unit. She tried to limit her work and the day would soon come when she would stop completely, but she feared boredom. She was older than her sister Jill, and her sudden appearance on the doorstep was welcome; now she had someone to talk to and give her some ideas on how she could occupy her time. Dermott Donnelly had a reputation as a man into everything, and some of his activities were very worrying to his wife. His speciality was recovering and restoring antique furniture, much of which came from Northern Ireland, and it usually fetched good prices in his shop near their home, usually after several doses of sandpaper, old wood stain and varnish. However his business interests didn't stop at furniture and the Irishman had a good and regular business selling swords, knives and a variety of other weapons, legally and without reproach from the authorities. He was the man to see if someone needed a pistol, rifle or shotgun and could pay well in cash. These weapons passed through his hands without paperwork and with the buyers remaining totally anonymous.

Due to his activities in the past during troubled times in Belfast he was constantly watched and sometimes interviewed by the local police if a crime with a firearm had occurred, or any crime in the area where violence had been used. He hated the police and the feeling was mutual; one day they hoped and prayed to see him slip up and then they would swoop, complete with search warrants for his home and shop. Dermott was always very careful and used third parties to carry out deliveries and collect payments to keep him out of the firing line; some smart guys tried to double-cross him but only once, and they were taught a swift lesson via a mild beating that discouraged any repetition. It was said he could get anything on the weapons front that could be used for robbery and violence, but nothing had ever been proved in spite of many long interrogations at Brighton police station. It seemed to some officers that maybe Dermott Donnelly had friends in high places in the police who helped him if he was pulled in, but nobody knew who, and more importantly why. What they did know is that his visits to the police station ended swiftly after he was allowed to make a single phone call. In the past old friends in Northern Ireland had found him anything he wanted on his shopping list, and he sailed close to the wind on some big deals on prohibited items to get the money to pay off his mortgage. After it was all paid for, Penny had pestered him to stop his dodgy deals and stick to furniture; he had agreed but she saw the twinkle in his eye as he smiled at her. He needed a challenge, but knowing that one day he could do a deal too many and get himself into trouble could not sort him out.

Nobody really knew Dermott's background; even his wife had not been able to drag all the information on his life out of him. He left the British army suddenly but with a good record; his brother Liam had a rough deal in front line operations and one day was found dead from a self-inflicted bullet wound to the temple. Dermott vowed vengeance, but nobody knew whom he blamed for his brother's suicide. It was not a subject for discussion with his wife, and like many other men after army careers he kept silent about the pain he had seen, and even more so had suffered in his own family.

Jill's arrival in Brighton was in some ways a pleasant surprise for her sister but she knew that she had problems with her husband Larry; what she didn't realise was how serious they were. To make matters worse, Dermott and Larry were old acquaintances: they had served together in the army and it was through Penny and Dermott that Larry and Jill had first met. Larry had been a career soldier but Dermott only signed up for six years, and after an initial three years in England he was posted to his home town of Belfast to help keep the peace, a job which he enjoyed as he was dealing with people he grew up with. The response he got when his accent was heard while he was wearing British uniform sometimes caused problems, but Dermott had an alert mind and he knew when it was best to retreat. He knew people on both sides and when he finally left the army he was a big loss to his regiment due to his knack of knowing about trouble before it happened on the streets of terror.

'Penny, I've been here two weeks now and heard nothing from Larry; I have to move on soon, and I know you said I could stay but this house is so tiny we can hear each other fart, or much worse, those animal noises when Dermott makes love to you.'

Penny laughed. Jill was good at making awkward situations humorous, and she was always the star at family parties.

'Yes, I understand, Jill but where will you go?' Before she could answer, Penny pointed through the front window. 'Look –

there's Larry now; he's talking to Dermott across the road. It looks like they're just coming out of the pub.'

'I don't want to see him, Penny; he's a dangerous man to start with, but even more so when he's had a few drinks.'

'They're coming in; you have no choice in this house, Jill. There's no place to hide.'

Larry Nixon was clean-shaven and looked smart in his sports jacket, white shirt and corduroy trousers. In contrast, Dermott was in his overalls and covered in sawdust straight from his workshop, and Larry had gone to see him first to make sure Jill was still around. Three pints of best bitter and a couple of whiskies later, they decided it was time for Larry to face his wife.

'Hi Penny, you look well.'

'Thanks, Larry. Come on Dermott, you smell of drink already so come and buy me one and let these two stay here and talk.'

Dermott did not need a second invitation, and took his wife's hand and all but dragged her out of the house before she changed her mind.

'Well, Larry, what the hell are we going to do? Have you calmed down now?'

'Jill, I know you're having an affair with Bill Knowles.'

'That's history. I'm sorry it happened, but it did; I've got him out of my system forever now, I promise you. So, Larry, a question for you: are you knocking off Marie?'

Larry could not look her in the face; he was a bad liar.

'So it's yes, and yes to both questions for the two of us?'

'If you say so, Larry, but as far as I'm concerned it was just a fling with Bill and it's very much over since I left the pub. I've had no contact with him, it's finished.'

'Same here. That Polish tart was ripping us off: she was nicking money from the cash till and some stock went missing last week. Next thing her brother turned up with a van when he thought I wasn't around. I caught him trying to load it with ten crates of bottled lager and a load of crisps and nuts. I liked the guy previous to that, so it shows what a bad judge of character I am.'

'What did you do?'

'I decided not to knock hell out of him – I could've done but I'd have needed a weapon; he's a big bloke and a lot younger and fitter than me. He drove away at high speed and left everything behind, so I kicked the girl out without any pay and he stopped to pick her up. She left all her clothes behind – by the way, some of them looked like yours. They're probably back home in Warsaw by now.'

'Well done, Larry. Look, I'm willing to give it another go if you are, but you have to see a doctor about the panic attacks, not just drink yourself to death. That doesn't work and you know it.'

'I'm ahead of you Jill, I've seen the doctor and for the first time yesterday a psychiatrist; in his opinion a lot of it's basically down to what happened to me in the army, but he said he can help me.

'That's great, Larry, but surely that doesn't mean getting pissed with Dermott?'

Larry bowed his head. 'I'm here to see you but I also wanted to speak with Dermott; that was important. You know what, Jill: when I'm with Dermott I'm under his spell; the bloke has so much history he should sit down and write a book. . .but maybe not, as he'd get sent to prison for sure. I've had a couple of hours with him on army days and even that frightens me; there's a lot you don't know and I'm going to be brave and try and find a way to handle it. Anyway, they've gone to the pub and they said they'll wait for us there; I told Dermott to do that.'

'Did you indeed? So what have you in mind to delay us?'

'Come with me and I'll show you.'

Larry stank of booze, but in spite of the odour she was turned on by him, and she still loved him dearly. They sat up in bed after making love in the spare bedroom with the paper-thin walls, after a session some 20 minutes longer than usual, in which Jill was bold and took the lead. Larry took his wife's hands and looked directly at her.

'I've one big problem and it's got to be dealt with as well: this bloke Parker is ripping me off and I need a plan to deal with him.'

'What's your problem?'

'I can't tell you at the moment, but now I know I can handle it without screwing myself up or you, I'll work out what to do and tell you soon.'

'I'll get my things together. Is the pub still closed? I heard you shut it when I left.'

'Yes, but we'll open it again tomorrow; I've two girls coming for interviews in the morning and you can see if one is any good to help you in the kitchen.'

'We've got to get rid of the pub, Larry – let's live in Spain!'

'Yes, but I'm not giving the place away to some foreigner for peanuts.'

'Come on, let's go and have one drink with Penny and Dermott. I'll drive your car; I hope it's clean inside.'

'The pub or the car?'

'The bloody car, you dope.'

'Jill, after all this you still ask me if the fucking car's clean. You're crazy.'

'I might be a bit mad but not as much as Dermott: he kept chasing me around the house! He was desperate to get me into bed, but Penny made sure she was always around. She said he did it just for fun, but he was like a 20-year-old sometimes.'

'That man's a special case, Jill, but I'm convinced that the fact they can't have kids is down to that bomb blast. He damaged his balls and he told me he's convinced that he's just been firing blanks since he was discharged from hospital. It's too late now anyway, but it's ironic that she's a midwife.'

'Did they ever consider adopting? She never told me if they did.'

'No, I don't think so. Dermott said to me once that kids were only around for 25 years or maybe less, and after that they have their own life and you never see them. Not like in the old days in Northern Ireland when they all met at least twice a week. Families were a lot different 40 years ago.'

'Perhaps he has a point; we don't hear much from our kids, after all. But if we do move to Spain, that could all change with Terry in Barcelona and Lucy just over the border in France. I got a call from Terry the other day; he was asking me about Alan Fisher. He'd heard that his parents had been killed by a bomb and he wondered what Alan was doing. You threw him out of the pub, remember?'

'Yes, his old man and I had a bit of a falling-out once and I didn't want him around.'

'That's a bit harsh, Larry, especially as they're dead and so is Alan's brother. Do you know who killed them?'

'You don't want to know, Jill, and that's close to the big problem I have: I was convinced Alan's brother's death was not an accident and somebody then went on to murder the Fishers in their own home. I've a good idea what happened on the day of Ben's death but that's all, and up to now I've not been able to deal with it. Now I can see some options in front of me.'

'Bloody hell, no wonder you've been sick, darling; that's some big problem.'

'Yes, but one I have to tackle even if it means I've to deal with someone. Come on, let's go home.'

'OK, but you've got to tell me more as we drive back and then I can try to help you, but please listen to me this time, Larry.'

'I will, but no names. If I'm killed you've got to get on with your life or you are in danger as well, and I mean big danger, Jill.'

They left the cottage, and a note for Penny. More alcohol was not a good idea that night and Jill wanted to get back to the pub, which was still the only home she knew.

Chapter 24
Not the Best of Friends

'Sit down, Norman, you look aggressive when you just stand there and point.'

Chief Superintendent Dick White pushed a chair in front of him.

'I'm pissed off, sir, and I'll explain why.'

DI Norman Hubbard had just received a phone call from Jason Harris.

'Our colleagues in SIS have suddenly decided that the key to unlocking the Fisher case is in the photographs that are currently missing from Gordon Fisher's office, that is if they ever existed at all. Now they've discovered that someone on their list of bad boys knew about explosives, so they're back on the case to find who made the bomb and who planted it. I was under the impression that they'd passed it all to us, but now they're sniffing around, and today one of their blokes went to see Harold Penny, the Fisher family lawyer and an old friend who Alan now confides in. I got a call from Harold after he got burgled and the computer got nicked; he's kept his head down since that happened, so to speak, and is getting on with the complex probate issues for Alan. What do they want from him, sir?'

'Yes, sorry – they did speak to me briefly about Harold. I didn't tell you as I thought you knew, so my apologies but at least we're all working in the same direction. I suspect your anger is because you've hit a brick wall.'

'No, actually I've the same lead as Harris and that's what annoyed me; I think he had it first and I'll explain why.'

'Get to the point, Norman, it's nearly lunchtime.'

'We discovered an army guy called Major William Barrington, "Bomber Barrington" to everyone he knows. It seems he knows the man who went on the mission with Alan this week and they worked together in Northern Ireland, and his speciality believe it or not is explosives. He's called Charlie Baxter and is the nephew of the SIS director.'

'I see, no wonder they're involved again and so they should be; no doubt they're looking under every stone Baxter ever walked on.'

'Actually, it all came to light when Baxter was screened for the flight to this mystery destination with Alan and they found traces of explosive on his clothes. The bottom line is that Barrington and Baxter could be involved in the deaths of the Fishers, but the feeling is that they were a band of three and someone else is involved. SIS are back on the case and we both need to jump on Alan when he's back to give us what he's got so far on the photographs.'

'Cooperate, Norman: speak to Harris daily and forget politics. Let's find the bomber.'

'Yes, but they asked me something else today; completely in another direction, but then it could be connected in some way.'

'What was that?'

'As the activities in Northern Ireland have now hopefully come to an end, SIS believe from information they have that there's still a big stockpile of weapons and explosives somewhere, and the main supplies of explosive are from Libya. There is no way the IRA bought direct and I discovered they had a local agent in Northern Ireland who handled it for them, buying through an Arab dealer. We believe that local agent was a guy called Paddy Mulligan who was found dead a few weeks ago. SIS suspect that he supplied somebody with the explosives that killed the Fishers; the detonator that Alan found at the house was also from Libya.'

'Is that it, Norman?'

'Yes, sir. With your permission I'll fly to Belfast in two days and get a meeting with the RUC; I've checked with SIS and they're in agreement. Paddy Mulligan couldn't have worked alone, so let's find out who he worked with. I'm going back to Guildford tomorrow to look again at the bits and pieces we got from the Fisher house to see if we or Alan have missed something. He should be back in a few days and then we can talk again. I hope he doesn't have problems on that job he's doing for SIS; I can't really understand why he's bothering to help them.'

'He's a professional and a specialist, and totally in the wrong job as a planning officer, but under current circumstances his trip will help sort his mind out. I hope the security people have got the right man for the assignment; they probably have a career job in mind for him. That's of course if he does get back.'

Hubbard did not like his boss' throwaway comments, which made it clear he didn't like Alan. Superintendent White's assistant knocked on the door and walked in without waiting, but both men knew she only did that if it was urgent.

'Sorry to interrupt, sir, but I think you need to know this information: Molly from SIS rang and asked me to give you this message now, and more details will be sent securely by email later today.'

'Spit it out then, Linda.'

'A bomb has exploded at a house near Greenwich and a man is reported dead. At first they thought it was a gas leak and for the moment that's what's being reported, but a full alert has gone out – the usual stuff: airports, stations and docks. SIS say it's just a precaution as they believe the bomb was specifically targeted at the man.'

'And who might that be?'

'A Major William Barrington; a hero, I understand, during the Northern Ireland conflict.'

'Well 30 minutes ago we hadn't even discussed this Barrington man; now I assume he's dead. A pattern of some description is developing here – Norman, go and see Jason Harris today and I'll call the director. We're back on board with them now on this one and I'm sure they'll agree; don't go to Belfast straight away until we've spoken again, but you must go eventually as you suggested.'

'Sorry, sir, one more thing: the blast destroyed only the major's office, which he was sat in at the time.'

'Thanks, Linda; anything new copy to DI Hubbard as well please.'

She left the room, and White was gazing into space when Hubbard spoke. 'You sounded at first as if you didn't know Barrington. Did you know him, sir?'

'Yes, yes, I knew of him. Now off you go.' White pointed to the door. Hubbard left without ceremony; just a brief wave as White picked up the phone and dialled a number from memory. His DI had hit a nerve on something and he wanted to end the meeting.

'Look, things are getting very hot. Meet me in an hour in Clandon Regis Golf Club bar; it's quiet and the only people we'll see are golfers.'

The man at the other end of the phone was surprised at the abrupt call, and did not reply immediately to the request. After a pause, he asked a question in a quick, nervous voice.

'Why a meeting now? Every time we have one it's trouble; what is it now?'

'Your old friend Wild Bill Barrington has been killed by a bomb, or maybe you know already. Did you plant it?'

'In that case we'd better meet, and no I damn well didn't kill him.'

'Fine, see you at three o'clock.'

Aaron hung up the phone, and his wife was waiting for him. 'Who was that, Aaron? Who didn't you kill?'

'One of our friendly protection policeman, Chief Superintendent Dick White – you know, the one who keeps forgetting what he should be doing; I only hear from him when he's got a problem – just asked me if I'd planted a bomb.'

'Is this connected to the death of Paddy Mulligan?'

'Could be, I really don't know, Leah. I didn't know anything about a bomb killing Bill Barrington until White phoned.'

'Wild Bill Barrington, that mad man. If I remember rightly, when I met him for the first time he was with you when we went to that trade dinner near Stormont. You must remember: the longer the evening went on, the more threats were discussed by him and his two English cronies, mainly against British army people. It was difficult to tell whose side he was on. I remember him well; he told me minutes before he groped my backside that his father was born in Dublin and his mother was the daughter of a general in the British army, and he liked dark Mediterranean women like me. He was a repulsive creep.'

'Yes, I remember it all, Leah, as if it was yesterday. You're right about him, but he wasn't just creepy, he was arrogant with it, just like those days in Beirut with the different war leaders. You never knew who was on your side.'

'You played both sides, Aaron, and now you could be well and truly stuck in the middle. We can't leave here, we'd be killed without trace in most Middle East countries, and most other countries wouldn't give us a visa.'

'Don't worry, Leah – nothing's new as we've been in this situation for a long time and have lived with it. I'm going now; ring Larry Nixon for me and tell him I can't get to see him today, but I'll call him tomorrow morning.'

'He won't like that, Aaron; I think he already suspects you're screwing him after you told him the deal was off, and then a few days later back on again.'

'So what? Another day won't make a difference. If he gets really nasty go and see him; you know what the deal is and he may take the offer better from you than me. I hear his wife's back at the pub now, so maybe he's going to be more difficult, or on the other hand he may be ready to close a deal.'

'Sounds like you're still talking to Bill Knowles, if you have such good information.'

'Yes; maybe I'll give him an extra bonus if it all works out. See you later, Leah; keep me in touch if you see Nixon.'

He drove away from the apartment, oblivious to the dark car parked across the road, observing all his movements.

The driver picked up a mobile phone. 'He's on the move at last. Shall I let him go?'

'No, just follow him; anything new we can learn from him should tell us if he's working alone or not.'

'His wife just came out of the apartment as well and has gone in the opposite direction on foot with a mobile in her hand. What shall I do about her?'

'Follow him only. Leave her, but as I said, don't do anything other than watch him and let me know where he goes.'

Leah Parker put her phone away. She had decided to just turn up at the pub rather than have a phone argument with Larry Nixon. Her car was in the multi-storey car park: the apartment came with only one parking space and Aaron's new Mercedes took pride of place over her discreet little red Honda Jazz. The journey to the pub was long enough for her to get worried about her husband. She knew his business was supplying weapons and explosives; a dangerous but lucrative family business, and well-connected in the Middle East and Europe, with many years of profitable success under its belt. She could deal with that as she had known the risks when she married her husband, but now she was getting older and she feared that as a childless, ageing partner she had been pushed firmly into the background. She more than suspected that Aaron had a lover – he was out many evenings, arriving back very late and sometimes the next day with thin stories or excuses regarding his whereabouts during the previous day.

The week before, Leah had found something that made her even more suspicious about somebody she had heard Aaron talking about. She had found a piece of paper screwed up into a ball in the inside pocket of his winter overcoat, which he had given to her for dry cleaning. The piece of paper had an unfinished handwritten address and no phone number: *Sheila new address – 16 Old Farm Yard Buildings.* Leah decided that after her meeting with Larry Nixon she might pay the young lady an unannounced visit; she would Google the address, which had to be somewhere within a 20 mile radius, and then at least she could see for herself where Sheila lived.

The pub car park was busy for early evening, and inside she was surprised to see a group of men already eating, with the small tables all pushed together.

'I see he's sent you to do the dirty work, Mrs Parker?' said Larry, laughing at the sudden appearance of the small foreign lady.

'No, an urgent matter came up that couldn't wait so Aaron asked me to come and talk to you. Who are all these people?'

'A new idea from my wife; we've started to cater for funerals and as we're near to the crematorium and three churches, we have a special menu for the wake.'

'It looks like a good idea with 30 people at a time.'

'Yes, Mrs Parker, and that's what I need to keep hold of this pub: new ideas, new business and preferably more food customers.'

'What do you mean, "keep hold"?'

'The price your husband mentioned is a joke. An old friend is interested in buying it and he's talking £100,000 more than your last offer.'

'That's ridiculous – you can't do that, we had a deal!'

'No we didn't, this is England, not some Lebanese market where you barter all day.'

'How did you know we're from the Lebanon?'

'I didn't, just a guess, but now you've confirmed it for me.'

'That was a long time ago and we want to buy a pub here now and make a new business. We have some small investments already.'

'You still can buy it: make me an offer over £350,000 and I'll consider it for a cash deal, otherwise we've nothing to discuss.'

'I'll ask Aaron to call you tomorrow, but that sounds far too high.'

'You can, but it's simple – you know the minimum amount I'll accept, and if I don't have an offer in writing by Monday I'll sell to the other party. Would you like a drink before you leave?'

Leah was in shock and she needed a drink, but she also guessed that Larry would talk more if she stayed and listened to

271

him. Maybe he was just bluffing. The funeral party were paying their bill to Jill Nixon, and Larry brought Leah a glass of cold white Chardonnay.

'Does he let you out much, Mrs Parker?'

'Leah, please, Larry – you don't mind if I call you that, do you?'

'No, not at all; my wife knows who you are and she's not jealous, or at least not today.'

Larry's joke was missed by Leah: the man was right; she was not let out very often other than to the shops, the hairdresser's or her bridge club.

'Yes, I go out, but I don't have many friends. Without Aaron I'm nervous and shy.'

Larry fell for her charm; she was telling him the opposite of what she was really like as a way to get his sympathy and his confidence to go back to the deal on the pub. She also found him very interesting, and he told her that he had been in the army, but not in the Lebanon other than a transit visit when he was based in Cyprus.

'We spent a lot of our life in Cyprus before we came here. Both sets of parents were from Beirut and after the city was wrecked we all ended up there for safety, then later we came here.'

'Why?'

'My husband's work. So how did you guess we came from Lebanon?'

'Because I was told by a friend who knows your family: an Irishman called Dermott Donnelly.'

Leah gasped, and Larry saw the colour drain away from her face. 'It looks like you need another drink, Leah. Do you know Dermott?'

'Yes. Another drink and I'm paying; here, take my car keys and lock it for me, and I'll get a taxi and collect my car tomorrow. We'll tell my husband I ran out of fuel or I'll find a story; I want to talk to you. Can we go somewhere private?'

Leah's motives were clear: she had to get Larry talking and find out if their cover had been compromised or if Larry just guessing; and whether Dermott Donnelly was really a friend of his or not. She had no immediate loving thoughts about her husband; he had to be having an affair with this girl Sheila – his stories about her didn't add up, and Leah was not going to stand by and be made a fool of. She needed time to think and there was nowhere better than the pub: she would spend the evening having a meal and more drinks. Maybe she would learn more from Larry or maybe not, but she would think more about that the next day.

Chapter 25
The Front Line
Turkey

The route to the mountains and the hiding place of Deniz Korham was in front of Alan and Charlie as the sun was almost at its highest point of the day.

'My arse has gone to sleep from the truck seat. Here, Charlie – just rub it against a tree like a bear.'

Charlie smiled and did as Alan suggested; the first smile for days.

'Yes, well done Alan, that's better.'

'The first kilometre is easy but keep your eyes skinned. I'll be concentrating on the route; you keep your eyes open for unwanted guests.'

The gradient increased and the men's fitness was put to the test. After an hour they stopped for water and Alan checked their position.

'We're 980 metres above sea level and 800 metres higher than the drop off-point. Everything is spot on, Charlie.'

'No it fucking well isn't, mate; look up there, below that crag.'

The path had disappeared into the valley below, and a gorge, about five metres in length, opened out before them with no path or way of getting over it and back on the track.

'Shit, I see what you mean. I reckon the only way we can do it is to rope up together and loop that large tree; we then jump out and swing across the gap to the other side. The worse that can happen is that we swing back to the starting point.'

In his analysis of the situation Alan realised that his life could depend on his colleague, and he still could not work out if he was on his side or not.

'Do we have to go this route? Is there an alternative?'

'We have no alternative, Charlie: the distance round this range is too far for us if we're to keep to the schedule. I'll go first.'

He decided to go first in the dangerous manoeuvre for more than one reason; he knew he could control the situation once he had made the jump.

'Yes, OK: looking at your map I reckon we'd have to detour for about eight kilometres to avoid it.'

'OK, let's do it.'

Alan tied the rope around his waist and made a slipknot to thread through the loop he had made. Charlie threw the other rope around the tree and held it around his waist to test it.

'When I go, Alan, you'll have to knot the rope around that large stone on the other side, then steady it as I make my jump.'

'I know that, but unfortunately we can't have a practice run. Let's check all these knots again together.'

Both men didn't think too long about the jump as time was precious and they needed to clear the mountains while they still had some daylight.

'See you in a couple of minutes, mate.'

Alan walked back several paces and checked that all his gear was tight and in place. The AK47s were tied further down the rope, and they would just pull them up when they were safely across the valley. Alan ran to the edge of the path, then jumped. Charlie took the 80-kilo weight of his colleague and his backpack; the rope tightened, then slackened as Alan hit the ground on the other side.

'OK, Charlie; let me just tie this rope around the rock. Remember that there's nothing behind you once you've undone it from the tree.'

'Yes, no problem. Catch this end.'

Alan caught the rope and braced himself for his jump. Charlie was not as fit as Alan, and heavier, and although he swung in the right direction his jump was short of the opposite landing point. He swung back to his original point and kicked off again, but as he did so he started to fall down the gap between him and Alan.

'Don't look down; look at me!'

Alan could see the fear in his face; a look he had seen on men wounded or dying in action, and a look that he knew meant that

276

his colleague was crippled with the fear of falling over 200 metres to his death. The rope tightened almost unbearably around Alan's waist; his ribs were pushing against his lungs, and he could see the part of the rope around the rock starting to break with the strain. He had one chance to save Charlie. He stepped backwards, and with one large pull took his whole weight and pulled Charlie out of the gap and onto the rocks. The men fell safely on top of each other, laughing.

'Thanks mate; you're some bloody strong soldier.'

'Ah, but I'm not a soldier any longer, Charlie; but still fit enough to lift you up.'

They coiled the rope and released the AK47s, then strapped them to their backs. After they had taken a few minutes' rest, they continued to clamber up a further 300 metres, walking along a two-kilometre ridge to the path leading down the crag to their overnight stop.

'Shouldn't we have oxygen, Alan? I can't breathe.'

'No, at this height we can control our breathing. You're probably in shock; come on, keep going. We've got about an hour's light left and from memory I'm sure there's a hut about 30 minutes from here. If it's still there we get luxury, if it's gone we've a small wood to put the tent up in. The place is in a sheltered spot behind a wood; the winds blow off the mountain and through the valley, and we may have to share the area with a wolf or two so we must remember to stick the silencers onto the Berettas.'

'I hope the hut's intact, I hate bloody camping, especially with four-legged creatures around.'

Charlie's worst fears were about to come true: they reached the hut and it looked like the Turkish army had used it for target practice. Only on side of the building remained, and the rest was a heap of rubble.

'Can't we put our tent up here, Alan, and use the remaining wall as cover against the wind?'

'No, unfortunately not – look on the floor at all the shell cases. This damage has been done in the last few days; whoever was here was gun-happy and we have no real cover if they return. There's one other option, but it'll be nearly dark unless we go now so we need a quick decision.'

'What is it? Tell me quick; I don't want to camp.'

'There's a stone cottage built for travellers, but it's closed for another two months as nobody comes up here at this time. We'd have to break in, so that would tell people we're around.'

'Come on, we must do that; if we can't get in we can camp behind it. Let's go – not easy with these AK47s strapped to our backs, though. Why have we got them, anyway? Surely we won't shoot at the Turkish army, or even the Iranian one; we'd be outnumbered.'

'Only if we're attacked by either army, and avoiding a confrontation's a priority: that's why we're travelling this circular route. We shouldn't be here at all but the real reason we've the guns is in case we meet bandits – maybe Kurds, or just plain bandits after anything they can lay their hands on.'

The men's speed quickened as the light faded, and just before it became totally dark a silhouette of a stone building appeared in the distance. Alan circled it on one side and Charlie the other. The wooden rear door was padlocked, and the small front door was covered by a steel frame and double-padlocked.

'Got to be the back, Alan; this one's down to me.' Charlie produced a piece of wire and in seconds the lock was on the ground. Inside was a steel frame, like on the front door. 'Shit, the padlocks are on the inside, so when they locked up they went out of the front. That's odd: for some reason they're telling intruders go to the front. Surely they don't alarm the place?'

'No, Charlie, I'm not certain about that: it's a government-owned lodge house and they could have any sort of device to protect it.'

'Yes, but not one that would destroy the building. We should use the front, but carefully; I'll lock this up again.'

By this time both men wanted sleep and Alan just wanted Charlie to get the place open so they could have some food and drink. Charlie showed his prowess again by removing the locks on the steel frame in seconds and then carefully picking the old lock on the wooden door.

'Alan, wait – have they alarmed this area somehow? Pass me a torch.'

The torch lit up the interior. It was simple and compact, with four bunks, a washing area in the corner, a table and several chairs. A curtain, which separated a small area from the main room, screened a chemical toilet, the smell giving away its presence.

'Nothing on the door or around it; come in behind and don't move unless I do.'

The torch lit up the curtain.

'We're pissing outside tonight, Alan.'

'Why?'

'Look over my shoulder.'

The torch picked up two small boxes, one on each side of the curtain. The left-hand one had a small red light on it, emitting a beam to the other box on the right.

'That's the security measure, Alan.'

'What is it?'

'It's a simple radio beam; if it's broken it sends a warning somewhere. Relatively short range; say, maximum five kilometres.'

'That makes some sense: there's a checkpoint post about three kilometres from here. It must have a radio link to there so they keep an eye on it. We'll pass near to it tomorrow, so you'll see it for yourself.'

'I'll check the rest of the place. Why don't you unpack outside, then bring the gear inside and we can have some food?'

Alan did a double-take at Charlie's instructions, but agreed and went to get the two rucksacks and the AK47s. He started to unpack the food, but through a crack in the wall illuminated by Charlie's torch he could see his friend and what he was doing. The search of his pack was over, and Charlie was sending a text. Alan decided that now was not the time to tackle him about who he was texting; it was obvious he was reporting to someone, but why from the Turkish mountains? Alan knew he would have to find out who he was contacting, and why, very soon.

Apart from the eerie noises of wolves the noises of the night were few, and morning light arrived early. The two men shared a bottle of water and a trip to the woods, each one guarding the other during morning bowel action, which was rather rapid for Charlie after his brush with death the day before. The remainder of the day's journey was uneventful until they reached the checkpoint that Alan had mentioned the previous day.

'That's it, Charlie: on the right north east at about two o'clock. It gives them a view of the road from both directions; we should just about get the glasses on it. Have a look, but keep the lenses away from the sun.'

'I'm no novice, Alan.'

Charlie was back to his grumpy self, and always after he had used his phone. The message he had sent had received a reply, and Charlie didn't think Alan had heard the vibration noise, but he underestimated him. Alan missed nothing.

'Yes, two guys in soldiers' uniform inside and two more outside looking inside a truck.'

'Is that all? Check again.'

'Yes, definitely – look over there for yourself.'

Alan grabbed the binoculars and concurred with his colleague's assessment.

'What does that mean? Shouldn't there be four soldiers?'

'No, there should be six unless they recently changed routines; I know some of those guys, remember – I worked here. We trained them and shared tactics all to do with UK, USA and Turkish cooperation. We're well enough away and unfortunately we must keep our distance and take the long route into the village where Korham's waiting in case the missing two are on patrol. Once we reach the road we're safe as we'll be hidden by the trees and banking. Out here we're sitting ducks: they won't shoot unless they see the AK47s pointing at them, but I don't have a story, do you, Charlie?'

'No; my Turkish may be handy but I haven't got any believable lies ready.'

The route Alan had planned did exactly as he had said and kept them a safe distance from the checkpoint. The village came into view, but suddenly so too did an old Nissan 4x4 car. They scrambled behind a rock as the vehicle sped past them, and as they started to move out into the open again an army Jeep shot past them, catching the old car up very quickly. To their horror, the Nissan turned back towards them.

'We've got to do something or those soldiers will see us. Have you still got your Beretta silencer handy? I repacked mine in my pack.'

'Yes, Alan – here, take it. What are you going to do?'

'Watch, and keep your head down!'

As the car got closer Alan took careful aim at the offside front tyre and put three bullets into it, two of them hitting the middle of the Dunlop trademark. The vehicle carried on for another hundred metres, then as the tyre ripped apart from the wheel, the Nissan turned over and burst into flames. The chasing army Jeep stopped and saw the men still inside, and left for the checkpoint to report what had happened. The emergency services in Turkey did not operate in many areas, and unless the patrol came back it would be likely that the bodies would be eaten by wolves before the burnt-out car was inspected and removed.

'Well done, that was good shooting.'

'Yes, but I killed two people, Charlie.'

'You had no choice. If we'd been discovered those army guys would have opened fire; they both had guns in their hands as they chased the Nissan.'

'I saw that, Charlie, but it doesn't make me feel any better.'

The men completed the journey to the town of Muradiye, taking cover behind the banking of the road which kept them completely out of sight. After a few minutes they found the house from the map provided by Brian Wilson.

'So this is it, Charlie: a day and a half to get here, roughly to plan, and the same hopefully to get back, with or without Deniz Korham. Now, before we go in: who are you texting on your phone, and who did you speak to in the house when I was in my room?'

For the first time since they started Charlie Baxter looked annoyed, and his eyes flashed Alan a warning.

'Alan, it's not important to this trip. One day I'll have to square things with you and I will, but I'm asking you now to please trust me. We can talk as soon as we're back home, I promise.'

'Don't like it, Charlie, but for old times' sake I'll wait, but don't let me down on this mission. You realise that if I find you are a threat to my safety I'll have to deal with you?'

'I know Alan, and I also know you'll trust me.'

Fisher just nodded. Charlie had seen how easily Alan killed the men in the car, and he knew that if he messed up his partner would be ruthless.

Chapter 26
Clandon Regis Golf Club

The golf club was an ideal meeting place for Chief Superintendent Dick White and Aaron Parker. Both were unknown at the club – they didn't play golf, but the general public were always welcome, provided they bought a drink or had some food.

'Aaron Parker, my apologies. Please take a seat.'

'Hello, Chief Superintendent. What are you apologising for?'

'Just that we haven't spoken much recently, but my men are keeping an eye out for your safety, of course.'

'I think you say here in the UK, "And pigs might fly." Appropriate, don't you think?'

'That's not very nice, Mr Parker; maybe we don't watch you as much as we should have been doing, but that's because we know you can handle yourself and we respect your privacy.'

'To the point please, Chief, I've another meeting soon.'

'You knew Major Barrington well, didn't you? Please don't give me any of that crap that he was just a friend.'

'OK, you know my background; you know what my business was, and the British government was one of my biggest customers. Barrington was another customer; he paid well and I'd no problems with him.'

'So who killed him, then?'

'Not me. I'll ask around, but as Paddy Mulligan is also dead I'd say it could be the same person; it's like a clean-up operation. If you consider the Fisher deaths as well, Barrington may have lost the plot – perhaps he committed suicide. I heard he used to get depressed, and often spent weeks in the army sick bay.'

'On my desk I've got three cases and three deaths: the Fishers, one death; Barrington, a fake bomb in Tolworth, plus the RUC have the death of Paddy Mulligan at the top of their list. The connection to all of this is you, as no doubt Mulligan supplied the explosives and you supplied him, even though it was many years ago. This isn't my war, Aaron, for many reasons: I've my own issue and that's nearly been dealt with. If we can say Barrington committed suicide we will, but that's out of my hands.'

'Talk with your colleagues at SIS. They must know who Paddy Mulligan worked with, or the RUC should know. I've no other connections that spring to mind.'

'That's what I wanted to hear. Thanks, Aaron; let's keep in touch, and if you hear anything at all please call me immediately.'

The sudden change in the policeman's attitude worried Parker, and he guessed that he'd said something that calmed Chief Superintendent White down.

'All right, but I'm not involved now; I'm concentrating on a different line of business which is more secure.'

'Tell me more.'

'No, it's confidential: my customers are countries again, but not materials, just information; and without information decisions on the future plans of many nations can't be made.'

'Sounds like something big. Perhaps I should watch you more.'

'You can if you like; it's all legal.'

'That brings me to my last question: how well did you know the late Gordon Fisher?'

Aaron Parker was not prepared for that question, and he crossed his arms and stared at White.

'Lost your tongue, Aaron?'

'That man did his job very well – perhaps even too well. He was the best man in a shit job, and calmly helped put away the bad soldiers without fuss. How well did I know him? Not very well personally, although I once had dinner with him as he wanted to tap my brain on some logistical issues. I did have a short meeting with him afterwards in Cyprus, but he'd convicted the soldiers without my evidence, so really we'd nothing to talk about.

'You know Alan Fisher's brother was killed in action. The enquiry was held in Kabul, but not of course with his father involved; after a hearing and ignoring conflicting evidence from the SIB, the enquiry – not, in this case, a court martial – gave a verdict of accidental death. It was all based on the forensic evidence and an enemy bullet found in his temple. No British soldier appeared to be involved, and it was logged as a pure accident. Are you saying, Aaron, that it wasn't an accident?'

'No, of course not, but at that dinner I had with Gordon I felt he was telling me to pass on a message to an Irishman I met once.'

'What was the message?'

'He just said, "You know my eldest boy died and they said it was an accident. I know more, and one day I'll sort it."'

'It was strange for him to tell you about his son.'

'At the time I thought it was, then I realised my connection was the only way for him to get a message passed to the right man. When we briefly met in Cyprus he just told me in passing that the other business we discussed would be resolved, and he thanked me. I assumed he'd found out what really happened, and I never saw Gordon Fisher again after that.'

'You didn't tell me who the Irishman was.'

'Didn't I? Mulligan, of course, but he was just a postbox for others and I don't know who the actual message was given to.'

'Another brick wall, Aaron.'

'Depends on how good you guys are, but there're a lot of Irishmen who don't like the British, remember?'

'I don't need reminding of that, Aaron. Thanks for the meeting, and if your memory finds its conscience give me a call. Doubt it will, but you never know.'

'Wait a minute, Chief Superintendent: you asked me about Gordon Fisher, but Paddy Mulligan told me you and he were good friends once but you fell out over something.'

'Forget it; it's not your business, Aaron. Off you go.'

Parker knew that one day he might need a favour from Dick White, although he suspected he was holding something back in the investigation of the Fishers' deaths. He decided not to push him further on Gordon Fisher: he needed the artificial help of the British government and they both knew it. He was uneasy about the policeman; the meeting had more concerned with what each of them knew about the Fishers, Mulligan and Barrington, and not much else.

As he left Clandon Regis Golf Club on the narrow road with speed humps, Dick White waited for Parker to pass him, then he pulled over onto the verge near the 16th tee box – a dangerous spot to stay for too long – and dialled a mobile number.

'It's me, and I've got to be brief. I had a meeting with Parker and he's about to guess some of the recent activities; no more from me other than we're even now and you don't owe me anything. I suggest we both stay away from Belfast.'

The answering machine was convenient as he didn't want to talk to the person at the other end. He was a dangerous man, and one Dick White hoped not to see again.

Aaron Parker's day was yet to begin. He arrived back at his apartment and was puzzled to find his wife out – still with Larry

Nixon, he presumed. He laughed to himself at the thought of her sat with him drinking pints of Courage Bitter, but had he known the truth, he wouldn't have been laughing. He made a call to Sheila Hamilton and had a shower, and then the phone rang. He expected it to be his wife, but then an angry voice shouted down the phone.

'Aaron, it's Mohammed here; you promised to phone me.'

'I'm really sorry, Mohammed, I got stopped by the police.'

'Not serious, I hope?'

'No, just clearing up an old matter. So what's happening?'

'The information we want is coming. Contact has been made and I hope to have something for you next week for certain. It's worth £1 million to you, so make sure I get it.'

'No, Mohammed; £2 million if it's as good as I think it'll be.'

'We'll see. Call me the minute it arrives.'

Parker was not short of money, but £2 million could be easily used in his next project, although he knew he had to verify that the information he was getting was reliable, which wouldn't be easy with the product he would be analysing and selling.

Chapter 27
Alice Miller, née Smith

'Aaron's coming round here soon; you'd better go, Alice.'

'Yes, I spent the afternoon following him round Surrey. He met a guy I've seen before; I think he's a policeman who interviewed me once. They drove separately to Clandon Regis Golf Club and talked for half an hour.'

'How much is Bill Knowles paying you for this surveillance work?'

'Not a lot, but it's easy money and if it helps me get that fat introduction fee from him it's worth it. I've also done some debt collecting for him; it's amazing how quickly people pay up when they see me – men, that is; he doesn't give me debts owed by women. It's my last day tomorrow, then I think Bill is going to risk it and go and see Larry Nixon himself; he's still his accountant and they need to wrap things up, and he owes him money. I reckon Leah Parker has gone to see Nixon today; she left the apartment at the same time as Aaron and drove off in the direction of the pub.'

'I doubt it, Alice, she's a lightweight.'

'Yes, but she's a lot of sex appeal and definitely someone Larry Nixon would fancy so maybe they could do a deal, but on the other hand I hear Jill's back and will be watching every move Larry makes. No doubt Larry will be watching Bill as well in case he has another go at Jill.'

'He wouldn't dare – Larry would sort him out properly this time. By the way, I bumped into that hunk Alan Fisher the other day, you remember him?'

'Yes I sure do, who could forget him? Are we seeing him again, then?'

'Nothing arranged but he said he'd call me; he has a girlfriend but we could do him a special price.'

'You could; he could have me for free, Sheila. I've still got to be careful though: changing my name from Miller to Smith got rid of the police for the moment and I don't want them to get on my back every time there's a vice case.'

'Why not? The undercover work you did was brilliant, and they caught everyone in that group of Chinese prostitutes.'

'For my own safety I can't help them again; I think there are still people looking for me. At least two of the men who gave evidence took photographs as I left the Old Bailey after the trial.'

'Did you have to take on any punters when you were on your undercover job?'

'Yes, just one; he turned out to be a policeman which is another reason I don't want them finding me. If Alan Fisher's working with the police to find his parents' killers my name could come up as he's local and knows a lot of people.'

'I doubt it, Alice – if we entertain him we could be very discreet and use the rear entrance etc.'

'Quick, let me out that back door – I can hear someone coming along the corridor.'

Alice left her friend's apartment with only one thing on her mind: Alan Fisher. She'd tried to divert her friend's attention away from him, as she wanted him all to herself. How could she find him? He lived locally; maybe Bill knew his address. She walked past Aaron Parker's car and kicked the front wheel. She hated him for his arrogance and the way he treated her friend. He was getting to her, and she didn't want anything more to do with him once the pub deal was closed. She needed the money she had been promised for the introduction of Parker to Nixon and she had to hope that Larry Nixon fell for Leah Parker's charm; the contract he should have signed with Bill Knowles was still valid, providing that Parker was the buyer.

Sheila delayed opening the door to her apartment to give Alice time to get away unseen. Parker suspected someone had been with her as he noticed the two coffee cups on the table, and as Sheila pulled the curtains he put his hand on the cups, which were still warm.

'You've been busy today. Who's been here?'

'Nobody you know, and anyway, that's my business.'

'Look, Sheila, I pay you for near-exclusivity. If I find you're doing a job or two on the side, I'll find someone else.'

'Yes, sorry. It was just an old school friend: a girl called Anita. She left just before you arrived.'

Parker was not convinced, but he needed Sheila: she suited his lifestyle and he dropped the inquisition as she made him a cocktail.

'You're late, Aaron. What have you been doing?'

'Not a lot, just a brief meeting with the police. They wanted some information on a guy I knew who just died.'

'Oh dear. Was he a local man?'

'No, it was in London and it was nasty but nobody will be crying over him.'

Chapter 28
Deniz Korham

The two men didn't need to knock; they had arrived at the agreed time as Deniz Korham was making coffee in the kitchen area of the very small house. They entered with the Berettas cocked, but he was alone. Charlie checked the other rooms, and apart from a camp bed and a rucksack the place was empty of any furniture. In the kitchen there was some fresh food: bread rolls and cheese prepared for the visitors.

'Hello. You're the men from England, I know that.'

His voice was heavily accented, a cross between American and European, but he seemed to be getting his words more or less correct as he spoke, and Alan went through his rucksack to find the paperwork he had been given. The first sheet was a computer-printed photograph, which perfectly matched Korham.

'Yes, I'm Alan and this is Charlie. We're working for the British government and they sent us here to talk to you, so first we've some questions. Charlie speaks some Turkish and I have the translation for the questions; I'll record everything. Please reply in your language, especially on the technical points. I'll then ask you some questions in English; simple ones and not connected to the nuclear information which we're told you'll give us. We've no longer than one hour to do this interview as we all have to get back to our overnight stop before it's completely dark. Do you understand, Mr Korham?'

The man nodded and offered the visitors Turkish coffee in small cups. They took it from him so as not to offend him, but the sweet taste almost made Charlie retch. Alan had drunk it many times before and took a small sip to be polite. Charlie sat directly across from the Turk and stared at him, but Korham made no attempt to look away from his interviewer; he simply folded his arms and sat up square to the small table. He was nervous but professional, and it was obvious that he had been trained by someone on how to deal with interrogation. His controlled body language was noted by Alan, and details of it would later be passed to the SIS.

Charlie slowly asked the questions in what sounded like perfect Turkish. Alan knew some of the words, but with paragraphs and sentences it was difficult for him to make out where Charlie was up to as he looked at the copy script.

'Mr Korham, I'll call you Deniz; you call me Charlie and my colleague Alan.'

The Turk smiled and answered 'Yes' in perfect English.

'What was your job at the Lasop Plant, and what's made there?'

'I am an engineer and responsible for the plant's power. We make electronic components.'

'What power is that?'

'Today one part is coal-powered and other areas are oil-powered.'

'Have or are the company building nuclear power to operate the plant?'

'Yes, one reactor.'

'When will that be ready?'

'Soon, I think; maybe it's nearly ready to use. Maybe two months' time.'

'You say maybe; why don't you know?'

Korham shuffled on his chair and looked at Alan. In English he said, 'Look, I don't know everything; the company are careful not to be specific on many things that would present a security risk. Gentlemen, please let's talk in English and if it's a complicated question Charlie can put it in Turkish to satisfy your bosses. I was brought up first in the USA, and although I had to give up my passport some days I still feel like a westerner.'

'I agree; carry on, Charlie, but read the English lines and Deniz you must say if you don't understand.'

Charlie picked up his crib sheet and continued in English. 'Does the plant have the ability to make anything else other than electronic components?'

'Not to the best of my knowledge.'

'Has anybody told you or have you heard about plans to use the plant to make a nuclear weapon of mass destruction?'

Korham paused for the first time. 'Give it me in Turkish, Charlie, so I give you the right answer?'

Charlie was irritated: one minute he was speaking in English and now he was back in Turkish. He guessed it was a delaying tactic so Korham could think how to best word his vital reply.

'I can only answer that question to your superiors when we're in England. Understand please that doesn't mean yes or no.'

Charlie repeated the question in both languages. He hated the delaying tactic, and looked at Alan for support. Korham kept silent and Charlie started to sweat; he wondered if he had phrased the question correctly and repeated it.

'Yes or no? It's a straightforward question.'

'You have my answer,' said Korham quickly in an excited voice.

Alan interrupted. 'For my benefit, in English the question from Charlie is "Are there any plans at your plant, or other plants near it or that you know of, to make nuclear weapons in the near future?" Sorry, to keep it simple I should add the words "and can they be made soon?"'

The Turk replied in English. 'I know what you say both in my language and yours, and my answer is that as far as I know at the moment no nuclear weapons have been made, but the equipment at the plant I work at could be changed to make a nuclear device. I know nothing about what other plants make.'

'That's it, is it Mr Korham?'

In his impatience, Alan decided to address their new friend formally, which seemed to annoy him.

'No. I've this package for you, and inside it there is information which may better answer your questions. It's what you call my passage to England.'

Korham handed Alan a large brown leather book tied with a black ribbon, and some damage that showed that at some time it had been sealed with wax. It was packed with line drawings of components, with a key numbering system for each one of them and a glossary at the back of the book. Each component was described in detail, with measurements for each part, and cross- referenced to a section in the book with photographs.

'What the fuck is that thing, Charlie?'

'My guess is that it's a manual describing how to assemble a nuclear weapon. It looks like it's from the USA and been very well used. Maybe it's just been spread out and photographed and copies made, as you can see several folds on the pages.'

Alan abandoned the Turkish questioning. 'Mr Korham, your English is good enough for us but we need to carry on quickly. Where did the book come from and how did you get it?

'I got it from my boss. He got it from USA and they paid many millions of dollars.'

'Are they using any of the information?'

'I don't think so yet, but they've made many copies and translated them into the Persian language.'

'I have to make a call. Stay here with Charlie and have another coffee.'

Alan left the house and dialled a preset number on the sat phone and pressed a scrambler switch.

'Molly, it's me, Alan; the contact has a leather-bound manual with *GHT2016* stamped in red on the cover and below *Detroit Engineering*, it's dated 2007 and it looks genuine. One question: does that warrant me bringing the guy back? Call me in fifteen minutes.'

'Understood Alan, bye.'

SIS were being given a short time to say yes or no, but as they had full authority and clear instructions on what to expect from the Americans the book was a new development, and a phone call to Washington was needed. Alan went back inside to find Charlie and Korham talking in Turkish about football.

'Our office will call me back very soon, so let's do the questions I'd planned.'

Korham looked worried, but nodded.

'You were born and lived in the USA, and have an American and a Turkish passport?'

'I was born in the USA and I did have a US passport, but it expired and if you have a US passport you can't have one for another country. I therefore have a Turkish passport and an Iranian work permit.'

'What would happen if you went back to Iran? They must be looking for you.'

'I would probably be sent for trial in Tehran and then I could be deported or executed for treason; almost definitely if they found I have this book. Actually I do have two options, the other being Israel. People are looking for me from Iran but so far not round here – some Turkish troops arrived today for a training session and are camped a kilometre south, and I heard they're everywhere tomorrow but they won't be interested in me.'

'OK, that's a problem we may have to deal with on the journey, Deniz.'

Charlie was jumping up and down; he needed to speak to Alan alone. He pointed to the front door and Alan followed him outside.

'That book is genuine, I'm certain, and I actually think he's OK. He's a lot to tell when he's safe but his answers are his passport to safety; my view is we should take him back.'

The sat phone made one bleep and Molly spoke. 'Yes, but you must get the book as well. Send a message to the house in Van: the code word's *Jell*, and we'll be at the place tomorrow.'

The phone went dead, and Alan smiled. 'OK, let's get going. You speak to Korham and tell him we're moving, but no details. You take the book; he'll guess we're going back, so quickly reassure him then pack up.'

Alan left the building and switched the recorder back to check he had the conversations recorded. Everything was in order. He did it outside so Charlie couldn't see him, then he called Almas on the sat phone.

'I haven't time to play the recorder now – please come tomorrow and we can play it together; I need your view. The man will be with us.'

'Fine, see you then.'

Alan went back inside. 'Right, have you briefed him, Charlie? Ask Mr Korham the code word, then we go.'

'It's OK, I heard the question, Alan. The code word is *Beckham*. No, sorry; it's *Jell*; I was joking.'

Nobody smiled. Alan put the Berretta back in the holster.

'Good job, Mr Korham, or I'd have had to shoot you.'

Charlie was amused at the joke, but Alan was in charge and he just scowled as the man tried to be clever. They packed up to leave in silence. The house was locked and Korham put the key under a stone; the coffee cups were put in his bag and all traces of rubbish were pushed into his anorak pockets. The three men left Muradiye just in time.

'Look over there: it's a lot less than 200 soldiers; more like 12 or 15 that are on the exercise. What you think, Mr Korham?'

'I think problem – we have to run now; the soldiers are Iranian.'

Without hesitation the three men took the route they had used into Muradiye, but keeping out of the line of vision of the Iranians.

'We run for ten minutes, then stop and assess the position on a one-minute break; then run for another 15 minutes until we can see the path to the stone cottage. Then we just walk quickly and we'll get there before dark.' Alan made his instructions very clear, and Charlie and Korham both nodded in agreement. The one-minute break came quickly; they drank water and saw the Iranians go in the opposite direction.

'They're going to Muradiye to grab somebody; they'll know within an hour that I've left and am with you. We'll have been seen and the locals will be frightened and tell them everything.'

The Turk was excited and his English was breaking down, but Alan and Charlie understood and nodded their agreement. After nearly 30 minutes the path came into sight and the three had a short break behind a large rock face.

'OK, now we make for the stone hut; we stopped there last night, Mr Korham, so we know it's comfortable and quite safe provided we don't set the alarm off.'

As they stood up they looked down the valley in horror, the Turkish army was about 500 metres away.

'Get down!' Alan hissed. 'What are they doing?'

'They're inspecting that car, Alan, and by the look of it they're pulling the bodies out of it. The wolves wouldn't have had time to get them it yet.'

Korham pointed at the vehicle. 'That's the type of car used by bandits. They're old cars; I think they steal them and eventually crash them. The soldiers at the checkpoint must have caught them.'

Alan and Charlie didn't speak. They knew what had happened, and Korham should not be told about it. The light was starting to fail and they carefully climbed away from the valley, and eventually the stone cottage came into sight. From the outside it was as they had left it, and Charlie pointed out the beam security device, which highly amused the Turk.

'It's Russian. There are many in Iran, and the problem is that sometimes a mobile phone signal can set off the alarm.' Korham was critical of the cheap device, but Charlie had an idea for it.

'Thanks, good to know that,' Alan remarked. 'So none of your dodgy texts tonight please, Charlie.'

After the race to the cottage the three men were exhausted.

'I've some bread and cheese we can share and Charlie has some water. Save the bottle; you pee in it here, not outside; if you need a shit you have to wait, do you understand?'

With zero light in the cottage the three men ate their supper, and 'Deniz' Korham was given the spare blanket as he prepared for sleep. Charlie checked the doors were locked and put a small device on the window.

'What's that, Charlie?'

'It's a movement censor, but it makes no noise. I've a receiver halfway up my arm; if anyone comes within 50 metres outside we'll know: it just presses my arm.'

'Slick. Is it foolproof?'

'No, sometimes it gets a bird, but not out here.'

The weak joke was the last thing said as the three men fell asleep.

The night seemed short; daylight was starting to appear through the cracks in the shutters as Alan pushed Charlie and Korham to wake them up.

'Get up you two, we've company. It looks like they aren't coming this way, but they'll hit our ridge path in about 20 minutes if they keep going straight.'

Korham looked at them through his binoculars. 'They're my countrymen: they're Kurds, and not many. They'll walk the ridge path, then go back to their mountain camp; I think it's a regular route and when I came back from the USA I had to serve in the army for two years. They quietly train here; it annoys the Turks and occasionally there's violence.'

'I thought you said you were a Turk? That must have been awkward for you.'

'I'm a Kurd, but as I lived out of the country and then returned with my father I stayed away from our past. My father did not; he's here somewhere but I'll never see him. I keep quiet that my family were Kurds, and there's nothing more to say.'

Charlie was unhappy about his comment and the way he said it, but Korham didn't want to discuss the Kurds or his Turkish army career. The three men set off again, walking quickly to keep ahead of the army group. With the main road in sight and about two kilometres from the waiting truck, they stopped and took cover in a wood.

'What's the matter, Alan, are we nearly there?'

'Look, it's two more of those cars. Are they bandits, Mr Korham?'

'Yes, they're waiting for any traffic coming down the main road.'

'Shit, our pickup will be there soon and he's unarmed. He'll be attacked and shot, and they'll take the truck. What do you reckon, Charlie?'

'We could take them out, but it looks like there are six or more and I bet they've similar guns to us.'

Korham put his hands up. 'No, they have better – they'll have a rocket launcher and they'll get us before you can get near enough to open fire.'

Charlie shook his head. 'I guessed something like this might happen, and I think it's time to attract the attention of the Turkish army, who I think will be near the checkpoint. We know they're just about a kilometre behind us so I wired up a little device. I couldn't sleep last night so I dismantled that beam alarm in the cottage and what behind it was a little surprise. It didn't send a message to the checkpoint, Alan, it was worse than that: it was wired up to a detonator attached to a small pack of plastic explosive in the fireplace.'

Korham went white. 'Fuck me,' he said in a perfect, but American sounding accent.

Alan and Charlie laughed.

'Don't worry, Korham; trust us. You're an important person and we don't intend to lose you now, so please save your swear words for England. I think I can guess what you've done, Charlie.'

'Yes, mate; lucky I had my phone now, isn't it?'

'Go for it: that patrol will go straight in the direction of those two cars, and they'll think those bandits have caused the explosion. Hope it works, Charlie.'

'So do I, Alan. I'm sure it will, and I didn't like that front door anyway.'

Charlie went out into the open, but still camouflaged himself from the cars in the valley as he took the back plate off the phone and connected the transmitter.

'I bet it's the hash key, Charlie.'

'Dead right, mate. Here goes.'

The explosion was deafening as it resonated around the mountains. The two cars didn't move for a fatal minute or two as they had no idea where the noise was coming from, but eventually they worked it out as they could see the dust in the distance. They raced off towards the road, and the army Jeeps suddenly appeared, 600 metres behind them and gaining all the time.

'Come on, we're going now as well; we'll be at the truck in ten minutes and off in the opposite direction. Well done, Charlie.'

'Thanks, Alan – regrettably explosives and IED devices are my baby, but I'm not proud of it.'

Alan let the comment go; he would ask him what he meant later.

The truck was just about to leave when the driver saw the three men running towards him.

'Jell,' said Alan; as it was a different truck he had to be sure. Before the driver could speak, a man dressed in khaki jumped from the front passenger seat and without any discussion he pulled an old revolver from his belt, pointed it at Charlie and shot him in the shoulder. He then turned the gun towards Alan and Korham. Alan had already anticipated the man's next move, and in a flying leap knocked him to the ground, but not before he had pulled the trigger again. Charlie crawled under the truck, in pain from the flesh wound in his shoulder, but in even more desperate need to get to his rucksack, which had fallen on the floor with him. He needed his Beretta quickly. The second bullet from the revolver missed its target but hit the driver between the eyes and he slumped over the wheel of the truck as blood gushed from the wound.

Alan wrestled with the killer and the gun finally fell to the ground. The next move happened so quickly that Korham and Charlie couldn't believe it. Alan somehow got behind the man, and although he was at least four inches taller he got his right arm in the position he wanted. The faint crack like a twig was followed by the man falling to the floor like a sack of potatoes; he twitched, and then was totally still. Alan leaned over him checked his pulse, then turned away and was sick next to the wheel of the truck. The man was dead; Alan had broken his neck.

Alan pulled the body to the side of the dirt track road and pushed it over a gap between the road and a slope down to a deep crag some 50 metres below them. The wolves would get this body, and it might never be found. Charlie jumped to his feet and checked through his binoculars, and saw the Turkish army vehicles through clouds of freshly disturbed roadside dust. He estimated they were four or five kilometres away from them.

'We've got a maximum five or six minutes before the Turkish army get here; let's hope they don't start shooting before we get out of range. Come on, Alan, the bandit is dead; let's get out of here pronto.'

Alan nodded. 'Deniz, push the driver into the back through the canvas sheet cover then sit in the front with me; Charlie, jump in the back with him and loop his trouser belt to the lorry framework to secure him – he's past help. We have to drive like hell now, so fasten a rope to your body and tie it to the truck frame. I'll drive, but give me my AK47 and get yours cocked as well as your Beretta. I'm really sorry, mate, are you OK? You were standing up with your back to me so I assumed the bandit's bullet missed you, but now I can see the blood down your arm.'

'I think so; the slug took a piece of flesh right out of my shoulder so it hurts like hell but hopefully the bullet didn't lodge in my skin. Let's go, though, and I'll get it looked at properly later.

'Get yourself cleaned up: the first aid kit is bolted to the floor somewhere, Wilson told me before we left, and Charlie for fuck's sake make sure that rope to the frame is tight otherwise you'll finish up in the road. You ready, Deniz?'

The engine was still running and Alan quickly worked out the gearbox with a manoeuvre that suddenly had them going backwards. He expertly spun the truck and accelerated away to a top speed of about 25 miles an hour, crashing up and down as the potholes grabbed the thick-treaded tyres.

'Sorry guys, hold tight; fortunately I know a lot of this area and also a couple of short cuts through the woods. We've got to get away from those guys behind us and we can't start shooting at the Turkish army unless it's us or them and that's not a battle I'd relish. It's definitely a problem, win or lose.'

The bottles of water and a flask of Turkish coffee had been left for them in the lorry, but most of it was spilled as Alan flung the vehicle around a couple of bends through an area of forest full of hairpin bends.

'You sure you know where you're going, mate?'

'I do, thankfully, Charlie; just like you know your explosives.'

Charlie didn't reply. The pain from his shoulder had got much worse, and he found the first aid box and managed to wrap a bandage around the wound.

'Can you pick up the binoculars, Charlie; they're behind my seat somewhere, and see if those trucks are catching up with us?'

After groping around on the truck floor Charlie finally found the scuffed binoculars, but to use them he had to move to the back of the truck. He slackened his improvised safety belt and undid a canvas flap, a move that would save his life.

'Nobody behind, Alan, but I can see dust on the hill to our le—'

His speech stopped as a dozen or more bullets ripped through the canvas in the exact spot where he had been sitting. Their pursuers had taken a bigger shortcut than Alan, and they were almost alongside them, like in a western cowboy film.

'Shall I return fire, Alan?'

'No, stay down – and you, Deniz. I have a job to do; we're stopping.'

The truck came to an abrupt halt about 30 metres from a narrow wooden suspension bridge, just wide enough for one vehicle with a gorge some one hundred metres below. Alan jumped out and inspected the construction, then quickly jumped back in the truck and accelerated across the bridge. The construction of the bridge was crude yet effective, but Alan was taking no chances. He slammed the truck directly into second gear and drove very slowly, and after what seemed like an age they reached the other side.

'Deniz, stay here, mate, and if I cock up, drive off. You know where to go, and you may be lucky and outrun the people behind.'

Alan left the truck with an army knife in his hand. He climbed down into the ravine to examine the ropes that held the bridge together. Fortunately they were not metal but a strong twisted twine; four ropes held the base and two the top. He knew that if he succeeded in cutting the bottom ones the bridge could fall on him, so like a sailor going up a mast he climbed up to the top ones, which for some reason were thinner and easy to cut. He quickly released them, then slid down to the ones holding the road slats. He had cut through two when the trucks reached the bridge.

'Deniz, take the truck 50 metres away; those guys will be shooting in a few seconds.'

The truck moved away into the forest, and Alan Fisher was on his own. At first the Turkish soldiers couldn't work out what was happening, but then they saw Alan and started to fire at him, and he was a sitting duck as he cut through the last rope. The flimsy bridge slipped past him into the ravine as bullets smashed into the wood, which was the break Alan needed to clamber back up onto the road. As he jumped into the passenger seat of the truck bullets hit the wheel arches and the fuel tank, but they had escaped. Deniz accelerated through more forest, then suddenly the road into Patnos appeared in front of them and the unwelcome escort was marooned behind them on the wrong side of the ravine.

'Pull over, Deniz, I've one more diversion tour to do so we avoid going past the police compound.'

The two men swopped seats and Charlie took the opportunity to pull some canvas back and investigate the petrol smell that was almost knocking him out.

'Alan, I reckon we've little fuel left; one of those bullets hit the tank and it's been dripping out since we left the bridge.'

'Yes, I can smell it, but if we stop we'll have a big problem as there's nowhere to hide here until it's dark and that's hours away. We just have to hope this tank lasts us; contingency plan comes later.'

Nothing was said in the last few kilometres before Patnos. Eventually buildings came in sight and Alan took a risk: he went straight behind the police compound and they were lucky – the place looked deserted, with no police to be seen. The truck stopped dead in its tracks 30 metres from the house: it was out of fuel, and the three men laughed as Brian Wilson shouted at them from the top step where he was waiting.

'Don't park there, you'll get towed away. Tell the driver.'

Wilson then saw that something was wrong with Alan behind the wheel, and he joined him at the back of the truck. With

Korham at the wheel, they pushed it behind the house and out of sight.

'Please to meet you, Mr Korham; your room is number eight and we leave at 6am tomorrow for the flight back to the UK. I have many questions for you, and Mr Fisher and Mr Baxter's work is now over. We can talk as we travel.'

Wilson changed his tone when he caught sight of Charlie Baxter. 'Shit, what happened to you, Charlie, and where's the driver?'

Alan looked grim. 'We had a major incident, Brian, and I need to debrief you fully; we weren't compromised but it was a very close call. Charlie needs urgent treatment.'

'Yes, come inside: through the second door there's a room for medical problems; it happens now and then. Almas is next door, I believe – tell her about everything that happened to your shoulder and she'll deal with it or get someone to help you.'

Alan Fisher just looked at the truck as Brian Wilson talked to Charlie. One tyre was flat and the fuel tank had not one but three holes in it – why it hadn't blown was a miracle. One of the canvas sides must have had fifty holes in it and resembled a string vest.

'We were very lucky, but Charlie and I were always a good team. Then again—'

'Yes, you were very lucky by the state of that vehicle. I'll phone in a minute to get the driver's body moved; what did you mean when you said "Then again"?'

314

'You don't miss much, Brian; it must be your training. Something's not right with Charlie, but that's for another day; he did well on this trip and one day he might tell me what's eating him.'

'Alan, give me the book now, please, for safekeeping. I'll take it and then you'll be free of the responsibility; it will leave for London tonight on the overnight plane which leaves in two hours. By the time we get back our security people will have studied it and will want to talk to you, so get a good rest and I'll see you at the airfield tomorrow.'

'I get it: you don't want me to read it and know how to make a weapon of mass destruction.'

'No, don't be silly – your job's over; please relax.'

Alan went to his room and Korham to his. Almas had patched Charlie up, and while he waited for the doctor he slipped out unseen to the toilet to send a text, which simply said *He's interested.* Alan had guessed he was up to something, but as the mission was nearly over he couldn't be bothered to question him that day, but he would when the time was right. There was a knock on his door, and Almas Mehmet walked in and kissed him.

'You obviously had a few problems?'

'Yes, everyone was out in the area we were working: bandits, soldiers and a couple of unforeseen obstacles, but we did it and stayed alive. I'm really sorry about the driver. It was nothing to do with our mission; those guys just wanted his truck. He died instantly.'

'I know his wife and family and I'll go and see her tomorrow. She'll be very well paid by your bosses as they don't want any problems with the police, and they'll be paid as well.'

'Are you going to stay a while here in Patnos, Almas?'

'No, only a day or so to make sure loose ends are tied, and then before you leave I want to see you again; I'll come back after you've had dinner and stay with you.'

Alan's groin tingled in anticipation, and guilt hit hard for ten seconds. Then he relaxed and thought to himself, *What the hell am I worried about? I'm a free man; yes, I've a girlfriend, but that's for another day.*

'Give me your AK47, Alan; I have the other one from Charlie and his Beretta as well. Did you fire either of your weapons?'

'Just the Beretta. Can I keep it, Almas?'

'You shouldn't really, but later I'll just say you've still got it if they ask. Take this spare magazine and the silencer, and be careful, Alan; it sounds like you're planning to use it in the UK.'

'No, but it's insurance just in case. This baby is like gold dust in England; I hope it's not needed.'

'Tell the First Officer on the plane that you have the gun. He stays here regularly and knows me, and I'll clear the weapon with him. He may take it off you and give it back after you've passed through your arrival checks.'

316

'Yes, great, Almas; thanks. Can you listen to the second recording I made? The first I'm not worried about, so can you take the machine and translate that one later, and do the second one now, please?'

'Yes, give it to me.'

He handed her the recorder and she scribbled down the conversation in English, stopping occasionally to correct her words. From her facial expression she didn't like the two-minute conversation between Charlie and Korham – neither of them had seen Alan switch the machine on or off, and so the dialogue was quite interesting. Almas played it through twice to make sure she had got it right.

'That's it, Alan, but I don't quite understand it.'

Charlie had said the same thing to Korham three times so he understood it: another government wanted the information he had, and they would pay a big price for a copy of the book. Korham said he understood, and the book was on a micro camera film in his bag. Charlie asked for it and Korham said they would discuss a price when they were back in England, and they argued a bit but in the end Charlie agreed.

'What does it all mean, Alan?'

'The book is from an engineering company in the USA; it's highly confidential stuff but on its own it's nothing special to us. The interesting part is what else Korham can tell us about where he was working, and not the just about the book. Our security people will get inside his head for a few days, and if he cooperates he'll be allowed to stay in the UK with a British passport, but I discovered that he doesn't have an American one as he had to give it up once he got a Turkish one. The Yanks are sure to want to speak to him; he could finish up back in the USA. Lots of scenarios, Almas, but I'll be free of it all once I hand him over to the security services.'

Morning arrived quickly after the three men talked for hours and finally went to bed at midnight. Korham was a Kurd, but he kept his stories to himself as he was going to the UK as a Turk and that would be his identity. He was frightened that he would be left behind now that he had passed the book over to the Englishman, but Charlie in particular seemed to have every reason to make sure he got to Brize Norton in one piece. Almas arrived at Alan's bedroom two hours before he was due to leave and gave him her goodbyes like a loving wife in the morning, and her final kiss would stay in his mind forever as she left him to dress and went to make the breakfast.

Chapter 29
Many Clues and Much Evidence
SIS HQ, March 2010

Jason Harris gave the news they had already. 'The plane has arrived at Brize Norton and we've put Alan, Charlie, Brian Wilson and the Turk in a hotel just off the M4. They're having a meal and then we'll join them for a meeting before the Americans arrive tomorrow.'

'OK Jason, now it's up to you to find out what this guy knows before the Yanks work him over.'

'Thanks chief, I bet they will want to know how he got the book.'

'I think we know. Read this download; Molly found it yesterday. It's a page she's copied out a November 2009 morning issue of *The New York Times*. It describes a break-in at an engineering company making energy recovery systems in Detroit, and look at the wording: *Due to the possibly sensitive nature of the material stolen, the FBI has been informed and has taken over the case.* She checked after that date and it wasn't mentioned again; the CIA must have taken over and that was the end of it. That's it, Jason; anything else that happened has been suppressed by the CIA, but if Korham is released to them he could be for the high jump.'

'What do I do, sir?'

'Go down there now and talk to him, then call me with the main points. I'll speak to the Home Secretary and get a ruling.'

'OK, I'm on my way, but one thing before I go: I just had a call from DI Hubbard. He's in Belfast and had a meeting with the RUC about the deceased Paddy Mulligan, and an assumption on the death of Major Bill Barrington.'

'Spit it out, Jason, you've got to get going.'

'A summary, sir: Paddy Mulligan got his plastic explosives and weapons from Libya. The actual supplier is one from a shortlist they gave me, and the likely person is someone we're protecting or at least the police are, so that's a problem we've to sort out. Bill Barrington recently bought supplies from Mulligan and then he was found dead soon after. The RUC are sure it was Barrington who killed him as he'd been seen near his house, and the way the wire that was hooked around his neck had the smell of a commando-style killing. The smell is strongly Barrington, but they're keeping their options open and saying they can't be 100% sure yet. If it was him, he travelled back here to London immediately after he did it. A car was seen near Mulligan's house with two men inside it just before the RUC got an anonymous phone call to say Mulligan was dead; the caller said "All square now, gentlemen." They think the driver was the man who called;

it's a pattern used before but it's unusual for the RUC. They don't know who he is or they're not guessing; they want to be sure first. DI Hubbard wants our help, and he's checking now if the explosive and detonators found in a lockup garage belonging to Mulligan were the same type used to kill the Fishers. We'll know in a few days and Hubbard will call us.

'OK sir, I'm off now to the hotel, but just one thing: the pathologist on Major Barrington's case reckons it could be suicide – that's a new one to throw in, and he's promised Hubbard a report by Friday. The RUC were in the process of dragging Barrington back to Belfast as they'd found a lot of evidence on his activities and they wanted to interview him on other crimes as well as Mulligan's death. DI Hubbard said the RUC seem pleased that both men are dead, so virtually ending the story, but they still have to link up with us on this one as both coroners will want to know every piece of the puzzle.'

'I see. Molly, come in a minute, please.'

Jason ran to the door before his boss asked any more questions. He had only one thing on his mind and that was Deniz Korham.

'I know you've been itching to speak to me; I'm sorry Molly but the Turkish guy has been picked up and Jason wanted to tell me about Barrington and Mulligan. Have we got a pattern developing? I know the police are onto it all but anything we can do to get the people who killed the Fishers is personally one of my priorities, that is until we have to deal with that group of renegade Pakistanis who are now threatening their own people here.'

'Yes sir; I've some information on that, but this is what I've found on links to the Fishers. I haven't passed this to Chief Superintendent White yet as it needs your approval. Gordon Fisher, as we know, was a Judge Advocate. He must've had some enemies or people with grudges about the sentences he gave them, and he was in charge of many a court martial in the past ten years. Note, by the way: the court martial is singular in the English language; weird, really. I went through every one: the witnesses if any, the accused, the defence, the jury – which, of course, was made up of officers – and at first I didn't think I was getting anywhere. Then after reading one of many sad coroners' reports from Kabul I realised I was looking in the wrong direction. Gordon Fisher had two sons: Alan, whose history we know well, and his brother who was killed in an accident in Afghanistan, just near Kabul.

'The enquiry into the death had two pieces of evidence: a bullet in his temple and the gun that fired it, both belonging to an Afghanistan regular soldier. He stated he was cleaning the weapon and had forgotten to clear the bullet in the breach; young Lieutenant Ben Fisher was killed instantly. Open and shut case possibly, or at least it seemed so, but in the notes is a profile of the Afghanistan soldier which was no doubt read but totally ignored by the people who investigated. The bit that interested me was his family: Sergeant Sandi had been in the army for five years, but his family were trapped in a remote area between the Taliban front line and the Allies, and he needed to get them out. I checked and they're back in Kabul in a nice apartment, so he succeeded.

'This is the email I got today from our man in Kabul: *Re. Sgt S and your enquiry, funds arrived from overseas a week after death of Lt Fisher. Apartment owned 100% by Sgt S.* So where did the Afghan get the money from? Nobody's asked him that; shall I get our local guy to pay him another visit?'

'No, Molly, but this is good stuff – if we assume that someone paid the sergeant for killing the Fisher boy we have to look at the possibility that his father Gordon was the judge when a soldier was convicted for something under doubtful circumstances.'

'Yes, that's possible and I've done all that and unfortunately there are so many possible people with grudges due to convictions we could have fifty suspects; it's difficult to know where to start.'

'Molly, this is a job for the police, not us, but my opinion is that for someone to do something as violent as kill in revenge they must be very sick. Gordon must have been involved with more than one incident if someone wanted revenge – or it was some form of vendetta? Call Superintendent Dick White and tell him what you told me.'

'OK, will do.'

'Molly, you didn't forget the Pakistanis, did you?'

'I told Jason; he obviously didn't mention it to you.'

'No. What have you found out?'

'Mr Mohammed Ana arrived last Thursday morning from Dubai on Emirates flight EK2 in first class seat no. 1C.'

'Yes all right, Molly, I didn't want his inside leg measurement. Where is he now?'

'Lucy followed his free airline taxi; he went shopping at Harrods and bought lots of clothes and an iPhone, then checked in at the Ritz. The airline taxi waited for him at the shop, then took him on to the hotel; he must be a regular customer. The front desk told her, after some resistance, that Mr Ana will be staying for two weeks. Everything's in place, and Lucy will report daily.'

'What about his new phone? Can we find out who he calls, if anyone? He has to contact somebody here.'

'He's two mobiles, sir: Lucy saw a BlackBerry in his hand but we haven't got a tap on it now, do you want me to set one up? Maybe he's bought the iPhone as well for a specific reason? He used the hotel phone twice and called a mobile: it's on the O2 network and the billing goes to a Mr Aaron Parker. Why are you laughing, sir?'

'The police should be protecting him discreetly. He helped the government a couple of times; in fact, more than a couple of times. In practice they can't be bothered and don't watch people for very long unless they're crime suspects; we need to meet with White and Hubbard before we stand on each other's toes again. Please set it up, then tell Jason about this and go with him to meet them tomorrow, you deserve a day out.'

'Thanks sir, it'll make a change, but you need to stay here in case Mr Korham needs to be dealt with.'

'I hope not, Molly, but I'll speak to Brian Wilson in a minute and find out the latest on our Turkish friend. Also ask Lucy to find Aaron Parker and follow him for a couple of days to see what he does with himself.'

'Sorry sir, I got ahead again on that instruction: I asked Lucy yesterday to find him and do just that.'

'Smart girl, but tell me first next time.'

'Sorry sir, but I knew you were busy on the Turkish job.'

'Did she find anything out on him?'

'He went out just once to an apartment in South London; we're checking the owner. Lucy can be a bit paranoid, that's why she's so good, and she said that someone was already following him. She's got the car number but it had false plates and although the driver wore a baseball cap she thought it was a woman as she could see a ponytail. When he left the apartment Lucy was amazed as he went to the Ritz and met our new acquaintance Mohammed Ana.'

'That's good, we know now where to find them both. What a can of worms, Molly. Set the meeting up with the police and find out what's going on; either Lucy got the registration number wrong or Mr Parker may have a secret or two. Get a picture of Mrs Parker – from memory she looks a bit like a debutante.'

The director had a memory like an elephant, and he could recall faces even after brief meetings. If Leah Parker was following her husband it was because she suspected him of adultery, which was not one for SIS unless it was a threat to the country.

Chapter 30
Open All Hours
The Brown Cow

'I didn't expect that, Larry.'

'It's only a kiss, Leah, and a friendly one as you're leaving here on good terms. I've to be careful now as I was a bad boy recently and I promised Jill I'd be good as gold and concentrate on selling this pub. The days of the local are over and The Brown Cow needs someone to turn it into a gourmet restaurant. I'm sure your husband can do that, so the bottom line is, make me an offer over £350,000 and we might have a deal. Jill is the licensee for the place so I can't run it without her being on the premises. She's said she'll stay on to help you until you get a change of licensee accepted, and that's all part of the deal.'

'But we're not the only prospective buyer now, are we Larry?'

'That'd be telling. Off you go – your cab is outside, and both of you come here tomorrow and we can see if we can make an agreement, but tell your husband to leave his bloody arrogance behind.'

'Yes, I get the picture. See you tomorrow.'

Larry found Jill unpacking the food shopping from her car and told her the story.

'Unfortunately though, Jill, I have a difficult matter to sort out.'

'What's that? Not more young girls?'

'No, it's your ex-boyfriend Bill Knowles; he's got something on me. Actually, you'll probably guess: it's my tax. He's massaged it for years, and although I'm still very angry about your affair with him I have to sort things out before we can sell the pub. I discovered that he hasn't been handling the sale of the pub in the way I wanted him to: he was going to buy it and sell it on to Parker in a back-to-back deal; making a load of money from me, but I suppose that's business. I spoke to Bill on the phone before Leah arrived and he's coming here in an hour. Keep out of sight; I promise not to hit him.'

'I don't want to see him anyway. You know, in some ways it was funny that you thought I was playing around with Alan Fisher when you saw me talking to him.

'Why not? The bloke's had a rough time and you'd be a good shoulder to cry on. I know I was out of order throwing him out of the pub, though: he was just trying to help me. Please understand, Jill – it was that other business I mentioned in Brighton that was eating me up. Alan is welcome here as long as we own the place; I'll square it with him one day soon.'

'There's a phone call for you in the bar, Mr Nixon.'

'Thanks, Mia. Lovely girl, Jill – she's a good choice.'

'Leave it, Larry, or I'll cut your balls off in your sleep.'

He appeared to ignore her but actually he got the message loud and clear.

'Hello Larry, it's Harold Penny here. Can you help me with something if I pop in, or am I still barred?'

'No, of course not, Harold. I'm really sorry about my behaviour; I seem to be apologising to everyone at the moment. Come in for a pint and it's on me.'

'I'll be on my way in a few minutes as I need to get a taxi; I had a burglary so I've been staying at Alan Fisher's place while he was away. I just got home and I'd like a chat.'

'OK, but take your time. Bill Knowles may be here, but we can break away from him and still have a talk in private.'

'Yes Larry, not one for in the bar.'

'All right, see you soon.'

Larry hung up the phone. 'It's a night for visitors, Jill: first Leah Parker, then Bill, and now Harold Penny wants my help with something.'

'You're a popular man all of sudden. We only need Alan Fisher and you've a group for a game of cards.'

'Don't look now, but he's behind you.'

Alan smiled. 'Hi Larry. Can we shake hands? I don't know what I did but Harold is on his way and we need to talk to you.'

'Look, I'm really sorry about that night, Alan, and I know you were only trying to help. Anyway, I thought you were abroad on holiday or something? I bumped into your girl Cheryl the other day.'

'I was on business; she was being discreet. I came back this lunchtime and had a call from Harold, so I decided to join him here. He's just coming now – I can see the taxi, so can you get us two pints of bitter please, Larry, and can we go into the snug bar? It looks empty.'

'Sure, in you go and I'll get the beer.'

Alan greeted Harold as he entered the pub. 'Hi Harold, sorry I couldn't pick you up – I got a lift in a police car of all things. DI Hubbard was on my back again so I cadged a lift with him.'

'That's OK, Alan. Now, as I said on the phone, once I saw Larry in some of your father's pictures I thought he could help us, but they weren't from any computer. I can't operate that Mac thing you got me: Janet next door brought it round to your place for me after she'd set it up, but it beats me. I had a power cut and then I couldn't find the on and off button, but I don't want to keep bothering her.'

'I'll show you tomorrow, Harold; it's simple, don't panic. I just hope Larry plays ball – if not we'd better run and forget our pints.'

Larry came back into the snug bar with three pints and spilt them as he put them on the table. He was very shaky, and both

330

Harold and Alan noticed it but didn't comment. A small thing like that could tip Larry over the edge.

'What can I do for you, gentlemen? Do you want to buy the pub?'

'No, perhaps one day, but not now. This is what we want your help on.'

Harold had two photos: one with four people in it and one with three; all in Mediterranean-type clothes, and in the background were soldiers in uniform. He put them on the table in front of Larry, who grabbed his own pint, stood up and shut the door. He was shaking more than usual, and the colour had left his face.

'I knew one day I'd have to face up to this, but I'm not ready to cope with it yet. I'll tell you who some of the people are and a little about them, but you've got to find out the rest and I'll tell you who from; then I'm off the case. Afterwards, drink up your pints and go, and don't come back until you've the complete answer. I want to stay alive, but keep in contact please, and I'm sorry.'

'OK Larry, we understand. Just ten minutes – all I want is to find my parents' killers.'

Larry picked up one of the photos. 'This first picture was in Baghdad, Iraq, outside a temporary building. I'm on the end of the line and your dad is next to me – we'd just had a beer together and you can see the sand blown by the wind sticking to our moustaches while they're still white from the froth; that's why we're laughing. Your dad was angry with the news reporter who took the picture without permission, and he made him give him a copy but it was never published. The other people in the picture are a bloke called Major Bill Barrington, who committed suicide recently so he won't tell you much, and the other bloke I think must have worked with your dad. I gave prosecution evidence on a soldier on a manslaughter charge.'

'Who was the soldier in the dock?'

Larry paused. Alan guessed he knew but wasn't saying.

'He was an Irishman; I've forgotten his name. Your father just did his job and didn't accept flimsy defence evidence, so the man got life imprisonment, which from memory was a minimum of fifteen years. Then later there was an appeal, a different Judge Advocate allowed some new defence evidence and the soldier was given a full discharge and sent back to his unit. I gave evidence on the weapon and the shell trajectory in both hearings, and really he should never have got away with it.'

'Why did he?'

'I never really found out. The rumour was that is was a technicality; some bloke whose name I don't know got the case reviewed and got him free.'

'So let's go to the other picture. What's the matter, Larry? Why are you shaking your head, mate?'

'It's real bad news for both of us, Alan, it's just a fucking nightmare. The bloke who got off the charge in the first picture went to Kabul, and another soldier was killed – not by him, although he was there, but by an Afghan sergeant supposedly cleaning his gun. I'm sorry but that death was your brother, Alan.'

'You're right, Larry, this is a nightmare so let's get it right: the soldier got away somehow with manslaughter after my dad nailed him; his next tour was in Kabul and by chance he bumps into my brother Ben, shoots him and blames it on an Afghan soldier?'

'You've got it, Alan. I'm really sorry, son, but there was nothing I could do; the bastard must've borrowed the Afghan soldier's gun for a payoff. I was sent to check it out and it all fitted; the shell was from the gun. I saw your dad as he left for the UK with the body in the plane: he was in shock and didn't speak to me, and I saw little of him after that until he turned up one day in the pub, but I was busy and didn't really get a chance to talk to him.

'So where was this picture taken? That's my dad in the middle, and Harold said this photo was attached to the other with a paperclip. The person you didn't identify in picture one is there again, and I know who the other bloke is.'

'Yes, he's the explosives man, Charlie Baxter.'

'I knew I was right. He must have supplied the explosive to kill my parents, and I just spent a week with him!'

'Wrong, Alan – your Charlie Baxter is not really a supplier, he's just a technician, and as you know, a bloody good one. After the bomb killed your parents last year I rang Charlie and he was devastated; he'd possibly set the device up for someone he didn't know, but he didn't know the target; he thought it was being used in Spain. He's on extended leave from the army as he probably told you, and I don't know why except that he desperately needs money and at the moment that's all he's interested in; maybe it's family. Look, that's all I can tell you: find the mystery man in the picture – both shots show his face slightly under that hat, and if you can identify him you could have your parents' killer. If that bloke didn't do it, someone close to him did. I've told you who can help and that's Charlie; he'll know everyone in those pictures.'

'I should've guessed. I knew something was wrong with him; he had difficulty looking me straight in the face. The problem with the mystery man is that he has a thick beard and desert glasses – he looks vaguely familiar but I need a shot with him clean-shaven. I think the police could play with it, but then I've to involve DI Hubbard. It's much too complicated to go through with the police at the moment, but I will do as soon as I have a more complete picture. Thanks, Larry, you've really helped me – is it OK if I call you again?'

'Yes, but only when you've something new.'

Harold and Alan shook Larry's hand and left the pub. In the car park, Alan paused.

'Sorry, we need a taxi – I'll go back in and call one. Wait here.'

Jill was waiting for him on the step. 'I've done it for you; it'll be here in a minute.' She lowered her voice. 'Alan, please find the killer – it's not just you who's suffering; as you can see it's Larry as well.'

'Does he know the other bloke in the picture?'

'I don't know, which one? Show me.'

Alan beckoned Harold over, and Harold pointed to the man in both pictures.

'His uniform collar is so big, and behind the beard and glasses you can't really see his face. If Larry knows his name and isn't saying, it's for a good reason.'

Harold nodded. 'There are a few more pictures in the folder, but not taken in the Middle East.'

'Where did you say you found them, Harold?' Alan asked

'The folder was in with your dad's will; I think perhaps he knew there could be a problem and these were left with me for safekeeping.'

The taxi delivered both men back to Alan's apartment. Harold was ready to go home – he had stayed in Epsom while Alan was away, but now he wanted to go back to his own home and work on Alan's parents' estate. The new security arrangements on Alan's apartment building were a welcome addition, although the cost would be reflected in the service charge. The number of his flat on the entry phone had no name next to it, as he could see no reason to advertise where he lived or give strangers his name.

'Evening, Mr Fisher. Your girlfriend called but she didn't have her key, so she said she'll be back at 9pm. She's shopping in Waitrose.'

'Thanks Jack, let her in when she arrives.'

Alan sat in front of his TV, chewing over the meeting at The Brown Cow. In his mind he was clear that Larry Nixon could help solve the mystery of his parents' deaths. He knew that until the killer was found, he was in as much danger as Larry. He made a decision that on Friday he would resign from his planning job at the council – they had been good employers and given him time off, but since his trip to Turkey he'd realised that town planning was not his future. His thoughts were interrupted as the new entry phone burst into life.

'Hi, come up, Cheryl.

She entered the flat, setting her shopping bags down at her feet. 'That's a good idea, that phone; makes you feel a bit safer when you arrive here.'

'Yes, they put it in last week. I'll give you a special key which you hold up to the box inside the lift door; that'll get you up here, and the security man leaves at ten o'clock so it'll get you out as well.'

'Come here, big boy, I've missed you.'

The girl crushed her sizeable breasts against his chest and Alan kissed her, then pulled away.

'Are you OK, darling?'

'Yes, but I've made a decision: I'm not going back to work. I've enough money to keep me going until probate comes through for my parents' estate, and I want to wrap up the case on their deaths. The insurance company and the probate office know about the situation, so they'll sit on their hands until everything is done and dusted. The inquest date has changed twice but now it's definitely next week. Will you come with me?'

'Yes, I was going to ask you anyway. Harold phoned and told me and said there's a new time of 11am, so can you pick me up?'

'Yes, sure – I think it's in Woking which is about 25 minutes from your mum's place. We can put it in my computer and use Google Maps to get the address.'

'What're we eating, Alan? The fridge looks a bit bare.'

'I've got some food but can't be bothered to cook it, I just want to be with you. Shall we have a drink across the road, then get a takeaway?'

'Yes – unhealthy with loads of salt, but why not?'

Within minutes the couple were sat in the pub and Cheryl went through her week in the shop in detail.

'Mum's been driving me nuts; she keeps looking at that identikit picture you got from the police of that bloke who came to our shop.'

'Well, has she any clues?'

'She keeps saying "I know him" but when I ask her who he is and where she knows him from she can't remember. It's very annoying.'

'The best thing is if she tries to forget it, then it may come back to her.'

'The one thing she said was that she's seen the face in the newspaper; it's not someone she's seen in the flesh.'

'Which paper?'

'National one, not a local.'

'Ask her tomorrow, then I can give it to DI Hubbard and he can send it to the paper with the identikit; it's worth a try. Have you got the day off tomorrow, Cheryl?'

'Yes, two days in fact, just for me to make endless filthy love to you.'

Alan smiled, but only as she reminded him of Almas. Then he pulled himself together.

'Top of the agenda, I promise, but then I need your help at Harold's. We've to look through lots of photographs to see if we can find someone.'

'Let's go, Alan, I want your body and urgently.'

As they crossed the precinct, a car mounted the pavement, Alan instinctively pushed Cheryl away as the car leapt over the raised kerb and drove straight at them, but it was too quick for him to avoid completely and it hit his forearm, then accelerated away. It was no accident. Someone had tried to run him over.

The ambulance took five minutes and the trip to the hospital two minutes. The arm was broken, but the break was a clean one and the hospital said it would only be in a sling for a few days, after which a special bandage would hold it in place until it mended. Alan's face was white – delayed shock had hit him hard as he waited for the taxi to take them back to his flat.

'It's bloody killing me, Cheryl; the drugs haven't taken effect yet.'

'The nurse gave me more so you can have some before we go to bed.'

'Stay tonight, Cheryl, you're totally in control now for a change. I'll ring the police tomorrow if the hospital haven't done it already, but I want to sleep now.'

'Yes of course, darling; all you have to do when we get back is lay still and I'll give you your medicine.'

The image of Almas was still in Alan's mind, but the pain of his arm made him forget the guilt for now. It would return in the morning when the drugs had worn off.

Chapter 31
The Door Opens Wide

It was a long night, but Cheryl had made sure Alan took his drugs and the pain had eased. He pulled himself out of bed as his mobile phone burst into life.

'Alan, it's Larry Nixon here. I heard about your accident; one of my customers was telling everybody in the pub. He was your ambulance man, and he was also at your parents' house that night. Anyway, we need to talk: can I come over to your place in about an hour?'

'OK Larry, sure. Security is a bit tighter here now so I'll ring the guy on reception downstairs to warn him you're coming.'

Larry was early, and the security man let him into the lift and pressed for the fifth floor. As the door closed he started to sweat, and suddenly he felt as though someone was going to strangle him, but before he had a full-blown panic attack the lift doors opened. Alan stood at the door of his flat as Larry went inside, still shaking from his daydream.

'Are you OK, Larry?'

'Another of my fucking phobias, Alan; as soon as I got in that lift I felt like I was being strangled.'

'Come on, I know it's early but I'm in pain; we'll have a large Scotch, but you do it as I might fall on my arse, or just spill it.'

Nixon laughed, picked up the bottle and grabbed two teacups, then poured two large measures.

'Are you on your own, Alan?'

'Yes, Cheryl's gone for a few hours as her mum's really busy in the shop. By the way, this arm was no accident: I think someone is making serious attempts to kill me. It's not dummy bombs in my girlfriend's shop or hooded guys following me in beat-up cars now, it's someone who wants me out of the way, and I'm fucking angry and also a bit scared. It's not one for the police, I have to deal with it myself.'

'How do you propose to do that with an arm in a sling?'

'With difficulty, but I can still fire my gun. I kept one from a small job I did.'

'No, Alan – these people won't approach you face-to-face, and the accident yesterday was to let you know they're around. They're sure to use a bomb like in your parents' house or similar, and you'll never know what hit you. I think I know who they are, and if I'm right they're capable of doing anything, or at least one man is. I want to help you; I've a shadow hanging over me and somehow I have to deal with it.'

Alan went quiet as the Scotch started to hit home. He was in turmoil: his life was upside down and the job in Turkey had unsettled him. That was the type of work he wanted, and he knew that when he was fit SIS would make him a proposal. He also guessed that if he accepted a post with SIS it would be the end of his relationship with Cheryl, as his lifestyle would change and he did not want her faced with danger. He was still well below 40 and marriage was not on his agenda until he had made a sound career for himself.

Larry Nixon went to the toilet; the lift incident had loosened his guts. While he was in there, Alan's mobile phone rang, the screen displaying a blocked number. He answered it, but his nerves were on edge and at first he didn't speak.

'Alan, it's Jason Harris. Look, I know you're suffering so I've got something to cheer you up.'

'Go for it.'

'Deniz Korham is genuine. The Yanks have finished grilling him and now they're taking him back to the USA for debriefing; they aren't charging him with stealing the book. Some new information he gave them is just what they wanted – they aren't telling us what it is but we think it confirms that they know what Iran has, good or bad we don't know, and frankly we're happy to take a back seat on the whole business. You and Charlie will get a nice letter from the Home Secretary, and as soon as your arm is better the director wants to see you, so come up here.'

'Yes, fine. So what did you do about Charlie and the other offer to the Turk?'

342

'That was all a set-up by the director to get a nasty bloke called Mohammed Ana sent back to Pakistan and hopefully get Aaron Parker deported for good. We don't want an incident. Parker helped the British government once or twice; perhaps more, although we're not proud of that and it's best left under the carpet. We found his apartment but he'd already left when we went to get him. He'll be deported. Did you find that Alice girl, or her friend Sheila? From what we know he was a regular visitor to her place, but she's moved as well and we've lost the tag on her. Molly Smart, one of our internal people, found an apartment for Alice near you, so if we text you, can you check it out?'

Alan wasn't sure he should give Jason Sheila Hamilton's phone number, but he couldn't avoid it if she was harbouring a wanted man. Still, he would need to explain to Jason face-to-face why he knew her. He wondered if it could jeopardise a job with SIS if he admitted that he'd an evening with both girls a few years before. He would ignore Jason's request on Alice Smith as Sheila Hamilton was a safer bet for SIS, and she was the one sleeping with Parker.

'I'll try now, Jason – can you and DI Hubbard call in at my place tomorrow? I need to talk to you about my parents' case and Charlie.'

'Yes, I'll arrange to come down to Surrey with Hubbard; he'll text you the time, but Charlie isn't for discussion. Charlie was told not to tell you what the other deal with Korham was so you wouldn't be concerned, but as it turned out it had a reverse effect with you becoming suspicious. Anyway, it worked out OK in the end. That shoulder injury has slowed him down a bit; it's a bit of a coincidence that you're both one-armed at the moment.'

'You heard already? You don't miss much. Hang on a minute, Jason, I've a visitor and he's been in the toilet for five minutes. Are you all right Larry? The smell's bloody awful.'

'Yes mate, I'm being sick and shitting at the same time. Leave me alone.'

'OK, stay there, I'm on the phone. Sorry Jason, a small technical problem with my friend but carry on, I've locked him in the toilet. You were talking about Charlie – what's he going to do now? He's a clever bloke, Jason, but I've difficulty looking him in the eye as I know he's hiding something.'

'Since we told him you'd discovered he was an explosives man he's scared to talk to you, but he really didn't know that the bombs he made were supplied to a third party and that they were the ones that killed your parents. He tells everybody his wife left him, but that's his own way of dealing with her illness: she's very sick with leukaemia, she needs 24hour care, he hasn't any medical insurance, so every penny he can spare goes on her treatment. The prognosis is she won't last more than a few more months. The kids live with his sister-in-law as he just couldn't cope with them.'

'Why didn't he tell me, Jason?'

'He couldn't tell you about his wife without touching on the money issue – he still has this guilt complex about the bomb-making, and so he should have. He is technically still in the army but seconded to us; his CO wants him out so we'll arrange it with the MOD, but then there's his latest offence before your trip. If it's confirmed that he supplied the explosives that killed your parents he'll have to be charged; the director isn't happy about it but it's a civil offence and Charlie can't hide behind a court martial. When something happens with his wife, which could be very soon, we'll have to consider what we do with him – a problem for another day, and thankfully not mine.'

'I understand Charlie's situation; it's like someone killing a member of your family by supplying a defective car that crashes. In my parents' case he should have known the bomb wasn't for use in Spain before he agreed to make it. I'm going to have another look at pictures – I found some clues but there must be more that could help. Have you still got that identikit sketch from when my girl Cheryl had the visitor at the shop? It's possible he was the bloke watching me outside here; trouble was, the police were also watching me and helping in their own way, but in the end it all got very confusing.'

'What happened to you the other day, then?'

'I was pleased to be home, and I met Cheryl here at my place. We went out to Wetherspoon's, and after we'd had a couple of drinks we came out of the place and a car mounted the kerb and came straight for me. I pushed her out of the way and jumped back as the car wing hit my arm; I broke it just below the elbow, but fortunately it's the left one so I can still write and wipe my arse.'

'Good to see you've still got a sense of humour, Alan.'

'Yes, but only because I think I'm getting close to who's behind my parents' deaths. They obviously want me dead so that means I'm getting warm; I want closure and then I can move on. Got to go now, Jason, I've to let my mate out of the toilet; he's banging on the door. See you and Hubbard here tomorrow, and ask him to bring that identikit picture as well.'

'OK Alan, but can you make sure the front door is locked?'

Alan agreed, then hung up the phone. 'Are you still in one piece, Larry? That smell's still bloody awful.'

'Yes, fine now. I was just looking out of the toilet window as I needed some air and I can see a car parked in the far corner with someone in it. My suspicious mind is working overtime, Alan.'

'Hang on a minute.' Alan left the room and quickly returned with a small pack. 'I just found my night binoculars; we used these last week and you can see a fly on the wall in the dark through them. Yes, there's someone in the car but he's got a hooded jacket almost covering his face.'

'Do you reckon he's watching you, Alan?'

'For certain; he must be waiting for me to leave. As soon as he sees me, open the door downstairs – he could jump me from behind the dustbins.'

'What're you going to do, call the police?'

'No, I'm restricted with this broken arm. I told you I've got a gun, but to use it I've got to be really sure he's after me otherwise I'll be in deep shit. This is Epsom not downtown Kabul.'

'Look I can help – unarmed combat was my speciality before the trauma of the army got to me. Come on, we've got to find out what this is about; it may help me as well.'

'Why, Larry?'

'Because until we know for sure who the other person in your dad's pictures is we can't work out who actually carried out the murders. As I said, I've an idea or two but I need a few more pieces of the puzzle to get the complete picture.'

The men shook hands, and just in case of real trouble Alan forgot his cautious approach and stuffed the Beretta down the back of his trousers. The lift arrived, and Alan stood near the door and Larry to the left of the control panel so that he couldn't be seen when the doors reopened on the ground floor. The lift crashed as it stopped, and the security lights came on as Alan stepped out of the back entrance of the building. He took four steps behind the first green bin. Whoever was watching him was waiting to see if it really was Alan leaving the building.

The man was out of the car. Alan looked left and right, but kept behind the bins as the security camera could not see behind them. He was on his own, and just as he turned a figure appeared in front of him with a baseball bat in his hand. He swung it at

Alan's head, but even with his broken arm Alan managed to kick him in the stomach, and he lost his balance before he fell to the ground. Larry was shaking with fear. He couldn't move; he was frozen. The man jumped on top of Alan and raised the baseball bat.

The next thing Alan could remember was being helped to his feet.

'Sorry for the delay, mate but at first I was shit-scared; then suddenly it all came back and I went into combat like the big green man in the films and I nailed that bloke.'

'Where is he, and who is he?'

'He's gone. I ripped his hood off and then got three punches in, and with your kick I think he'd had enough for one night. He got my ear and I may need a stitch but that's nothing. Are you OK?'

'Yes. I just got away with it again; this time thanks to you, Larry.'

'No problem. To answer your question about who the man is, by my reckoning he's just a hired thug. He said just one thing as the blood poured out of his mouth: "The big boss will get you for this." I told him that now I know his face, if I saw it again I'd finish the job. He had an Irish accent which has got me thinking.'

'Good one Larry, come on let's get back in the flat. We need a beer and a dressing for your lughole.'

348

As they started to drink all the beer in the fridge and patched up Larry's damaged ear, they chewed over what had just happened to them, and they both came to the same conclusion that calling the police was not a good idea.

'Look out the window, Alan: that car's on fire! He must've come back and torched it, the cheeky sod.'

'That might be on CCTV. I 'll get the security bloke to check it tomorrow, that is if he still has the tape. Look down there: the old bill and fire service are here. Come on Larry, let's go to the pub, as it won't be long before the police start knocking on my door. We can go out the front down the stairs; no lifts to make you shit yourself.'

The two men left the building as a second fire engine turned up, and the acrid smoke bellowing from the burning rubber gave them a smokescreen as they ran across the main road and into The Vestry pub.

'That's going to explode in a minute so we could be in here for some time.'

'I can think of worst places, Larry – excluding The Brown Cow, of course.'

'You cheeky sod. I had to come over here in case Jill's ears started to flap; she's not involved with my past and I don't want her to be. When I tell you more you'll understand.'

'I think I'm getting the picture already. Please carry on.'

'I can't remember the exact dates but as you know your old man had been a Judge Advocate for a few years. People in the army and security services remembered his work in Northern Ireland, Bosnia, Kuwait, Baghdad and later of course Kabul before the courts were all set up here. His appointment was a bit controversial at first as although he was well trained in his time with the RAF, and of course he was an experienced legal man, his early working life had almost always been spent in civil courts, not the military court martial. The control of the jurors was different as officers made up the alternative jury, known as a board. Opinions could be very one-sided, and Gordon had to deal with them and make sure the defendant got a fair hearing; a difficult job sometimes. Few people remember that one of his very first appearances as a recently appointed Judge Advocate was in Northern Ireland – after the Troubles, but still a place simmering with hatred. The difficulty of that place speaks for itself, with consideration of the religious and political situation having a bearing on the man in the dock. Your father would probably agree that a portion of the court decisions made by the board were pretty uncompromising – they had to be. Northern Ireland in the past had a similarity to the killing fields of Vietnam some weeks, and servicemen were under extreme pressure every time they reported for duty.

'My point, Alan, is that being the judge at the hearings in Northern Ireland made your father very unpopular with some factions. I'll give you a summary of what happened during those times, and why I'm at war with myself and need an end to it. Your father had jealous enemies at top level. The Judge Advocate General, a man as high as you can go, supported Gordon 100%; his predecessor appointed him but he also had total confidence in him. I met the JAG, as he was called, at a dinner in Sandhurst, and he told me he worried about appointing judges as it was always a tough role, and very specialised in adjudicating cases in dangerous war zones. Everybody knew your father and he was determined one day to get a top job; his goal I guess was probably a senior circuit judge, as he was about the right age and the view was that he would be the perfect candidate.'

'Yes, I remember him talking about that once.'

Larry nodded. 'What many people didn't know was that in the early days Gordon had constant pressure from sectors of the Irish public to deal severely with cases that involved the discipline of army personnel, usually linked to interrogation methods and the treatment of prisoners. It was clear he worked under extreme provocation, and I wondered if it was getting to him when I met him at a hearing one day. He looked ill, and my guess was that he'd received death threats but it blew over, I think, or your father learned to cope with it, and the next time I saw him away from court he seemed confident and relaxed.'

'This is all news to me, Larry. So who were the individuals who had problems with my father?'

'My best friend in the RAF, Dermott Donnelly, was one of them; he's my brother-in-law. I say my best friend because he saved my skin twice in separate incidents: he had eyesight like a hawk and twice spotted road bombs, which were invisible to me, and if they'd gone off we would both have been killed. One day an IED did go off very close to us, and men in our platoon were badly injured. We lost two of our colleagues, and three others just about made it back to the UK. Neither Donnelly or I could speak for hours afterwards – the shock was something I still have problems with; the quacks call it post-traumatic stress disorder. Dermott Donnelly you saw in the photo; he's a Catholic Irishman but we never discuss religion. We fought together, played football together and occasionally had a drunken scrap together – you get the picture, Alan?

'Yes I do, but why did he fall out with my dad, and did he kill my parents?'

'On the first question, Dermott never liked your father; his brother Liam, a tearaway soldier, was arrested in Londonderry for beating up two civilians. I can't remember the full details but it went to a court martial – normally the CO would have dealt with it but the SIB had Liam branded as a troublemaker, especially if he'd been on the booze. The jury convicted him and Gordon gave him the maximum sentence without concessions. He served two years in Colchester, then I heard he somehow finished up back in service in Baghdad; bizarrely, someone got his sentence reduced. Two incidents followed in the Middle East and amazingly, in spite of sound evidence Liam got off again. In both cases Dermott must have got to officers on the board; don't ask me how, but he did it and Liam was cleared.

'I mentioned your brother's death yesterday, and in my opinion Liam must have been the person who fired the bullet from the Afghan's gun that killed him, and the reason was black and white: it was because of your father. The final case brought against Liam was the shooting of a woman in Baghdad, who from the defence evidence was supposed to have been carrying a rifle and aiming it at him. In mitigation, Liam had just seen the horror of two of his buddies being killed by an IED. His mind was in turmoil and when he saw what he believed was a person pointing a rifle at him and preparing to shoot, he fired, and he had the right to shoot. The victim was a woman and no weapon – rifle or other firearm – could be found near her body. All the evidence was against him. His CO told him he couldn't help; SIB moved in and he was charged. The court martial board were new officers fresh to court and they found him guilty of manslaughter – correctly, your father didn't guide them otherwise. I never knew what the jail sentence was as Liam was also dismissed from the army, and he hung himself in his cell at Colchester Military Prison.

'Dermott was devastated. He blamed everybody, but the man he hated most was your father. Shortly after he left the army, he moved from Northern Ireland to Brighton, married Penny and continued with a business he had set up a few years before but done very little with. He buys, sells and restores antiques, and sometimes weapons if he get his hands on any. Most of the stuff comes from Northern Ireland or Éire, and he's been pulled in many times for suspected firearm offences but he always gets off. He's a clever bloke, but drinks too much, and although I see him once or twice a year I try to keep my hair on when he goes back to the past; he gets very nasty. I saw him a couple of weeks ago and he was as happy as I've ever seen him.'

'Larry, do you know if he killed my parents? He had a good motive, and he would also have wanted the photographs to destroy them; any connection to my father would immediately make a good copper suspicious, and a lead worth following up.'

'My feeling is yes, Dermott could have done it; he would have got the bomb from an old store hidden by the late Paddy Mulligan for a rainy day. Maybe Charlie Baxter gave him a new detonator set up and ready, or maybe he set up the whole device.'

'So no chance the bomb was going to Spain?'

'No, Baxter probably convinced himself that it would but underneath he knew it was for use in the UK, but unless he had been told specifically I doubt he knew it was to be used on your family. He just wanted the money and then to be out of it.'

'Should we tell the police now or later?'

'Look, Alan, this is the living nightmare I've had since my mates were blown up next to me. It doesn't go away; in fact because of your parents' deaths it has got a lot worse. Jill left me and the pub was and still is in serious debt because of me, but thankfully she has come back now. I've a plan to get out of the mess and I want you and your young brain to help me.'

'Don't piss about with me: you want some of my money in return for finding the killers!'

'Spot on, Alan. Dermott is behind it in my mind, but he won't have done it himself and something tells me there's someone else in on it. We should think hard who that could be.'

'Don't get me wrong, Larry, I'm really grateful you came tonight and that you're helping, and yes I'll help you with the pub. There are a few options we can discuss with Harold later but can I trust you to keep all this to yourself until the time is right?'

'Yes you can trust me – if Dermott got wind of anything bullets would fly, so it's far too big a risk for me to get pissed and loosen my tongue. If you help me keep the pub afloat you have my word that I'll talk to nobody.'

'I take it that Aaron Parker is now out of the frame?'

'Yes, that's why I went to Brighton to see Dermott. I knew Parker was an explosive supplier but not who he was working with. Parker wanted to buy the pub and was screwing me on the price. I reckon he'd no idea your parents were the target for his old supplies of plastic explosive.'

'I see, so if you could get something on Parker you might have got the price you wanted?

'Yes. Parker tried to do a deal with Bill Knowles, my accountant, but for more than one reason that backfired on him big time. I still have to settle with Bill. Even though he's been doing something behind my back, once he's finished my accounts I want to pay him in full and give him the sack, and I think he'll be relieved.'

'Did he have a sniff at Jill?'

'You're like a bloody detective, Alan Fisher – yes, and mind your own fucking business.'

Alan laughed, but Larry scowled at him.

'I'm trying to mind my business, but you keep giving me more revelations and this was the first thing I could smile at.'

'Yes, and I deserved it but that's another story.'

'So where do we go from here, Larry? By the way, see this belt buckle – do you recognise it? I'd like to know which regiment it's from, but I haven't had time to look it up properly.'

Larry looked grim. 'That confirms Donnelly's involved, I think.'

'Why?'

'Where did you get it, Alan?'

'The burglar who broke into Harold Penny's house and stole his computer caught his belt on the window catch and left the buckle on the sill.'

'Snap, that's it then: the young man I had the first discussion with a few hours ago outside your place had an Irish accent. My guess now is that he's Shaun Donnelly; he was in the Ulster Defence Regiment just as his two uncles were before, when it was called the Royal Irish Rangers. That's the old Rangers belt badge, and it probably belonged to Liam – Shaun's father – or Dermott.'

Alan nodded. 'The jigsaw is fitting together and I think we're really close; maybe Shaun planted the bomb for Dermott, or somebody was paying through Dermott. All he had to do was detonate and scarper, and that could account for why the office bomb didn't work right and detonators were found on the floor.'

'Could be, Alan, but Dermott would have to be pulling the strings as moving high explosives is very difficult. Baxter would have done a deal with Paddy Mulligan once, but to get here from Northern Ireland with a device ready to use would take some doing.' Larry looked at his watch. 'Shit, is that the time? I'm off home otherwise Jill will think I'm with another woman. Can you drive?'

'No, but Cheryl can and she's some time off work tomorrow. I'll check and call you; can we meet up?'

'Yes, come over early evening and Jill can give Cheryl a cup of tea while we talk.'

'Thanks mate. I don't know what I'd have done without you, Larry; I was almost at a dead end.'

357

'It's not one-sided: I have problems and if this helps me sort them out I'll be in your debt. Maybe you'll get a discount in the pub in future.'

'It should be free. Off you go Larry, if you go out of the front door with the security guard he can get you a cab as you'll need one after the booze we've had. Don't wait for the bus; the cabs queue up outside the station opposite now so no fear of being jumped by anybody.'

'Thanks, Alan. My car's in the multi-storey; I'll come and get it in the morning. If that bloke is Shaun Donnelly I can handle him, and it could be interesting if I tell his uncle I met him.'

'Don't, Larry – think what could happen if Shaun tells him what happened.'

'He's bound to tell him, Alan, and that's a confrontation I'll have to deal with alone, and probably soon.'

After Larry had gone, Alan sat down and took in the evening's events. He put his head in his hands as the pain from his broken arm was getting past the booze, and he thought only about one thing: who was the mystery man?

He picked up the phone. 'Harold, sorry it's late but I'll be over for lunch tomorrow. I have the police in the morning, then Cheryl will drive me to you. I'll bring the Apple Mac with me.'

'Yes Alan, I've worked it out now with Janet next door. She's bought a new one and we've been looking at Facebook: Cheryl is on there and we've found lots of people from the past.'

'Really? That's given me an idea. Harold, can you ask my Uncle Ted who my dad worked with at senior level when he became a judge? Anyone he can think of – he has a perfect memory. It might just be someone we know or have come across who's played a big part in my parents' deaths. I've got lots to tell you; see you tomorrow.'

Chapter 32
Leah
The Parkers' Apartment

The front door of the apartment was slightly open. It was 6am and Aaron Parker had stayed the night with Sheila Hamilton. Inside everything was in place, but with no sign of his wife.

'Are you looking for your wife?' said a loud female voice from along the corridor. 'She's on the first floor with the porter; they have a story for you.'

Aaron knew the woman vaguely and she had obviously seen his wife leave, but he had no idea why. He walked down two flights of stairs to the porter's flat and office.

'Hello, good of you to turn up. Where've you been, Aaron?'

'Why are you here and not in the flat?'

'We had visitors, but let me have your story first; the porter will be back soon. He's just gone to lock our front door.'

'Sit down, I've something to tell you, Leah.'

'Is it about your woman?'

'What woman? No, it's about Mohammed Ana. I was out to dinner with him last night at the Ritz; he called and asked me to join him but it ended in disaster.'

'What do you mean?'

'By luck – and it was luck – I went to the toilet after the meal; in fact I called you here at the same time, but all I got was a continuous ring. Were you out or in the bath?'

'I'll tell you more in a minute. What happened?'

'When I was walking back to the table I was just in time to see Mohammed being taken out of the hotel by two suited men – they looked like security services or plain clothes policemen. On the table Mohammed had scribbled on a napkin; it said *Deported – watch your back*. I went to the desk and asked if he'd left anything in his room, but the desk clerk wouldn't give me any information until I put £50 into her sweaty hand. Then she looked around and said, "Mr Mohammed Ana was checked out by the visitors and they got his clothes from his room. He's on his way to Heathrow airport." So something has gone wrong with our deal; I had the call as expected about the book from Turkey, and Mohammed said he had the money and we were just waiting in the Ritz for Baxter to turn up when I went to the toilet. It was either the police or SIS who took him away; they'll be after me next and this address is easy to find. The odd thing is that maybe Superintendent White didn't know about this man being deported as if he did he'd have called me, or perhaps he did know and if that's the case it's bad for us. I've tried to phone him but it just goes to his voicemail – not like him, I wonder if he's avoiding me? I'll pack my bags then find a place to hide, but I'll leave

England as soon as possible. I have to meet with White first and find out how we stand.'

'That all adds up, Aaron: the police must have been here looking for you. I thought we had been burgled and I came down here to get the porter; someone has been inside but nothing's been moved. It must be over that deal you did from Northern Ireland – I told you it was a mistake to trust that Charlie Baxter.'

'He was just doing a job and he needed the money for his wife; she's seriously ill and needs very expensive treatment.'

'Did you give him anything?'

'No, just money I owed him from a job he was doing for me in Spain. He must have double-crossed me and told SIS; they must be paying him too.'

'I don't believe you, Aaron; you're a liar. I guess you and Baxter were selling explosives, and not to Spain. What have you done?'

'Look, Leah, I need to get away for a while.'

Aaron Parker restricted his wife's knowledge of his shady business and this time was no different. He knew he had to get away, and alone.

'Where will you go?'

'Best not to know, then you've no need to lie when they come back here. I'll go through our paperwork which I have safe and it will go to Zurich by DHL tonight. I'll deliver it personally to their office on my way to the airport and my sister will keep

362

everything safe for me. Get your passport, my dear, and leave England tomorrow: the police will be looking for me and they could also be watching you. They may take your passport; have you got your Lebanese one?'

'Yes I have, but you're the one who has to go quickly, Aaron. Do you think White will contact you? After all, he's supposed to be looking out for us.'

'He'd better.'

'Why?'

'You'll find out one day.'

'More puzzles, Aaron – I've had enough of all these games! By the way, aren't you going to ask me about the pub?'

'I guess he threw you out.'

'No, just the opposite: he was pleased to see me; he just hates you. I had too much to drink and when he finally said that he wanted £350,000 for the pub I told him to forget it. He didn't seem bothered at all, and I was getting on well with him until his wife joined us. I left by taxi – Harold Penny turned up when I was leaving; he doesn't know me but I know him.'

'That's why your car's not here. So what happened before you got drunk?'

'Nothing. As I said, once Jill gave me the evil eye we didn't talk about the sale of the pub anymore. He must have another buyer.'

'It's history for us, Leah, and for him as well unless Bill Knowles scrapes him out of a hole.'

Leah nodded. 'Right, I want to talk about us, Aaron.'

'What do you mean?'

'We don't have a marriage; it's a sham, and our relationship is just that of business colleagues married for convenience. I know you've a mistress so don't deny it – you can afford it but it's an insult to me and I've had it with you; I want a divorce. You take your money and I'll take mine, I've enough and you've plenty but you may need all of it if some of your old friends catch up with you.'

Aaron sat down. It was just what he had wanted to hear for the past five years, but when it finally came to it he was nervous about a split as Leah knew a lot about him and his business. Still, he knew he had to take that chance.

'I'm sorry, Leah, you're probably right. I'll contact you in a couple of weeks and we can talk, but not here in England.' Parker made the statement to keep things calm, but he had no intention of contacting her again or giving her any documents.

'Aaron, if you try to go to your sister in Zurich you won't be allowed to stay. The Swiss are tough on unwanted visitors and you're already on their blacklist.'

'That was a long time ago.'

'It's on their computer: weapons and explosives dealer, and this time you won't have an invitation from the government.'

364

'Then I'll have to risk somewhere else, and the best place is the Middle East but I'll be moving around all the time. Anyway, what's new? I've had a life of watching every doorway and looking over my shoulder for potential danger; that's why I've moved so frequently, and you knew the risks when you married me.'

The porter returned to his room and Leah started to cry. By the time he found her a tissue, Aaron had left. He was ready for this day but he had never been sure that it would happen: he was a coward at heart and as his wife was making the play he would leave before she changed her mind. He returned to their flat and quickly packed three bags with his favourite clothes, and as he did so she rushed into the room and grabbed his arm.

'I'm sorry, Aaron; but it probably is the best thing for both of us.'

'Goodbye, Leah. Have a good life; you own this place so sell it and buy a boat.'

Leah didn't speak. She bowed her head and held back her tears, but as the door slammed she felt better already. Her life would start again from that day, and she had plans. Packing her clothes was easy: they had moved so many times that they rented furniture rather than buying it, and their main purchase was always a heavyweight category five safe fitted into every apartment, which always stayed behind when they moved, but empty. Aaron had already taken his own paperwork, money and passport, and what was left was in her name and totally hers. It was more than enough for her to live comfortably for the rest of her life.

Chapter 33
Bill Knowles' Last Stand, and the Exodus to Follow

The phone call was expected.

'Larry, thanks for our chat the other day. I've been thinking about our discussion, and the tax part is the easy bit to sort out: I'll do everything you need to bring you up to date, and you owe me £1238 plus VAT in total for past and present. With regards to the pub, I'm prepared to offer you £340,000 subject to survey, no chain and completion by July 1st. Simple and straightforward; you have five days to accept or decline and of course Aaron Parker doesn't feature in the deal.'

'OK Bill, I'll think about it and let you know.'

'What happened to Parker, by the way? He's suddenly gone missing, and he left me a number which is now unobtainable.'

'No idea, he sent his wife to the pub to see me. She's a lovely lady but not much of a business person.'

'She also came here recently, and I know what you mean; she's a lovely woman and she's coming to take me to lunch today.'

'Anything that keeps you away from my Jill is good, Bill, but be careful. Aaron Parker could be a dangerous guy to do business with and I'm the only one allowed to beat you up.'

'Yes I know, mate, and that's history. I look forward to hearing from you.'

Bill stood in front of the mirror. He had told Larry only half a story, but he wanted him to know that his affair with Jill was finished and he knew that was all Larry really wanted to hear. He had given his secretary the day off, and he had big plans as he put the closed notice on the door. The knock from the back door was the one he was waiting for.

'Come in Leah, you look fabulous.'

'You look smart as well, Bill. So where do we go first?'

'Have you got your bags?'

'Yes, all four; that's all I have in the world. One bag has a load of cash in it: over £3 million in bonds in my name, and the deeds to our apartment, which are also in my name.'

'I didn't think you had that much. Is that more than Aaron has?'

'No, he's worth over £20 million but one phone call from me to the wrong people and he'd lose it all.'

'All made from supplying guns, explosives etc?'

'Yes and it doesn't worry him, or the number of deaths that were caused by his products; he has a crocodile skin. I've been following him for months, and so did my friend the other day when he thought I was safely away talking to Larry Nixon. She told me he went to the address I gave her which I found in Aaron's pocket; it was that girl Sheila Hamilton's apartment.'

'I was surprised when you called yesterday; it's all happened so quickly.

'I've just had more than enough of Aaron and his girls. My decision is on the floor in front of me; my bags are my answer to your invitation. I had one final short discussion with him about her as he left and he just wouldn't accept that she was nothing more than a hooker. He was blind to her magic but now he has nobody and he'll be deported if he doesn't get away quickly. He tried to do one deal too many with that Pakistani Mohammed Ana.'

'So that's why he left so quickly. Wasn't he the guy who double-crossed the Yanks?'

'Yes I think so, but with him and Aaron it's a long story and instead of keeping away from him he tried to do one final deal with the Pakistani and I guess the security people followed him to the Ritz and then grabbed and deported him. It'll be much easier for them to deport the man from the UK rather than have awkward discussions with the Yanks on extradition; they obviously wanted to see who he met and my husband fell into the trap. You won't read about it in the newspapers'

'Did you know that Alice Smith works for me sometimes? She's a friend of that hooker Sheila Hamilton, your husband's friend. She works as a private detective, usually on identity theft or checking up on people who've defaulted on loan payments for banks and building societies.'

'I didn't know what she did but Aaron did mention her once. I thought she was called Miller, though.'

Bill laughed at Alice's new name. 'It's funny, really: she did some unofficial work for some police guys on a nasty internal corruption case for cash. It was very unofficial and they gave her the new surname to protect her, but almost as a joke. But she did the right thing and gave them the slip as soon as they wanted her to do more. They were frightened of what she knew, so they've been trying to keep tabs on her in case she started to blackmail one of the top police guys. It seems national security is involved, so she keeps her head down with her new name of Smith.'

'Is she one of your girlfriends, Bill?'

'No, Leah, she's nearly 20 years younger than us. By the way, you look more like 38 than 48 – how do you do it?'

'By doing nothing but spending money on myself. The sex I had with you was the first in five years – I desperately wanted to be touched and loved but Aaron never tried; he obviously had someone else. My relationship with him was non-existent and I've been looking for a way out. Don't misunderstand me though, Bill: I'm not in love with you but I do like you very much and if you'll have me I'll sleep with you and look after your house. This is all if I don't get problems from the police – really they shouldn't bother me as they protected Aaron for years and we paid our taxes. I'll have to see what happens once he's gone, but I've done nothing wrong.'

'Thanks for being so direct. I understand how you feel: everything's a risk but since my wife died and I haven't taken many, but let's just get on with it and see what happens.'

'I'll drink to that, and I've only just started again; I all but gave up five years ago. Can you put the money and paperwork in your safe and we can sort out where to put it later?'

'Yes, sure. Leah, do you still want to buy The Brown Cow? I made Larry that offer we discussed today, and I'm sure he'll accept.'

'Come on, let's talk about it over lunch.'

Bill put the dowry in the safe and locked it, smiling as he did so. Was he dreaming? He would pinch himself later. He wondered where Aaron Parker wa,s and if he would really leave the country.

The answer was at Sheila Hamilton's apartment. Her doorbell sounded and she opened the door slowly as the entrance camera showed only the back of a head. Then a loud knocking started as well, and she knew it was the police.

'Is Aaron Parker here?'

'Yes,' said Sheila, shaking as she spoke.

'I'm Inspector Curtis and this man is from the immigration service.'

Parker appeared from the bedroom with just two suitcases, one in each hand. He glanced at the visitor's ID and smiled.

'I'm ready, gentlemen, so tell me what my destination is?'

'Well, we understand you have dual passports: British and Lebanese. Your British one has been cancelled, so you have a choice: Beirut at 22.00 or Nicosia at 21.40. The British government will pay for your one-way ticket, but sorry, it's not business class.'

'Nicosia it is. No contest, as you people would say.'

The policeman pointed to the door. 'One of our local colleagues, DI Hubbard, is waiting downstairs with an immigration officer. They'll take you to Heathrow, where they'll interview you then accompany you to the aircraft, so come and have your last ride in the UK.'

Aaron turned and kissed Sheila on the cheek. 'Take this, Sheila – it'll keep you in clothes for a few years. Here are my spare car keys; you can collect the car from my apartment and I've already filled out a transfer form in case this ever happened. The car and all the documents are inside the glove box: just date it, sign it and send it of to the DVLA; the car is yours and the signed letter with it states that clearly, so do whatever you want with it. You may get £10,000 for the number plate alone.'

'Thanks Aaron, you're a good man.'

'No, not really Sheila, but that's another story. Try not to bump into my wife, so pick the car up at night.'

Parker smiled to himself. Leah would think that she would be getting his Mercedes, and there could be a serious handbag fight when she learnt that it was not the case. Sheila closed the door, poured herself a Martini and lifted the glass to toast Aaron's departure. He had never been more than just a customer, but he was the best one she ever had and probably irreplaceable.

Conversation was non-existent as the unmarked police car joined the M25 on route for Terminal 5, London Heathrow Airport. Parker took his last look at the lush green countryside with some sadness. He was leaving his wife and his adopted country and the survival price was high; he had no choice but would still ask a question or two if he got the opportunity. Detective Inspector Hubbard climbed out of the car first and then held the door for his passenger.

'Welcome to Heathrow, Mr Parker. I understand your chosen destination is Cyprus, and we have an hour and a half before boarding commences. This young man will check you in; give him your passport, then we'll have a brief meeting here in this lounge. It isn't a very private place but we can find a quiet corner and I'll even buy you a coffee.'

The BA ground staff man returned very quickly with a boarding pass and Aaron Parker's Lebanese passport, then took his two bags, tagged them and put them on the conveyor. He started a conversation on whether Aaron had packed them himself, but Parker and DI Hubbard were already on their way through security with an immigration officer. Like anyone else Aaron had to go through the scanner, and as a matter of routine he was thoroughly searched. Hubbard was edgy: the last thing he wanted was for Parker's departure to be delayed due to the security staff finding something on him. He passed through the security area and another immigration officer came up to them.

'DI Hubbard, you can have my office for 30 minutes; it's the blue door over there. Help yourself to coffee – come with me and I'll show you.'

The two men went into the office with the officer; it turned out to be an immigration interview room, and was totally bare other than a table, a few chairs and a bubbling coffee machine.

'Thanks; we'll return the favour sometime if you're in Guildford. So, Mr Parker, we've got our own business lounge; those immigration people are very keen to make sure you have the correct send-off and they seem pretty anxious that I stay with you all the way to the plane.'

'I am a VIP at last. Now what I can do for you, Inspector?'

'OK, let me explain. My job at the moment is not directly connected to you; it's to find the killers of Gordon and Fay Fisher who died in the bomb attack on their house.'

Parker nodded; he knew exactly what DI Hubbard wanted.

'I've just spoken with their son Alan, and he's told me about the supplies of explosive materials from you and a Mr Baxter, whom we are told worked with you. I also know that we're supposed to be giving you some limited protection as I'm told the British government bought from you once.'

'Yes Inspector, all correct, and actually it was a lot more than once and it's common knowledge in Whitehall. So what do you want?'

'I want the killers, and I think I'm getting warm. Alan tells me that a Mr Larry Nixon has given him a summary of what happened during his father's career. In the time we've got I want to discuss it with you, and if I'm not satisfied you will not leave.'

Parker remained motionless. He would definitely be leaving: the policeman was bluffing, and not very well.

'So far, my conclusions are firstly that you supplied explosives many years ago via Libya to Northern Ireland to a local IRA man, a certain Mr Paddy Mulligan, who still had some supplies left over when he died. He sold some to a Mr Charlie Baxter to set up a bomb. Somebody as yet unidentified wanted Gordon killed, so he hired an Irishman called Dermott Donnelly, who we think gave the contract killing to a novice, his nephew Shaun Donnelly. The bomb was given to Shaun Donnelly by Baxter, who allegedly believed the job was in Spain; Donnelly knew what to do as he'd had some training but we believe had never used explosives before. I think the young man made mistakes during his setup, but the bomb planted in the car worked perfectly and was deadly: the Fishers had no chance of survival.

The amount of plastic explosive used must have been massive, judging by the damage it did.

'The Donnellys and their friends had problems with Judge Advocate Gordon Fisher, and rumour goes that the threats he received were from them. Other Irishmen made abusive phone calls; others sent him intimidating letters, but they could've been from anyone. He was a target for their anger simply as the man in charge of several court martials, and he had justifiably sentenced some of their family and friends relating to offences they had committed in action. The irony is that it was Northern Irishmen serving in the British army who faced charges and the relationship with Mulligan, a devout Catholic, must have been purely business.' The Inspector interrupted. 'What we want to know is whether Mulligan was supplying both sides during the Troubles in Belfast? Then it may make some sense.'

Aaron shook his head. 'No way, but from memory he was terrified of Donnelly and if Donnelly wanted something, Mulligan couldn't refuse and nor could Baxter.'

'Fascinating, Aaron, and from what you've told me I've a better understanding of the background to the case. I have most parts of the puzzle that I didn't know already, thanks. But I still don't have the final lead on who placed the contract to kill the Fishers; if I knew just a little more it might take me to a name. Come on, we're running out of time; you must know something else as I believe there was another motive for the murders.'

Parker shook his head.

'All right, but before we go to the departure gate, I still have some questions which I'd like you to answer for me. You aren't obliged to do so but I think you're going to help me convict the killer, after all you're finished with all this now.'

Parker looked at the clock on the wall and put his hands flat on the table.

'You're nearly there, I think I know your questions. I'm sure Charlie Baxter met and gave Dermott Donnelly the bomb, probably at his house in Brighton, but Donnelly wouldn't have discussed the target with him. Shaun Donnelly wouldn't have been trusted to carry the device a long distance, so Dermott probably met his nephew near the Fisher house. Your colleagues in the RUC regularly watch young Shaun – you probably didn't know that, and yes, before you ask that is sometimes here in the UK. Shaun is public enemy number one and how he stays out of jail beats me, and that goes with the fact that Dermott must have had help from a special person or persons to make sure he wasn't picked up with the device in his possession. But Inspector, I'm sure that even from my limited knowledge of him it seemed pretty certain to me that Baxter wouldn't have given him the devices if he'd known they were for use here in England.

'The deaths of Gordon Fisher and his wife weren't ordered by any Irish political group: the murders were carried out by Shaun Donnelly for his uncle, and he did it for the cash. I'll write on this piece of paper the name of the man I believe is connected to the murders and the reason why. I'll sign and date it; you may get away with it as a statement, but anyway it's all you're getting from me now, Inspector. I hope you get a confession.'

Aaron Parker wrote on the A4 piece of paper in good clear writing the name of the man he thought was behind the crime committed by Shaun Donnelly. He passed it, folded, to DI Norman Hubbard. The policeman unfolded it and looked Parker straight in the eyes.

'Are you sure? This is massive.'

'Yes, that's it; now take me to my plane and on the way I need something stronger than coffee.'

Hubbard took the man by the arm. He had what he wanted, but he had no idea how he would start to deal with it. The first thing was to go and see Alan Fisher; he was probably one of only a few people left whom Hubbard could trust in what was becoming a unique situation.

Chapter 34
Inquest
Surrey Coroner's Court, Woking

The coroner's court was in session and had two cases on the list for the day, but it was unlikely that they would get to the second case due to the magnitude of the first. One of the most senior coroners in the country, Maurice Davis, was in attendance; it was not a day for one of his colleagues to stand in for him. The police had a private theory that someone might turn up to watch the proceedings to see how far the investigation had got in four months. The court and surrounding areas had additional CCTV and there would be many plain-clothed police around the court.

The brutal murder of Gordon and Fay Fisher in their own home had rocked the nation. Could the IRA be back in the UK, or was it Al Qaeda, or just some madman with a grudge? All these questions had been put indirectly to the authorities. Maurice Davis did not respond to pressure to speed up the inquest, especially from the police or even the Home Office. He would commence proceedings when he had all the information he needed and not before.

That day had arrived and he saw his court full, with no visitor seats free as he briefed the jury on their duties for the day. As usual the mixture of people chosen varied from an out-of-work labourer to a midwife, several teachers, a footballer and an army officer. In an unusual move the coroner immediately replaced the army officer with a vicar, then he thanked him for attending and gave no reason why he should not be on the jury. The clerk stood up and addressed the court.

'Ladies and gentlemen, our first case today is the inquest into the deaths of Gordon Alexander Fisher and Fay Fisher, who resided on the Tyrells Wood estate, Leatherhead, Surrey. Full details of the deceased are posted on the board behind the gallery, and the jury has a copy of these details.'

The coroner looked up from his paperwork. 'The deaths will be presented separately as some medical facts are obviously different. The verdicts must be considered and noted separately. Does the foreman of the jury understand this point of order?'

The footballer was the appointed foreman, and nodded in agreement.

'Please answer in words, I need to hear it.'

'Yes, I understand, your honour.'

'Just address me as sir; that's sufficient. We firstly deal with Mr Fisher, then afterwards Mrs Fisher.'

The proceedings followed the usual pattern, with the police report followed by the pathologist's, and special evidence given by an SIS representative who described himself just as a civil servant. Alan gripped Cheryl's arm throughout the proceedings – today he felt that reasons didn't matter; it was just the question of who did it that was on his mind. DI Hubbard gave his evidence, adding that the case was still very much open and enquiries were continuing. He spoke with confidence, and had arranged to see Alan after the hearing to discuss Aaron Parker's theories. Hubbard had the file of photographs downloaded from his father's files, plus the photographs Harold had found with the will and the identikit sketch of the man who had gone into Mandy Rix's shop. On their own they were all relevant, but it would be Parker's information that could reveal the killers. Hubbard had to hold back Parker's revelations and he knew the coroner would not demand details on every piece of evidence as long as the cause of death was clear.

After nearly two hours of hearing evidence the coroner pushed his papers together and removed his spectacles.

'Ladies and gentlemen of the jury, you have heard the reports, evidence and technical details regarding the deaths of these two people. The delay in holding this inquest was caused by a piece of evidence that was difficult for the pathologist to deal with, namely the presence of a revolver found on the floor of the car on the driver's side, with two bullets missing from a magazine of six. When I read the first report from the pathologist I asked for more work to be done to see if these two bullets could be found, and that included checking the car and the remains of the bodies. Thanks to technology and detailed comprehensive forensic work carried out by the pathologist and the police, we know for certain that the gun had not been fired recently and no bullet wounds were found on the Fishers' bodies.

'My advice to you is to record the case firstly on Gordon Fisher as unlawful death by explosion, which of course is sometimes stated as a murder committed by a person or persons unknown. The evidence is such that whoever did this terrible thing meant to kill. I then ask you to record on the case of Fay Fisher the same verdict of unlawful death by explosion, and again that it was a murder committed by a person or persons unknown, and who meant to kill. I ask you now to leave the court and follow the instructions given to you by the bailiff on a majority verdict. You return firstly on the case of Mr Fisher, then retire and return on the case of Mrs Fisher. Is that understood?'

'Yes sir,' replied the footballer. By this time had seen and heard enough, and his white face confirmed his disposition. The coroner left the court and the remainder of the gallery stood up and muttered to each other. The coroner was confident they would be back in court very soon.

'Harold, what happens next?'

'Not much, Alan – today is almost a formality as your parents' deaths were plainly caused by a bomb. The court is here to make sure the cause of death is correctly confirmed; if they had any doubts now the coroner would have mentioned that an open verdict could possibly be recorded, but not today, I'm absolutely sure. It's unusual to hear two cases like this together, but the coroner has the discretion within usual law guidelines. What about the gun, Alan?'

'I didn't know about the revolver in the car, only that my father had one. I wonder why he had it with him? Most unusual, but we may never know why.'

The footballer led the jury back into the court after a deliberation of just 30 minutes. The clerk opened the door for the coroner, who had papers under his arm. He whispered in his ear and the clerk nodded and turned to face the jury.

'Have you reached a verdict?'

'Yes sir. We find the cause of death of Mr Gordon Fisher was unlawful death by a person or persons unknown.'

'That has been noted; thank you. Now retire the case concerning Mrs Fay Fisher.

The journey to and from the deliberation room was longer than the discussion and the jury returned within five minutes.

'Have you reached a verdict on the death of Mrs Fay Fisher?'

The coroner scribbled on his paper the word *Hubbard*, and looked up as the foreman of the jury spoke.

'We also find that the cause of death of Mrs Fay Fisher was unlawful death by a person or persons unknown.'

'Thank you, please be seated.'

The coroner looked up from his paperwork. 'The verdict of the jury is recorded. However, in my position I'm allowed to make a comment or two, but I would like to do that in private with the police. We'll have a recess for 30 minutes.'

The court clerk went up to Norman Hubbard. 'Inspector Hubbard, could you join the coroner in his room? Tea or coffee?'

Hubbard was already halfway out of the door of the court. He wanted to see Alan Fisher, and his stomach turned over nervously at the coroner's request. He had no idea what he wanted.

'Yes of course; tea please, I'll be right with you. Alan, a minute please?'

'Yes Norman, are you coming over later in the week? Not today as I'd sort of forgotten that the inquest was today, but can we meet on Saturday?'

'OK, but let's talk on the phone later.'

'We've been through all the pictures and tonight we're having dinner at my Uncle Ted's place as a sort of wake for my parents; we thought afterwards we could go through everything we've got. Did you see Parker on his way out?'

'Yes, he'll be in Cyprus by now. I'm not sure what questions he'll be asked or if he'll be allowed to stay in the country; the immigration people have already been on the phone to us. I'll tell you more on Saturday – the coroner's waiting for me now, so I must go.'

The formality of the day had not upset Alan. He knew that the death of his parents was the work of a madman or contract killer and he guessed DI Hubbard had something new to discuss. Saturday could not come quickly enough. Alan and Cheryl jumped into his Uncle Ted's car. He had invited Harold Penny and Cheryl's mother Mandy, but if he had invited all the people he knew at the coroner's court he would have filled a football ground. Everyone wanted to know what had happened that December afternoon in Leatherhead.

The coroner was waiting for Hubbard in his office. 'Come in, Inspector, and collect a cup of tea. We don't have long.'

'This is a first sir, I don't think I've ever had a conversation with a coroner outside the witness box.'

'Yes Inspector; hopefully it's the first and last time. I just wanted a quick word with you, now listen.'

Hubbard took the deserved reprimand and listened to the Coroner.

'You didn't know this, but once I was a copper and I knew Gordon Fisher well. I first met him when he was a barrister and occasionally we had a beer together; he was a great bloke and I miss him. I had no idea originally that I'd be the coroner today, and I could hardly contain my sadness but I wanted to take the hearing. You have to get the bastards who did this, Inspector. What I'm going to tell you is not official but it could help you –

most irregular I know, but I'd deny it came from me if anyone asked me later about what I'm telling you. Do you understand that, Inspector Hubbard?'

'Yes sir, please carry on.'

'One day when I was young sergeant I was leaving the Old Bailey after we'd lost a fraud case on a technicality. It didn't happen often, but when it did it made the police look like bloody fools. The defence lawyer was Gordon Fisher; he found a reason for the charges to be dismissed due to some incorrect interview techniques. The senior policeman responsible got a very serious telling off from the chief constable – he escaped losing his stripes but he lost face and it was several years before he got promoted, and to be fair to him at the time he was a good policeman. As we walked together down the steps away from the court he said, "That's the second time that bloody man has done me up, and if I ever got the chance I'd sort him out good and proper." It was all a bit over-the-top, and something said on the spur of the moment.

'Then later I heard that Gordon had got the Judge Advocate job dealing with military court martials. He was ideal as he had served in the RAF, then done some security service work and of course he was also a barrister. I thought at the time that the post Gordon was given could possibly lead to the very top position in the judiciary; when we met I teased him about it, but of course he wouldn't discuss it. Gordon just smiled at me, which must have meant he knew something about his future but he was certainly not telling me. The policeman he'd upset that day in court was the other candidate for the original Judge Advocate job; he'd initially had a legal education but decided to join the police after serving in the army. I heard on the grapevine that he went absolutely mental with disappointment when Gordon got the job over him.

'The Chief Constable of Surrey was told about the policeman's expectations and gave him a consolation prize of a promotion, which was followed by several more over the next few years. He was doing a good job until one day he and Fisher clashed over something and nothing on a case where he had to give evidence to a military trial. His evidence was clearly biased, as the policeman made it clear that if the trial had been in a civil court the case would have been thrown out. He was seriously reprimanded by your father and his own boss, resulting in a transfer to the RUC which he regarded as a punishment.

'Unfortunately during his time in Belfast he befriended some of the wrong people, and one was a man called Dermott Donnelly who had somehow got away with all sorts of nonsense in the army. After he left under a cloud I heard he'd been pulled in for dealing in explosives, guns and even forgery, most of which involved weapon sales to the UK, and that he was using his antiques business as a cover. Donnelly was never charged with anything in Northern Ireland and I'm pretty sure that applies here as well. I think he lives in the south of England now. I was told all this by SIS – in those days, MI6 – as a case came up which the security service were very unhappy about. A hearing on an officer killed in Londonderry was recorded as misadventure when it was clearly murder, although I was never sure why MI6 were in Northern Ireland in the first place.

'All attempts by the RUC to get to the truth failed, and Donnelly made sure nobody would give evidence to put the actual killer in the frame. The result was that the person I'm talking about was put in the spotlight in the RUC and all sorts of things came to the surface. He was eventually demoted and moved back to England, but is still in a reasonably senior position, which I could never understand other than that he must have friends in high places. My view, Detective Inspector Hubbard, is that this man arranged the killings of Gordon Fisher and his wife. That's it, I must get back now; you know what to do.'

At first Hubbard just stared at the coroner; his mouth would not open to say the words. 'Who is he, sir?' he asked eventually.

'You know him very well and I'm sure you have your own suspicions; if not you shouldn't be a copper. Best of luck, and goodbye, Inspector.'

Norman Hubbard now had a list of one, confirmed by two people, but he was trying to work out in his mind how to deal with it. Firstly he had to get photo evidence of the man with Gordon, then somehow get the Donnelly duo pulled in for questioning. His mind was racing ahead but then it hit him: if Dermott Donnelly organised the Fishers' death and carried it out by delegating the task to his nephew Shaun, he was the one they had to find first. No doubt Shaun had been told to frighten and maybe kill Alan Fisher, because at some stage Dermott would regard him as a risk. Alan had been a good, careful soldier and it would have needed a clever plan to catch him unawares.

Hubbard took a few minutes' break in the car park before driving back to his office in Guildford. He had two missed calls on his mobile, and one message was from Brighton police, who said they had a book the size of the New Testament on Dermott Donnelly, but that he had never even been charged with anything. Could he ring them as soon as possible? The second call was from his boss Chief Superintendent White, who didn't leave a message. He had probably thought that Hubbard would be at the inquest all day.

Chapter 35
Pictures and Pictures
Ted Fisher's House, Leatherhead

'Come in all of you, sensible to order taxis for later. I've quite a lot of food and booze to get through but I hope we can get a little work done beforehand.'

Alan shook hands with guests as they arrived, but his mind was elsewhere. His uncle handed him a glass of sherry.

'It's been a shit day, Ted, but it had to be done and I thought the coroner did his job without any fuss. The killers must know the verdict by now, and at my next meeting with the police I want us to be able to tell them something from these boxes of photos I've printed off. I spent £100 on Kodak paper so we've got good images. I've asked Janet Ash to join us; she's Harold's next door neighbour and is pretty good on the computer and she collated most of the pictures. To get us started, would Cheryl and Mandy help my housekeeper Jean to lay the table and sort us all out with a beer? Then we'll go into the library for a few minutes and try and find someone we know in this lot.'

Alan was eager to get going, and encouraged everyone into the library except Cheryl and Mandy, though to Cheryl's annoyance her mum got a kiss as well from him as they left for the kitchen. His mobile phone rang and Norman Hubbard's number came up on the display.

'Alan, lots happening and I know you're looking at the photos tonight but be really careful when you leave and tell your friends the same because we've had a call from the *Daily Mail*. They've matched that identikit picture of the man at your girlfriend's mother's shop with a picture of a man working at a concert as a bouncer. Cheryl's mum saw the picture of him in the newspaper dragging a young kid away from the stage and he got the sack. By the way, tell her a big thank-you from me. The company who employed him said he worked at four gigs for them in London and they paid him cash, and they said that he was Irish and his name was Sam Brown, an alias, I believe, for a certain Shaun Donnelly. The address he gave them was of course false.

'We then asked MI5 to try and find him in London via the street camera equipment – we've the same gear but they're better at using it. They took all day, but then they found him living in a bedsit in Tottenham. We went to the place 30 minutes after we got the address but somehow he must have had a tip-off. But that's not possible, really: only a few of us knew about him, or maybe it was a coincidence and he was just too quick for us. Anyway, he got clean away. We searched his place and found all sorts of stuff: maps and an old Webley 38 calibre handgun, probably made in the 1960s. It was in good condition and no doubt it would still work if you could find ammunition for it. We also found a few photos of the outside of your flat in Epsom but it was difficult to see the registrations plates apart from your new doorman's car; he was on duty so I would guess it was taken very recently.

'I've put someone on permanent guard at your flat for the weekend – check in with him when you get home; I'll text you his number. He lives in Epsom so he knows the back doubles if Shaun turns up and gets away from him. We can blanket the town quickly once we get a sighting, but we doubt it'll be tonight; he must have a stash of money and a gun, perhaps in a left luggage box waiting to be collected. We've cameras everywhere at all the London stations, and the people on duty have his photograph.'

'Thanks, Norman. Have you got a mole in the police, or someone who knows Shaun Donnelly? I doubt they would know what we're about to do; more likely Dermott's been tipped off and told Shaun to get moving.'

'From information I got today it seems Dermott may know most of what we're doing so we've to be careful. I'm going to see the director at SIS tonight with the latest developments, and I think we're back on a full-scale operation together with Surrey Police and SIS. They have to be involved as national interest is their area and they need to help us finally clean the Irish connection up for good; it seems a lot of weapons have still been coming through Dermott Donnelly and someone's been turning a blind eye to it all.'

'OK, I understand. Please keep in contact, and we'll call you from here if we find an interesting photo.'

During Hubbard's phone call Alan had a missed call with no message, and the number wasn't blocked so he redialled it.

'Larry, sorry mate, I didn't put your number in my phone but I saw your missed call.'

'Yes, I just had a call from Dermott Donnelly. That in itself is not unusual but he said he was on the way here to meet me, and he'll be here in about 20 minutes. What do you think, does he know we're near to getting him arrested?'

'Could be, Larry, but we can't take any chances as we know he was involved with my parents' death but we're still looking for the big man. If we get Donnelly arrested now we might lose the trail and the police always fail to get any charges to stick when he's pulled in.'

'All right, I'll see what he wants; I'll make sure Jill is with me when we talk and hopefully we can confine him to the snug bar.'

'If you need me, call – I'm five minutes away on the estate but once he sees me he'll know you're on to him.'

'I think he knows that already, but I'll call you when he's left.'

Alan was uncomfortable: Donnelly was a dangerous man and Larry had grassed him up. Alan knew he couldn't leave him to face Donnelly with just his wife helping him, so he made a quick decision to go to the pub and be there when Donnelly met his old friend Larry Nixon.

'Sorry folks, I've got to go out for half an hour or so. Larry Nixon has something for me and he's just down the road at his pub; I'll be back as soon as I can.'

'You can't drive, Alan, because of your arm,' said Cheryl.

'Yes, I forgot – my brain is only working in one direction. Take me in your car, and if we go now dinner will be ready by the time we get back. You'll have to stay in the car, though – Larry wants to see me in private.'

In anticipation of a situation like this Alan had hidden the Beretta in his computer bag, but he had no room for the silencer. He took the gun out and checked the magazine, then pushed it down the back of his trousers without Cheryl seeing him.

'Harold, do me a favour and call DI Norman Hubbard. Here's his number; ask him to send a patrol car with the siren off to The Brown Cow. Explain that I'm going to meet Larry Nixon and Dermott Donnelly could be there.'

'OK, but be careful, Alan and remember you only have one good arm.'

Alan smiled and waved at him as he fastened his seatbelt, and Cheryl did a rally turn into the road. She could see the pub lights already; everything looked calm.

'Park here near the exit, Cheryl and give me a kiss. I won't go into the snug bar unless I need to help Larry; Donnelly doesn't know me. When the patrol car comes flag it down as it comes through the entrance, explain where I am and wait for me to return.'

'I'm frightened, Alan.'

'Don't be, we're nearly out of this nightmare and then we can start living our lives again. See you in a few minutes.'

Alan surveyed the car park and guessed that the Range Rover parked near the pub door belonged to Donnelly. He put his hand on the bonnet: the engine was hot and it must have stopped only minutes before. The police patrol car entered the car park with all its lights off; the driver had the message about the situation loud and clear. Cheryl jumped out of the Mini and told the two policemen what was happening.

'We'll just wait here; DI Hubbard told us not to approach the pub unless we hear or see a problem. My colleague Sergeant Fred Lowry is armed and I've a Taser gun. I'm Sergeant Jack Rix.'

'*The* Jack Rix?'

'Yes, who're you?'

'I'm Cheryl, your cousin – do you not recognise me?'

'I haven't seen you for over ten years, Cheryl.'

'That's because my old man pissed off with a younger model to replace my mum, so my uncle has been off the Christmas card list since then.'

The family catch-up was interrupted by the sound of a gun, and the two policemen fastened their coats and ran towards the pub.

'Remember, my boyfriend has a yellow jacket on!'

'OK, we know him, Cheryl.'

As they approached the door a bleeding Larry Nixon was dragging Dermott Donnelly out of the pub by his hair.

'Leave him to us, Mr Nixon.'

Larry released his grip and Donnelly started to run away as Sergeant Rix pulled out his Taser and fired. The zip of the gun was similar to the machine used to light gas stoves, but much more effective. Donnelly rolled over: the stun gun had done its job, and the policemen lifted him up and handcuffed him to the door handle on the back seat.

Cheryl turned to Larry. 'Where's Alan? Who fired the shot?'

'I'm here, Cheryl.'

She rushed up and hugged him.

'Larry needs to go to hospital, Donnelly shot him in the foot. As I waited outside the snug I heard a terrible argument. Jill Nixon ran out in tears and as the door opened I saw Dermott pull the gun out. I smashed the door open as he was just about to fire the gun into Larry's chest. The gun still fired but into Larry's foot, Donnelly went mad and jumped at Larry, swearing and spitting. I managed to pull him off and kicked the gun away, Larry recovered and punched Donnelly three times below his breastbone and as the Irishman fell to the ground Larry grabbed his hair and here he is.'

'I'll need statements, Mr Nixon and Mr Fisher, but they can wait until tomorrow. Once Donnelly comes round he'll find he's in a secure hospital unit at Guildford to get him checked out. He'll then be charged with assault with a firearm, which will keep him locked in the cells until DI Hubbard gets hold of him.'

'Thanks. We'll take Larry to Epsom Hospital; its only a few miles away. They'll probably call you about the wound, but looking at it I reckon the bullet is in the snug bar floor. It went straight through his foot.'

Jill Nixon ran towards them. 'I've closed the pub and everyone is leaving. Go back to your flat Alan, and I'll take Larry to the hospital in my car. He can walk OK, if I need you I'll call.'

'Thanks, we'll get back to my Uncle Ted's house.'

Cheryl was still shaking as she drove the car. 'I need a stiff drink, Alan.'

'So do I. It should be an interesting phone call from Jill to her sister Penny Donnelly. I can't see that man ever getting out now; once Larry has given DI Hubbard the full story I guarantee they'll find stuff under the carpet to put him away for life.'

'It's long overdue and I think we'll soon find out how he managed to keep out of jail all these years. By the way, that sergeant was my cousin Jack.'

'Which one?'

'The driver; the one who fired the stun gun. I haven't seen him for years as he's on my dad's side of the family that we didn't see.'

'Did you get much chance to talk to him?'

'For a few minutes; he said this had been his first call of the day as one of the chief superintendents based at Surrey Police HQ had grabbed him in the car park and told him to take him to Heathrow this afternoon. Jack said his governor told him off for not telling him until he was halfway to the airport.'

'I wonder who that was, and why did he want to leave so quickly?'

'That's what he said. He saw his ticket as he left it on the seat when he was getting out; he was going to the Bahamas.'

'I'll tell Norman Hubbard that; he may be interested. I'll ring him when we get inside.'

As the rasp of Mini's exhaust echoed around Ted Fisher's forecourt everyone came out and Alan got another big kiss from Mandy Rix. He was beginning to worry about her, and Cheryl did not look at all pleased.

'We've been busy while you were at the pub and it's Mandy again who's come up with a possibility.'

'It's a certainty, Harold; it's as definite as that my tits are real.'

Mandy's crude joke helped deal with the situation: the evidence was conclusive. Alan and Cheryl looked at each other and smiled.

'For once, mother, you may be right and by the way, we bumped into Jack – he's a copper now.'

'Yes, someone told me. I married the wrong brother.'

Mandy picked up three photographs, and one of those Ted had found with Gordon Fisher's will. She got a December issue of *Surrey Life* and folded back a page with a large photograph of a man in uniform.

'Look, all of you: the four pictures are of the same man except he had a beard; now he's much fatter in the last picture with no beard, and it's got to be very recent as it's at the October county dog show in Guildford. From his size he looks like he's been enjoying life a bit too well. Alan, your father's never near him in the photos and he's always last in the line. Didn't Gordon like him?'

'Well done Mandy, I agree with you. It's the same man, and as my father never mentioned him I didn't know how well he knew him.

'He's in a couple of other pictures as well but he seems camera-shy and they only show half his face through his beard, and he always has those glasses on.'

'So Alan,' Harold interjected, 'can you tell us what these pictures mean, and also what tonight's episode was all about?'

'Yes I will, and please all of you listen carefully. The man in those pictures, who we're now certain arranged for my parents' deaths, is Chief Superintendent Dick White. DI Hubbard knows this already and the man's rapid exit to the Bahamas today tells me he's on the run. I know the reasons and will explain later when I have the full story, but basically I can't understand why I didn't guess earlier: he worked in Northern Ireland and with my father abroad, and over a period of time they must have fallen out. I think I even know why my brother Ben died.'

'Stop, Alan; tell us later.' Ted Fisher pointed outside. 'The security lights are on. The ones on the back path are hidden to intruders until they go off, but it's probably only that mangy old fox again. I borrowed your father's revolver before he died and I'm certain I shot the animal twice, but somehow he's still alive.'

'So that's another thing you didn't tell me, Ted, and it could solve another mystery. Did my father take the gun back from you?'

'Yes, it was Fay who let me borrow it and I was going to return it before your father knew about it – that fox was a menace. When he saw it in my kitchen he was very cross, but he just threw it into the seat pocket of his car and cursed me for taking it without his permission.'

'Stop – look over there now, Ted; I can see somebody in the shadows. I'll find out who it is – phone Hubbard and tell him to have someone on standby, he's expecting this. We'll watch and wait; keep the curtains closed, we can see the back well enough from the toilet window.'

'Alan, quick – he's making for the Mini and ignoring the lights! What's he doing, is he letting the air out of the tyres?'

'No, he's attaching a package to the underneath of the driver's door and putting a strip at the bottom. It's a crude bomb that will detonate when I open the door.'

The ring of the house phone made them all jump.

'Ted Fisher here, who's calling? OK right, I understand. I'll tell Alan.' He hung up. 'Alan, that was Sergeant Rix; he's next to our front gate. He and his colleague will seal off the exit with the police car and backup is already on the way from the police armed response unit. They'll be here in two or three minutes.'

'Good. What did they do with Donnelly, then? Surely they can't have got to Guildford hospital and back here in such a short time, we only left them about 25 minutes ago.'

'No, Rix said they didn't take him to Guildford but to Epsom Hospital A&E on instructions from their station. A local policeman is watching Donnelly until a police van collects him in a couple of hours.'

'Now why the hell have they done that? He'd been stunned with the Taser but it wears off pretty quickly, and as soon as he comes round fully he'll be looking for Larry Nixon who he'll guess must be in the same hospital.'

'OK Alan, but first we have to sort out this visitor. Do you know him?'

'Yes, it's most probably my parents' killer; he's called Shaun Donnelly, the nephew of Dermott Donnelly who was in the incident at the pub tonight. Dermott was one of the people who gave the job to Shaun – we believe for a lot of cash and a trip to South America, after I'd been killed as well. All of which leads back to what I've just told you: Shaun was also the man who came to the salon and planted the dummy bomb. It was just a message to me not to try and find my parents' killers, and when I ignored it Shaun was given the contract to kill me. He obviously had little or no explosive left; his supplies had all been used, but he managed in the end to get some, we think from a bloke called Major Bill Barrington, then he must have knocked him out and strapped half of it to the man's body and murdered him. The irony is we now believe Barrington had killed one of his old buddies in Northern Ireland, a man known as Paddy Mulligan – he suspected that he'd supplied explosive for the murder of my parents. Barrington went to Belfast to confront him about it, and they argued so Barrington throttled him with steel wire.

'Shaun got the short straw from his uncle and must have been told to fix Barrington and make it look like suicide, which he somehow managed to do. I was suspicious as it takes a lot of guts to kill a trained senior soldier in his own home, and I think it was the last job Dermott may have done himself. Charlie Baxter, an English army mate and the one I've just spent a week with in Turkey, got the explosives from Mulligan and set it up with detonators he had kept at his own home, but allegedly didn't know the bomb was to be used here as they told him it was for Spain. At the time he didn't care: he needed money urgently as

402

his wife is very sick. These are all still theories but DI Hubbard and I are convinced this is the outline of what is happening. We are certain we know why my parents were killed and tomorrow Hubbard will make a statement; that's when the killer has been caught as well.'

'Alan, quick, look – he's leaving by the side gate! The police will miss him.'

Donnelly was climbing over the gate onto a path, which went behind the house and joined the road 200 yards nearer the gate exiting the estate.

'Ring Hubbard quickly, I'm going to stop him.'

'No, Alan, wait! Please stop!'

'No, Cheryl, this is what I'm trained for, even with this smashed-up arm.'

Alan took the Beretta out of his computer bag for the second time that evening. He checked the magazine and ran around the garden, waiting for Shaun Donnelly. The wait was too long, and he began to sweat. Where had he gone? Had he done a U-turn, or had he climbed into somebody else's garden? Alan was thinking about what to do when he heard movement behind. A large, slim figure was sat on the top of the wall, looking at him with an automatic pistol in his hand, cocked and pointing at Alan.

'Good evening Fisher, at last I finish the job. You thought you were smart and that I'd use this path as a way out, but I think like you and you fucked up. I should've run you over last week; you were lucky then but now you'll join the Fisher family grave as well.'

'Wait, Shaun – just one thing, please. Tell me who your Uncle Dermott was working for. Who gave you the job of killing my parents? I think I know, but please tell me.'

'Simple, it's that copper bloke Dick White. He's my godfather in more ways than —'

Three bullets hit Donnelly in the back of his head, and he fell to the ground in front of Alan. The gate into the road burst open and two armed response unit policemen ran to the body. One lifted his helmet visor and spoke to his colleague.

'He's dead; no expensive trial for this bastard. As soon as we saw his finger touch the trigger we knew that was as far as it could go – someone had to shoot him. We need to take your gun for forensic, Mr Fisher; sorry but it's procedure. Put it in this polythene bag, please; an ambulance is on the way and forensic and someone from the pathologist's department will follow shortly. It's going to be a long night; I'll tape the area off, then hopefully we can get a cup of tea to calm our nerves. Are you OK?'

'Yes, just about. I nearly messed that up; he outsmarted me. I'd be dead but for you guys.'

Cheryl and the others were at the end of the path. She couldn't wait any longer, and ran to Alan. 'Are you OK?'

'Yes, fine – it's all over. The missing man who organised the murder of my parents is definitely Chief Superintendent Dick

White. I don't know how he was allowed to get away with it for so long, covering up for the Donnellys – it's a mystery but we'll know soon. There'll be a big, long and expensive enquiry; he couldn't have been helping them alone, so he must be connected to someone or something bigger.'

'Come inside Alan, you're shaking.'

One of the officers held up a hand to detain him. 'Mr Fisher, before you go in, have you another weapon on you?'

'No officer, you have my Beretta and that's all I've got. I didn't get time to use it; your bullets hit him before I moved.'

'Your gun wasn't fired and neither were ours – we thought you'd done it.'

'Shit, it must be Dermott Donnelly: he's got out of the hospital and somehow got in here. Where are the two patrol policemen?'

The three men looked at each other and no one spoke.

'No, surely not,' shouted Alan.

They ran to the police car. Both officers were slumped with their faces down on the dashboard; somehow Dermott had managed to get hold of the Taser gun and stunned both of them. The armed sergeant's pistol holster was empty: Dermott now had a real gun as well as the one he shot Shaun with before he could grass him up.

'I just had DI Hubbard on my radio – Dermott Donnelly attacked the policeman watching him when he heard Larry Nixon's voice, and the biggest punch-up of all time followed.

Nixon has been sedated and put in a private room with an armed guard: he's alive but his face is a mess, though nothing seems to be broken. Jill Nixon is badly bruised but she's discharged herself and has gone to friends in Epsom. It seems everything was used in the fight from chairs to fire extinguishers, and Donnelly threatened to cut Jill if she didn't tell him your address. Then he stole an ambulance and left it on the main road.'

'Where is he now? He won't leave here without trying to kill me.'

Ted shook his head. 'He might, Alan, as he needs to regroup. Shaun was a loose end even though he was family, and he would eventually have told the police everything about Dermott's business setup. He was almost more important to kill than you; Shaun getting arrested would have been a disaster.'

'Yes, Ted, you're right, and there's no sign of him on this side of the house so let's go inside.'

'We've got more of our guys coming, Mr Fisher, and they'll seal off the estate within minutes. We'll get him; lock yourselves in the house please. Go in a back room and wait for us to phone.'

The group were stunned into silence. Only Alan and Ted Fisher could speak; everyone else was in shock and wishing it was daylight.

'Ted, what routes has he got?' asked Alan.

'He can only escape through the back of the golf course, down the hill and on to that back road up to the downs. He may know that route as he might have played golf sometime on the Tyrells Wood course. He must know the estate, then, as it's not easy to find even if Jill Nixon gave him directions.'

'I'll just tell the officer that exit theory; he'd probably do it best in my Mini.'

The room went silent. The bomb placed on the car door by Shaun was in place, but only for two more seconds. The blast broke several windows in the house and in cars parked near Alan's Mini. Dermott Donnelly's body was blown onto a flowerbed near the compost heap: a fitting end for the murderer. Alan and Cheryl took sanctuary in the library. As an internal room it had no windows, but the hiss from a bent central heating pipe clearly reminded them of what had happened that night. They curled up together on a large settee and Alan's phone started to flash – the ringtone was off but in the semi-darkness he could not escape from it.

'Hi, it's Norman, sorry to hear about everything.'

'Dermott is finally dead; he blew himself up by mistake with a bomb meant for me under my car.'

'Shit, sorry Alan; the officer there has just told me about the blast.'

'Yes Norman, and I don't care about the car – to me it's closure and now there are no loose ends other than your boss Dick White. He must have had some help in keeping Donnelly out of jail, and it all links to my parents' deaths.'

'We're looking into that, Alan, but first we've to get Dick back from the Bahamas. He won't staying there long so we need to move quickly. You and I are more or less finished for today: get some sleep if you can and we can catch up tomorrow with the statements, but not now. Call me and we can talk in Guildford.'

'Are the two coppers OK? '

'They will be – sore heads and a few days' leave. Larry Nixon will leave hospital tomorrow. I just spoke to the duty sister in A&E and they want to get rid of him a soon as possible. He's told them to send a bill to Dermott Donnelly's address; he said he was only defending himself. Fair comment, and I managed a brief smile. Goodnight Alan, and thanks, mate.'

Chapter 36
Loose Ends
The One and Only Palace at the Royal Mirage, Dubai
8 months later

'This is the first time I've relaxed since I met you, Alan. Our lives changed that night your parents died. You were happy in your new job in planning and now you seem uncertain which direction to move in.'

'I've given in my notice at the planning office, Cheryl, and they weren't surprised as after my parents' estate had been estimated and put in that article in *The Times* people knew how much I was worth. I feel very selfish – in the last months I've just been totally involved in finding my parents' killers and now that's over I'm trying to make a decision on what my next move should be. This is a great place to think it all through.'

'I know that Alan, but I'm not sure I'm the right person for you. I know you want to join SIS and I also know that the job will be dangerous and would give me many anxious times, especially if children came along.'

'So if I was to propose to you, you'd say "No thanks"?'

'I didn't say that and I won't answer the question. I think we have to give things more time and I don't want to be a widow; we've a lot of life in front of us.'

'Very serious, Cheryl, but I see where you're coming from. For the moment I think we should do nothing; the answer will come one day soon. Shall we go and have that camel ride now? It'll calm us down a bit.'

'Calm me down? It'll probably give me a very sore bum. I'll go and get changed; see you in the bar.'

Alan laughed. The crudeness of her mother came through at regular intervals, but he loved it and underneath he frequently thought that he did want to marry Cheryl. His meeting with SIS the following week would help him decide on his life's direction. He didn't know whether he should put Cheryl first or his career. As he drank his cold beer and devoured the bowl of nuts his mobile phone rang.

'Hello Harold, how is it with you?'

'I'm getting on well with your parents' estate. The tax authorities have agreed my figures and all the valuations are done, but one insurance policy has been much reduced due to your father stopping the payments. Financially he did a few other strange things, some only in the months before he died.'

'What do you mean, Harold?'

'The first thing was that he had a meeting with both Dermott Donnelly and Dick White last summer – separate meetings, and after them he wrote a report.'

'What happened to it? Come on Harold, don't be a boring old man; this is big, please get to the point.'

'I may be old but I'm not boring, and to prove it Janet next door has asked me to marry her.'

'What, she has asked you?'

'Yes, I know it's unusual but at my age I'm thrilled to bits. I know it's naughty but I did stay at her house one night and in her room. Single beds of course, but I quite liked it.'

'Stop that now, you randy old sod. Just tell me about the report and then I can go and have my camel ride.'

'Right, there is a sealed envelope addressed to the Home Secretary; it seems I sat near him at your parents' funeral. I didn't remember him but then I'd forgotten who he was, as they keep changing.'

'Me as well, Harold. All I know is that his name's Kendall – he didn't look well and said he had stomach problems, I think it was cancer. All he talked about was the bloke he replaced in the government who was fiddling his expenses and left quickly, which I think was common knowledge. Have you any idea what my father's report says, assuming that is what's in the envelope?'

'The notes with it are for your mother; he obviously didn't expect to die with her, but in case they did he was covering all eventualities. The report describes his meeting with Donnelly and White held privately somewhere in London: it goes into many pages and the first page is addressed to the Home Secretary; the theme is very much about corruption. The police commissioner could not ignore information given to him by somebody like your father; the notes to your mother indicate that this report was done in detail, and that if he died and the commissioner did nothing she should take it to the Home Secretary. Another letter was addressed to him, and the bottom line was that some people could be for the high jump. According to your father, the letter was specifically about individuals working for the RUC and SIS, and some Irish civilians who tried to pervert the course of justice.'

'This is terrible, Harold – we have to decide what to do with the report. It means that once the commissioner saw the information my dad feared for his life if he was also involved, but that was just like him: he hated corruption and backhanders.'

'Correct – Donnelly and White may have colluded to get your parents murdered, but someone much higher gave the order and that's what your father must have said in his report.'

'Anything else? My camel and girlfriend await.'

'No, we can discuss it when you come back but I think it's best if the report is burnt.'

'Keep it very safe, Harold; in fact make a copy, lock one in the safe and put the other in that cushion you use as a safe place as I need to read it thoroughly. Anything else?'

412

'No, other than that a wedding invitation in the post for you from Janet and I, and Bill Knowles has bought The Brown Cow from Larry Nixon after all.'

'Congratulations, you old goat; take it easy. You've got to watch that heart.'

'Thanks Alan. I take it you'll come to the wedding?'

'Yes, provided I'm in the UK.'

'Make sure you are – oh, I forgot: Leah Parker is living with Bill Knowles. I met them the other day; they seem very happy. Aaron is in jail in Cyprus on some gun-running charge I think, but Bill told me Parker has so many enemies he's probably safer in jail. They haven't found Dick White yet and DI Hubbard is being promoted to chief inspector, and my football team Crawley Town keep winning and it looks like they may get in the second division next year; I reckon no chance, but hope I'm wrong.'

'Thanks, Harold. Bye.'

Cheryl was waiting for Alan as he hung up the phone. 'Bloody hell, he had a lot to say.'

'Paperwork, Cheryl – just stick to your nails, it's all very boring.'

'Get in the taxi and put that phone away.'

'Yes I will, but hold on – I just got an email from an old friend.'

Alan turned his eyes to the screen.

Hi,

Hope you are now safe and well. Read a lot about you on the net; it sounds like everything got sorted out at your home. I have news for you: your son was born two days ago here in Ankara. He is 2.5 kilos, blue eyes like yours but my legs. Going to call him Alan.

All my love,

Almas xxx

'You've gone quiet, Alan, is everything OK?'

'Yes, I think my decision has become much easier. Let's go.'

Chapter 37
Alan Fisher's Apartment, Leatherhead, Surrey
A Year Later

'Come in, Ted. Have you got the plans?'

'Yes, I'll put them on the dining table. How was your trip to Turkey, Alan? It was very short – did you see the child?'

'A sad one really, Ted: I knew I couldn't marry Cheryl without telling her about the baby and Almas, so I went to see her yesterday and told her. She took it very badly and I thought her mother was going to attack me; maybe I had a close shave but to split up was the right thing. When I got to Ankara last week Almas' husband was with her and he begged me not to take her away. He said he loved the baby, and in a way this sorted out the problem: they are staying together, Almas is pregnant again and whatever happened between us got her insides sorted out. We left as friends, I agreed to pay for the boy's education and he will come here when he's ready for senior school. I am his Uncle Alan and hopefully he will continue here at university, but definitely not training for the army – that's part of the deal.

'The job with SIS is working out well so far: I'm not front line but I will be next year; I can't ever tell you any more, then you won't have to lie about me. Just say I'm working in import and export, with no details. One thing for sure: I never want to be a Judge Advocate.'

'That's no surprise, Alan. So now we can start building this new house?'

'Yes, but my job is full-on and I'm afraid it's down to you Ted. Maybe Harold Penny can help a bit with the paperwork?'

'Yes, that's a good idea, I'll ask him. He may help me with the payments; my timescale is about 15 months from now and the plans we agreed on are all approved, subject to a few small amendments. These are the council's comments and they are all OK.'

'Good. I have a new girlfriend, Ted, and at the moment that's all she is, but you'll meet her soon.'

'Anyone I know?'

'Not sure, she's called Alice Smith and is a registered private detective. The police know her and she has plenty of work – we get on really well so let's see what happens when the house is finished. She changed her name once so you may have heard me talk about Alice Miller, but she is definitely a Smith now.'

'No, never met her – I remember the name but not what she did.'

'Good, just checking. Best you didn't, Ted. By the way, I heard from Norman Hubbard today: he phoned just before he left

Heathrow for the USA. He said Chief Superintendent Dick White had been found shot dead in a Miami apartment, so he's now officially off the missing persons list. He was going to meet the local police and identify the body for them – it seems that White had no adult relatives; in fact he had almost nobody his own age. Very strange, and I might get Alice to check it out one day. His killer was believed to have left the country immediately and the FBI have an open file if he ever returns – they said that the description could have fitted Aaron Parker, although Hubbard said he'd only seen him once and he couldn't be certain it was him. The Miami police think it was Parker as they discovered from the Nicosia security people that he managed to bribe a guard in the main Cyprus jail and escape in a food truck.

'Then a week later White was killed in an apartment near the beach. A man fitting Parker's description arrived from Beirut two days before the murder, and the same man left the USA with a Lebanese passport a day after the murder and headed for Beirut via Zurich. The passport and visa were not in Parker's name, but they were genuine, with a photograph that matched his – very clever and he must have paid big money for them, but then he had plenty if he could get his hands on it. He must have been in contact with Dick White otherwise he would never have found him; maybe he owed Dick money. Lots of questions but frankly I don't care; he's best dead.'

'Good. Let's hope Parker stays in Beirut or Zurich – we don't want him and his bombs here in Surrey. So what happened to Charlie Baxter?'

'Nothing as far as I know, Ted: his wife died and I think he might be working in Afghanistan on the bomb disposal teams. He never officially left the army, he was just on extended leave because of his wife's illness. With his technical knowledge he would be very useful; he's probably training the teams on IEDs and how to deal with them.'

'I see. I had an interesting chat with Larry Nixon, too: they've moved into their house in Spain permanently now. He'd flown over for the day from Malaga to close his bank account at NatWest and said it would be the last time he'd be here. He looked well, and even though I only talked to him briefly he seemed a changed man and much calmer. He sent his regards to you, Alan. I don't know what happened to his sister-in-law but at the time the inquest finished she was probably just pleased it was all over; she must've known what Donnelly was up to. By the way, what happened to that report your father did?'

'I shredded it, and the copy as well. As White is dead the only man left in the cover-up, if that's what we call it, is the old Home Secretary and he died nine months ago. You did say that he looked ill at the funeral. My boss in SIS said the government knew about his collaboration with White and Donnelly and they'd sat on the information in case anything came out of the

418

woodwork later, but like a lot of things in security it will be filed just for the record. I'm satisfied now – my father had enemies and as far as I can tell all the doors are closed, so now I have to get on with my life. The Turkey trip helped me to grieve at the right time; if I hadn't done that job I don't know how I would have dealt with my parents' deaths, and the job I have now is my destiny and I know my dad would be pleased. Right, Ted, open those house drawings and I'll get Harold over here, then it's all systems go. What are you looking at?'

'That car outside – it's been here ever since you arrived.'

Alan laughed. 'This time I know who it is. Don't worry, Ted.'

Also by Keith Wild

The Station
The Betting Shop

Information available on KeithWild.Com or from Pen Press.